C000220251

A Time To Every Purpose

Ian Andrew

Helping Writers Become Independent Authors

For Jacki

10 July 1997
and
28 March 1998

Two times that had purpose.

Ranks

A full glossary of terms is included at the rear of the book. The majority of ranks used throughout are rendered in English, but the correct German translations are given here for completeness.

SS Officer Grades
SS Officers normally held Gestapo ranks as well but these are omitted for clarity.

Reichsführer-SS, Empire-Leader of the SS, no equivalent.

SS-Gruppenführer, Major General.

SS-Standartenführer, Colonel.

SS-Sturmbannführer, Major.

SS-Hauptsturmführer, Captain.

SS-Untersturmführer, 2nd Lieutenant.

SS Non-Commissioned Officer Grades

SS-Hauptscharführer, Battalion Sergeant Major.

SS-Unterscharführer, Sergeant.

SS Enlisted Grades

SS-Sturmmann, Lance Corporal.

SS-Oberschütze, SS-Head (Senior) Private, no equivalent.

SS-Schütze, Private.

SS-Totenkopfverbände (SS-TV)

Death's Head Units responsible for administration of Concentration Camps (Female ranks and English translation only).

Chef Oberaufseherin, Chief Senior Overseer.

Oberaufseherin, Senior Overseer.

Lagerführerin, Camp Leader.

Erstaufseherin, First Guard.

Rapportführerin, Report Leader.

Wärterin, Female Guard.

Kriegsmarine *(Navy)* Ranks

Fregattenkapitän, Commander.

Kapitänleutnant, Lieutenant.

Wehrmacht *(Army)* Ranks

Hauptmann, Captain

Obergefreiter, Corporal.

Schütze, Private.

Part One

A Time to Speak

and

A Time to Kill

1

20:15 Sunday, May 17, 2020 – London

She stood on the Mall opposite the entrance to Horse Guards and gazed along the flag-lined boulevard towards the Palace. A soft spring breeze gently billowed and caressed its way down the two parallel lines of red, white and black. The folds of the nearest flag shook out and the Swastika unfurled against the turquoise blue of a London sky.

She looked away from the symbol of the Reich as the Fore-Fone buzzed on her arm. The unknown number icon flashed on the screen but she reached up to her earpiece and clicked the connect toggle anyway.

"Leigh Wilson, hello."

"Doctor Wilson, it's Heinrich Steinmann, I'm so sorry to disturb you on your weekend." The language was English, the accent clipped, precise and stereotypical of an Oxbridge education. Yet just in his vowels there was the trace of mid-Germanic origins. Leigh's senses sharpened. Mid-Germanic yet educated at the best universities in England normally indicated a particular type of Party operative. That alone would have made her cautious but the fact that she didn't know who Heinrich Steinmann was added to her sense of foreboding. Her mobile number was not in any directory listing due to her status as a Senior Government Science Officer yet here was this stranger calling her.

Leigh responded cautiously, "Guten Tag Herr Steinmann, Wie geht es Ihnen?"

"Thank you Doctor Wilson but English will be fine and yes, I'm fine too, thank you for asking. I was wondering where you were at present?"

"I'm sorry, but would you mind telling me who you are before I tell you where I am?"

"Ah, my apologies, I forgot. You've been on leave. I'm Major Lohse's replacement."

"His replacement? I didn't know he was leaving."

There was a momentary pause and when Steinmann spoke again his accent had softened, subtly. "No. That's right. It was rather sudden. A family emergency in the Homeland. It would appear his eldest boy was involved in some... mmm, unpleasantness, at the Munich Institute. We do all trust the Major will return to duty swiftly but," he paused a beat before continuing, "as you can imagine, it will depend on the outcome of enquiries. Yes?"

"Yes, I see," and she did, clearly. Although she had no idea what the unpleasantness referred to was, it didn't matter. A Major in the Reich Security Directorate did not, could not, have members of their family being anything less than model citizens. Depending on what young Lohse had gotten himself into, Lohse senior was facing a halt to his career, perhaps a demotion or two or... She didn't finish the thought. "So is it Major Steinmann?" Leigh asked.

"Well, no. Formally I suppose I am Colonel Steinmann of the Allgemeine-SS, Special Investigations and Security Directorate. But please call me Heinrich, we shall be working together after all and I find formality, so, um, formal." Heinrich laughed lightly at his own humour.

Leigh felt a stab of adrenaline in her stomach. Her breathing had quickened and she could feel sweat running down the back of her neck. The temperature was a seasonal fifteen degrees Celsius, the normal average for London in May, yet her whole body convulsed in small shakes more associated with a freezing winter wind. She struggled for control of her voice.

"Oh!" She was high by an octave. She covered her mouth and coughed. Her mind screamed at her to get a grip on herself. She coughed again. "Excuse me Heinrich, my apologies. So, what can I do for you?" She knew he would have expected his title to get a reaction and she was annoyed at herself for allowing it to show so obviously. She imagined him smiling at her discomfort as he spoke again.

"As I said, I was just wondering where you were?" He asked plainly and without offering any explanation as to why he wished to know.

"In the Mall, opposite Horse Guards, I was going for a walk," she answered quickly. Her mind shouted so loudly to calm down she almost flinched from the noise in her head. "Why do you ask?" she managed to say a little slower and a lot more calmly than she felt.

"Excellent, I'm so pleased to have caught you nearby. My apologies for interrupting your walk, but I was wondering if you could come into work? Just for a short while. We have a little query with regard to the experiment Professor Faber has left running and I'm afraid he isn't available. I realise my request is terribly inconvenient on a Sunday evening but I would appreciate your input." Heinrich spoke in such a non-confrontational, pleasant and charming way that anyone with no knowledge of his professional specialisation would have felt flattered to be asked.

Leigh knew it was all just for effect. She knew from his title exactly what Heinrich Steinmann was and no one, not even the Chiefs of Staff of the Reich forces, would have turned down his 'request' for 'input'.

"Of course," she heard herself say. "I can be there in half an hour."

"Oh no, please. Please allow me to have a car pick you up. Just stay where you are and we'll save you the walk. I'll see you shortly Doctor Wilson."

The call had already disconnected but she distractedly pressed the end call button on the wireless earpiece. Continuing to stare at the Fone's blank screen, she played out the scenarios in her head. There was nowhere to run to and nothing to do but wait for the car. If they had finally caught up to her then the best she could hope for was a swift processing. At worst, if they thought she had information on others, then her next seventy-two hours would not be so pleasant. She reached inside the concealed double-lined pocket in her light jacket and fingered the small gelatine capsule that nestled there. She would wait for the car. It wouldn't take long to figure out what was going to happen.

If they travelled east to her work in the Todt Laboratories then maybe things were not as bad as she feared. Although there was a newly built detention facility in the compound she would know straight away if they headed for it. She would stay alert to the possibilities that Colonel Steinmann was playing a game with her, but she would wait. But if they took her north-west to the Harrow Holding Centre, then there would be nothing to wait for.

Leigh smiled. For her thirty-five years of life she had worked her way through the system, gained academic honours and achieved a senior government role. She was a leading scientist on the most far-reaching scientific experiment ever undertaken in the eighty years of the Greater Germanic Reich, or arguably in the whole history of humanity. She had run a good race. If it ended now, well that was what God intended. If not, she would continue her work to undo everything; in His name.

2

It was a 1930s built, three-bedroom, detached property. Solid, reliable and updated to include what were once luxuries but were now essentials for a man of his social position. Thomas Dunhill reflected on the amount of effort he had expended to fit-in where he shouldn't be.

The solar-panel central heating, water management system, triple-glazing and multipoint recycling did at least make him feel he was contributing to the environment. Aside from the energy improvements, he had also overseen the construction of an en-suite bathroom, a state-of-the-art kitchen and an extension into the large rear garden for the domestic help. Finally, he had designed and installed a stunning audio-visual entertainment system. The furniture and décor that dressed the property reflected money and excellent taste. The former quite common but the latter, sadly, in short supply in the leafy suburbs of North London.

His house was situated near to the end of a quiet, tree-lined street that was home to a few doctors, a pharmacist, some military officers, a professional singer and a scattering of City business types. The predominant cars in the driveways were high-end BMW, Porsche or Mercedes fleet cars. The majority of residents were native English, like Thomas, but there were one or two Homeland-ers in the bigger houses at the far end of the road. A Dutch family lived next door but one and the singer, who lived opposite, was originally from Paris. The traffic was never heavy as the road was not a cut-through from anywhere to anywhere.

Thomas did love his street and how, at this time of the year, the muted squeals of pleasure from playing children would accompany the sun as it dipped into the serrated hues of a yellow, orange and red setting. The domesticity of the suburb given exotic overtones by an evening chorus of shrieking Swifts, fresh in from their migratory flights from Sub-Saharan Africa.

But Thomas couldn't hear any of those sounds tonight. Nor could he see the setting sun. His lounge room was cloistered by heavy curtains across the bay windows to his back and the only illumination came from a soft glow uplighter in the corner of the room. The designer furniture had been moved against the walls and he stood in the central cleared area with five others.

All six stood in a loose circle facing toward a small table that had been covered with a white linen cloth. To his left were Amanda and Terrance. To his right, Liza and Ben. Opposite him at the far side of the table and in front of the entrance door to the lounge, was Christine. He had been friends with these six since their university days in Newcastle. They had lived apart from each other, they had lived in the same house as each other, they had loved and fallen out and made up, but throughout all their friendship remained.

He had watched Amanda and Terrance as their university fling grew into a love that was solid and strong. Eventually they became husband and wife. Liza and Ben also grew together and while they hadn't married, they had lived with each other for almost seven years. Thomas and Christine remained just good friends, as they always had. Every time he saw her his mental clock of missed opportunities clicked up by another one. So many clicks he didn't even sigh inwardly anymore. He smiled at Christine and then looked down to the table that stood in the middle of the six friends.

On it stood a single item.

A small porcelain statue, standing fifteen centimetres tall. A perfect circle mounted on a small, pyramid base. Within the circle six finely twisted strands of porcelain formed six spokes radiating into a smaller circle at the centre. The wheel had been in Thomas's family since the 17th Century. Created by a master craftsman in the North of England, it represented the last physical link Thomas had with his heritage. He had changed his family name, his personal history, he had forsworn in public any connection to the family he had loved and respected. He had broken any links that could have traced him back to the people he came from. Yet he had kept his belief inside and he had kept the wheel. Safe and protected. The way he felt when, in private with trusted friends, he professed his true self.

Christine led them as if prompted by Thomas's thoughts. She raised her hands in a welcoming gesture and spoke in a soft and gentle rhythm.

"Dear friends, in the presence of God, amidst this circle and in our own company let us profess our beliefs."

Bowing their heads, the six, in hushed and reverent tones, began to speak the sacred words that had sustained mankind for almost two thousand years. Beliefs that had grown and adapted as each new Messenger of God was revealed through the centuries.

"We believe in One True God, Creator of all that is seen and unseen. We believe in the Holy messengers, led by the First Prophet, Abraham, who taught us the word. We believe in the Holy Prophet, Jesus, who was heralded as the one Messiah, embraced by all the peoples of Earth. He banished discord and united the world in peace. We believe in the Last Prophet, who made us stronger. We believe in the realisation of Moksha, in the way of the light through Buddha and in the unifying force of harmony within the universe."

They raised their heads to look at the person opposite them in the circle. Thomas looked into Christine's eyes and as always, was amazed by how truly beautiful she was. He smiled as he began, with the others, to profess the central tenets.

"We believe that blessed are the peacemakers, who shall be called children of God. We promise to love one another as we would be loved and to turn the other cheek to aggressors. We look for forgiveness and await the world to come."

They paused in harmony, bowed their heads and reflected on their own acts since the last time they had met. At no set moment one of them would feel the urge to speak and recount the good and the bad that had influenced their life in the intervening time.

Thomas looked to Ben. Since last they had gathered Ben and Liza had discovered they were to become parents. Liza was due in six to seven months. Thomas thought a winter solstice baby would be a fine thing. He watched as Ben raised his bowed head and began to speak.

But Thomas did not hear him.

The shaped-charge explosive that had been placed around the bay window detonated with a force that took all sound away.

Simultaneously the front door to Thomas's house was blown off its hinges, the back door was smashed in by a leaden entry ram and all power was cut, taking away what little light had been in the lounge room. In a smooth, well-practised and much used manoeuvre, the black-clad Kommando moved into the house. Three soldiers entered directly into the lounge room through the remnants of the shattered window and shredded curtains. Each man trained the laser sighting of their Heckler & Koch machine pistols onto the head of their designated target.

Four more Kommando entered through what was left of the front door frame. One covered the hallway and bottom of the stairs while the rest moved swiftly into the lounge room through the door opposite the bay window. They also trained their weapons on their designated targets. The four Kommando personnel who entered through the back door cleared the rest of the house in little more than a minute. It was swift, professional and brutal.

The six targets were not expected to put up any resistance. Even if they hadn't been guided by their beliefs, the friends could not have resisted. In the shock wave caused by the initial explosions Thomas had his eardrums ruptured. He had instinctively crouched at the noise but had stayed up on his feet. Peering through the dust and the swirling black shapes around him, he could see Ben lying on the floor. A piece of window frame had smashed into his friend's face and he lay bloodied beside the debris. Thomas looked left and right and saw the rest of his friends crouching, like he was. Frightened, shocked and cowed. Except Christine.

Christine stood tall, looking down at him. In the faint blue-black light of dusk filtering in through the obliterated window he saw a smile on her lips. He tilted his head in query and looked at the woman he had loved for the last fifteen years. She looked back at him and then down at the table. He followed her gaze but stopped as he saw the stain of red spreading across her shirt. What looked like a finely crafted crystal spear jutted out of her right breast. He couldn't understand what he was looking at. He frowned and looked back at Christine's face. She gazed into his eyes and then he saw her lips move.

"I love you Thomas."

He watched as she began to fall but saw nothing else as his world plunged into black. He felt the hood's fabric around his face just as his hands were yanked behind his back and tight restraints jolted onto his wrists. He was pushed, pulled, lifted and then forcibly thrown down. He braced for a hard surface but felt the soft yield of a lawn. He lay still and tried to hear through deafened ears. Had he been able to see he would have been amazed.

The quiet suburban street was transformed from its norm. Three detachments of Special Forces had sealed off both ends of the road. They had, quietly and with their normal efficiency, moved all the other residents out of their houses. The cordon had been secured before the commander, Johan Lowther, gave the 'Go' order. He now stood and listened to the radio chatter from his Kommandos. A small, charred tear of curtain fabric fluttered silently down, twisted in the air and landed gently on Lowther's lapel. He reached up and, with a delicate touch, dusted off his pristine uniform. The blackened remnant fell away and revealed again his subdued-pattern, double lightning strike insignia.

"Building clear. Tango-Three unconscious from flying debris, Tango-Four is dead from a glass shard. Looks like one of the detonator cords on the window slipped and blew in the bottom left of the frame. Other targets secured and on way out now, your orders?"

SS-Major Lowther raised his right hand to the throat mic he wore and acknowledged the report.

"Good work and don't worry about the det cord, it saves us transporting six of them. I don't want to waste time lifting unconscious bodies, just finish it here. Leave the corpses, torch the house. Escort the others to the transport. Liaise with the Fire Department so it's only this piece of shit that is razed. The good citizens of Stanmore might object otherwise. I want you all up and out of here within the half hour. See you back in Northwood. Oh, and Carl, remember to post the sign." Lowther keyed off his mic and turned on his heel towards his transport. He was very satisfied and knew that his senior operators could look after the rest of the night's necessities without him hovering over them.

SS-Sergeant-Major Carl Schern looked down at the slumped figure of Ben Stevens. He moved the sight of his HK-MP19 so that the small red dot of the laser illuminated onto Ben's brow and pulled the trigger twice. He then nodded to his remaining squad members to carry out the rest of their orders. The main power switch was tripped back on so they could work with more haste. It also allowed his men to see what was worth 'saving' from the house before they set it on fire.

The kerosene cans were emptied throughout the upper and lower floors and once done the final squad members made their way out. Carl stopped and checked by radio that all his men were clear. He took a last look around and was about to leave when he saw the table in the middle of the lounge room. Its white cloth was soiled by dust and debris and Tango-Four's blood. But sitting upright on it, unharmed in any way, was the six-spoke wheel. He walked over to the table, picked the statue up and shook his head. He was slightly incredulous that something so fine and delicate and obviously very old could survive the violence that had been visited upon this place. Somewhere deep in his psyche he knew there was a larger significance to the symbolism but he ignored it. He looked again at the statue and momentarily thought about pocketing it. He smiled as he remembered this little flimsy statue carried a death sentence for anyone found possessing it. The spoils of war were not that important. He dropped it on the floor between the two bodies and crushed it underfoot.

Less than twenty minutes after the initial blast, the street was cleared of Special Forces, the remaining prisoners were being transported to the Harrow Holding Centre, the Fire Department were monitoring the blazing house and a sign had been posted on the front lawn:

**This property has been identified
as a gathering place for the
Turner Religious Sect.**

**Its use is outlawed by order of the
Reich High Command.**

**All citizens are forbidden to congregate
in its vicinity on
Pain of Death.**

It was the same wording that had been in use since the beginning of the Reich. It was the same wording that had been posted throughout the world from the German Southern African Colonies to the west coast of the German States of America and to the east coast of Germanic Russia. The High Command boasted of two things; the sun never set on the Reich and the Reich never stopped in its hunt of Turners.

3

The sun had set and the street lamps had come on. Leigh still waited for the car. A few couples walked here and there. A young and obviously single Lieutenant of the Kriegsmarine had approached her to ask directions to the Palace, which was in plain sight from where he stood. She had taken her time to point it out to him.

She knew she fit the Aryan mould and, as such, she was held as a thing of beauty in the culture she despised. She was fairly tall and her shoulder length hair framed pale skin and a face that men had told her was beautiful and younger than her actual years. She was aware that her figure was slim, her legs shapely, her bust full enough to cause men's eyes to drift. She knew that wearing an A-line skirt and simple court shoes, a white blouse and a thin cardigan under her light jacket made her look plain and refined all in one. She knew the handsome mariner was going to ask her to accompany him. Smiling up at him, she thanked him for his kind offer but told him, in as casual a voice as possible, that she was waiting for a Schutzstaffel car to pick her up and take her to work. He stepped backward a little too quickly and couldn't hide the apprehension on his face. He nodded in the uniquely old-Prussian manner and set off in the direction of the Palace. Leigh sighed to see that even a handsome sailor was terrified at the very mention of the Siegrune.

She lit a cigarette and watched a group of excited tourists from Spain follow their guide into the entrance way to Horse Guards Parade. Leigh's Spanish was not all that good but she could make out the odd word of excited chatter and surmised that the tourists had seen the Trooping the Colour ceremony for the Founding Führer's Birthday celebrations on State Television the previous month. Now they appeared to be extremely buoyant about seeing the actual parade ground in real life. The mass floodlights surrounding the square allowed visitors to come and go at all hours of the day and night in complete, halogen-lit safety. There was to be no fear of being accosted in the second capital of the Empire.

The tour guide was stopped by the on-duty Police Officer and, without hesitation, she swiped her fingerprint over the biometric input station set into the external wall of the sentry post and looked into the small camera lens mounted above. The familiar tones of the elektronische Bürgerdatei warbled their way through their scale as the biometric data was processed. Inside the post a second Police Officer sat watching a bank of terminals. Leigh could see the dark shape of his head through the small, bullet-resistant windows, but his features were not visible against the low lighting reflected from the computer screens.

Leigh had worked on the cross-reference algorithms for the eBü back when she was a Junior Scientific Intern at the Reich Security Directorate's Technical Division. An interesting summer spent learning about just how some of the State's apparatus worked. She knew that on one of the small screens inside the sentry post a green-bordered box would pop up within three seconds of the fingerprint being swiped, confirming both the name of the subject and displaying an ID photograph taken within the last five years. This image was digitally face-matched to the young woman looking up at the camera outside. The popping up of the box corresponded with an audio confirmation tone passed directly to the wireless earpieces both Officers wore.

Well, Leigh presumed, this would be what happened. She didn't imagine a Spanish tourist guide would cause the other possible outcome. A red-bordered box popping up on-screen details of an outstanding arrest warrant, a mismatched face recognition image or some other breach of security. That would cause a very different audible note to be passed to the two Officers.

As it was, the Police Officer smiled at the pretty tourist guide and nodded for her to proceed. She nodded politely, stepped onto the pathway that led down to the parade square and waited for her brood of followers to pass through the checkpoint. Fourteen people, all undergoing the same process, all cleared through by the affable and smiling Police Officer and on their way in less than a minute of total time. Leigh noticed one of those strange emotions she often felt. A surge of simple pride that the system worked so well. A comfortable pleasure that she and her colleagues had produced a very, very good piece of equipment. Yet this pride and pleasure was corrupted by the knowledge of what that system actually did.

Of what would happen to the individual if the red box popped up. Of why the smiling and affable Police Officer carried a chest-slung modernised HK-MP5 machine pistol and a hip-holster that contained a HK-P8 side arm.

She sighed and checked her watch. It had been thirty-five minutes since Heinrich Steinmann had called her. She could have walked to the tube station in Westminster and been at her work by now, but she guessed what they were up to. Even in these days of advanced surveillance and CCTV cameras there were parts of the city that were unobserved. It was the nature of physical space and dimensions. Walls were just not see-through. So they had her wait. In plain sight of at least four cameras and just across from a manned security checkpoint. Clever.

But she was clever too. She had initially sat on the small raised kerb with her back to one of the ceremonial masts, glancing upward to see the drape of the Nationalflagge hanging over her head. Producing a notebook and a pen from her bag, she had busily scribbled down notes, invented to make it look like she was thinking about the good professor's experiments and what could have gone wrong. She made no phone calls, she made no furtive gestures, she behaved like a model citizen waiting to serve her country. She had continued to write and look thoughtful about potential work problems. She had observed the passers-by on the street, talked to the young sailor and watched the tourists. She had also watched the sky darkening.

Now a slight chill was creeping into the evening air and she pulled her cardigan and jacket closer. It had only been her inten-tion to go for a short walk. Through James's Park and out at the exit across from the Palace, up through Green Park and onto Piccadilly opposite the Luftwaffe Club. Along the busy road and back into her flat in Old Bond Street. All done, she would have been out of her home for just over an hour.

She liked walking in the city on a Sunday evening. It reminded her of the times when, as a little girl, her father had taken her for evening walks through the small village in Cambridgeshire where she had grown up. The memory made her smile. She still missed him. She missed her mother too but she supposed that, like most little girls, her father was the one she had been closer to. Although it was six years since they had gone she could see them in her mind as clear as the lights of the parade square. The thought of them smiling at her on her graduation from The Führer's College, Cambridge was the image that was always the clearest. Her mother had been crying and her father had said that she had done well.

That simple phrase, "You've done well Lee-Lee."

She had hugged them both and had cried. They had walked arm in arm down to the Backs and hired a punt. Her father had asked if there was anything more stereotypical to do in Cambridge but it was good natured and they had bumbled along the Cam, trying to avoid the athletic young men whose coordination and capabilities with the long pole outstripped theirs. It was a memory that her mind had perhaps made more idyllic since her loss, but she was sure that it had been just as special as she recalled. Her memory shifted backwards. She was thirteen.

"The years leave a mark." Her mother's voice. "Constantly hiding who you really are and what you really believe, oh Leigh, it takes a toll on you. We know you're clever and strong, but this double life you think you want. It has consequences. We know sweetheart, we've lived it for ourselves."

"It's okay mum," Leigh had replied, so sure of her convictions and commitment. Sometimes she just wished that she could have a few more moments with her mother to tell her.

"You were right mum. So right. Playing a role, being the other Leigh. Oh mum, it is so hard sometimes. Being a good Party member. Mixing with the senior officials, having to listen to their intolerance, living in their company, smiling at their base humour, going home each and every night and praying for my heart's salvation. Willing Him to find me and help me. It's been hard mum. You were so right. The years leave a mark." But she had always kept the pain to herself.

The temperature had dropped more and she buttoned her cardigan and fastened her jacket. The breeze had picked up and the flags above her unfurled their full length. In the overspill glow of the floodlights surrounding Horse Guards the flags looked somehow less threatening. Their colours were washed out and that symbol was not as visible.

She gazed at the flag and remembered back to when she was nine, maybe ten. Her father and mother had spoken in quiet tones about how the true nature of humanity was being crushed. How the very symbol of the Reich was a sign of love and peace and harmony that had been corrupted. During that summer she had learnt that the barbarism, insanity and elitism of the world that surrounded her was not the way it was meant to be. That was not the teaching of God. That was not what had brought nearly two thousand years of peace.

She had been taught the Turner Creed and had learned how the people of Earth had embraced the way of love. She listened to the distant voices of her childhood and she could see how everything had led her to where she was now. As her grandfather in Scotland had prepared her father to become influential in the Party so she had been prepared.

She was sent to good schools that were open to her because of her father's money and influence. But it was her natural intelligence that allowed her to rise into the top ranks of the scientific community. Alone now, with her grandparents and parents gone, she was the torchbearer of her family. The latest and maybe the last in a generational plan to keep the beliefs, work a way into the system and watch for an opportunity to crack it apart.

Her parents had told her, "The reason we're still here as a family Leigh, is because we don't force anything. Your grandfather said to let the wheel turn at its own pace and God will place you where you need to be and send the people he needs to send."

She was taught to be careful and cautious. To only allow others to see what she chose them to see. Again and again she was schooled to trust no one outside of the family. No one. Her father had sat her down in front of the six-spoke Wheel of the Messengers that was their family relic.

"Leigh, you can trust God, your mother and me. But even then, don't tell your mother and me any specifics of any plans you may be working on. You keep them between you and Him. Promise?"

"I promise, daddy."

She had joined the Bund Deutscher Mädel on her fourteenth birthday. She studied the lore and traditions of the Party, the Reich and the history of the Führer. Her mother had told her that to wreak havoc on the system she needed to know that system inside and out.

On her sixteenth birthday she had received the Reichsführer-SS Prize for an essay she had written about Hitler's thoughts and motivations in saving the world and humanity. The version she wanted to write, but couldn't, would have belittled the penniless artist who had blamed his circumstances on anything but himself and his own shortcomings. How his inner thoughts had manifested themselves into a warped and sick political ideology. She knew the sequence of events in the early 1900's that led to the Great Famine. She could recite how and when the Spanish Flu had broken out and how, eventually, the global economy had collapsed into depression. She had studied the growth of his polluted ideas into a firm doctrine and how he had manipulated the early forms of mass communication to get his message out.

She knew in detail how he had masterfully manipulated the theories of Darwinism. Twisting the survival of the fittest in the animal kingdom and pointing to the futility of the world's powers in assisting everyone during the disasters that were befalling them.

He had blamed the Turner Religion and its teachings of non-aggression for debasing true human nature. He said the Turner's doctrine that insisted all should be loved and protected, even the weakest, had left humanity with no fight. The weakness was a cancer at the heart of the people. It pandered to the weak and allowed the sick to survive. It denied the strong their rightful spoils.

He sought out those who had been most affected by the natural disasters that had befallen the world in those years. The ones who had lost family, friends, prosperity and security, and he offered them an easy solution. He told them they deserved better and together they would take it. They were easily manipulated and quickly transformed into thugs and murderers.

The next step was to find a soft target for his bullies, and all around him stood Turners. He knew they would not, could not, fight back. His mantra remained that the poor were being subjugated and destroyed by the elite of the ruling classes. That all the Nations on the Earth were being controlled by the puppets of the Turner Religion. The Turners were the real evil in the world. Threatening the survival of the fit by the inclusion of the weak.

He had uniforms produced to regulate the appearance of his followers. He drilled them and paraded them, held rallies and processions. When they were seen as a separate identity to the rest of society he united them further by saying that they were, in fact, a superior race. He wrote that the races were not equal. He said the long history of humanity proved that there were stronger nations and cleverer people than others. How in ancient pre-history the White Homo-Sapiens had evolved out of the Black. A superior race, a different species, as different as the Cheetah was from the Tortoise. How could the Aryan peoples allow the base, pre-evolved races to survive? Not only to survive but to own land and property and harvest food that the strong should have. How could they be allowed to rule and to spread their weakness?

He railed that had humanity bowed to the strength and fury of Mother Nature, the one true force, visible everywhere, society would have weeded these miscreants out by now. The world would have been filled with a stronger, cleverer people. He avowed that it was people who were weak and animals that were strong. He said it was forgivable to kill weak and pathetic humans but a base crime to harm strong and majestic animals.

Leigh turned her back against the wind that was now a strong cold force from the east. The flags above her flapped and danced in the artificial light. They threw shadows across her and onto the road in a way that reminded her of the famous footage shown to all schoolchildren of the Reich. The 1929 rally; a little man, animated on a big stage. The crowd noise ebbing and flowing. Waves of cheers building and breaking on each point. Made to watch it at least four times a year in school assembly, Leigh could still recite the whole speech. Waiting in the cold, she allowed her mind to recall the images.

Stage-managed to perfection, the old banners of the Legions of Rome, updated to reflect his doctrinal mantras and surmounted with the reversed Swastika, had been unfurled around the stage. The light of torches had caused the flags' shadows to fall on him as he spoke.

"Blessed are the peacemakers? What nonsense," he had paused and raised his fist, bringing it down onto the podium in rhythm with his next sentences.

"Blessed are the strong who protect their children from the weak and feeble minded!"

"Blessed are the strong who protect their friends and family from the weak!"

"Blessed are the strong who protect our Homeland!" The cheers erupted.

Leigh remembered the noise the crowd had made and how the roar had actually made the camera shake. The force of the crowd's passion even now, still so strong, through the scratchy, disjointed newsreel footage. The noise ripped across the distance of history and reached into the room where she had sat, transfixed by the birth throes of a terrible creature. She recalled how he had waited, with a calmness born from practise, for the crowd to quieten.

"I know we are strong. But what are we to do? Are we to wander unguided? I know that we need a leader and so tonight I come to you to ask that question. To ask us to begin to search for one to lead us."

On reflection, it had been a masterful ploy. He knew all they lacked was a leader. He wanted them all to have a leader. He would search to find a leader for them. His final play was to refuse the mantle of Leader. He expertly managed and manipulated the whole drama. He was elevated on the shoulders of his followers, he was paraded through the narrow streets of Munich and his Lieutenants started the spread of the whispers; 'Why not him to be our leader?' The whisper became a murmur which grew to become a cry that ripped the world to its foundations.

Leigh knew the dates and the events and the history of the changing of the world like it was her own life history. The Führer consolidated his power, took supreme command of the German nation in 1933, built up the strength of the armed forces and all the while the Governments of the world, bound by Turner Doctrine, opposed him with nothing but words and prayers. He sponsored similar movements in Japan, Italy and Spain. He did it all in plain view and denied he was doing it.

The rest of the world failed to see the evil that was truly in their midst. When the realisation that appeasement and turning the other cheek would not stop the force that was coming, it was much too late. With no military forces, with nothing but love and peaceful protestations, the free nations of the world were annihilated.

Their final surrender and the declaration of the Greater Germanic Reich happened on the Twentieth of August 1940. He had stood on the steps of the defunct parliament of the people and declared, 'It is finished.'

She'd always thought it was the strangest thing to say. It hadn't been the end. It had only been the beginning. The transformation of the world into an image of his making had only just started.

***

Boredom of sitting on a roadside kerb caused her to light her third cigarette of the previous forty minutes. Typically, just as she had taken the first two draws from it, a Horch staff car with SS pennants flying swept through the archway at the head of the Mall and approached her.

She stood, put her notebook and cigarettes away, smoothed her skirt down and adjusted her jacket. Crushing out the cigarette on the side of the adjacent waste bin, she walked forward and stepped to the roadside. The headlights from the Horch swept along the right hand side of the road and lit her so that she had to shield her eyes with her hand. The car slowed and stopped almost gracefully, its large V8 engine softly purring in the evening. A Lance-Corporal in the uniform of the Großbritannien Division of the Waffen-SS stepped out briskly from the passenger side door and saluted her. She nodded as he reached for the right side rear door but also realised he was not one of the normal security detail that she was familiar with. She ducked under the sill and stepped into the spacious rear compartment taking her seat behind where the Lance-Corporal was regaining his.

Glancing forward and left to the driver, she didn't recognise that man either. He was anything between mid-thirties and mid-forties, brown hair with a few small flecks of grey beginning to appear at the temples. She guessed at him being slightly taller than she was, lean but toned. He had a pleasant profile, deep set eyes, straight nose and generally appeared to Leigh as quite a handsome man. He wasn't wearing the normal SS uniform. In fact he was in civilian attire. Denim jeans and a close fitting black tee-shirt. She noticed he was looking at her in the rear-view mirror. She looked back into his eyes.

"Hello Doctor Wilson. I'm Heinrich Steinmann."

4

"You're late. I thought you'd forgotten about me."

"Oh no, that was hardly likely, just delayed a little. I hope you are not too cold, shall I turn the heating up?" He glanced from the road to the rear-view mirror as he spoke.

Leigh was uncomfortably aware that the man's eyes were unnervingly... What? Not mean or threatening. She had expected him to be as cold as all the other Security Police she had ever encountered. Their eyes tended to be hooded, with a coldness that belied either the deeds they had seen or the deeds they had done. But this man's eyes were different. She realised, with a flush of guilt accompanied by a blush of colour to her cheeks, that this man's eyes were unnervingly attractive. Even in the dim light cast from the interior dashboard displays she could see a hint of green in them but it was their depth that held her. She realised she was staring. She glanced out the side window as she answered.

"No, the temperature's quite comfortable, thank you. I must admit I expected a pool driver to pick me up. To what do I owe the honour of being chauffeured by a man who has direct access to the Führer?" Leigh tried to make the question sound light-hearted but inside she felt sure he was here to take her directly to an interrogation centre. She casually moved her hand inside her jacket and slipped her fingers around the small tablet concealed there.

"Oh, you know, sometimes you just can't get the staff," he laughed lightly, "To be honest Doctor Wilson..."

She interrupted him, "Please, call me Leigh. You did say you didn't like formality."

"Okay, well, to be honest, Leigh, I fancied having a look around the town again and I don't like being a passenger. So I asked young Lance-Corporal Wiehaden here," he nodded in the direction of the young man in the passenger seat, "if I could drive. I think it might be a control thing?" He smiled and glanced at her in the mirror. The young Waffen-SS Lance-Corporal remained silent and the conversation progressed around him like he wasn't there.

"I would imagine it might well be a control thing. I could see that of you. You said 'again?' You've been to London before Heinrich?" She once more caught his eye in the mirror as she said his name. She was used to acting in an innocent manner in front of all sorts of Nazi Party members but this was something different, unusual. She needed to be careful. She did notice that the car had powered around the Memorial and was now speeding back down the Mall, heading north-east.

"Yes, I was an undergraduate at Balliol, Oxford. Used to escape and come up to the big city at the weekends, you know to, um, study. But it was a while ago, I'm older than I look."

"Ah, but your modesty covers for you, yes?" she asked mockingly.

"Something like that, yes," he laughed and she put on her best fake smile in response.

"So what did you study at the second tier University of England?"

"Now, now, Miss Wilson, just because we're being informal doesn't mean you can have a sneaky dig at me for being an Oxford Alumni. Keep that up and I'll drop you here and you'll have to walk in the cold." His voice was light and almost playful. "Anyway, I studied Criminal Psychology and bizarrely then decided to do a Masters in English Literature," he said.

"I see. So not only can you understand and read the language that is my native tongue but you can study all my body language and tell me what I am thinking, eh?" Leigh asked in a comically sarcastic tone.

"Well, sort of I suppose," he glanced into the rear-view mirror and held her eyes for slightly longer than was safe as he sped east through London.

"Very astute. Do you think I could ask you to maybe pay close attention to the road, given the speed we're doing? I'm not the world's best passenger."

This conversation was not what Leigh had prepared for. She had composed herself while she waited on the Mall. She had reminded herself why she was doing what she was doing. She was ready to face the monster and, if necessary, she would use the final option in her jacket. What she hadn't expected was to be in a slightly flirtatious conversation with the man who was quite likely preparing to interrogate and execute her. She had experienced adrenaline rushes before but none of them ever made her feel like this. She found herself looking through the gap in the front seats and appraising the right side of Heinrich's body as the car went quiet for a moment. She could see his muscles outlined through his tee-shirt. She noticed his arm as it reached to the steering wheel, toned and slightly tanned. She also noted that the car had continued to head east towards her work and not north-west to Harrow. She relaxed a little, took her hand from her jacket and turned to look out the side window again. She wondered about the nature of the man up ahead.

He spoke more seriously than before and shocked her back into reality. "I'm sorry Leigh, I never meant to make you feel unsafe in a vehicle. I assure you I'm a competent driver. But, please accept my apology."

Leigh looked round at him. She was instantly angry with herself and with him. "So, Herr Steinmann, you've read my file, very good," she said it coldly, almost spitting the words out.

The car was quiet, he didn't speak again. She sat back and watched the Thames pass on her right. They had sped along the special traffic lanes used exclusively by the Security Forces and had made the journey from the West End to the Isle of Dogs in just under fifteen minutes. Leigh watched the old docks pass on the left as the car drove the loop road down to the southernmost tip of the Isle. She saw the lights of the Todt Laboratories as the car turned left into the main approach road. She began to feel sweat on her palms again and a rising panic. She knew that she was either going to work or going to a cell, depending on where the car stopped. She was determined to remain on her guard and not give herself away too early. Especially with this cunning bastard who had made her feel like a flirting teenager, then reminded her that he had studied her file and knew about her history before coming to pick her up. She calmed her breathing. Getting angry was not a good idea. Her hand slipped inside her jacket.

He turned off the headlights as they slowed so as not to blind the gate guards. He slowed more, opened the side window and was recognised by the on-duty soldier who had seen him leave the complex not long before. A smart salute was delivered, which Steinmann acknowledged with a cursory nod of the head. He powered the staff car through as the automatic boom gate came up. Leigh's heart rate raced as she watched to see if they would head to the small holding facility over on the eastern side of the compound. She was conscious of breathing a deep sigh as, instead, they made straight for the main entrance steps of the laboratory complex. Lance-Corporal Wiehaden had his door open and was out, opening Leigh's door before she had actually acknowledged the car had stopped. She slipped her hand from inside her jacket, clutched her bag and stepped into the neon security lighting that flooded the area. Steinmann was coming around to the front of the car. He told Wiehaden to take the Horch back to the motor transport yard, fuel it, park it up and have a relaxing night. He would see him in the crew room at 07:30. Wiehaden snapped a drill-book salute, shut Leigh's door, walked around and climbed into the driver's seat. He pulled away from the entrance steps without causing so much as one gravel-chip to fly up.

Leigh turned to walk up the ten steps that led to the marble and glass fronted atrium of the main reception building for the Todt Laboratories. The building was nothing more than a double-storey, medium sized office block, but it sat atop the entrance to the Deep Underground Engineering Laboratory. She was primarily responsible for the most sensitive of the experiments it was now conducting. Steinmann came close to her ear as she started to ascend the entrance steps. "No Leigh, I didn't have to read your file. I knew your parents. I miss them too."

5

Thomas's ears were still ringing from the earlier explosions, but he felt the noise of heavy metal doors being opened and swung back against the sides of the van. He sensed a change of light through the dark material of the hood. He felt hands on his shoulders. Dragged clear of the van, he was dropped. He hoped for the soft yield of grass again but he hit the concrete floor hard and the wind was knocked out of him. He tried to gasp for breath but the hood sucked into his gaping mouth. Thomas tried to gasp again. He couldn't get enough air and with his hands and feet still bound he couldn't stand to help his lungs. He began to panic. His breathing accelerated but he got less oxygen with each frantic attempt. The buzzing in his ears was drowned out by the pounding of his heart. He twisted and writhed on the ground. He felt like a fish, out of water and desperate for life. Finally, he heard insane crying, screaming for him to calm down. Thomas realised it was his own inner voice. He listened. He mustered all his personal control and forced himself to breathe through his nose. His lungs expanded.

Leigh and Heinrich were walking up the steps to the Todt Laboratory as Thomas Dunhill and his three surviving friends, were being dragged out of an armoured car in the reception processing area of the Franz Six Memorial Centre, Protective Custody Camp, Northwick Park. It was commonly known as the Harrow Holding Centre and was one of five such facilities in the British Isles.

Advertised in all official documents, official Government websites and State Broadcasting channels as being *'Situated in the north-*

west London suburb of Harrow it is a one-kilometre square Protective Custody and Rehabilitation Centre for the re-education of those persons posing a threat to the orderly society enjoyed by the citizenry of the Greater Germanic Reich. Within the confines of the centre the inmates enjoy University-level education classes to provide those opportunities they may have missed out on in earlier life. Sports and recreation facilities to engender their social and team-building skills. Excellent nutritional and health care to build the bodies that will, on reintroduction into society, contribute to the good of the people. Like all rehabilitation centres throughout our Great Reich, the Franz Six Memorial Centre builds a strong person for a strong nation.'

***

The reality was somewhat different.

The reception processing area was, counter-intuitively, the central compound within the facility. After the prisoner transport had driven in through the last set of four security gates it entered a two hundred-metre by one hundred-metre, unroofed concrete box. Walled by seven-metre high, plain grey concrete unbroken to the two long sides, the south side was breached only by the electrically operated vehicle gates that allowed the transports in. The gates themselves would only open when the outer gates in the surrounding compound had been closed. The north wall of the compound was blank with the exception of a flush-fitted, metal personnel door that led to the administration offices and two aluminium roller doors, almost garage-type, two-metres wide and three-metres high, set on either side near the corners of the wall. Above each roller door was a large stencil, one marking the left door for Men and the right for Women.

The compound floor sloped gently, almost imperceptibly, from each wall to six equally spaced central storm drain covers that ensured, even in the foulest of weather, the compound remained flood free. Small sangars mounted on top of the walls at each corner were only accessible by ladders running externally to the compound. Each sangar was manned by one member of the SS-Totenkopfverbände with a MG-42 Mk6 laser sighted machine gun. Sodium spotlights, mounted at ten-metre intervals around the top of the walls, turned the darkest of nights into noon. There was no noise save for the laboured breathing of the four hooded bodies lying curled on the ground and the quiet ticking of the armoured car's engine as it cooled.

The evening paused.

An electronic click broke the still and echoed around the compound. The soft whirring of servos on a drive mechanism accompanied the solid steel door of the administration office swinging open on its motorised hinge. A woman dressed in the black of the SS-Totenkopfverbände, Great Britain Rehabilitation Service stepped out. In any setting she would have attracted attention. In the compound the effect was startling. She was twenty-five years old, well above average height, with a figure that was classically proportioned. Her long strawberry blonde hair, secured in a pony tail that reached halfway down her back, complimented her typically northern European complexion. Her eyes were the ice blue of an Arctic sea and looked older than her years. The rest of her expression was as cold and stark as the concrete walls that enclosed her. She wore her black combat trousers bunched like a paratrooper's above glistening black boots. Her pristinely pressed black blouse was decorated with the silver oak leaves for meritorious service and the Death's Head collar insignia. She wore no rank or headdress. The only other addition to her uniform was a Sam-Browne belt and holster in polished black leather that held a Glock-46 pistol, the latest model service-issued pistol. She had wanted to keep her old Glock-17 but had been won over by the weight and feel of the new model. It still took 9mm rounds and held seventeen of them in its magazine.

She was followed out of the door by two, much shorter, male administrators dressed in conservative business suits and carrying A-4 sized electronic tablets. The effect was of an Amazonian being followed by mice.

Behind these three came six Waffen-SS riflemen dressed in the standard issue grey-green uniforms and with shoulder slung, new model, semi-automatic Karibiners.

The prisoners remained on the concrete, their hands still cuffed with plastic ties and their heads still hooded. Behind them stood SS-Sergeant-Major Carl Schern and three of his men. Carl looked up at the approaching entourage and thought, 'Fuck me, she's gorgeous!' He had never dropped anyone off at Harrow before, but he had heard the stories about the Chief Overseer. He had always thought them just the exaggerations of men making good on a fantasy. In reality, the stories had fallen short. He waited until the black-clad Chief was within speaking distance.

"Turner prisoners from the raid on Stanmore. Can we get them signed over so my men and I can be on our way please?"

"Certainly Sergeant-Major, but aren't you a little short?"

Carl hesitated. He stood one hundred and seventy-eight centimetres tall, so he was a bit shorter than her but he was an elite NCO of an elite force, no one took the piss out of him, not even a woman this stunning. He was still thinking about how to phrase a response when she spoke again.

"I was told to expect six of them?"

"Oh, I see, um, yes." He felt foolish but recovered his composure. "Two of them never made the trip, saves you the hassle I suppose." He smiled as he said it, trying to sound nonchalant and wondering if he was cutting an impressive figure in her eyes.

"Well, that would be an error in your thinking Sergeant-Major. Hassle free would have been six, not hassle free is four, as my men here," she waved in a dismissive gesture over her shoulder at the two behind her, "now have to redo all the paper work for the incoming and outgoing processing."

"Sorry." Carl stumbled over the word. He thought, 'Sorry? Why am I apologising for this shit. Who the hell does she think she is? Uppity bitch! It's only a generation since we even allowed women to take on command roles.' Again his thoughts went unspoken. He glanced at his own men to see if they were smirking but they were as shell shocked as he was at the woman.

She spoke again, "Well, I suppose you could stand them up for me and take their hoods off. Yes? Then you and your men can go and wash your faces. Yes?"

Carl's hand instinctively moved to his jaw. He knew as he felt the familiar texture of the camouflage cream on his face that the look he was presenting to her was not the best. He probably appeared like a clown with green and black makeup.

He nodded to his men and they stepped forward. Carl grabbed the male prisoner who had been wriggling like a fish and lifted him straight up and on to his feet. His men did the same with the other three bodies curled in front of them on the cold ground.

As the blonde dominatrix moved down the line, Carl and his men removed each prisoner's hood and identified who she was looking at in turn.

"Thomas Dunhill, designated Tango-One, householder of the raid address."

"Liza Carpelli, designated Tango-Two."

"Amanda Baxter, designated Tango-Five, wife of,"

"Terrance Baxter, designated Tango-Six."

The male administrators followed her, but not too closely. Using electronic pads they entered the data they needed and tagged each of the prisoners with a small data dot. When she got to the end of the line she moved behind the prisoners and looked along to where Carl stood.

"Right, Sergeant-Major, that's all I need. You may go," she said dismissively.

Carl had had enough of this shit, so he nodded to his men to mount up and get out of the place. They moved past her to get into the transport. She stopped him with a hand on his arm as he walked to her left side.

Very quietly she said, "Only teasing Carl, I know who you are and you should call me sometime. Now, fuck off and be a discreet boy, yes?"

He felt the business card being pushed into the gap between his thumb and palm. He looked at her but she was looking straight past him. He pocketed the card and never said a word about it on the way back to their Northwood base. His lads did notice that he was in a good mood, but they put it down to the high they were all on after the earlier raid.

Chief Senior Overseer Mary Reid nodded to her two junior administrators as Carl and his team exited the inner compound.

The older of the two spoke, "Yes, that's fine Ma'am, we have all we need. Christine Kelly and Ben Stevens are the two that are missing, but we'll look after that."

"Okay Harold. Once you and Fredrick have completed the paperwork, lock up the vault and go home."

"Ma'am," Harold nodded.

With that, the two men went back into the administration office. Mary walked down behind the prisoners, checking their wrist cuffs were still secure. A small sly grin crossed her face when she thought of Carl Schern. She had seen his picture in an edition of Signal a few weeks before and been struck by the handsome face looking back at her. He hadn't been the main feature of the article, obviously. The Wehrmacht were unlikely to make heroes of Waffen-SS Kommandos but, occasionally they would a run a 'colleagues-in-arms' story that tried to paper over the wide cracks of inter-service rivalry. As per usual, Signal had attempted to make a simple story enigmatic and mysterious by alluding to a top secret Kommando unit stationed 'somewhere in London'. Then it had named all the members of the team and published photos of them. Rather than helping relations it had, no doubt, pissed off the Kommando hierarchy and made the average Wehrmacht soldier either envious or dismissive. Bloody idiots working in Wedel Straße couldn't produce a decent story if they ran into one. Still, they had given her a very nice image to fantasise over. She knew that if he really was in London then it would be at Northwood and, given his role in life, it was inevitable that their paths would cross sooner or later. She had decided that if or when she did meet him, and if he was as impressive in the flesh as in the flash, then she would indulge herself. After all, it wasn't often she fucked for pleasure.

She had recognised him as soon as she walked out into the compound and decided straight away that the photograph had been an injustice. Carl Schern was gorgeous. Carl Schern would be a real pleasure. Coming back around to the front of the prisoners, she stopped opposite Thomas Dunhill.

Thomas had been blinking his eyes since the hood had been removed. It had taken a few minutes to see the details of his surroundings in the exceptionally bright spotlights that illuminated the compound. He'd first watched a tall blonde woman in black uniform and two smaller, suit clad men walk past him. One of the men stuck a small badge onto him. He sensed rather than saw an armoured car moving in his peripheral vision. He looked to his right and saw Liza, tears running down her face, beyond her Amanda, and at the end of the row Terrance. He looked right and left slowly but could not see Christine. He had figured out what the crystal shape jutting from Christine had been as he was in the back of the armoured car, yet had still hoped she would be here. But he had known the reality. Now he also realised that Ben was missing. He looked back at Liza and she turned her head to look at him. His world was silent, save for the incessant ringing in his ears, but he could see Liza's tears and he could see her mouth, "Ben's gone." He simply nodded.

The tall blonde woman in the black uniform had come to stand in front of him. She was taller than him and looked down into his face with an expression of complete disinterest. Like she was looking at a specimen in a jar that she knew was once alive but was now just a passing irrelevance. When he looked into her eyes Thomas's first thought was that he was gazing into a godless soul. But his Turner Creed dismissed the notion. No one, not even an unbeliever, was less than him. This woman was not interested in anything he might know or anything he had to say. But he had a sudden clarity of thought and knew that his beliefs would give him the strength to bear whatever was coming.

Behind her he could see six uniformed guards carrying long rifles slung over their shoulders. The woman turned on her heel and walked away. Thomas nudged Liza's foot with his and nodded toward Amanda and Terrance. The four friends looked at one another and moved closer so that they stood shoulder to shoulder. Thomas began to speak and although none of the friends had recovered their hearing from the earlier blasts, they knew what he was saying and they added their voices to his.

"Our Father, who guides us, let your name be known."

Mary Reid stopped in front of her riflemen and turned back to look at the prisoners. She was always amazed that they never ran. They just stood there, meekly accepting their fate. Sometimes they held hands, sometimes they wept, sometimes they prayed and sometimes all three at once. But they never ran. Not even a stumbling attempt from the ones with bound hands and feet, not even an effort. Of course there was nowhere to run to but she always thought someone would have tried, if only to live for a second longer.

Before her time in the Service it used to be that they would all be lined up and forced to kneel. Each one of them would be dispatched with a single shot to the back of the head. That had changed when it was found to take too long and caused the ones further down the line to soil themselves from fear or alternatively, faint and fall over. If they fainted it meant that when they were shot the bullet would likely exit the head and embed itself deeply into the concrete.

Neither of these were good outcomes for the efficient bureaucracy that was the SS-Totenkopfverbände. The extra mess and blood needed to be washed away and the concrete had to be fixed. So a time and motion study into the best way to execute millions was carried out. New rules were brought in. Firing squads of twelve were assigned to four prisoners at a time. It speeded things up but not enough. Eventually, it was felt that a single rifleman could be assigned to each target. Numbers of up to thirty would be dealt with in batches of ten or less by a single rifle squad. Any more than thirty and they were processed using the chambers. It was still the way.

"Senior-Private Williams, as you can see we are two short, so choose who is needed. They're all yours. Carry on."

"Yes Ma'am. Do you wish to give the order?"

"No. Now we have spares it's all yours. I'll be right behind you."

"Yes Ma'am."

The four friends' voices carried over the compound, "In heaven and on earth. You are God, you are Allah, you are Yahweh."

Senior-Private Williams nodded to one of the riflemen to move away. The others unslung their rifles from their shoulders. Each member of the squad checked their magazines were fitted properly and stood with their muzzles pointing down to the ground.

"Guide us today and every day to be your vessel."

"Squad!"

The squad nestled the butts of their rifles comfortably into their shoulders.

"Be with us and help us to love one another."

"Make ready!"

They checked the safety catches, pulled the weapons into their shoulders, cocked the bolts back and released the cocking handles. The breaches rammed forward as each rifle chambered a round.

"And teach us to love those that care not for us."

"Aim!"

The firing party leant forward into their weapons and aimed at their targets. A sharp click echoed as the safety catches on the rifles were flicked off.

"For we need your help to turn and turn and turn again. Amen."

"Fire!"

The four rifles fired in one single explosion of sound that echoed and rumbled around the concrete compound. The squad members relaxed their aim as Chief Senior Overseer Reid stepped beyond them and over to the bodies on the ground.

She walked forward and went to Terrance Baxter, bent down and checked the pulse in his carotid artery. Nothing.

She stepped over him to check on his wife. No pulse.

The woman with the Italian sounding name had fallen sideways. It made it slightly easier to access the artery but Mary didn't really have to. The bullet had gone high, straight through the woman's forehead. Dead centre and her eyes had been frozen open in shock and terror. But it was in the regulation book that Mary had to check the pulse and so she checked the pulse. Nothing.

She moved to kneel next to the leader of the group, or at least the one whose house it had been, Thomas Dunhill. He lay still and quiet but again she followed the rules and leant over him to check that he was dead. She almost fell backwards when, as she reached her hand to his neck, he opened his eyes and looked directly at her. She jerked upright and fumbled at her holster.

"I forgive you," he said in as strong a voice as he could manage.

"Fuck you, I don't need your forgiveness!" Mary spat back at him. Her gun wouldn't pull clear from the leather flap that held it securely in place. She glanced down at her side and then beyond as she noticed blood spreading around the prisoner on the concrete. She looked closer at him and saw that he had only been hit in his shoulder. She glanced back at the rifle detail and thought, 'How the fuck could a trained rifleman miss centre mass at that range? Their lives are misery for the next month.' She half smiled as she began to think of the shitty jobs she could have them do as a punishment for sloppy marksmanship. Her thoughts were interrupted by the wounded man speaking again.

"I love you, my friend," he said.

"I'm not your fucking friend and your love is worth fuck all. You don't even know me, you prick. How the fuck could you love me?" Mary flung the words at him but the man, this Thomas Dunhill, just looked at her in a calm and serene way. She looked back down at her sidearm and finally managed to release the pistol. She brought it up and shifted the iron sight until it fell squarely in the middle of his forehead and began to squeeze the trigger.

"I love you for who you are," he said and closed his eyes.

Mary's finger froze. Her hand trembled slightly.

"What did you say?" she managed to whisper. The man's eyes reopened and he looked at her.

"I love you for who you are," he repeated, softer than before. "God loves you. He is inside you. He dwells in you. I love you for who you are." He gave her such a warm and beguiling smile.

"You don't know me. You can't love me." She held his gaze but her eyes narrowed.

"Of course I can love you... Our Lord teaches me to love you... You are His creation... Sent to do His will," he spoke in shallow, panted snatches as his breath began to catch on the pain in his body.

Mary felt a rising tide of anger. She spoke through gritted teeth, "Really, his will? So, he wants me to kill you. How's that working out for you?" She put her foot on to the wound in Thomas's shoulder.

"He has His reasons," he gasped.

"Ma'am? Is everything alright?" It was Williams and he had begun to walk forward to her.

"It's fine, stand still!" She ordered.

"You were saying you loved me?" She pressed harder on Thomas's shoulder.

"Yes," Thomas drew in a gulp of air and grimaced against the pain, "and I will, no matter what you do, for I believe you are His instrument."

"You little prick, you're nothing to me. Don't say you love me you conceited piece of Turner shit."

Thomas looked up at the woman's face and noticed the hurt in her expression. "I love you for who you are," he said it softly and watched as her gun hand fell to her side and she looked away, seemingly immersed in a memory of some other time and place. He felt the true force of his belief as he watched this woman and he relaxed his head onto the cold concrete. He noticed the wetness of his blood on his hair. He watched her memories play through her eyes and then she seemed to refocus. She looked back at him. Her face, momentarily lightened and youthful, changed again. Her eyes stared into his. He knew it was over.

"Do what you must. Though you know it not, you do it for Him. My God will not forsake me. Through Him I forgive you," he said quietly with his last breath.

Mary forgot the regulations about firing into bodies on the ground. In a haze of intense emotions rekindled by his words, she fired four times into his body. She stayed looking down at the ground for a long moment and his dead eyes held her gaze.

She shouted without turning round, "Senior-Private Williams, get your team inside, get your weapons cleaned and be in my office in fifteen minutes, your marksmanship is pathetic. And send the cleaners out here. NOW!" She almost screamed the last word. Williams and his squad checked the safety catches on their weapons and hastened away. Mary holstered her pistol and tried to compose herself. She was shaking. Her mind could still hear Thomas's voice, truthful and caring, 'I love you for who you are.'

She had killed before. Countless times before in the previous seven years. She had started in the Service as a Female Guard back in 2013, not so much as a calling but because it was a steady job. It offered her a decent wage and she could choose where to serve with a fair amount of certainty. She had to admit that when the careers officer in school had gone through the various roles open to women she had been struck by the uniform. Black suited her. But she hadn't been a silly teenage girl thinking that a uniform was a reason for a job.

She knew the real attraction was the sense of control it offered. A control so missing in her own life. She wanted to get far away from home. She had closely guarded skeletons in her personal closet. Skeletons that she had wanted to purge and getting into the Service offered her a vehicle to do it.

Her beauty had been with her since she was a little girl. Her father was a physically strong man, a welder and fabricator at the Middlesbrough steel works. Her mother; a stay at home alcoholic. Mary had been the youngest of three girls, a surprise late addition to the family. Her two elder sisters left the house as soon as they had been old enough to travel independently. Janey was somewhere in Spain and Kasey was just somewhere. She knew why they had left, not then, but later. She had been only nine when Janey left and eleven when Kasey came to see her in her room late on an August night.

"Mary. Mary, wake up." The girl had eased the golden hair from her younger sister's face and held her close.

"Mary, I'm sorry but I won't be here for you." Kasey had half spoken, half sobbed the words. Mary had just looked at her sleepily.

"Be strong Mary, survive, like Janey and I. Survive. I love you. My beautiful little sister, I love you for who you are. Never forget that." Then she had left.

Mary knew that was the last time anyone had said 'I love you' to her and truly meant it. Until Thomas Dunhill tonight.

When Kasey left her room Mary had gone back to sleep. When she woke in the morning she was effectively an only child. Her father took her for the first time two weeks later. He continued to come to her room for the next seven years. Her mother did nothing although Mary was convinced she knew, had always known, what was going on under her roof.

Her father said that if Mary told anyone about what they did together then he would be taken away and her mother would be taken away and they would be killed and it would be her fault. Mary would be at fault. Mary would be to blame and no one would ever love her or forgive her or allow her to live. She would forever be known as the girl who killed her parents. He was almost prophetic.

So she had kept quiet. For seven years she had not mumbled or screamed or cried out. She would fall asleep sobbing quietly after her father had left her room. She stayed quiet in school. She was studious. She kept all her emotions inside herself and she slowly lost her ability to feel, because the feelings hurt. She compart-mentalised her life. She loved no one and would not let anyone in school become close to her. She wouldn't bring people home after school because her mother might be drunk. She wouldn't bring people home at weekends because her father would be there and he would be jealous. Later he would go into a rage and hurt her more than normal.

She left for the Service on her eighteenth birthday. The life she was leaving behind was sealed in a box in a part of her brain that she never needed to visit again. Yet it sat within her every day. She asked to be assigned to Harrow after her basic training rather than be near to her childhood home.

She knew her looks attracted the attention of the senior com-manders. Sex was not an emotional response with her. So she used it as a tool to curry favour.

She was promoted to Report Leader four months after arriving at Harrow and promoted again to First Guard a little over a year later. During the 2015 purges instigated by the new Führer, Joseph Adolf, she led the main reception squads and thrived in the command role as the concrete compound processed two hundred prisoners per day for almost two months. That had been the last time the roller door entry points had seen the men and women split up and the full mechanisms of the Konzentrationslager compounds kicked into motion. The prisoners stripped of their clothing, given camp uniforms, tagged with the purple circles that marked them as Turners, or the inverted triangles that marked out the other categories of prisoners. Housed in the prefabricated dormitories, fed and kept alive until Mary and her staff could finish the record-keeping so important to the Reich. During that time, when the incumbent was forced to take leave due to the stress of the job, Mary had been selected to fill the temporary role of Camp Leader and led the detachments that ensured the enemies of the strong were exterminated and disposed of quickly.

The things she saw and the things she did were added to little secure compartments inside her mind and never looked at, examined or questioned. She was capable of operating with no impact on her conscience for that too was tucked away in its own dungeon.

Toward the end of May 2015 when the number of incoming prisoners slowed to a more traditional norm of twenty to thirty a day, she learned that her mother had died in a pool of her own vomit while her father had been out at work. With her access to the security reporting systems she wrote an allegation of paedophilia against her own father and sent it to the north-east headquarters of the Reich Security Division. She followed it with a fraudulent command authorisation that instructed him to be sent, not to the northern holding centre in Bradford, but to Harrow. She was present at his arrival into the centre.

When her father stepped into line in the secondary roll call area of the facility, she personally pinned the pink triangle onto his shirt and smiled sarcastically at him. He tried to grab her arms as she leant near to him to whisper that she was going to make his stay as miserable as possible. The compartment in her mind, where he had been for so long sealed, popped like a jack-in-the-box and her anger and fury poured out. She threw him off, pushed him backwards and kicked him in the chest, sending him sprawling.

Her protection squads went to move forward but she yelled at them to stay where they were. The commotion drew the attention of a VIP Reich Ministry tour that was reviewing procedures. Their close protection detail tried to shield them from whatever potential threat was arising, but Reichsminister Joyce stood atop the steps looking over the roll call area. He watched as this beautiful woman drew her service pistol and emptied the entire magazine into the prisoner.

She had been introduced to the Minister, at Joyce's request, and later that night became his mistress. A role she was perfectly designed for. She wanted no commitment, she was discreet and she was never going to cause problems for the Minister with responsibility for all Great Britain's Custody Centres.

Five years later she was Chief Senior Overseer of the Harrow facility. She expected, in due course, to be the first woman Kommandant of a Konzentrationslager in the Reich.

Mary Reid's life was on track and she had maintained control of the monsters in her mind. She had locked them away and ignored them. Until Thomas Dunhill had forgiven her and truly loved her as she shot him. Now, as she continued to stare down at his body, she felt a new emotion. One she didn't know how to deal with. She felt a deep, sorrowful guilt in her heart. A tear fell from her cheek and into his blood.

6

Leigh and Heinrich sat opposite each other in the darkened cafeteria of the Todt Laboratories. Lit only by the over-counter neon strips that bounced a silvery light off the stainless steel counter tops, the cafeteria facility was on the second floor of the main reception building. During the normal working day the twenty tables were constantly occupied with a flow of administration and science officers. But on a Sunday evening the security personnel would use their small kitchen on the ground floor while the on-duty science teams, six-storeys down in the laboratories, would not come up above ground until the end of their shifts. With no likelihood of customers, there were never any cafeteria staff on duty at the weekends, but vending machines were still capable of dispensing plastic coffee.

Since he had spoken to her on the steps into the building they hadn't uttered another word. Walking in silence, Leigh followed him as he led her through the security barriers that blocked the entrance, across the open foyer, up the main stairway and into the empty cafeteria. She had nodded when he indicated the coffee machine, picked up a handful of saccharin sachets, two wooden stirrers and taken a seat at the windows that overlooked the building entrance.

Now they sat facing one another over the coffees and she still didn't know what to say.

"Are you okay?" he asked.

"I'm not sure!" She glared at him. "About an hour ago I got a phone call from you, a member of the Allgemeine-SS, Special

Investigations and Security Directorate. That would mark you out as one of only, what? Twenty-five, less, people in the Reich with that security level? I'm told there's a problem with an experiment but instead you bring me into the cafeteria. Your rank and your phone call and your ruse to get me here, for I assume it was a ruse, would make me think I am about to be whisked away for interrogation. You know? I think I'll be seeing the other side of the security apparatus that I've often worked for. But as soon as we're alone you tell me you knew my parents and that you miss them too. So, am I alright? I don't know Heinrich, you tell me. What's going on?" She finished and took a breath, then another that turned into a sigh.

Heinrich sipped his coffee and grimaced before setting his cup back on the table. "It's complicated would be a trite statement now, wouldn't it?" He smiled.

Leigh looked at him without returning the smile. "Yes, it would Heinrich, yes it would."

"Okay, well, I was posted in here on Wednesday from Senior Staff College. You were on leave and I figured that you had taken the week off to go home to Cambridgeshire."

Leigh looked at him with a frown.

"The anniversary of your parents?" Heinrich said.

She nodded.

"So, I needed to talk to you as soon as I could. Waiting until tomorrow was not an option as there would be a lot of people around and Sundays would appear to be quiet," he said as he cast his eyes around the empty room to reinforce his point.

"But why?" Leigh asked. Her mind was racing. If this was an interrogation it was not like any she had prepared herself for. It could just be a masterful stroke on the part of this member of the Gestapo or he could be, however remote the possibility, genuine. But genuine what? He knew her parents, so what? She held her judgement and waited.

"I had to make it look like the full weight of my office was being brought to bear to resolve a problem at work, hence the stiff and formal phone call, the car and the escort, but the reason was to get you in here to talk, unobserved. I couldn't just drive round to your apartment."

"Unobserved? We're in the most open room of the whole facility Heinrich. How is this unobserved?" She almost spat the words at him and realised she was angry and something much more worrying. She was frightened. She tried to calm herself.

"Because this is one of only three rooms in the whole facility above ground that isn't monitored or wired. People think that they're in the privacy of their own offices but they aren't. Small spaces are easy to bug. Cafeterias are open spaces and people don't talk about anything they shouldn't when they're in here. They fear being overheard. That, plus all the coming and going, make an audio surveillance on the place almost impossible," he said with a confidence that came from knowing his subject. "Even given the systems we have now we don't have the resources to make it worth our while. People just don't betray themselves and talk in unguarded ways in areas where they don't feel safe. So, ironically, we're sitting in the safest place in the complex." Heinrich paused and looked at her.

"None of the labs underground are monitored. There aren't even cameras in there because of the classification of the work we do. So we could have gone there," she countered.

"Yes, but to get underground we have to go past monitored and manned security posts. That means a timestamp of our coming and going. I'd rather not be logged."

She tried to hold his eyes but the unexpected feeling she had had in the car returned and she looked down at her coffee cup.

"Okay, so why do you want to talk to me Heinrich? What would make you think that I have anything to discuss with you that couldn't be spoken about in the full glare of daylight and in the company of my colleagues. Even if you did know my parents, why all the cloak and dagger drama? What is it you want from me?" She spoke the final sentence with strength in her voice.

"I want to tell you that you're no longer alone. I want to tell you what Donald told me when I Turned."

Leigh's head snapped up when he used her father's name. She studied Heinrich's face and he looked at her with a mix of compassion and tenderness. There was silence between them for a long while.

Eventually she said, "Heinrich, you have me wrong. And you know that I have to report you for what you said. You know that don't you?" She moved her chair back and began to stand. Her mind screamed to keep her well-crafted mask in place.

Heinrich ignored her movement and continued, "He said that I was never to force any of my career. He said that I would eventually end up where I was going to do the most good. He said I would, if God was willing, end up meeting his daughter and maybe we could help each other to achieve the goal."

Leigh was now turning away from the table and walking toward the door.

Heinrich raised his voice slightly so she could still hear him clearly, "Donald told me to trust no one, no one except God and you."

Leigh stopped.

Heinrich continued, speaking to her back, "Donald told me that he had made you promise to trust no one except your parents and God. Even then keep your council with God alone. He told me that he would talk to you and advise you that one day I would be in touch and you could trust me."

Leigh turned, "Really, that's all terribly interesting," she said sarcastically but with venom in her voice that she couldn't hide. "And when did this miraculous conversation take place with my father Heinrich, when?"

"The morning after I Turned to God and believed. The morning after I said the Creed in the study of your parent's house. The morning of the Thirteenth of May, 2014."

Leigh felt a physical pain in her chest. She felt tears welling up in her eyes. She managed to control her voice. Her delivery was disdainful and dismissive, "So Colonel Steinmann, member of the Gestapo, let's not call your organisation anything other than what it is. Your story is that my father was a Turner and he converted you. That he told you to work with me for some unknown cause or reason. That he had a conversation with you about me and his only advice to you was trust no one." Her voice grew stronger.

"Trust no one; pretty good advice when your charlatan religion gets you a summary execution. But no, you have this conversion and he, my beautiful, supportive father was obviously going to tell me all about you. Except this happened on the day that my parents flew out to visit me in Paderborn," Leigh paused. She could feel the tears streaming down her face, but she realised that in the dull half-light of the cafeteria he would not be able to see them. She breathed and her voice carried nothing but coldness. She knew she was delivering a speech that would save her life or condemn her to death.

"And you know, because you are a thorough investigator, that when I picked them up from the airport, on our way back to my digs we had an accident. It's unlikely my father, a significant contributor to the Reich, a senior lecturer in leadership at your own SS staff schools, an independently wealthy man, it is unlikely he was going to tell me this great revelation about you as we walked through the airport or drove in a Reich Security Directorate vehicle," her voice had risen and her tone had turned bitter.

"So they died. They died and my father wasn't likely to have informed me that my great hero was coming to help me, but you know that, and this pathetic attempt to try and entrap me with a fucking sham of a story is beneath even your type. I shall see to it that you are removed from your post. You are not the only one with friends in high places. You fucking scum!"

She delivered the final words with a passion that betrayed her real emotions. She was scared. She turned to the door and started walking in measured steps, trying to maintain some control. She was almost into the corridor when he spoke.

"The years leave a mark, Lee-Lee."

7

Mary Reid sat very still. She eyed the men standing rigidly to attention in front of her desk. Each man concentrated on staring at a fixed point on the wall above and behind her as her gaze moved from face to face. She finally looked away from them and picked her own fixed spot on the desk to contemplate as she spoke softly, "Senior-Private Williams, what is your role here at Harrow?"

"Security Protectorate Ma'am."

"No Williams. Your specific role?"

"Camp guard Ma'am."

"And part of those duties requires you to occasionally control and take part in firing details, yes?"

"Yes Ma'am."

"Do you have to do much administration?"

"No Ma'am."

"Much in the way of cooking?"

"Ma'am?" Williams looked down at her with a slightly confused look on his face.

Without raising her eyes from her desk Mary quietly rephrased her question, "Do you have to cook for yourself?"

"Um, no Ma'am," Williams said hesitantly.

"What about painting walls, maintaining prison facilities, fixing broken locks, preparing the disposal pits, washing down the courtyards. Do you have to do any of those jobs?"

"No Ma'am," Williams said it a little more forcibly. Mary considered he had finally worked out where the conversation was going.

"No Ma'am," she echoed his tone. "In fact you have really only one task as a senior rifleman in the SS. Your one guiding light in life. To be an expert in the use of a rifle. That would be it. Lock, stock and barrel if you will pardon the pun. Is that, more or less, correct Senior-Private Williams?"

"Yes Ma'am," he said half sullenly, half apologetically. Like a child who had to admit their wrong doing.

Mary paused.

In the forefront of her mind she knew what should happen next. She knew she should look up and hold him in her glare. She should build a gathering momentum. A rising, yet controlled, tone. An increasing volume and a cacophony of scorn directed toward the Senior Rifleman and his squad Riflemen. Leaving each in no doubt at her disgust at their failure during this evening's proceedings. Making them feel guilt and shame at the waste of the Reich's resources that their training obviously was. Finally, rising from her seat to stand before them, she should remind them that weak and pathetic was not tolerated. Weak soldiers were not soldiers. They might have been able to scrape a living in the ranks of the Wehrmacht but not in the SS. She would see to it personally that he was reduced back to SS-Private rank and all of them would be reassigned for remedial training and...

...and she did none of it. She calmed her thoughts. She saw and heard Thomas Dunhill and she smelt the aroma of her sister Kasey. She drew a quiet breath, looked up from her desk and said flatly, "Just go home."

All the men looked down at her with surprised expressions. Then they looked at one another before Williams spoke up for them, "Pardon Ma'am?"

"Just go back to your billets. You know what you did wrong. You know you won't do it again. You know what happens if you do," she sighed. "I don't need to tear you all a new arsehole. Just get out."

They mumbled variously, "Thank you Ma'am" and "Yes Ma'am," saluted and left her office as quickly as they could.

Mary stayed sitting alone, illuminated in the small pool of light coming from her angled desk lamp. She had a planned rendezvous in the city but she didn't need to leave for another hour or so. She felt numb and the words played in a loop in her head. 'I love you for who you are.' Such a peculiar phrase.

She had never heard it since Kasey said it to her the night she had left. Now she had heard it again. A sudden deep pain hit her in the stomach. What if Thomas Dunhill had heard it from Kasey? What if he had known Kasey? What if he had known where she was? A possible link to her remaining family and she had crushed it. Stood on it, turned her boot into the agony of the man and finally dismissed his life as an irrelevance. He might have known where her sister was.

"For fuck's sake you pathetic man," she said it aloud to the empty office. "Why could you not stand up for yourself, why does your fucking religion have to be so fucking weak?"

The touch screen linked to the central administration database beeped and slowly awoke out of its hibernation mode. A new email message lit the screen. The records of the evening's processing had been entered by Harold prior to his going home and the final confirmations had traversed their way through the systems and protocols so beloved of an orderly Reich. The text on screen was a receipt.

```
Attention:
Chief Senior Overseer Reid,
Franz Six Memorial Centre,
PCC, Northwick Park
Confirmed OP43.99821/17052020
Processing complete
#Thomas Dunhill #Liza Carpelli #Ben Stevens
#Christine Kelly #Terrance Baxter #Amanda Baxter
Designated TR
RxDis SS_Amt_D_GB03/14/249956
```

She glanced at it, not really reading it. She had seen countless receipts before. The light from the screen was not bright but was penetrating. She reached out to mute the screen display but stopped short.

It wasn't countless receipts. That was the point. Nothing in the Reich was countless. She focussed on the last line.

RxDis SS_Amt_D_GB03/14/249956

The Inspectorate of Camps, Amt D, designated the Harrow Centre as the third of the five facilities in the Großbritannien Division. It had been in operation for fourteen years, having replaced an older centre on the same site. The last figure was the total number of collated process events that had occurred either within the walls or as part of an arrest operation within the jurisdiction. Process events. Deaths.

Mary looked at the number. Nearly a quarter of a million in fourteen years. Albeit the numbers had slowed recently. But this was only one of five centres in Great Britain and they were only five out of hundreds throughout the Empire.

"Why could your Jesus not let you stand up for yourselves? A fucking quarter of a million, here alone. You could have swept us away in a day. You weak bastards."

She held her head in her hands and massaged her temples with her fingers and felt the tear roll down her cheek. She knew why they hadn't stood up for themselves. For the same reason she hadn't. Her sisters hadn't. Her mother hadn't. It was weakness but a weakness born of the worst fears. They had been four in a house with one man and yet they had been cowed by him. Scared of him. Paralysed by fear and picked off one by one. Until she had broken free. Grown strong. Fearless. Angry. She had stood up for her sisters, her dead mother. She had beaten down and killed the bully, the tyrant.

She thought of Thomas Dunhill. Wasn't she the bully, the tyrant? She had never thought of it as that before. She had just been doing her job. One of the compartments in her mind that protected her and kept her safe, even from herself, slowly opened.

No one had asked her to defend the weak. No one had asked her to be their strength. But Thomas said he loved her. You protect those who you love or who love you. Her head hurt with the memories and the searing emotions. She saw her sister's faces, Janey and Kasey, laughing and smiling at her as she played. She tried desperately to see her mother's face but it was lost in the folds of her own pain.

Her tears dropped steadily onto her desk. She cried for the memory of her sisters, her mother, her own innocence. And she cried for Thomas and all the others that she had killed. She cried until she had nothing left inside but hollow, racking sobs. She became still as they slowly subsided and she heard again, 'You are His creation. Sent to do His will.'

"Oh, Thomas, you chose the wrong God."

She rose to her feet, wiped her face, switched out the light and left the office.

8

He retrieved some serviettes from the counter and handed them over. She sat opposite, her eyes red rimmed and sniffed quietly. He waited. When the tears stopped she looked up.

"More coffee?" Heinrich asked.

"Please," said Leigh.

By the time he returned to the table she was as composed as she thought she was likely to get. He put the coffee in front of her and resumed his seat opposite.

"You have questions?" he asked quietly.

She laughed and said sarcastically, "Questions, oh nooo, none that I can think of." She stirred the saccharin into her coffee as she continued, "Let's see, what questions could I possibly have that, if I asked, wouldn't get me immediately arrested and shot?"

"Okay, that was dumb."

"You think?"

"No, I know. I've had a lot longer to deal with this. I knew when I was coming here that I would have this conversation, but you've had it all sprung on you. I realise it's a shock and that your emotions are battered. I know and I'm sorry, but there was no other way."

"Heinrich, let's play a game, okay?" she asked.

"What?"

"A game, indulge me."

"Um, okay?"

"Suppose, for arguments sake that I am one of the leading physicists in the Greater Germanic Reich?"

"You are Leigh."

"Yes but let's just suppose, okay?"

"Okay."

"Suppose, that in my position I have briefed the Reich Chiefs and the Führer himself."

"Okay," he agreed, knowing she had.

"Do you honestly think that I wouldn't have been checked so thoroughly that someone would have found out about my supposed Turner affiliation and my duplicitous mother and father."

"Well," he countered, "let's suppose that your mother and father were incredibly clever people, schooled and trained by incredibly clever and devoted parents themselves. Let's suppose that your grandfather knew from the earliest days of the Reich that the only way to break this tyranny was to play a long game and wait for the right moment, whenever or whatever that would be. Let's suppose your mother's family were stubborn Celtic Irish who genuinely believed in the way of our Lord and even more tenaciously believed in freedom. Given that 'suppose,' then yes, I could believe it." He smiled, almost cheekily, at her.

Leigh was confused by her own reactions and emotions. She was sitting at a table with a man who might just be a very clever interrogator, but mixed in with her fear was a large element of excitement. She looked away and took a breath.

"Okay, Heinrich, you asked for questions. I want the truth. Why did you say that years would leave a mark?"

"I didn't. I said the years leave a mark. There's a difference. You know what the difference is."

The first time he had said it his words had physically shaken her. This time they dug into her skull. She felt a hollow weight in the pit of her stomach. She saw the face of her mother saying the same phrase to her all those years ago. No one had said anything remotely like it to her since.

"How do you feel Leigh?"

"Honestly, I feel tired." She looked into the coffee cup and realised that that was the truth. She felt tired of it all. Thirty-five years old and most of it spent living a completely false persona.

She sat quietly, thinking. Unbidden into her head came the words that she said each night before she slept. 'I call upon the Messengers of God to hear me. My life is a wheel. Please help me to turn it to your purpose. Light my way, guard my being, rule my mind and guide my decisions.'

She decided to trust her God as she had done her whole life. If she was wrong then so be it. "Heinrich, if this is true, if you are genuine, tell me why did my father trust you?"

Heinrich looked at her and shook his head slowly, "I wish it could be a simple answer. Unfortunately, there isn't a thing or a place that's the key to why. Just my story."

"Great, you haven't started and I'm confused. Just answer me, why did he trust you?" Leigh asked.

"At first I didn't know. I'd joined up as a soldier when I was eighteen but was selected for commission from the ranks in 2002 and was sent to SS-Junkerschulen at Bad Tölz. He met me, or I met him rather, when he came to Bad Tölz in September 2003 as one of the guest lecturers in my final month of Waffen-SS Officer Training."

She looked hard at him, "You're kidding?"

"Leigh, why would I kid about that, it's a fact you could check."

"I don't need to, I know he lectured at Bad Tölz on the Twenty-second of September 2003," she said.

"What, are you some sort of date freak with a photographic memory?" Now Heinrich looked a little startled.

"No, but I started at Cambridge on the Twenty-first of September 2003. He'd dropped me off with all my stuff on the Sunday night. He was on his way to the airport to fly out. It was a big day in my life, so I remember it." She smiled a sad smile and added, "Sorry, I interrupted you, go on."

"Well, he lectured about leadership and he was a really excellent speaker. It was interesting and that was that. We met at the reception event in the Officers' Mess afterwards and I remember that when he spoke to me he had the knack of making me feel like I was the only person in the room. I couldn't even shake his hand properly as I had a sling on my arm from a broken collar bone. I was desperate for it to be better in time for the Graduation ceremony in October. He shook my left hand and told me that he was sure I would make it. If jockeys could recover in a matter of weeks, he reckoned, a Waffen-SS Officer would bounce back. He was right as it turned out. But that night we spoke about my village and, unlike anyone else I had ever met, he knew where it was."

"I guessed you were from Lower Saxony based on your accent," Leigh said.

"My accent? I thought my English was accent 'less.'" Heinrich sounded almost offended.

"Heinrich, focus," she said exasperated. "Where are you from?"

"Well, you're quite close. I'm from Deuna."

"Where?"

"Deuna, it's a small village in the Eichsfeld district of Thüringen."

Leigh looked at him blankly.

"The Harz mountains?" He tried vainly to get some recognition over to her.

"Give me a reference Heinrich, I'm a physicist. Geography was never that big on my list."

"Okay, it's about two hundred and fifty kilometres south-west of Berlin and one hundred and fifty south-south-east of Hannover. Does that help?"

"Sort of." She had no idea where Deuna was, but it didn't actually matter to her.

Heinrich laughed. "See that's the normal reaction I get. But your father said 'Ah! Deuna,' like he knew it. I asked him how he recognised the name and he said it had an interesting history. He asked me if I knew of the Deuna Crest."

"The what?"

"It's the ancient heraldic coat that the village used until the rise of the Reich. Anyway, I said I knew nothing of it, but I said it a little too quickly. Your father knew I was lying and yet he just smiled. He said, 'Don't worry, all is good,' wished me luck and went on his way."

"So what's the significance of a crest?"

"I told you; it was the ancient sign of the village. But it had some particular imagery in it that didn't sit too well with the new government. So it was banned and all copies of it purged from the records."

"How come you knew about it?"

"When I was nine years old, my grandmother was dying. The night before she passed she gave me a pendant that she had carried with her since childhood. She told me it was for me and not to tell anyone about it. She made me promise her. I didn't realise the implications of it until I was older, but I loved her an awful lot so I kept the promise and the pendant. I still have it."

Heinrich reached into his pocket and slipped a small shield-shaped, enamelled, copper pendant onto the table. It was only three centimetres by two and although its colours were a little faded they were still bright enough to show the detailed design. The curved bottom half of the shield was white with a stylistic three-spire building atop a representation of water. The top half of the tiny shield had a red background. Centrally mounted in this, picked out in white enamel, was a six-spoke wheel.

Leigh looked down at the pendant, before picking it up and examining it closely. She got up from the table and moved to the counters so she could examine the pendant under the counter lights. She knew little about antiquities but anyone could see that this was old. She was still staring at the pendant as she said, "Are you insane carrying this around? It has a Turner wheel on it." She looked over at him.

"Well, it has a Turner Church on it too. That's what the building in the bottom half represents. The three spires for the three peoples of the Book."

Leigh nodded.

"But no, I'm not insane. I said I kept it, not that I keep it on my person, not normally. Tonight is an exception. When I joined the Hitler Youth and began to learn about the enemies of the Reich, obviously I figured out what my grandmother had given to me. So I hid it. I kept it hidden. No one knew I had it, no one. In fact, since my grandmother placed it in my hand that pendant has only been seen by me, your parents just before they died, and now you."

Leigh retook her seat opposite him, "What about your parents?"

"No. My father was ex-army but after nine years he left the Service and went to work at the Power Station that's just outside Deuna. He died in a fire on the site six months before I was born."

"I'm sorry," Leigh said and meant it.

"It's okay, I never knew him. To be honest I don't think my mum ever recovered properly. So her mum came to live with us and help out with me. Like I said, I was a little boy and I loved my grandmother dearly. She made me promise not to tell anyone about the pendant, so I didn't. Then, when I learnt just what she had bequeathed to me, telling anyone at all was out of the question."

"Is your mum still alive?"

"No, she died a few years ago. But Leigh, let me get through this. I'll tell you about my mum later, okay?" Heinrich looked at her.

"Okay," she said softly. "So no one knew about it. What did my father say to you?" Leigh set the pendant down on the table and realised that this interrogation had completely switched around. She was asking the questions.

"Nothing. That was it. I didn't produce the pendant and say, 'Da-Dah!' Actually, yes I know about the crest, I have a copy here." He framed his hands like a stage-magician pointing out his box of tricks.

Leigh felt some of the tension slip away. She was still unsure where this was going but she was beginning to think it might not be headed for a cell or a firing squad.

"It was just like I said, he knew the village, asked me about the crest, I lied to him and he told me not to worry. He had obviously figured I knew about the symbol and was embarrassed by it. I was young and not that good at lying to anyone, let alone a man like your father. That was it." Heinrich took a sip of his coffee. He picked up the pendant and slipped it carefully back into his pocket.

"Okay, so you met him in '03, how do you go from there to his study?"

"In a series of steps that seemed unconnected then, but now seem like a well-worn path."

"Go on," she encouraged.

"I met him and your mother at a formal reception in Berchtes-gaden for the New Year celebrations in December 2004. Your mother had been invited to play for the Führer. I guess you remember that as well."

"Yeah, that was a major honour for mum," Leigh lied. She knew her mother had dreaded the event. "I remember the Führer had heard one of her recordings of Quantz's Flute compositions and asked for her to play at a reception at the retreat. Everything was very easy to organise as dad was a well-known supporter of the Party. I didn't go. I was too busy having a ball in Cambridge." She smiled at the memories of that time before thinking she had spotted a major flaw in Heinrich's story.

"Hang on Heinrich. You would have been a Junior Officer. What were you doing at a private function at the Kehlsteinhaus?" she asked.

"I was a member of the Leibstandarte SS Adolf Hitler. Got posted there after Officer training. All the best did, you know." He stopped and looked for a reaction from her.

"Yes, I imagine they did and occasionally the odd one like you would slip through," she offered back to him, her face neutral. He laughed out loud and dipped his head in mock submission.

"Go on Heinrich, tell me about that night."

"We were just a regular troop deployment but on formal events we would be turned out as pretty guards all standing around looking shiny. The Führer always used us if the Japanese or Spanish or Italians were turning up. I think he wanted them to see us as his own Praetorian Guard. I guess we were. Anyway, I was on duty in the reception area. Your father spotted me and wandered over to talk to me. I thought it was remarkable that he remembered me from the lecture over a year beforehand, but he said that he was pleased to see me 'Sans-Sling' and laughed."

Leigh smiled at the thought of her father cracking one of his lame jokes. He had a manner that seemed to relax the people around him. It had allowed a man so devoted to the overthrow of the Reich to mix freely with the men he despised.

"He spoke to me about generalities and then said, 'So Heinrich, what ambition do you hold?' I told him straight away. I remember my youthful enthusiasm all bubbly and confident and it makes me cringe now. But then I was just cocky, so I told him I was happy in the Division but I wanted to be on the Führer's close protection unit. Your father just looked at me and said, 'You will be, you will be. If you want it enough and you frame the thought in your mind, you can make it happen.' That was it." Heinrich paused and looked at Leigh.

"That's it?"

"Well yes, what did you expect? I was a show pony on a massive night for the Führer and your father was a VIP. He could hardly spend the night talking to me could he? Your mother came over and he introduced me but then they left."

"You remember this passing conversation from fifteen years ago?"

"Well, no Leigh, I didn't. I did remember his advice about positive thinking, but no, I doubt I would have remembered the details. But as the years progressed and I met your parents again then, yes, those memories became more important. They weren't just passing irrelevances anymore. As we talked and remembered them so they became reinforced. Like memories with friends do." Heinrich voice had taken on an edge. Leigh recognised it as a rising annoyance that she still mistrusted his story.

"Okay, sorry, go on. Please go on."

"I worked hard and I don't mean it to sound prideful, but I was good. In October 2005, after two years in the Division, I was selected for specialist training and posted to the Führer's Close Protection Detail."

"What? You were one of the guys with the earpieces and the sunglasses?" Leigh asked.

"Yes, the guys with the sunglasses. But we did do a bit more than look cool. Although, to be fair, we did do cool quite well." Heinrich smiled and asked her, "Do you remember March 2006?"

She shook her head, "I was still at University, in my third year. Why, what happened?"

"Berlin, March 2006, you don't remember?" He paused for her to think. The look on her face changed, she registered disbelief.

"The assassination attempt on the Führer? You were there?" She blurted the question out. He said nothing, just nodded and smiled a strange half-smile, half-grimace. She looked at him and saw the strength in the man. She saw his eyes that for the most part sparkled and laughed but occasionally held memories that were deep and dark. She studied his face and then she realised.

"My God, you're *him?*"

9

Heinrich leant back and raised his tee-shirt on the left side. There was a deep and ugly scar running the length of his lower ribs. A skilled surgeon had attempted to make the best of a horrendous wound but cosmetic grafts couldn't hide the damage.

"Yes, him. The man who saved the Führer. Who took the bullet and saved the day. Well, not the bullet obviously, but the very sharp knife." He smiled. "All the publicity that surrounded it and, thankfully, because of the nature of our jobs, we were never exposed. The whole of the close protection team were assured anonymity. All the reports and all the enquiries and never once was my identity released to the public. But yes, I was him. I am him."

They were quiet. She watched as he lowered his tee-shirt and she waited for him to push the pain of the memory into wherever he kept it sealed.

"Your father flew out to visit me in hospital, did you know that?"

"No!" Leigh said, surprised.

"He stood by my bedside and handed me a small parcel. He said he was sorry he hadn't been farsighted enough to bring it the last time he met me and laughed at his own joke. I didn't get it and he just said, 'Don't worry Heinrich, but I thought you would appreciate the story and like the irony. It's proof of the value of a classical education.'"

"What was in the parcel?" Leigh sounded intrigued.

"Calm down, nothing exciting. Well, I thought nothing exciting at first. He had brought me a copy of Shakespeare's Julius Cesar. I wasn't going anywhere so I read it and to be honest I struggled through it. But after that I was kind of hooked on Shakespeare." Heinrich looked at her. She was looking at him, watching him closely. "You are too Leigh, I know. Your mum and dad told me."

"Well, I like it but not like my dad did. Anyway, what's this got to do with you and him?" She said it abruptly.

"I read it and laughed and really appreciated Donald's sense of humour. I knew he'd taken a chance making even a slight joke out of the events and I felt very honoured that he had taken the time to share it with me."

"I don't understand Heinrich, what has Julius Caesar got to do with this?"

"You're telling me you've never read the play?"

"No, it's boring and all about ancient Rome. Give me a break. I like Shakespeare but I'm not a freak."

"The Ides of March?" Heinrich paused and looked at her. She registered the same look as she had when he had mentioned his home village.

"The Fifteenth of March was the day Caesar was attacked inside the Senate. It's also, of course, the date of the Founding Führer's death. On the Fifteenth of March 2006, the third Führer and his wife were going to the Reichstag Museum to unveil a new portrait of his father. Given the circumstances, if I'd read Shakespeare, I might have been a bit more wary. That was what your dad meant about the value of a classical education. Anyway, I didn't have one of those and I guess neither did the rest of the guys on the Detail. So when the attacker ran from the crowd we didn't react quickly enough. It was obvious we weren't going to get shots off before he covered the distance so, instead, I moved into his path and took the blade into the ribs. The rest of the team dragged him off me. You've seen the news reports. It was all over in seconds. I was the hero. Stabbed four times and the Führer was saved." He looked down at the table as he said it. He reached for his coffee and took a sip. It was still vile and getting cold but he drank it.

"You got the Führer's personal award, the Deutscher Orden. It was a massive thing, I remember the headlines. Only the what? The twentieth in the whole history of the Reich?" she looked at him with amazement on her face.

"Twenty-second."

"What?"

"Twenty-second. There was an oversight on the Propaganda Ministry's part. There had been twenty-one previous awards, but yes, it was a big deal. I was only the eighth to get it non-posthumously."

"Anyway, I was laid up in hospital and medically down-graded so I couldn't go back on to the Detail. All in all I was in convalescence and physiotherapy for months. I was fairly down. My exuberance and cockiness had evaporated. I thought my career was over and was getting quietly depressed."

Heinrich looked out the cafeteria window. He was looking at the first flecks of rain marking the glass but his focus was far off in time. Leigh was quiet and waited. She knew the emotions he would have faced in the hospital bed. She had faced them during her life. The frustration of not being able to do the things you took for granted. The shock of having nearly died, the realisation that life and career may be destroyed. She watched him watching the increasingly frequent raindrops.

Heinrich spoke to the drops on the window, as if lost in his memories, "Your father came to see me a couple of times a month while I was in hospital. He spoke to me about life and opportunity and generally just chatted to me about the things that interested me. He became a friend to me. He told me that he was sure things would work out. It was the fifth time he came to see me that I finally got the courage up to tell him I knew about the Deuna Crest. He asked me how and I told him about my grandmother's gift. I didn't show him it. It was hidden far away from the hospital, I didn't even tell him I still had it. I just told him about it."

Leigh realised the enormity of what Heinrich had done. "But you only knew my father as a massive supporter of the Party. By telling him that your grandmother had been a Turner, you faced losing everything. They would have stripped you of your Commission, your awards, possibly even your life, Heinrich. What were you thinking?"

Heinrich turned back into the room and looked deep into Leigh's eyes. "I was thinking he was my friend and I didn't want to keep anything from him."

She held his gaze and began to realise her father had seen the same as she was seeing now. Heinrich was an intelligent, thoughtful and sensitive man. He might have followed a specific path through life but he was not a blinkered serf of the State.

"Donald just said 'thank you for telling me' and that he would never reveal anything of our conversation. He continued to visit and in the June he brought your mother out to see me. She was a very special woman, but I guess I don't need to tell you that, do I?"

Leigh smiled and shook her head. A classically trained flautist and harpist, Rosalyn Wilson had been a featured soloist for the London Philharmonic, the Berlin Symphony and the New Munich Philharmonic Orchestras. She had released three award-winning albums, played for the Führer, the Spanish, Italian and Japanese Emperors, was the recipient of the German Classical Societies Honoured Fellowship Award and held an Honorary Doctorate in Music from the University of Belfast. Being a native of Belfast, the latter had made her smile more than any other plaudit. She was also a lifelong hater of the regime she had grown up in.

"She was so kind to me and told me that life would turn out the way it was meant. That I shouldn't force my career or my plans and things would be okay." Heinrich smiled at the memory. "Your father said that I had nothing to worry about. That the man who saved the Führer's life would be looked after. He last visited me on the day I was being released from the physiotherapy-convalescent centre. I was allegedly 'all cured' and thought I was going to be met by a driver, taken to SS administration and medically discharged. There was no position in the Waffen-SS for someone who had no chance of being medically upgraded again. The damage to the lung was always going to mean a lack of full fitness. I was sitting on the side of the bed just waiting when your father came in and said he had brought someone to see me. In walked Reichsführer-SS Jason Friedrichand. When he came into the room, I leapt up so quickly I nearly ruptured my side."

"Hmm," Leigh said. "Jason and dad went back a long way. Dad called him the most evil man who..." Leigh stopped herself. She realised that if this was a clever interrogation being constructed by Heinrich, then she had just provided him his coup de grâce. She looked away into the empty room.

"Leigh, it's okay. The most evil man who ever held that post. He said the same to me, later. In comparison to Himmler's legacy, your father said that Friedrichand was worse in every regard. Yet on the day he introduced me he just said that the Reichsführer wanted to talk to me about a job. I was not to be discharged from the Service. Instead Jason Friedrichand himself asked me..."

Leigh's eyebrows raised.

"...asked me, yes. Not told me, he asked me if I would like to transfer to the Allgemeine-SS and onto the Gestapo Graduate program."

"That's impressive," said Leigh and realised she genuinely meant it. It was an elite way into the SS and not many were afforded it. Even less a transferee from the Waffen-SS that was injured.

"I know. To be honest, I was dumbstruck. Literally, I couldn't think of what to say or do. I just stared at him and after a short time nodded, mumbled a thank you and saluted. Not exactly the most auspicious of meetings."

"My father set that up for you?" Leigh almost asked it to herself.

"Yes. He was a good man." Heinrich smiled at her.

Leigh genuinely smiled back at him.

"Your father mentioned that it would mean having to go to Oxford University to study but he was sure I could cope. That was pretty much that. Friedrichand departed the building and I was escorted to Gestapo headquarters to complete the usual mound of paperwork."

"Heinrich?"

"Yes?"

"In all this time, did my father ever mention me?"

"He said he had a daughter, yes. He said you were a leading member of the University Officers' Corps at Cambridge and that you were a solid member of the Party. Later he told me you were working in Germany for the Security Directorate, but no details. That was all he or your mother ever mentioned until much later."

"Okay. Listen do you mind if I smoke? I'm gasping for one."

"Are you allowed to in here?"

"Heinrich, we… Well, you… are, possibly, talking about stuff that can get you shot and you want to know if there's a no-smoking policy?"

"Fair point." Heinrich got up and retrieved a side plate from one of the dish racks at the counter and returned. "You go right ahead. You do realise they're not good for you," he chided her.

"Yes, I do, but I also read a startling statistic the other month."

"What was that?"

"Well, apparently 100 per cent of non-smokers, that's one 100 per cent of them, will also," Leigh paused for comic effect, "die." She smiled smugly at him and lit her cigarette.

He leant back and laughed a gentle self-mocking laugh. "I'll remember not to tell you off for smoking again then."

She took a deep draw of the smoke and as she exhaled asked, "So you joined the Gestapo at the request of the Reichsführer-SS. What next?"

"I spent a few months doing all of the normal basic investigative courses and was attached to a senior investigator until my start date for Oxford in 2007. I selected Criminal Psychology and thoroughly enjoyed it. I was invited to your parent's house for the first time that September."

"Sorry Heinrich, September, why not earlier?"

"Your father had apologised it hadn't been sooner but he or your mother were always scheduled for one event or another. He also said it was good for me to find my own feet first."

Leigh realised the real reason may well have been because she was finishing at Cambridge and was around the house a lot in 2007. In the August she had secured a placement to study for her Postgraduate Degree in Stuttgart which saw her leaving on a permanent basis. She hadn't lived in her parent's house since then. That at least told her that in 2007 her father and mother still had a long way to go before they trusted Heinrich. She said nothing.

"Anyway, I would go up there and stay the odd weekend. I was going to do a Masters straight after my undergrad and with the time I spent at your parent's house, reading their library, I decided that English Literature would be an interesting subject. Simply put, your parents and I became friends. We would occasionally go to the theatre in Cambridge together. I was invited to attend some of your mother's performances in London. If they invited me for the weekend I sat with them and talked to them. I did see photographs of you around the house but we never spoke of you because of the nature of where you worked. You don't start a conversation by asking, 'oh, what's your daughter doing in the Security Directorate?' It wasn't like they worked at keeping you out of any discussions. It just was what it was."

She nodded and considered what he'd said.

He continued, "Sometimes we would talk about the world. The four Empires and how the planet was shaping up. Later, around December '09 or early '10 we started talking about the Reich and what scared it into doing some of the things it did. The conversations got deeper and more interesting. I looked forward so much to going up to their house." Heinrich stopped. He stared down at the table and his eyes looked profoundly sad.

"What is it?" Leigh asked.

"My mum died on the Twenty-first of December 2010. I was in England and she was back in Germany. I had gone back to see her during the summer break but she was on her own when she died. An aortic aneurysm. The doctors said it had probably taken less than ten minutes for her to die from the moment it burst and that she didn't feel anything. But I was full of thoughts that she had been so terribly alone when her time came." Heinrich's voice was laden with remembered grief.

"I'm really sorry Heinrich."

He gave a resigned smile and nod. "I obviously went back to Germany to sort things out. Once the funeral was over, I made arrangements to clear the house, lease it and then I returned to England. Your parents invited me up to Cambridgeshire for the Twenty-first of January. It was my thirtieth birthday and they had guessed I would be spending it getting quietly drunk and depressed. So they resolved to cheer me up, which they did. I had a great day with them. We got frozen as we walked through the Colleges of Cambridge and when we finally got back to the house in Warboys, we sat in the kitchen and drank mulled wine. That Saturday evening as we chatted I told them about my mum being alone. I cried for the first time since she had died. Your mother reached over and took my hand and said quite softly, 'She wasn't alone. Our Lord was with her.'" Heinrich looked at Leigh. She wasn't crying but he could see the emotion in her eyes. The glistening that bordered on tears. She nodded for him to go on.

"I looked at your mother and I didn't say anything. I just cried a bit more. Your father started to talk about the Turner Religion. Of the simple message that each of the Prophets had brought. Of the unification of all the Messengers of God. He spoke of the idea that God was one destination reached via many paths. He spoke of the binding together of the Old Book and the new way. He spoke of how Jesus's message of tolerance for the other beliefs in the world had been the single greatest event in history. Of how, once nonviolence and love had been shown to succeed in the face of opposition, humanity had entered its golden period."

"When he talked about the peaceful coexistence and gentle progress of humanity I began to doubt the Reich for the first time. I learnt about Jesus entering into Jerusalem in triumph. How the Pharisees welcomed him, the Discourse of the Pharisees on the Fast of the Firstborn, the conversion of Pilate, the delegation to Rome, the conversion of the Emperor and the building of the Temples in Rome, Alexandria and Constantinople."

"Your father was more animated and passionate than I had ever seen or heard him. Your mother taught me of the last Prophet and how He had continued the divine message. Of how He had united the factions and how the Council of Medina bound the religion together. I learnt how He had followed Jesus in ascending. I learnt how, as the centuries progressed, the great religions of the East were recognised as being just different paths to the same outcome. We talked and talked for hours. Eventually I looked at the two of them and asked them why they trusted me enough to talk to me like this. I could just go to the authorities. Your mother said, 'We let the wheel turn at its own pace. God places you where you need to be'..."

"...and sends the people he needs to send." Leigh finished the sentence for him.

The silence of the cafeteria bound them together and they sat quietly for a long time thinking of their separate memories of a shared phrase.

Eventually, Heinrich continued, "So in 2011, I finished at Oxford and returned to Germany, with an awful lot to think about."

"I need more coffee. You?" Leigh pushed herself up from the table. Heinrich nodded.

He watched her walk away to the vending machines. He had often looked at her photos in Donald and Rosalyn's house. He had always thought her pretty. But from the moment he saw her tonight he realised she was much more. Her prettiness had matured into beauty. Her body moved with a grace. A sensual grace that he found himself unable to look away from. Being one of the top scientists of her generation, she was obviously intelligent, but he hadn't expected her to be such a complete package of mind and body.

He smiled as he watched her from across the room. When she looked back over to him and held his gaze he felt that lurch in his heart and stomach. He knew it from first longings and first kisses and first loves. The emotional kick that the body loved and craved and the mind became intoxicated by. He tried not to break into a wider grin and failed.

She returned to her seat and slid his coffee over. "What were you smiling at?"

"Oh nothing really," he lied badly.

Leigh smiled back at him and almost reached across the table to take his hand. She stopped herself and simply said, "Go on with your story Heinrich."

"I was identified as an 'oaf.'"

Leigh looked puzzled, "An oaf? Really? Not exactly a compliment, surely?"

"Actually, it is. It stands for an Offiziersanwärter mit Herausragenden Führungsqualitäten. It's just pronounced 'oaf' and meant that they'd identified me as someone with the potential to achieve senior rank, so I was posted into the most demanding of the security divisions. On graduation from Oxford my Waffen-SS rank was aligned to that of a Gestapo Kriminaldirektor and I was assigned to Department B in Headquarters, Berlin."

Leigh's features hardened, "Sects and Churches; was that your choice?"

"No, I took your parent's advice and just went where I was sent. I worked some low-level investigations and continued to wrestle with the feelings and thoughts that had begun the night of my birthday. What do you know about Department B?" he asked.

"Only what's out in common knowledge. They're the 'hunters of the holy,' the 'scourge of the saved.'"

He gave a small, tight laugh. "B Department had been reorganised in the 1970s to have complete responsibility for matters regarding religious groups throughout the whole of the Reich. We also had special powers to liaise with and assist the Spanish, Italian and Japanese authorities. I got to visit the New Spanish Nations in South America to look at the ancient Aztec sites, Italy's African colonies to look at the Egyptian sites and even Tokyo and down to the Japanese Australian Territories. My first job was down there helping the Japanese to investigate a Turner sect in Hobart. They'd been discovered holding meetings in a park that used to be a cemetery. When they were rounded up their leader had a document in his possession that was later claimed to be an original Gospel manuscript. The Japanese knew that it was outside of their capabilities, so they handed it to us. I was given access to the Religious Archives in Berlin."

"How many Turners?" Leigh asked.

"Sixteen active members. But after their families were rounded up in the DNA screenings it was a total of one hundred and twenty eight."

"All of them?" she asked with a catch in her voice.

Heinrich just nodded his head in answer.

10

The spring rain fell more heavily outside the cafeteria windows. The lights of the security compound were transformed into a fuzzy, translucent haze that split into multi-coloured spikes as the droplets running down the pane acted as prisms.

Leigh and Heinrich both looked out at the night. He felt renewed guilt at how he had assisted in the murder of innocents and she was trying to come to terms with the possibility that Heinrich might well be what he professed to be.

Heinrich spoke quietly, "The Archives, Leigh. The place is fascinating. Back in the 1930s the plan was to destroy everything to do with any religion, but the old Nazi occultists wanted to study the writings to see if there was anything of relevance. In the end I think the German national obsession with record keeping kicked in. So they built a special repository and added to it over the years. Anything remotely of interest went in there. The writings and the documents that they hold are truly awe-inspiring. When the Hobart document came up I was given free access and spent a lot of time trying to authenticate it."

His voice carried the excitement he had felt on first entering the building on Berlin's Oranienburger Straße. "Oh Leigh, I've seen the oldest existing copy of the Gospel of Jesus. Actually seen it, and with the help of the archivists translated it from the original Hebrew. I even managed to become passable in Hebrew and Latin myself. I've seen a partial scroll of the first Sanhedrin, when He was initially heralded and an official Roman record from the

Conference of the Pharisees in AD 65. That's an actual transcription of the moment in history when the whole of the Jewish Nation of the Old Book formally adopted the teachings of the New."

Heinrich's eyes danced with enthusiasm as he continued, "I've held The Medina Accord from 622 when the Quraysh resolved to assist the Prophet, to end the persecutions and merge the teachings of the Messengers of God. It is amazing Leigh, I wish you could see it. It's no wonder the Archive is one of the most secure facilities in the Reich. That's where my conversion truly took hold. I read the documents outlining the events your father had told me about. I discovered a purpose."

"And all this time you kept in touch with my parents?" she asked, still trying to evaluate the man in front of her.

"During my tour of duty I would get to visit England, albeit infrequently, but I would always catch up with your parents. We talked of the documents. We spoke of the truth they held and the real evil of the Reich. We talked about how a conspiracy on a vast scale to bring down the regime would be impossible to achieve. They told me how a few well-placed people might just be able to stage a coup d'état. That was the plan your grandfather and others like him had worked out. The long term and slow infiltration of the system to its highest levels."

Leigh appraised him as he spoke. She could see that either he was a phenomenally good actor or he was telling her the truth. She had known this man for, she glanced at her watch, it was just two hours since she had received his first call. Two hours. Her life was changed either way.

"It was a slow process Leigh. It wasn't a sudden moment or flash revelation. But in May 2014 I had some leave owing and went to see your parents. I arrived on the Saturday night and told them that I wanted to become a Turner. We spent the next couple of days discussing how and what it would mean. The things I would have to do to continue doing my job, yet keep believing in the truth and the central tenets. They told me over and over that I'd have to resolve the struggle in my heart and soul each and every time I was forced to deny the love I felt. How, if I wanted to fulfil the destiny, I'd have to look for ways to defeat the tyranny. On the

Monday night I said the Turner Creed for the first time. Rosalyn warned me that the years of duplicity could wear you down and leave a mark. I showed them the Deuna Crest and it was, quite simply, the best night of my life." Heinrich smiled.

"The next morning, as I was leaving, they said they were going to catch a flight over to Paderborn to see you. For the first time they both spoke of you and what you did. Donald told me that he needed to talk to you. I thought he just meant he was going to tell you about me. But he said that when you were a little girl he'd made you promise to keep your beliefs a complete secret. To trust no one. They said that they now thought I could be an ally in the struggle and it was important that you knew as well. That perhaps the two of us might be able to help one another if the right opportunity came along. But that without him telling you, then you'd never accept me as a friend let alone a confidant. They couldn't exactly ring you up to discuss this so they were going to go and see you."

"Over the years I'd asked your parents many questions. The last ones I asked that morning were why they trusted me and why they were prepared to tell you to do the same. Your father said that, apart from having had ample opportunity to have him, Rosalyn, you and all your extended family lifted, no one had ever been arrested and taken away. But then he said the real reason was because he and Rosalyn regarded me as a friend and when I had professed my belief through the Creed they could see God in my heart. It was that simple. I said my goodbyes, we hugged and I drove off. They got ready to go to you." Heinrich stopped.

He could see the sadness in Leigh's eyes. "I am so sorry Leigh. I've regretted it every day since. If I had believed earlier, or later, they wouldn't have gone to see you. You wouldn't have been in the car."

He paused and took a drink of cold coffee. He emptied the cup and looked at her across the table. She still hadn't spoken and he could see she was clenching her jaw against the memories.

"I read the reports of the accident and I doubted that they had even had a chance to mention my name let alone tell you what was happening. They would have wanted to wait until they were somewhere private and secure."

He spoke quietly, "Leigh, didn't you ever wonder why they were coming out to see you on such short notice?"

"No I didn't," her voice was almost breaking with the emotion of recalling that day. "It wasn't unusual. They travelled to Germany a lot. I was in Paderborn on a research project and they would just ring up and say they were coming over. It wasn't unusual and seriously Heinrich, do you think they'd have mentioned the reason for their visit on an open phone line?"

He shook his head slowly, knowing what she had said was right. They sat quietly, both regretting the conversation that had never taken place.

"Did you go to their funeral?" Leigh asked.

"Yes I was there. I knew you were still in hospital on the critical list." Heinrich looked and felt older than his years when he thought back to that day. Watching the friends he loved being given a State Funeral by a state they despised.

"You never got in touch with me from then till now?"

"No."

"Why Heinrich?"

"Because you would never have accepted me."

"So if that was your thinking, if you knew I would never believe you, why are you telling me now?"

"Because now I'm here and I know the project that you're working on."

She looked at him and the realisation of what he had just said dawned on her. "What do you know?" she asked cautiously.

"Leigh, I've been posted in as head of security for a reason. Lohse was going to be replaced anyway, his son's antics in Munich just pre-empted what was coming. The Reich staff insisted the new head of security should be a Colonel and had to have special access clearances. Now that Project Thule is a proven concept, the Gestapo have been tasked to use it. They want to resolve some matters. The decision was taken at the highest level and the Führer decided that the man who would head up the security should be briefed on what the project is. Reichsführer Friedrichand made the appointment himself and for some reason I'm not exactly sure of, chose me. Unlike Lohse, who was always kept in the dark about the details of the project, I know what's going on here. I don't for one moment profess to understand the science and I admit to not believing it was possible at first. But I'm here now. I didn't ask for the post, I played the game as your mother and father taught me. But when I was selected and briefed on what the project can do, when I knew I would finally meet you, I thought..." Heinrich paused.

"You thought what Heinrich?"

"That you could use it to resolve this."

"What?!"

"Leigh, use Project Thule to answer your question. Use it to find out if your father trusted me."

11

Are you insane? You think I just walk in there and say, 'Oh I need to use the lab' and that's it? You think it's like a screwdriver?"

"No, I'm not insane although when they first told me what the project could do, I thought everyone else was. To be honest I have no idea how it works but there must be a way. You're the deputy head of the whole experiment. Are you telling me you can't do it?" Heinrich said it not as a challenge, but Leigh took it that way.

"What, are you daring me? This isn't some game to be played Heinrich, it isn't quite as easy as you might think."

"I don't know what to think, I don't know how it works. I was briefed on what it can do, not how." His voice had raised a little and he took a deep breath. "Look, Leigh, I didn't mean to sound trite and I haven't the first clue what would be required. But I thought if it was possible then a Sunday night would be the best time for it. Is it possible?"

"No Heinrich it isn't. Well, it is, but not without Berlin knowing that the system is being used and seeing what it's being used for. Which in effect means no, it isn't without massive repercussions that have to be thought through. I can't just walk in there, set a switch and hope no one is looking." She was angry at his naivety and angry at being angry. It wasn't his fault he didn't understand the science.

Heinrich ran both of his hands through his hair and exhaled deeply. "Well, what now?" he said flatly.

"Heinrich, it's late. I need to go back home. I've got to get up and come into work tomorrow. Can I get a car to take me?" She stood up and began to clear the table of the coffee cups, the sachets, stirrers and her improvised ashtray.

"I'll take you. I have my own car here."

"I thought you said dropping in to see me was not an option."

"Dropping you back home after you have cooperated on my fictitious problems earlier is not suspicious. In fact it would be expected. I live out past you." Heinrich stood and cleared his own cups.

"Will you at least consider what I suggested?" he said as she went to walk away from the table. "Heinrich, I imagine all I'll do over the next few days is think of what you said. If you don't surprise me and take me into custody as we're about to leave here."

"Leigh I wouldn't..."

"It's a joke, relax. And yes, of course I'll think about things. By the sound of it I'll also need to brief you on the actual project. I have no idea what they told you in Berlin, but I'm guessing they made it all sound so bloody easy."

"In truth, yes they did."

"Well, I'm not doing it tonight, I need to take you into the Jewel to show you how it works."

"The Jewel?"

"The Deep Underground Engineering Laboratories, D. U. E. L., it's what we're standing on top of Heinrich. Gee, you haven't been here long have you?"

"Not really. It was the inexperience that I used to get you here tonight."

They stopped next to the bins and dumped their rubbish in. Leigh could feel his physical presence next to her. She was awkwardly aware of the reaction her own body was having as he stood close. She turned to face him, "Yeah, what problem did you come up with to warrant ringing me on a Sunday, if we're asked?"

"There was an alarm that went off at nineteen hundred hours. It just flashed up to say that a digital lock on an isolation room in the Optical Systems Lab had released. I was paged as routine and knew it was because one of Professor Faber's experiments had ended and the door was released from a time-lock, but I made a fuss about it." Heinrich put a gruff tone to his voice as he re-enacted his earlier performance, "Why are doors being locked down and none of the security personnel, not even me, have override authority? It won't do."

"But the Wehrmacht guards have access to everywhere," Leigh said slightly puzzled.

"Yes they do but, I'm SS. You know how it goes. I'm only the project's security director. I don't actually have override access to any of the real estate. They have to inform me about any matters in the labs, but they have control of all the physical security and they're not about to share it."

"But that's daft."

"No that's inter-service rivalry and it's always been the same. They knew I'd end up looking like a twit."

"That's just ridiculous. I thought you were all meant to be a band of brothers?"

"Not so much. More like they are the strange cousins no one talks about."

"So what happened?"

"Well, you can see it from their point of view, a new SS com-mandant, all very strong-minded and stamping his authority. I pretended to be angry and ended my little tirade by saying some-thing along the lines of 'I'll show the bloody scientists this is not their personal chemistry set.' They could have easily said, 'Oh, we have access Sir' but I was banking on them not doing that. It wasn't much of a gamble. In fact it was a sure thing. When I was a junior soldier in the Waffen-SS I would have taken the opportunity to embarrass a senior Wehrmacht Officer."

"So you rang me?"

"Yes. At first I went through the motions of not being able to find Faber's number and so I called you. Allegedly I was getting you in to explain why it was locked down." Heinrich smiled at her.

"So don't we need to show our faces underground?"

"No, I'll just tell them you talked me around."

"Wouldn't it be better if, when I'm asked, I say you're a dick-head on too much of a power-trip for your own good?" Leigh held her face perfectly straight and looked at him. She watched his eyes falter just a little as he was deciding if she was being serious or not.

He frowned.

She relaxed and smiled. "Only kidding. I'll just say that I talked you round and now you understand why the safety factors are so important. Blah, blah, blah."

She turned away and walked out of the cafeteria and back down the stairs. Heinrich followed. They could see the rain falling in sheets across the compound as they got to the main doors.

"You wait here Leigh; I'll go get the car."

She just nodded.

He pushed the after-hours lock release and the doors slid open. There was no wind, the evening was calm and the rain deadened the noise of the city traffic in the distance. Heinrich jogged down the steps and then ran over to the staff car park. Leigh watched him as he faded into the grey and silver light.

She continued to stare into the middle distance toward the rain sodden car park, but her thoughts were focussed on Heinrich's story. The phrases he had used, the way he spoke of her parents. The regard he held them in, the sadness and joy she had seen in his eyes. She was convinced he was genuine, yet still there was hesitancy. She had already said things that would have implicated her. Did that mean it was too late already? If he wasn't genuine, wouldn't he have just arrested her? And what of his suggestion to use the project? She had thought about it before but dismissed it. Even if it had been possible to get permission from Berlin it wasn't like she could change things. She could go back and gaze on her parents but that would just make her loss all the more painful. It was six years and the pain was bearable. Still there, as it always would be, but bearable. To revisit it would just make it keen again.

12

A car horn shook her out of her thoughts. She hurried down the steps and after getting in to the passenger seat, laughed out loud. Heinrich was soaked from head to foot. His jeans looked almost black, his hair was dripping and his tee-shirt was wet through, clinging to his torso. Leigh couldn't help but linger on the damp fabric and the muscles outlined beneath. She apologised for laughing at him.

"Bloody English weather!" He scowled back in mock anger.

Putting his BMW into drive he pulled away, less smoothly than the young trooper had done with the Horch earlier. He headed for the gates and they were opened in time for him not to have to slow before he went through. He accelerated onto Eastferry Road and then swung onto Westferry Road that looped the Isle of Dogs. Leigh sat quietly but she was conscious that she found his ability to handle the car at speed in the dark and wet rather comforting. She normally detested being a passenger but somehow felt safe here. Heinrich gunned the car up towards Limehouse Link before turning left and heading back into the West End. Not being in an officially marked vehicle, he had to stay in the normal right hand lane and knew the journey would take twice as long as his previous run bringing Leigh from the Mall. He tried to rub his hair dry with his right hand. All he succeeded in doing was make himself look even more bedraggled.

Leigh looked over and suppressed a giggle. "Listen, I'm sorry for getting angry, it's just that the equipment is delicate..." She stopped when Heinrich put his hand on her leg. Her whole body tensed and she looked at him.

He moved his hand and placed his finger on his lips before saying, "I understand Leigh and I must genuinely thank you for coming in on a Sunday evening to help me. Especially on what was officially a leave day for you." He then circled his finger in the air and tapped his ear.

Leigh nodded and silently mouthed 'Oh, sorry'. She was genuinely surprised that even a senior rank like Heinrich assumed his car was bugged. She was also conscious of how her body had reacted when he had touched her.

"My pleasure Heinrich. I'm just happy it's all resolved. I'm also pleased to have had the opportunity to meet you. I always had my worries about Lohse. It's good to have a professional looking after our security now." Leigh was back to her normal controlled, concealed and calculating persona. The loyal Party member, zealously developing technologies for the good of the Reich.

Heinrich looked over at her and gave her a thumbs up.

They spent the rest of the journey in small talk about the city and the weather. She asked Heinrich where he was staying and he said he had rented a small apartment up on Gloucester Place. He aimed the car down the Strand just as the rain began to ease. Without hesitation he swung the powerful coupe into the Haymarket, around Piccadilly Circus, then into Piccadilly itself before turning right up the one-way Albemarle Street.

"I'm impressed, you do know your way around," she said.

"Told you, wasted youth while studying."

"Don't worry about going round the block, Heinrich, just drop me here. I can cut through Stafford and it saves you the hassle." Leigh had checked that it had actually stopped raining before making the offer.

"You sure?"

"Yes. My place is just across the other side of the junction."

Heinrich pulled the car into the right and turned to look at her. In the dark interior of the car he circled his heart with his right index finger and she responded by touching her forehead, heart and abdomen. The historic signs of the Turners.

"Well Leigh, thank you again and I shall see you in the morning." He sounded professional, aloof, the archetypal SS Officer. The look he gave her was not.

13

She got out, shut the door and watched as he drove off before turning and heading across the quiet road into Old Bond Street. Her apartment was on the fourth floor of what had been an impressive townhouse for a wealthy family in the Victorian age. It was now home to an exclusive watch showroom on the ground floor that also used the first floor for their offices and strong rooms. The second, third and fourth floors had been converted into luxury apartments. With just a single two-bedroom residence on each floor they were spacious for the city and, being central to almost everything, weren't cheap. Her father had bought theirs about fifteen years ago and it had been used as a handy family stopover in London when required. She now lived in it permanently, having sold her parent's large country house in Cambridgeshire after the accident. It had taken her the better part of two years to finally sell it, not for lack of buyers, but more that it marked a final goodbye. When she went to the village graveyard on the anniversary of their death she stayed in the local hotel, always assured of a friendly welcome.

She let herself in through the door set to the side of the watch showroom. Her only complaint about the apartment at first had been the stairs up to the top floor. She didn't mind them now. It was always a good check on her aerobic fitness. They also exercised her right leg, which still gave her problems six years after Paderborn and probably always would.

When she entered the apartment she dumped her bag on the table, went to the loo and then to the kitchen. From the small metal wine rack built into one of the cupboards she retrieved a bottle of red, unscrewed the top and poured a fairly large glass. She hadn't even read the label, she just knew she needed a drink. Grabbing a tea-towel, she went through the living room and up the spiral staircase to the roof garden. She wiped down the metal outdoor setting, drying the seats from the earlier rain. Looking out almost due south she could see the Palace, the official residence of the Führer when he came to visit his second Capital. To the south-east she could look over the city towards the river.

Leigh lit a cigarette and breathed the smoke in deeply. Feeling the bite of the smoke in her throat, she exhaled and sighed. Her thoughts were not profound, just 'What now?' She drank her wine and smoked her cigarette. She knew she should take a lot of time to think about what Heinrich had said. The truth was she didn't need to. She was convinced he was what he said he was. Having analysed the conversation over and over, she couldn't find a flaw. The alarm bells that had gone off inside her head when he rang her on the Mall had been silenced. In the course of their conversation, albeit such a brief amount of time, she had recognised that the things he had told her could only have been gained from long exposure to her parents. That alone told her enough.

The Reich security apparatus did not play the long game. They rounded up anyone suspected of being a Turner and summarily executed them and their families. A single Turner being arrested would eventually lead to a DNA sweep of the local area as the science of genetics had progressed. Anyone found to share even the slightest family link went to their deaths. Whole villages were depopulated overnight. The efficiency of the mechanisms increased as the years passed. In the eighty years of the regime an estimated one hundred and fifty million Turners had been exterminated. First, the prominent leaders, then the mid-level functionaries, then anybody who had shown even a tenuous link. A systematic, wholesale slaughter on an industrial scale. Added to the Turners were the Romany and the other Gypsy nations of mid-Europe, the poorest of the peoples of the Steppes, the richest and most powerful Arabian families, the leaders and elders of the African nations and the Royal Families of old Europe. The Japanese exterminated the Aboriginal peoples of Asia and large numbers of the other ethnic groups who had eventually resisted in Australia and New Zealand. All in all, the world had lost more than three hundred million souls. Those that weren't slaughtered were subdued and cowed. With the laws banning interracial marriage and the sterilisation of indigenous populations the world was still being reshaped to match the insane, perverted utopian ideals of Fascist madmen. It wasn't how it should be. She stubbed the cigarette out and reached for another one.

Her thoughts returned to Heinrich. Not only was she trying to process what he had said but she was struggling to understand the reactions she had experienced in his company. She couldn't help smiling when she thought of him. The physical attraction she had felt was surprisingly intense. His appearance was pleasant, but there was more to it than that. The reactions she had felt had been more than could be expected from seeing a handsome man. Something much deeper and rawer had been exposed. She had experienced emotions that she had long buried and denied to herself. Finishing the wine, she returned inside and went to bed, but couldn't sleep.

She made a decision while her mind continued to rush with the images of the evening. The promise her father had her make had been wholly designed to protect her. It didn't stop her from exercising her own judgement if the time ever came. Opportunities had been revealed previously with close friends and she had always kept her promise. But no one had ever had such deep and personal knowledge of her family. In the end the decision was simple.

If her father and mother had trusted him and they obviously had, then so would she.

She began to think of what he had said about the Archives. When she finally went to sleep it was almost 02:00.

14

Chief Senior Overseer Mary Reid was just getting up from Reichsminister Joyce's hotel bed. He watched her as she began to gather up her clothes.

"Mary, you could stay, no one's going to be disturbing me until about seven."

"No Uwe, I need to get home," she said abruptly.

"Are you okay, you seem sort of distant?"

"Distant? I just fucked you, how is that distant?"

"You know what I mean, you seem, I don't know, just a bit off. Is everything okay?"

"Everything's fine."

"Well, if I didn't think something was wrong before I do now. Fine? Seriously? You're using 'fine?'"

"I'm okay, just drop it will you?"

"What's with you? Did someone upset you today?"

"No!" she answered much too forcefully.

He sat up in the bed, "Mary, what is it? Come on, you can tell me. I can solve problems." He tried a half-smile for her.

"Look, even if there was a problem, don't sit there and tell me you give a fuck. I'm here to do one thing for you and in return you look after my meteoric rise. So please don't try to make me feel like we have anything beyond this." She pulled her underwear on followed by her uniform trousers and reached up to fasten her bra strap.

"Seriously, what is your problem?" His voice had hardened a little after her blunt assessment of the realities of their relationship. She reached out to the foot of the bed to retrieve her shirt from under a pillow.

He leant forward to take her hand but she shrugged it off. "Don't Uwe, I mean it."

"Mary, what the hell is with you? Did something go wrong at work?"

"No!" she yelled at him.

"Mary, just calm the fuck down. Did the Kommandos give you a hard time because, if they did, I can sort them out?"

"What Kommandos?" Mary asked. She had half buttoned her shirt and was looking down at him in the bed with a quizzical expression.

"The snatch squads. I know you had some prisoners coming in. Did one of the squads piss you off?"

"No, nothing like that. They came in, we took care of the..," she stopped and caught her breath.

"Mary?"

"It's fine. I did what I always do as per fucking usual. How the hell do you know I had prisoners coming in anyway?"

"Because my office signs off the custody terminations, you know that."

"Yes, but you don't. It's some grovelling little administrator."

"Ah, well it is and always was, but now there are so few of them coming through I like to take an interest. Especially with Turners. I do so enjoy signing them off personally and wondering if their fucking miraculous God is going to keep turning his other cheek." He laughed derisorily. "Or if some day he isn't going to get very, very annoyed and do some smoting down like he used to in the ancient myths." His comments were laced with a scornful sarcasm. "They're so pathetic. Anyway, if it all went without a hitch, then what is your problem? For fuck's sake, six Turners are hardly a reason for throwing a hissy fit."

"I am not throwing a fit." She buttoned the rest of her shirt and bent down to put her boots on. He shrugged and relaxed back into the bed.

"There were only four."

"What?"

"There were only four, the SS looked after the other two in the house."

"Well, even less reason to be pissed off." Uwe leaned away from her and over to the bedside table to get his cigarettes. He propped himself on one elbow trying to open the new packet while he continued, "Only four of the scum to waste your time on. I just despair of them, every time we think we've cleared whole areas of the country they keep crawling out from under some stone like fucking plague rats. Worthless pieces of weak shit. Telling us to love one another and be nice. Fucking nice!" He managed to open the packet and take a cigarette but fumbled the lighter. It dropped off the side of the bed. "Ah fuck it!" he said, leaning over to retrieve it. "Anyway, look where all that love and soft shit got them. I'll love them when they're all fucking gone." When he straightened back up in the bed and looked at Mary she was standing, fully clothed. Her service pistol was in her right hand pointing directly at his face.

"For fuck's sake Mary, what are you doing?"

"Do not call them that." Her voice was dispassionate.

"Have you gone fucking crazy? Put the fucking gun down."

"I said do not call them that. Apologise," She stated it slowly and deliberately.

"For what."

"For calling them weak."

"You're insane, you stupid bitch, I have your career and your life in my hands. Now put the fucking gun down."

"Apologise."

"I will not apologise to you for some pieces of Turner crap that don't deserve to breathe the same air as us. Now put the gun down and I'll try very hard to forget about this."

"They're not all bad people."

"Like fuck! I've had just about enough of this. I'm going to get up and you're going to put the gun down."

"You're wrong."

"No Mary, I'm not. That's what you're going to do and as for the parasite Turners, they deserve nothing, they are nothing.

They're weak fucking cancers that continue to spread and will continue to spread unless we stop them in their tracks."

"I didn't mean that."

"What the fuck are you talking about?"

"I meant you were wrong that you have *my* life in *your* hands."

Mary stepped forward, grabbed the pillow and in one movement put it next to Uwe Joyce's head. She pressed it hard into him with the muzzle of the pistol and pulled the trigger.

She was his mistress. She was discreet. No one ever knew she came to see him in his hotel when he was in the city. No one ever saw them together.

She went into the bathroom and folded all the used, damp towels into a tight stack that she placed beside the main room door. She took three clean towels from the bathroom. Using one of them, she wiped every surface she had touched since entering the room, stripped the bedding from under the shocked looking corpse of Uwe and placed it and the towel in a loose pile on top of his body. She took the second clean towel, soaked it and left it next to the room door. She took the third and secured it as tightly as possible around the sprinkler on the ceiling. She then took the battery out of the smoke detector and ripped out the wire supplying the mains power to the unit. The forensic teams wouldn't take long to figure out he had been shot, but she wasn't going to make their job easier by leaving copious amounts of evidence. Taking his lighter she set fire to a corner of the sheet she had placed over him and waited to ensure it had caught thoroughly. Picking up the soaked towel and the stack of used ones she left the room without looking back. She wedged the wet towel under the door gap like a draught excluder as the door shut, then checked it wasn't visible from the corridor. She then exited the hotel the way she always came in, through the staff corridors and service ways. Dropping the used towels into one of the many housekeeping laundry bins parked along the walls, she made her way to the entrance at the rear of the building.

Mary paused, listened and when she was confident she was alone used the key-card that had been stolen long ago for the purposes of ensuring the Minister was never publicly embarrassed by a scandal. She looked into the small alleyway, checked it was empty, and thought of Thomas Dunhill. 'I did what had to be done Thomas. You said I was sent to do his will. Maybe his will is that I reap vengeance for the weak. I'm doing what I must.' She walked into the dark and the door clicked closed behind her.

15

The stumpy, balding, overweight man was bustling through the door. Sweating, out of breath, his shirt pulled out of his trouser waistband at the front and a stain, from presumably his breakfast, prominent on the garish pink tie that hung in a loose knot around his chubby neck. He was propping the door open with one foot and trying not to drop his bulging attaché case from under his left arm while clutching a sheaf of papers in his right hand. He called in a friendly, albeit puffed voice, "Leigh, welcome back."

Leigh turned at the sound of her name and recognised the head of the Laser Research Department.

"Professor Faber! Would you like a hand?"

"No, no, I'm fine thank you," he said as he finally bludgeoned the door into submission and got through into the foyer.

Leigh stifled a small snigger. Professor Wolfgang Faber, outstanding physicist of his generation, holder of the Reich's National Prize for Art and Science, looked like a sack of shit tied in the middle. He always did. She remembered the last function the Todt Laboratories had hosted. As usual on the Twentieth of April they had held a formal black-tie affair in honour of the Founding Führer's Birthday. This year's dinner had coincided with the fiftieth anniversary of the opening of the Todt Laboratory Complex in London. Wolfgang had arrived for this most auspicious occasion wearing a dinner suit that was short in the trouser, a fact more remarkable for a man who was very short himself. His jacket had been the correct sleeve length but wouldn't have met around his girth had it been fastened with a bungee-cord and its left side sagged under the weight of his National Prize pendant. The red and white sash that accompanied the award sat crooked across his body and had been poked under a bow tie that looked as if it had been tied by a drunken sailor. His ensemble had been set off to perfection by an off-yellow dress shirt. Yet no one could doubt the man's intellect. People just forgave him his appearance.

Leigh walked back to the professor and took his attaché case. "Oh, thank you Leigh. I must say it is very good to see you back my dear, very good indeed. We have a new Gestapo head of security and he seems, well," Wolfgang searched for an appropriate phrase, "quite keen, I suppose one could say.

"Yes Professor, I had the pleasure," she dropped her voice, "if one can call it that, of meeting him last evening."

"Really, whatever for?"

Leigh recounted the story she and Heinrich had agreed on.

"Well, my dear, I shall go and have words..." Wolfgang was beginning to bluster but Leigh told him it was okay, she had diffused the situation and SS-Colonel Heinrich Steinmann was becalmed.

"I still don't think it's right that he takes my most brilliant scientist off the street in a SS car like a common criminal." They were walking side by side into the heart of the research complex which meant the senior scientist didn't see Leigh blushing.

She thought of Wolfgang as a brilliant and lovely old eccentric. He had been her boss since 2012 out in Canada and had never wavered in his support of her. He was the primary reason she was now the deputy-director of Project Thule.

"Thank you Professor, but really it's okay. I'm sure it's just because he's new and trying to be a little over-bearing."

"Yes dear, well, if you're sure."

They walked past the steps that led to the cafeteria and Leigh held a fire door open to allow Wolfgang to go through. She followed him down an eggshell blue corridor. There were doors along both walls that led variously to offices for administration staff, male and female toilets, a couple of stationery cupboards and the cleaner's store room. A further set of fire doors at the far end of the corridor were security locked by an electronic card reader. Leigh stepped in front of Wolfgang to save him the hassle of trying to fish his card out from whatever pocket he had forgotten it was in. She kept her own swipe card attached to a small, re-tractable-cord belt-clip. But when she tried to swipe it the reader gave a non-committal beep and the doors remained firmly shut. She tried again with the same result. After a third attempt she turned to Wolfgang and shrugged.

"It's okay Leigh, I have mine here," Wolfgang said as he re-trieved his own card from his shirt's breast pocket. Handing it to Leigh, she swiped it against the small black reader mounted on the door frame. The reader responded with a high pitched chirp and the automatic doors swung away from her, revealing what looked like a small square box.

But as they stepped into it, the wall turned sharp right and opened into a long narrow room, along the left side of which was a high counter topped by clear bullet-resistant plastic, reminiscent of a security counter at a branch of Deutsche Bank. Behind the security screen were members of the Wehrmacht security detail who controlled entry into the Deep Underground Engineering Laboratories. Four transparent circular doors were set into the far end wall. They were the only way in and out of the 'Jewel'.

Leigh headed over to the counter to report her misbehaving ID card and was thankful she had decided to come in early, even if the lack of sleep was going to catch up with her later. At 07:00 there were few people coming in and out. The main rush wouldn't start for another hour. Behind the security screen, raised up on a central plinth, were just two guards. Their numbers would also swell for the day shift. The younger of the two soldiers sat in a swivel chair behind a semicircular desk, his body mostly hidden by a raised front that housed recessed CCTV monitors. He sat placidly while his colleague, an older and much more jovial looking character, stepped forward to the small acoustic opening in the screen.

"Hello Leigh, welcome back. How are you after your week?" The old soldier asked the question with appropriate solemnity, given that he knew she had been up to see her parent's gravesite on the anniversary of their death.

"Oh, I'm very well Dieter, thank you. You know, it's never going to be painless but it gets easier each year."

Leigh reached her hand through the small gap at the bottom of the screen and the soldier gave it a gentle and caring squeeze. She smiled at him and he gave her the most caring look in return. Dieter Fischer was in his early fifties and only had a couple of years left to do before being able to retire on full pension from the Army. He wasn't much taller than Leigh and the years had turned his hair silver grey. His round face, heavy jowls and slightly bulbous nose betrayed his love of good wine and food. He had put on weight in the last few years and was now a sort of friendly grandfather figure around the complex. He wore the rank of Corporal and had done so for most of his career. The Dieters of the world were more common than not. Sign up, keep your nose clean, do nothing unusual, get paid, get married, have kids, retire. He had been posted in to the security detachment in 2013 and had recently asked to have his tour extended for the third time. His wife Margarethe and he had loved England from the first day of his posting. They had sold their house in Germany as soon as their youngest daughter had left home and had bought a small cottage in rural Essex, not too distant from the city. Dieter stayed in the soldiers' accommodation on-site when he worked his shifts but as soon as he could he headed home to what he called his 'Two Loves'. His Margarethe and his little cottage.

On each occasion Dieter asked for a tour extension his Commanding Officer at the time had acquiesced because Dieter was one of the steady old soldiers that Junior Officers liked to have around. The younger soldiers in the security detachment either liked him as a friendly old fellow or, as was the case with his current duty partner, thought he was a bumbling overweight old man. While it was true that he had only been promoted three rank levels since joining the Army, the soldiers who thought he was a foolish old soak overlooked the fact that Dieter had forgotten more about soldiering than they were ever going to learn.

Leigh had known him since her arrival in Stuttgart back in 2007. She had liked him straight away because he was always so nice to her. Margarethe, no doubt hearing from Dieter all about the young and shy little twenty-two year old scientist, insisted he invited her to dinner. She had often been invited to the Fischer's house after that and she and Margarethe became firm friends. They had continued to keep in touch after she had been posted to Toronto in 2012. When they heard about her car accident Margarethe had handmade a little knitted bear and sent it to the hospital with a card from her and Dieter wishing Leigh a speedy recovery. She was to hurry back to see them so they could give her a proper meal. Leigh had laughed on receiving the card and cried when she saw the bear. It was such a touching thing to do.

"But it's good to be back at work. Oh, can you tell Margarethe I'll give her a call this weekend, if that's okay?"

"Of course it's okay, I'll get her to call you," Dieter beamed, "Right, I shan't hold you up anymore, go on, off to work."

"Ah well, that's the problem, my swipe card isn't working."

"Oh give me that, it's probably just worn out, like myself. I'll get it fixed up for you." He indicated her swipe card, which she unclipped and handed over to him.

The younger soldier remained silent, staring at his screens. Dieter nodded over his shoulder and spoke lowly, "Well, I'll get young Herr Lukas there to do it, he of the friendly disposition. It'll take about ten minutes to run a new one. I'll send it down to you, but take this for now." With that he handed her one of the security detachment's master swipe cards. Similar to her own but without an ID photograph, fingerprint record or attendant security code. It was designed to be used by any of the soldiers for rapid access to most areas of the complex, without the need for biometric or numeric verification. Leigh looked past him to Lukas and then back, she winked and set off once more with Wolfgang.

They presented their cards into the reader slot when they got to the four circular doors. Leigh's door opened immediately with no further check. She retrieved the card and stepped in. Wolfgang swiped his fingerprint and looked into the camera mounted above. A few seconds later there was a chirp and his door rotated open. He stepped into the space and the door closed behind him. The door on the inner side opened after a momentary pause, allowing him into the laboratory complex proper. The doors were officially called circular locking, electronically controlled, ingress and egress points. To everyone who had to pass through them on a daily basis they were just known as the Tubes. A short corridor led to four lifts and, to the right and left of these, a set of emergency stairs. Leigh normally took the stairs down to help keep her leg supple, but with Wolfgang accompanying her she thought the lifts presented a much better option.

On stepping inside she swiped her card and selected the Sub-6th floor. The descent was rapid and the doors opening into a corridor that ran in a shallow left hand turn for about two hundred-metres. The floor was snugly lined with rubber matting and the walls were a shade of pastel pink. The lighting was subdued and, at strategic points, three cameras mounted on the ceiling provided complete coverage. Each fed its imagery to a small inner security booth situated on the other side of a wide and solid metal door that marked the end of the rubber walkway.

They walked the length of the space, passing the entrances to the emergency stairs where Leigh would normally have come out and when they were a few metres from the metal door it gave a loud, sharp click and swung open towards them. The quiet hum of servos drove the heavy steel into a slight recess set in the pink wall. Upon opening, it revealed a small security desk manned by a single soldier who had control of entry into the lower laboratories.

The corridor widened a little as they passed the security desk and arrived at a T-junction. The bar of the T was a wide thoroughfare running straight from west to east for two hundred-metres. On the north side, directly opposite the junction, beckoned the entrance to a central canteen and rest-area equipped with a library, televisions and soft furnishings. It also doubled as a meeting room, training space and staff party room if the occasion arose. Down each of the legs, again running off the northern side, were the entrances to a total of eight laboratories that constituted the Ladenburg Research Unit.

Each laboratory had an official and often pompous name. But each had also been given a slightly less formal moniker by the less than pompous scientists in the 'Jewel'. The lab furthest east, officially called the Armament and Explosives Research Facility, was always referred to as Arnie, while the one furthest west was the Optical Systems Calibration Laboratory but was affectionately called Oscar. To the south side of the main corridor, opposite each of the labs, were the offices of the Project Directors and senior managers. In the far south-west corner, right next to Wolfgang's office, was a secure briefing facility with direct communications to the Gestapo Offices in Whitehall and Berlin.

Marking the ends of the corridor at the east and west walls were wide electronically sealed and alarmed doors. They led to a shallow ramp that spiralled up to the surface and came out into a secure holding pen. Designed to be used for emergency evacuations, the ramp was subject to twenty-four-hour camera surveillance. Equipped with motion detectors and infrared sensors, it also had, just in case someone decided to use it as a backdoor into the labs, command-detonated anti-personnel mines embedded in its walls at regular intervals.

Wolfgang and Leigh headed left towards Oscar.

"Now, Leigh, I believe Konrad has a surprise for you."

"Really? What is it?" Leigh asked, as fond memories of her mentor Professor Dr–Ing Konrad Lippisch, the director of Project Thule, flooded her mind. He had been her supervising professor during her Doctorate in Stuttgart.

Back in 2007 when she had first arrived fresh out of Cambridge he had been a lecturer on her Master's Degree course. He'd told her she had great potential and encouraged her to stay for her doctorate as soon as possible. On his recommendation she was assigned to the prototype High Energy Laser Program and he gambled a lot of his personal credibility on her being capable of finishing her PhD in five years. Leigh had done it in four, graduated sub auspiciis Dux and Konrad was not surprised. For her part she not only respected him as a scientist but also cherished his friendship. He was witty and charming, full of fun yet utterly professional and his intelligence was not confined to science.

"Oh I think I'll let him tell you that. I wouldn't wish to spoil it," said Wolfgang, jolting her back to the present, as he continued down the corridor to his office.

"Have a good day Leigh."

"You too Professor," she called after him as she pushed open the heavy-duty, flexible PVC doors and entered into the main space of Oscar. The motion sensors detected her and turned on the lights.

16

Leigh sighed out loud. The Oscar Lab had been her second home since the team had relocated from Toronto almost four years before. A scientific laboratory was where she excelled. She loved her work. She always had, even from her earliest days in Stuttgart over a decade before. At first her conscience had balked at the idea of working on military systems but her parents had told her to trust that the Lord would place her where she needed to be. All she had to do was work as well as she could and trust in God. So that is what she had done.

She walked over to the small coffee percolator and set about making the first of many jugs that would be made during the day. Her thoughts returned to Konrad. When the Security Directorate had posted her to Toronto in late 2012 she had missed him a great deal. Then a year after her arrival in Canada, Konrad had been sent over to head up the research on the new Laser Acquisition systems. They had immediately slipped back into their easy way of working. They would go out to dinner together and had enjoyed each other's company in and out of work. Some people had thought they were having a romance and when Leigh heard the rumour she did nothing to scotch it. The gossip strengthened while she was convalescing after her crash as on each occasion Konrad travelled to Europe he would visit Leigh in hospital. It was quite easy to believe that she would have been his romantic liaison; even now he was a very young looking fifty-five year old, stood ramrod straight at one hundred and ninety five centimetres tall and reminded everyone who met him of an old fashioned movie star. Why wouldn't a woman, even twenty years his junior, be swept off her feet?

Leigh was happy to have people think that she and Konrad might be more than friends because she knew the truth was a lot more dangerous for her mentor. He had confided in her after too much red wine one night but Leigh had not shared her secrets. Konrad knew nothing of her religion or purpose in life. He was the one person who she had seriously considered telling but in the end decided she couldn't burden him with it. She knew if he was ever compromised it would not be pleasant. She loved him like a father and knew he loved her in a reciprocal manner. But, that wouldn't stop him talking in the right circumstances, so she maintained her own counsel.

She wandered round the lab as she waited for the water to flow through the percolator, just checking what was where and if anything significant had changed in the week she had been away. It was almost like a dog running circles in its kennel before it could comfortably settle down. It was Leigh's routine in any lab if she had been away. She paused and leant up against one of the small ring laser station benches. She thought that maybe this time was different.

For the first time in such a long time she might have a confidant. Someone to talk to about the Creed and devotion and emotions and memories. She had missed that so much since her parents had died. Her mind drifted back to Toronto, to the day she had come back after the car accident. Walking into a lab for the first time in almost six months had triggered such an explosion of emotions. She had been so relieved to be back in the comforting surrounds of science and yet that first day back had reinforced how desperately alone she was in life. She had no family left yet she knew that the Turner Creed would be her strength and her career would be her focus.

***

Her career had been on track. The PhD she had completed in Stuttgart had seen her contribute to existing theories on Micro and Nanostructures in Optoelectronics. Her posting to Toronto had made her a recognised authority in the field. When the Luftwaffe Procurement Command had instigated a specialist research project into electro-optical navigation systems in Paderborn, she was the obvious choice to head it up. She had left for Germany in January 2014 and was due back in Toronto by June that same year. But the car crash in May that took her parents had almost killed her as well. She suffered multiple fractures, severe internal injuries including a punctured lung and a ruptured spleen. But it had been the skull fracture and the resultant subdural-haematoma that had concerned her surgeons most. She had been kept in an induced coma for four weeks and operated on three times just to relieve the pressure building up in her skull. Her recovery was slow even after she had regained consciousness.

Professor Faber had flown over to see her twice in those weeks, but she didn't actually remember him visiting until the end of June. He had sat next to her bed and told her to take the time to heal. It wasn't like her job wasn't going to be there for her and she should focus on getting better.

She didn't want to take her time but she required further surgeries on her head, more to repair the damage to her internal organs and four separate procedures to save her right leg. Initially the damage to it had led her surgeons to contemplate amputation. Once the surgery had been completed, the long, slow process of physiotherapy began. She had tried to discharge herself from the hospital in the August, but the protestations of her doctors finally won out. They had said the only reason she had lived at all was that she had been young and fit, but that didn't mean she was capable of healing fully without a longer convalescence.

She tried to read the final report papers of the project she had been leading but that proved more difficult than she had expected. Her concentration drifted in and out, it sometimes took ten minutes to solve a simple mental arithmetic problem and most worrying, she couldn't remember things she was sure she should know. It was the memory loss that told her all was not well and that she should heed the advice of her surgeons. Her belief in God sustained her through the worst.

It took five months for her to be discharged. She still needed intensive physiotherapy to get the full movement back in her right knee, but her doctors agreed this could be done in Toronto. They offered her crutches, which she refused. They gave her a walking stick and insisted she take it. She did. Unfortunately she managed to leave it behind in the taxi that took her from the hospital back to her digs in Paderborn. She was determined to lose the limp on her right side as quickly as possible. She also wanted to get back to Canada simply to put distance between her and the place where her parents had died. She finally made the return trip in November 2014.

Professor Faber had kept her position open and insisted to the Institute of Physics in Potsdam, who kept offering him replacements, that he didn't want anyone else. He had been backed by a number of the senior faculty members in Toronto and at Paderborn who all recognised that Leigh Wilson was a one-in-a-generation mind. Faber had gone so far to say that, given time, he could see her as a future head of the whole Reich Technical Directorate.

***

The coffee percolator's beeping recalled her from the memories. She poured a cup and popped a little saccharin tablet in just as Francine Xu came through the door of the lab.

"Surprise!" Francine called and struck a dramatic pose.

Leigh smiled at her friend and the realisation of the surprise Wolfgang had mentioned. She was thrilled at the prospect of working with the full team again. Though she liked all her colleagues in varying degrees, she was closer to Francine than the rest. A native of Quebec, Francine Xu was arguably the world's most respected specialist in the design of the multilayered silicon wafers required for cascade lasers. Testimony to her intellect and ability was the fact that she was one of a rare few mixed-race members of the technical directorate. Her very survival into adulthood was proof of the Regime's capability to ignore its own boundaries and rules when it suited. Her French mother and Chinese father had both been senior lecturers in physics and their liaison had been tolerated due to their value to the Reich. The resultant Francine was the combination of her parents' intellect, temperament and looks. Short, slim and with a complexion that belied her forty-five years, she maintained a freshness of face and physique that put others a decade younger to shame. Her dark hair was always cut just below shoulder length and, with her dark eyes and her darker rimmed glasses, she was a very beautiful woman.

Francine had been seconded to the Marseille Institute of Technology in February to assist on a research project. Konrad must have worked very hard indeed to convince Professor Chabonne at Marseilles to send her back, thought Leigh, who was delighted at her return.

"Hi Franci, and yes it's a surprise alright. You could have phoned." Leigh set her cup down and hugged her friend.

"I didn't know. Konrad flew over last week and just pulled me back here. I thought old Chabonne was going to have a fit. But it's all good. I liked Marseille but seriously, they're even more fucked up than we are. Do you know what the security detail said to me when I arrived?"

Leigh shook her head.

"Oh, hello, are you the new cleaner?"

Leigh's mouth dropped open, "You're kidding!"

"Nope. The cleaner! That's what they said. I went ballistic. It took a couple of days but eventually I had the head of the Institute's security detachment muster all of his personnel and have them apologise publicly to me."

"And?"

"And what?" Francine grinned.

"And what did you say? If you had a whole Wehrmacht security detachment in front of you I can't imagine that the head of the Women in Science movement let them go without giving them at least a small lecture in equality."

"I may have said a few things." Francine smiled coyly.

"Did you get into trouble again?"

"Just another interview with the Kripo. They asked if I was trying to make them arrest me for public criticism of the Reich and the Party."

"And?"

"And I told them to fuck off and find someone else who could do what I do. Once they find her then I have no doubt Berlin will sanction my arrest. Until then I suggested they write up the report and file it with the others."

"Franci, do you ever think you might want to be a little careful?"

"No. Stuff them. Until they pay us equally and afford young women the same opportunities as men then the answer is no. You know me Leigh." Francine gave Leigh her best smile.

"Yes I do and I hope you never change. Love you! And I'm so glad you're back." She hugged her friend again.

"I'm glad I'm back too."

"Excuse me, Doctor Wilson?" the voice came from Private Lukas, who had just appeared at the door of Oscar.

"Yes?" said Leigh as she moved towards him.

"I have your swipe card."

"Excellent, thank you."

"Allow me," said Francine and took the card from the young soldier, deliberately brushing her hand against his. He blushed.

Francine reached up and gently stroked his cheek.

"Aww. You've gone quite red. Are you alright Herr Lieutenant?"

"Um, uh, no Ma'am. I mean, yes Ma'am, I am alright but, um, but I'm not an Lieutenant, I, I mean I'm only a Private. Ma'am."

"Oh Leigh, he called me Ma'am, how adorable." She stepped closer to the young soldier and continued to stroke his cheek.

"Francine, stop teasing him," Leigh rebuked in a soft tone. Private Lukas was backing toward the door yet somehow couldn't seem to break away completely from Francine. In the end she tapped him on the chin with her index finger.

"Be off with you or you'll get us both in trouble." She stepped away from him.

Lukas nearly fell over his own feet but somehow managed to turn and leave the laboratory as Francine turned back to Leigh and winked at her, "Oh I love my job."

"You're the only girl I know that can make soldiers of the Reich blush. That poor lad is young enough to..."

"Be exciting!" Francine finished for her. "Anyway, how come if he hit on me he'd be a stud but if I hit on him I'm a slutty girl?"

"Come on Franci, you know I'm on your side."

"Yeah but you're not enough. Everyone needs to accept it as normal. Imagine that, female equality as normal."

Leigh couldn't help but adore her friend. She was passionate, dedicated and a brilliant scientist to boot.

"Deep breath Franci."

Francine huffed a dramatic sigh and switched tack, "Guess what I did in Marseille?"

"Is this another conquest story?"

"No you cheeky cow," Francine laughed and added, "I'm not gonna tell you now. I'll make you read the paper."

"Yeah, and is it a thrilling title?"

"Advances in Graphene Oxide-Polymer Multilayer Films and Their Impact on the Silicon Wafer of the Future."

Leigh rolled her eyes and made a face and Franci play punched her in the arm.

During the next half hour the rest of the scientists on Project Thule arrived into the lab. Jerome Mills, originally from Larne, on the Irish coast, was the team's electronic expert. Wilhelm Darnell was from San Diego in the German States of America and an expert on Ring Laser design. Claire Bergen, from Salzburg, was Leigh's Optoelectronics sidekick and a specialist in semiconductor laser technologies. Dimitri Petrovlav was from Podolsk, just to the south of Moscow, and a theoretical scientist specialising in gravitational anomalies.

They stood around swapping their weekend stories and drinking coffee. The full team had worked together for the better part of five years. All of them were comfortable with one another both professionally and socially. The cross-talk and laughter was in mid-flow when a deep and melodic voice sounded.

"Right now, from what I can gather you bunch have an awful lot of work to do. I'd like to suggest you cut this frivolity out and get back to it." Konrad Lippisch was the last one into the lab as was his normal routine. His pronouncement was his best attempt at brusque and failed miserably as they all looked round at him. He was beaming and his eyes shone with good humour.

17

Now that Leigh and Francine are both back I want us to start getting into shape for the Führer's visit. It's just over three weeks away and I'd like a number of practise Projections just to get us fully up to speed. Our new head of security, Colonel Steinmann, will also be observing them. Leigh, I'm going to need you to run through things with him. He's received only the scantest of information from Berlin. As usual." The rest of the team gave a collective groan.

Leigh didn't say that she already knew Heinrich understood little about the science, she merely nodded her head.

Konrad continued, "He's been briefed on the safety and evacuation drills but other than knowing how to get out in case of a fire I doubt he understands anything about what we do. I ran into him on my way down and he said he would come in to see you this morning at ten if that's okay?"

"Yes, that's fine Konrad," she said in a mater-of-fact voice yet realised her stomach had given a little leap.

Leigh sat in her glass walled office in the far left corner from the entrance as the team went to their various cubicles and research benches dotted around the lab. She turned her PC on and looked at the plethora of emails that had built up since she had been on leave. She turned the screen back off and decided to use her time to arrange a demonstration for Heinrich. She also extracted some relevant documents that would help him understand exactly what he was head of security of.

He appeared in the doorway to Oscar punctually at 10:00. Leigh had been watching it off and on for the previous five minutes and was out of her office and on her way to meet him before he had managed to get a few metres into the space. He was dressed in the new style in-barracks uniform of black bloused combat trousers, belt with unit buckle and a black shirt. He wore no weapon and the only insignia was the Parteiadler on his right breast and two small Siegrune on each collar point surmounted by silver oak leaf rank tabs. She thought he looked remarkably handsome.

"Colonel Steinmann, welcome to Oscar."

"Ah, Doctor Wilson, please, after my false start yesterday evening, call me Heinrich and may I call you Leigh?"

They went through the formalities of shedding their formality as Leigh led him across to the small tea and coffee making area. She knew it had to look and sound to any other members of the team like she was hosting a man with whom she had only the briefest of meetings and who she knew practically nothing about. As she made them both drinks, she asked what he thought of the 'Jewel'.

"I've only been posted in a short time but what is it with the names?"

"Oh, you mean Oscar?" she said as she prepared the mugs. "How do you take yours?"

"White, none please and yes, I meant Oscar. And is it Alex?"

"Alec," she corrected. "It's just a way to refer to them without having to use their full, official titles. The people who come up with official names for these types of things tend to be," she paused trying to think of the right word.

"Full of their own self-importance?" he offered.

"Yeah, that would be a good way to say it. I was thinking more of eejits, as my mum would have said, but we'll go with yours. It's probably kinder."

He laughed with her and asked, "So what are the rest?"

"Let's see, Arnie, Penny, Alec, Mel, Toby, Cesar and Ella. And, of course, Oscar." She watched him running through the various labs trying to figure out how they had been given their nicknames.

"Okay," he said a little hesitantly, "I get Penny for the Propulsion and Engines Lab, Mel's obvious and even makes sense for the Mechanical Engineering Lab and I know Ella is the Electronic and Advanced something or other."

"Advanced Instrumentation," she said and handed him over a mug.

"Thanks. And the rest of them?" he asked.

"Arnie is armaments, Alec is electrical,"

"Shouldn't that be an E-something?"

"Probably, but they're electricians so be thankful it isn't a V."

"Fair enough." He said and rose to follow her through the lab.

"Cesar is the Computer Science and AI Research geeks, I mean division," she called over her shoulder, "and Oscar is for optical systems, or, as we like to think, Obviously Superior Clever And Revered." She stood aside and waved him towards the spare chair in her office.

"Obviously," he smiled at her and sat down. "That's only seven."

She moved past him and took the seat at her desk. "Who'd I miss?" She thought for a moment, "Oh yes, Toby." She laughed and said, "We have a whole bunch of other people, academics, researchers, scientists, all sorts who come and go all the time. They study all sorts of stuff from the traditional physical sciences to Nano-tech. They're never really here long enough for any of us to get to know them and their lab never had an official name. It was just the spare. But one of them insisted one day that their work set the yardstick for all of our work." She raised her eyes at the memory.

"I'm going to hazard a guess that wasn't the greatest suggestion?"

"No, not really, but it did give us the name for their lab, Toby. The Other Boffin's Yardstick."

"You're all nuts," he said.

"Thank you. We'd accept that as a compliment."

"So you're going to take me through what your crazy science has come up with and show me your magic toy?"

"No Heinrich, I'm going to let you read the important bits of the Project Thule file. Then, when you've managed to understand none of it, I shall give you the same brief and demonstrations we've given every senior leader of the Reich. Including the Führer." She said the last sentence as a punctuation to accompany her hefting a seven centimetre thick file onto her desk.

"You're kidding, that's going to take me all day!" he said, looking genuinely shocked.

"No, it's not. I've been very kind to you. The essential extracts you're interested in are here," she smiled as she slipped a few pages out of the file.

"However, Heinrich, before I can hand this to you I need to see your Thule card please."

Heinrich reached into his back pocket and took his wallet out. He retrieved a small electronically chipped card and handed it over. Leigh scanned it with the compact Security Point Reader on her desk. A dialogue box popped up on her PC screen and confirmed that the holder of the card had been briefed on the Security Classification rules for Codeword Thule.

"Well, that's okay then." Leigh handed him his card back and the pages she had taken from the file. "I'll leave you to it?"

He nodded and Leigh swivelled her chair round to her desk and began to catch up on her significant post-leave emails.

18

Top Secret Thule

Subject: Establishment of Project Thule
Ref: ReichHC/FD/191/1.3/4
Date: 1 October 2016

Authorities: Project Thule is hereby authorised by the
Reich High Command. The Project is to be used for
investigations commanded by the Office of the Führer,
through the personal authorisation of the incumbent
Reichsführer-SS. Live use of equipment will be the responsibility of the incumbent Head of Laser Research, Reich
Security Directorate (Technical Division).

Background: During investigations into navigational Ring
Lasers an anomalous discrepancy was discovered in
September 2015 by Dr Leigh Elisabeth Wilson (SS
No.TD2228228), Arcand Institute, Toronto, Germanic Common-
wealth of Canada. The discrepancy revealed a consistent
warping of gravitational fields. Subsequent experimentation
discovered an asynchronous disruption in the attendant time
fields. Following a catastrophic failure in June 2016 all
equipment and personnel were relocated to the Deep Underground Engineering Laboratories (Todt Laboratories Complex)
London. This move was
completed in September 2016.

Research Objectives: The research focus is to re-establish
a stable and controllable environment that will allow on-
demand and selective Time Window observations to enable
Intelligence Collection, Counter-Intelligence Surveillance
and Criminal Investigations to be conducted on operations
deemed essential to the Security of the State.

Funding: Project Thule is funded by the Office of the
Führer under special provisions and is designated Special
Operations Project 1A-657.

Top Secret Thule

108

Leigh looked round as Heinrich finished reading the first extract and asked, "All okay?" He looked up and frowned.

"Well, I'm one down and very confused. What's an asynchronous disruption in the attendant time fields?"

She swivelled her seat round, smiled at him and said, "Keep reading and once you've finished, I'll show you. And please, Heinrich, don't fret. I've only picked out those paragraphs and reports that give you the potted history of Thule. Don't get bogged down in the detail. I'm going to give you a demo later and show you a bit of archive footage. It'll be fun." She smiled again.

He frowned and picked up the other pages. They were just as confusing as the previous ones, but he persevered.

Top Secret Thule
(SS Eyes Only)
(Material attached must be safeguarded in accordance with
Reich Security Directive 49.137.3)

**Extract: Executive Summary, Arcand Institute
Report – 9/56/4, Dated 10 March 2016**

56. The time anomaly is best explained when compared to a telescope used for deep space observation. Light being observed from distant objects in space is thousands, hundreds of thousands and on occasion millions of years old. By increasing the power of a reflective telescope, observations of more distant objects may be achieved. In effect this allows the observer to look back along the timeline of the Universe. The time anomaly discovered by Doctor Leigh Wilson is a similar phenomenon but along the timeline of the Earth. Increasing the power of the laser disruption allows the timeline Window to observe events further back in Earth's history. It is equivalent to viewing the Earth from deep space with a high-powered telescope.

**Extract: Arcand Institute
Report – 9/134/6, Dated 16 April 2016**

9. Subsequent experiments have identified a carrier wave within the Time Observation Window that on isolation and amplification have revealed an audio component.

Extract: Arcand Institute
Report — 9/179/1, Dated 5 May 2016

3. Outgoing modulated audio streams can be transmitted
through the Time Window with reasonable success. However,
direct effect on previous events had unexpected outcomes.
Experiment 402H/2 placed an object in test position Alpha
and using compliant conditions influenced a test subject to
move the item. On movement being instigated the molecular
structure of the object in the present timeline suffered
catastrophic failure resulting in residual explosive
collapse of the molecular field.

Extract: RHSA Summary Findings,
Arcand Institute, Dated 30 June 2016

109. Recommendation. The unauthorised attempt of the
supervising scientist to directly manipulate the timeline
by introducing a foreign object into the Time Observation
Window resulted in a molecular disruption on a massive
scale. The standing reflective wave that entered by feedback into the output detection fields of the RL-01
apparatus caused a systematic collapse of the whole system.
Although the deaths of the personnel involved is regretta-
ble it is of primary concern that the resulting explosion,
despite local Propaganda Ministry intervention, created
unwanted coverage in the local media. It is recommended
that the whole time observation experiment is compart-
mentalised under a uniting Project and relocated to a
secure, preferably underground, experimentation
facility, namely the Todt Laboratory Complex in London.

Extract: Project Thule
Report — 191/60/5, Dated 13 September 2018

8. The successful reconstitution of a stable Time
Observation Window on-demand has now been achieved on a
complete and comprehensive basis. Despite this it is still
localised to a 100-metre sphere of influence centred on the
apparatus location.

Extract: Project Thule
Report — 191/60/109, Dated 18 December 2018

11. Direct geo-coordinate interlacing allows the time
observation apparatus to be steered to any point on the
Earth's surface. However, the time distance is limited to
4.6 light years.

Extract: Project Thule
Report - 191/60/854, Dated 21 November 2019

37. Given the incorporation of the advanced power amplification circuitry within the transformer stages it will now be possible to fully incorporate the increased power requirements into the apparatus. Limited virtual and theoretical testing has resulted in a distance of 2707 light years being achieved. It is unlikely that given current limitations in electronic technologies this distance will be extended further.

Extract: Project Thule, Theoretical Limits
191/60/854, Dated 6 March 2020

106. It is therefore recommended that the Time Observation Window is limited in its use to that which does not, nor cannot, influence or amend preceding events. All experiments have recorded that a singular timeline exists and any change to it will adversely alter the present time continuity with unpredictable results.

Extract: Project Thule
Standard Operating Procedures 191/61/001
Dated 6 March 2020

4. All activations of the Time Observation Window are to be documented with the Project Director, or Deputy Project Director. All safety protocol keys are to be engaged prior to operation of RL mechanisms and the Berlin Key has precedence.

(SS Eyes Only)
Top Secret Thule

Heinrich set the file down and looked over at Leigh.

"Questions, Heinrich?"

"I can't think of what to say, to be honest. When I was told what the project was in Berlin they made it sound that you could hop backwards and forwards and basically time travel. If I've got this right, from what I've just read you can look backwards and that's it. You can look back at previous events, but you can't interact with them?"

"Well, I'm sorry to disappoint you Heinrich. It's only taken us five years to get this far and let me be immodest. This is the biggest scientific breakthrough in history," Leigh said a little too defensively.

"No Leigh, I didn't mean I wasn't impressed. I am, truly. I just mean this actually makes more sense to me. Berlin had me thinking I could go forward and see what I would look like in my 70s, or go back and stop the knife attack so I wouldn't have the scar."

"Well, you could go back and stop the attack. Or rather you could go back and warn your other self by talking to him. Except for the fact that everything in the world after that moment might be irrevocably changed and we would have no way of predicting what changes would occur. Where or when. It's possible that as soon as you change the timeline you would in effect cease to be you." She looked at him and smiled sympathetically before continuing, "The truth is we don't have the first clue about what would happen except that we think the further back you go the more everything would be completely and utterly changed. Everything and everybody you know would be gone, probably. Maybe." Leigh shrugged her shoulders. "I can certainly say that sandwiches would not survive." She smiled at her own in-joke.

"What?" asked Heinrich.

"Never mind, I'll show you later. Come on, I'll take you into the lab and introduce you to my toy, as you called it."

Heinrich finished his coffee and got up to follow her.

"How did you discover this originally Leigh?"

"What are Berlin briefing you on?" She shook her head. "You know we insisted that anyone being inducted into Thule should come here first. There are currently less than eighty people within the project and only ten of them are in Berlin. None of those ten have any clue about the science or the history behind it. We've shown them what it does, we've briefed them on what it does, and we've tried to tell them again and again of the limitations but to no avail. Part of us dreads when we finally go live and the Chiefs of Staff make some ridiculous request." She was ushering him out of the office and into the main lab.

"To be fair, the Führer and the Reichsführer both fully grasp it." She stopped talking and looked sheepishly at him. "I'm sorry Heinrich. I do tend to rant when it comes to this."

He smiled at her and said, "It's okay. I get that you're passionate about it. But as I said, how did you discover it?"

"Accidentally, like all good discoveries I suppose."

She passed Francine's desk and tapped her on the shoulder, giving her a 'comear' nod for her to follow them. The three of them passed through a small, square cleanroom and headed back to the High Powered Laser Lab. Heinrich hesitated a little in the cleanroom as he walked over sticky-pad mats that he guessed took off any debris from the soles of his shoes. Leigh swiped her access card, keyed in her security code to the door and waited for Francine to do the same. Once the mechanism had accepted the dual entry protocol it clicked open.

"Thanks Franci."

"No problem."

Francine headed back to her desk while Leigh held the screening blackout curtains apart. "Come on Heinrich," she called to hurry him up.

The High Powered Laser Lab, it turned out, didn't have a nickname as such. It was simply known as the HP-Lab and was a long wide space with long, wide, solid wooden benches running most of the length of the walls. Within the rest of the room, set at irregular gaps and angles, were other workstations and fixed shelving. Most of these were loaded with an array of different shapes and sizes of equipment, none of which Heinrich recognised. Leigh motioned him over to the nearest workstation.

"What do you know about Lasers Heinrich?"

"I have a pointer that I use when I do briefings," he smiled lamely, before adding, "not a lot to be honest."

Leigh reached under a small bench and brought out a thirty centimetre long, twenty centimetre wide and fifteen centimetre deep metallic box.

"Okay, have you ever flown on a Luftwaffe transport or a Deutsche Lufthansa Jet?"

"Oh yes, many times."

"Ever end up in the wrong city?"

"Not me. Luggage yep, but no, not me."

"Well, this is one reason why not. It's a ring laser gyro." She looked at him and recognised on his face the look she must have given him when he had mentioned his village. She decided to start from scratch.

"Mmm, okay Heinrich, this is Basic Lasers 101, ready?"

He nodded.

"A standard laser works by bouncing a light beam back and forward between two mirrors. One of the mirrors is only semi-reflective so some light actually passes through it. The laser beam is the small part that escapes out after each reflection. But a ring laser gyroscope like this one," she removed the top cover of the box, "has four mirrors arranged in a closed ring. What we do then is send two laser beams around the ring, one clockwise, the other counter-clockwise. The equipment basically tunes itself so both of the beams have the same wavelength and, being lasers, the wavelength is pure and coherent." She looked at him. His brows had creased.

"Coherent Heinrich, they all go the same way and all together."

He was frowning.

She tried desperately hard not to sigh.

"OK. A normal light bulb scatters light everywhere. A laser light is like sheep being herded by a very diligent dog. We send light, or sheep, in one direction and the same number of sheep in the other direction. Imagine one set of sheep are white and one set are black. When they meet back at the start they cancel each other out. No sheep left. Got it?" He nodded so she continued quickly before he didn't get it again.

"So, when the beams of light come back together again after going around our four mirrors in opposite directions, they're sent to an output detector. Given that the speed of light is a constant and the cavity doesn't change, then both beams are identical and because they are going the opposite way from each other, they cancel each other out. Just like our sheep."

He nodded and smiled. She understood he understood. She hadn't the heart to tell him this is how she would have briefed first year high school kids. She reflected that even then it would only have been the slower ones that got this version. She decided to press on.

"However, imagine if the cavity where the mirrors are moves or twists. Because it's mounted in an aircraft and the aircraft moves, we can make that movement make the cavity change shape. If that happens then the distance around the circle for each set of sheep will be different." She paused and he nodded.

"Like warping a running track. To one of the beams the mirrors will be closer together while to the other beam the mirrors will have moved apart. Simply put, one of the beams will have to travel further and its wavelength will change. When both beams come back together they won't cancel exactly. We would have some white or black sheep left over. We can measure extremely small variations in the beams' wavelength and by calculating how much rotation took place we can determine motion. If we accurately know where the aircraft started from then we should know where we have moved to. Simple." She looked at him expecting to see his brows creased again.

Instead he said, "Okay, that makes sense. How do we get from this to looking back in time?"

"Ah, well, as is the way with simple things in science, it isn't as simple as I might have said."

"Now that's not a shock Doctor." Heinrich smiled at her and this time held her gaze. Leigh felt her heart skip again. She had an overwhelming desire to reach across, grab him and kiss him hard. She flushed at the imagery in her head.

"Right Heinrich, no shock at all," she struggled to control her voice "so, in 2015 ring lasers suffered from two problems, in fact they still do. Lock-in and frequency biasing. Frequency biasing is a peculiar effect only encountered with gas lasers. We used them in Luftwaffe kit, still do in the older stuff. The key to getting rid of it is to use something else and we proposed to use a Quantum Cascade Laser." She looked to see if he was still following her.

"Do I want to ask what one of those is?" he said.

"Probably not, no. Take it from me they are a good thing and very sexy." 'Like you' she didn't add.

He smiled, "Sexy science, I'm impressed. Okay, onwards."

"Well, as is the way in science, if we put a Quantum Cascade Laser in, then we solve the bias problem but compound the lock-in problem. It's caused when the ring laser is rotating very slowly, the wavelengths effectively become stuck and the beams lock to the same value."

She saw he was frowning again.

"Simply put, all the sheep stick together. There is no difference picked up by the output detectors so the device will not track its position accurately. Basically, we will have moved but there will be no spare sheep to count." Heinrich had stopped frowning and nodded.

"So we decided to go bigger and more powerful to see if we could get a workable solution. We needed to get the line width as narrow as possible. If we could get it narrow, then we could put more power into it and get more fidelity into each beam, thereby ensuring that even the tiniest differences were detected."

"I can safely assume that getting narrow width and increased power and therefore greater fidelity is the Rosetta Stone of Lasers?" Heinrich asked.

"Yep, you have it exactly. Well done. But we were confident, so we built a bigger version of this little ring laser. In fact we built one that was a metre in length on each side. The idea was to see if we could get it refined enough to sense the actual rotational motions of the Earth. Problem wasn't the laser, the problem was me," she paused.

"How'd you mean?"

"I had taken almost a year to come back into work full-time after the car crash. Even then I still had headaches, and my concentration lapsed occasionally. We had a problem with the kit and I was working late. I reversed the laser input streams to send the clockwise ones round counter-clockwise and vice-versa."

"Um, and that was bad?" Heinrich looked slightly puzzled.

"Well, it is if you take one of the most powerful lasers ever built and only reverse one stream. Basically, I sent sixty-four laser beams around and around a ring laser apparatus. We weren't really sure how at first but the output stages began to amplify the signals and a disturbance happened."

"A disturbance?" Heinrich asked quizzically.

"Come on, I'll show you, follow me and meet RL-04, it's even bigger than the one in Toronto was."

Leigh led him across to a double door set into a recess in the bottom left hand corner of the lab. The doors automatically slid open as they approached and revealed a stubby hallway leading to a set of manually operated, triple glazed, opaque-glass, sliding doors. Leigh slid them open and led him into a rectangular room that reminded him of the control hub he had seen in the Reich's missile defence centres.

"Welcome to the Thule Room," she said.

From just inside the door he could see eight separate control consoles arranged in a reversed-L with four of them facing to the front and four toward the left. Each one was a single curved desk into which were embedded, in some cases, two screens and, in others, five separate displays. On the flat portions of the desks were tracking balls, joysticks, keyboards and data entry pads in a variety of configurations. To the right of the space, set back from the consoles, was a small raised dais with about a dozen chairs. To the left, running the full length of the room, was a wall of very thick glass. Through the glass Heinrich could see a darkened space of unadorned concrete walls and floor within which sat a similar configuration of equipment as she had shown him on the small bench. The difference was the four mirrors of this laser were each two-metres in length.

"Bloody hell, that's big."

"Yep."

"Mmm, Leigh?"

"Yes," she said hesitantly.

"That ring laser's actually a big square."

She looked at him and tilted her head a little. "Ah, yes, yes it is. It could also have been three mirrors in a triangle but yep, it is square. And now you're going to ask me why it's called a ring?"

"Well, I was but I'm guessing that isn't important?"

"Spot on. You ready to see it work?"

"Uh-huh," was as eloquent as he could manage.

19

Leigh stepped up to the left foremost control console and began to flick various toggle switches on the panels.

"Right, I need your help," she said and motioned for him to step up to the right foremost console. "See that key in the console near to you?"

"Yes," he said, reflecting that it would have been difficult to miss. It resembled an old fashioned clock winding key and it stuck out of a port marked in red and yellow, 'Master Arm 2'.

"Well, it needs to be turned at the same time as the one I have over here."

"Okay," he said hesitantly.

"It's easy Heinrich, relax. I'll count three, two, one and turn. On turn you push down and turn clockwise 180 degrees. All good?"

He nodded.

"Okay, three, two, one, turn." They both turned the keys in a synchronous movement.

The first faint red beam began to show in the next room. When she flicked the final bank of controls, the centre of the cavity filled with a dazzling array of crisscrossing laser beams. Most were red but about a tenth of them showed as an indigo-violet shade. Leigh waited until the display looked like a stable set of crayon drawn lines suspended in mid-air before flicking a protective cover off a toggle switch labelled 'Master Alignment'. Although transparent to an observer, as she flicked the switch to 'On,' the thirty-two beams that had been circulating clockwise reversed and a total of sixty-four lasers began to feed their beams into the ring laser apparatus in a counter-clockwise direction. Their wavelengths became fully aligned and coherent as these beams raced around the ring. Each time they passed the output detection circuits their combined waves amplified each other like the feedback in a microphone and speaker. Instead of being cancelled out by counter-rotating waves they were all combining. Each time the beams completed their eight-metre circuit they amplified more. Given the speed of light, the eight-metres did not take long to traverse.

Heinrich stood, mesmerized. He watched as the beams became a blurring purple circle in the middle of the apparatus, but then he began to see something else. A glassy, translucent, almost watery whirlpool forming in the middle of the cavity one metre above the floor. Right at the heart of the effect, pulling down in the centre, was a small opening, no bigger than a table-tennis ball, but jet black. He could see the hole growing bigger and he could hear a distant rumble.

"The good news is that the glass in front of us is ten centimetres thick. When I did this by accident in Toronto, the noise was deafening and the rush of air blew me off my feet."

Even with the thick glass the noise could still be heard. It sounded like a train coming through a tunnel. He could also hear a faint high-pitched element that moved away in a Doppler effect, like a receding ambulance siren. The noise was rising incessantly but it was also focussing. He could tell the noise and the motion and everything that held him spellbound was centred on the hole in the middle of the whirlpool. The hole was getting bigger every second and the whirlpool effect itself was reaching out to fill the cavity between the mirrors. The red and indigo-violet beams he had first seen were now an intense purple light which appeared as an unbroken circle around the edge of the still glassy-surfaced whirlpool. Just as the noise was becoming hard to bear there was complete silence.

"What happened?" asked Heinrich turning to her, "Did you just switch it off?"

"No, we just reached stabilisation."

Heinrich looked back at the cavity. There was a steady circular ring of purple light forming an outer edge to a completely flat silver disc, one and a half metres in diameter and suspended one metre off the floor. The disc was featureless and looked like a large mirror, laying flat on its back in mid-air. Except that in the very centre was a hole about half a metre across. The hole was jet black in colour and completely opaque. Leigh pressed a few more buttons on one of the forward facing consoles and a screen slid down on the wall in front of her. At the press of another button a projector mounted on the ceiling flicked on.

"You'll probably want to turn round and watch this."

Heinrich reluctantly turned away from the scene through the glass and found himself looking at an image of the silver disc but from above. He looked back into the apparatus room and saw a small camera mounted on the ceiling looking down at the disc.

"Heinrich, this is the Time Observation Window or TOW in its raw state. What we're about to look at has become known simply as a Projection. What you'll see shortly is an image coming into focus inside the centre portal, or as it's normally called by anyone who sees it, the black hole. It isn't by the way."

"It isn't what?"

"A black hole, we'd be dead if it was, the whole lot of us, all sucked into a gravitational nightmare, but it isn't so we're not."

"Well that's good then isn-" Heinrich stopped as the screen on the wall began to show an image. He was looking at a plain brick wall with a LED-clock mounted on it. The clock showed the date and time.

"This clock, Heinrich, is on the wall at the far end of the room where the laser is. We don't know why but when the Window opens it always looks at the same place and always twelve hours from current time. We can't see back any sooner than twelve hours. Hence the reason the clock reads 23:12 on the Seventeenth of May, 2020."

Heinrich checked his watch and saw she was right. Leigh turned back to the control console and lifted a phone handset. She punched a speed dial button on the bank of switches.

"Hi, this is Doctor Leigh Wilson, I need an authorisation code for the Projection Request I sent earlier." She waited, punched a series of numbers into a keyboard, then hung up the phone. She moved to another console and entered in more commands. The image on the screen blanked out, and Leigh entered a last set of commands on a second keyboard off to her left. The screen flashed white and then refocussed. Heinrich stood in stunned silence as he watched the Projection. He saw Leigh take a couple of draws from a cigarette before standing, putting her notebook and cigarettes away, smoothing her skirt down and adjusting her jacket. He watched as she dropped the cigarette into a waste bin, walk forward to the roadside and shield her eyes from the approaching headlights. He saw the car stop and a Lance-Corporal in the uniform of the Waffen-SS step out of the passenger side door and salute Leigh. The image froze.

"51 degrees, 30 minutes and 21 seconds north, 0 degrees, 7 minutes and 51 seconds west, camera position altitude ten metres, 19:50 GMT on May 17, 2020." Leigh read the words off a piece of paper she had taken from her pocket. Heinrich looked at the image on the screen then back at her. He ran his hands through his hair and continued to stare.

"It would appear you are speechless, Colonel Steinmann."

"It would appear you are mostly right Doctor Wilson."

"Want to see anymore? Would you like me to zoom in so you can see yourself at the wheel of the car?"

"No, I think that's just fine. Thank you."

20

They were back in her office and drinking more coffee.

"You haven't said much?" she offered.

"Well, I'm a bit stunned really. I'll be honest, I was a bit disappointed when you told me the limitations but to actually see it in action. To have a window into the past and to have seen it actually working. What an investigative tool! It's amazing."

"Why thank you kind Sir." She dipped her head in a mock bow. "Okay, before I go through the next bit, any questions?"

"Probably lots, but not at the minute."

"Okay then. I opened the first Window in September 2015 but it took us months to figure out what it was and what it could do. After a lot of work we discovered it looked back through the timeline. Then we detected an audio signal. We decided to experiment with transmitting voice back through. We had these great ideas of asking Mozart how he had composed his masterpieces. We also thought we could use it to tell people not to get on the Titanic. That sort of thing. So we set up a test. We put a cheese sandwich, wrapped in greaseproof paper, on a table."

Heinrich chuckled, "A cheese sandwich, seriously?"

"Yes seriously," Leigh giggled with him, "I know it sounds pathetic now, but it was early days and we'd very limited funding. Remember this is back in Toronto and we were only a Research and Development project working on theoretical subjects. I have a bigger budget for stationery now than we did in total back then. We also didn't know what was going to happen, so the idea of using a BMW was out and we wanted to test the life state of an

122

object. If it aged or grew younger. We weren't prepared to use a puppy when we could test the freshness of a sandwich."

"Fair enough."

"Everyone on the team agreed to run the test and Bushy, I mean Jerome, have you met Jerome?"

Heinrich nodded, "He's the Irish one, yes?"

"That's right. Well, he volunteered. So we put the sandwich in place and we isolated Bushy for the day."

"Bushy?" Heinrich asked.

"Just a nickname for Jerome. Anyway, I can show you what happened." She stood up and turned on the large touch screen display on the wall. Pulling a directory across, she expanded a video set. Then choosing one of the files, Leigh made it full screen as it opened and came into focus. Heinrich was looking at a four-quadrant display. In the top half there were two rooms. Both appeared to be identical room layouts with a table, a fridge and a single bunk. The only difference he could see was that in the top left room Jerome was stretched out on the bunk. The top right room bunk was empty. On the table in both rooms was what he guessed was 'the' sandwich. In the bottom left screen was what looked like a control room with a number of people in it and in the bottom right screen was a close-up of Jerome sitting in a chair full-face onto the camera. Leigh paused the display.

"On the top left is the test room being viewed through the Time Window Projection. You're looking at the room but twenty-four hours in the past, hence why Bushy is lying on the bunk. The top right is the live feed CCTV from the room. As you can see, it's empty of Bushy and he is now in the bottom right about to be interviewed by Franci. Bottom left is the old Toronto control room. Make sense?"

Heinrich nodded and said, "By Franci I assume you mean Francine Xu?"

"Yep. We set up an experiment where one of the team would be isolated for twenty-four hours. We sent him into the room and he had no interactions with the rest of us in any way. He had food and water in the fridge and that was all. No radio, no TV, no anything else. We wanted as little interaction with the world as possible. We also put the star of the show, the sandwich, on the table and he was told not to touch it. That was it."

"And?"

"And nothing. He came out of the room after twenty-four hours and joined us back in the main lab. We put him into an isolation booth and Franci asked him questions. That's what you are looking at on this screen."

"Forgive me, but that doesn't seem like the most startling experiment."

"Well, no but the next bit was. When I play the video you'll hear Konrad, Franci, Bushy, various others and me. There's a bit of explanation of what the feeds are and then it begins. You ready?"

He nodded and she touched the screen.

The voice was deep, resonate and dispassionate, "Experiment 402H/2, Arcand Institute. Test Feed-1 subject room T-minus-24 hours via the TOW Projection. Test Feed-2 is subject room T-minus-0 via live CCTV. Test Feed-3 isolation interview response. Test Feed-4 control room environment. Initiate baseline response."

"Jerome, in the last twenty-four hours did you have any interaction with any members of the team?" Heinrich recognised Francine's voice asking the question.

"No." Jerome answered casually and without emotion.

"Do you remember any of us talking to you?"

"No."

"Did you move the sandwich from its place on the table?"

"No."

Heinrich saw Konrad lean forward in the control room display and key a microphone.

"Initiate command sequence."

"Bushy?" It was Leigh's voice in the control room.

The man on the bunk in the TOW Projection sat up and looked around.

"Jerome, in the last twenty-four hours did you have any interaction with any members of the team?" It was Francine repeating her earlier question.

"Yes." Jerome looked puzzled. His voice was hesitant.

"Do you remember any of us talking to you?"

"Yes. I do. It's like… It's like a strong sense of déjà vu. But I remember it. It was Leigh. She spoke to me. She just said my name. Or rather, she called me by my nickname. That was all. I'm sorry. I, I didn't mean to lie to you earlier. I just remembered it there now."

"How did her voice sound, was it clear, which direction did you hear it from?"

"It was clear, distinct," he hesitated. "But it didn't come from anywhere. Or rather, it came from everywhere. It was," he was looking increasing confused, "like she was in my head. Like when you listen to music through headphones. It's not in your ears; it's a spot inside you?"

"Did you move the sandwich from its place on the table?"

"No." Jerome was looking concerned.

"Initiate sequence 2."

Leigh's voice in the control room, "Bushy, can you please stand up for me and turn toward the table."

The Jerome on the bunk got up and turned toward the table.

Leigh's voice again, "Now, can you please move the sandwich from where it currently is to the other end of the table."

Heinrich watched as Jerome carried out the simple instruction.

As Jerome set the sandwich back down in its new spot a number of things happened on the screens. In the TOW Projection room the lights seemed to flicker and Jerome flinched and covered his ears. In the interview room Jerome had brought his hands up to cover his mouth and looked surprised, in the control room people were standing up and looking towards one another in an almost comedic double-take and the screen in the top right of the quadrant had gone blank.

"Jerome, in the last twenty-four hours did you have any interaction with any members of the team?" It was Francine again repeating her earlier question.

"Yes." Jerome's face registered surprise.

"Do you remember any of us talking to you?"

"Yes. Leigh asked me to stand up and move the sandwich."

"Did you move the sandwich from its place on the table?"

"Yes."

"And from your memory what occurred when you did?"

"When I set the sandwich back down on the bench there was an incredibly loud noise and the lights seemed to go off momentarily before coming straight back on. The noise was like a crack of thunder directly overhead. I remember covering my ears it was that loud and then it rumbled for a short while until it faded." Jerome paused, and looked into the camera.

"But Franci, I remember this now and I also remember telling you not two minutes ago that I didn't touch the thing. I wasn't lying. I know what I'm saying now is the truth but..." he just shook his head. "I also feel sick..." He bent forward and began to vomit. The screen went blank.

"What just happened?" asked Heinrich.

"Bushy threw up," Leigh said.

"Uh, yeah I saw that. I meant..."

Leigh cut him off by tapping on the upper left display. "We asked him to move the sandwich and he did. He describes hearing a loud noise that rumbled and faded but otherwise that was it. We didn't interact with him anymore and, as you saw, he remembered everything he had done as soon as we made him do it. He had no memory of the original day's events and his reality was what we had him do. Short term he suffered shock, confusion, physical nausea and vomiting but he survived. Longer term he had unnerving feelings of déjà vu that persisted for a while. It took about three weeks of clinical discussions with our resident psychs to get him squared away but, as I said, he survived."

"And the room in the top right?" Heinrich asked her.

"Ah. Well. Watch." Leigh collapsed the original quadrant displays and double-tapped on a new file. It expanded and was a close up of the table.

"This is a super slow-mo, frame by frame playback of what happened."

Heinrich leaned forward and watched intently. The sandwich instantly disappeared from one end of the table and appeared at the other. In the place where it had been was a shimmering, translucent, almost after-image of the sandwich. The next frame showed the outline around the shimmer intensify in brightness and the next showed that the outline had collapsed to a single, radiant point of light. Then the screen went white, then black."

"What happened?"

"The sandwich moved."

"I saw. That was truly amazing. But after that?"

"It took us quite a while to figure that out. When it disappeared from one end of the table it really disappeared. It left nothing. No molecular structure at all. The very space it had occupied was ripped out of our existence. It created a true vacuum. It turns out that nature really does abhor a vacuum and when she decided to fill this one, she did it with enough energy and resultant force to blow the sandwich, the table and everything else that was in the room into very tiny little shards."

"Oh!" Heinrich didn't really know what else to say.

"We ran the experiment over and over and changed the parameters but in general we replicated the same results. We increased the number of people in the room and that was interesting. They could all hear the audio signal in the same way Bushy described but after the experiment their disorientation was more severe. It was like they all had subtly different memories of the same thing but in a terribly disjointed way. Some suffered hallucinations, some became severely depressed while others were fine. It was weird and we never really got an adequate explanation for it." Leigh frowned, obviously still concerned at the lack of a proven outcome. "We increased and decreased the time delay and increased the size of the object being manipulated. In the end we stopped because it was always the same." She added almost as an afterthought, "And we couldn't control the size of the effect."

Heinrich just frowned at her. "The size?"

She returned to her seat and swivelled it toward him. "We had an isolated experimentation facility within a wooded area in the north of Ontario. We decided to use it because Bushy had been nearly deafened by moving a small object and we reckoned things might escalate. We were half right. We slewed the Time Observation Window and instructed the test candidates to push a trolley with a fifty kilogram weight from one end of a room to the other. The resultant explosion in the live-feed room was tiny. It didn't even splinter the table but there was a ten second blackout in the

Projection room accompanied by a noise that actually incapacitated the test subjects. Almost deafened them permanently. The next one we ran we increased the weight to a hundred kilograms, thinking bigger was obviously better, and the resultant explosion blew the whole live-feed room apart. Literally, not a shred of anything left. We even cleared the trees in the surrounding woods out to a fifty-metre radius and yet the test subjects in the Projection room hardly noticed a thing. Then, on a notable occasion that we never managed to replicate, we moved a remote control model vehicle around the room and there was no damage whatsoever. Nothing. It just arrived at the new spot and that was that. The bright image outline appeared for a second but other than that, nothing. We tried it again and it produced so much heat the room looked like it had been airbrushed with a welding rod. After three weeks we had seen enough. If we went back in time and manipulated physical things then the results were unpredictable at best and could be cataclysmic at worst."

"So, if we go back and alter anything, we lose everything here?" asked Heinrich.

"That's just it. We don't know. Maybe, maybe not. I know that doesn't explain much. You see we ran another set of tests where we just changed a person's behaviour. We got them to do things differently. Simple stuff, like read a different chapter in a book to the one they had read or do a different set of exercises, push-ups instead of sit-ups, that sort of thing."

"And?"

She shook her head, "Much like the other results. Very inconsistent. Some were not good at all and produced a lot of confusion and distress. A lot. Some took weeks to readjust. Other test subjects were fine. Couldn't actually recall any effects. And on one occasion the person could clearly remember both sets of events. Said it was like being able to see two things happening at the same time in her memory. She didn't need counselling, she just commented that it was an interesting phenomenon."

"So you stopped?"

"Yeah. We held quite a lot of seminars with some very impressive theoretical physicists and to be perfectly honest, we're still not really sure. Some reckon if we were to go back far enough and alter something then it would be like ripples on ponds. By the time they would catch up to us they wouldn't be noticeable. Others argue that they would build like waves and swamp us in a tsunami of change. Mind you, most of these theorists don't actually know we have Thule. Most thought it was a purely theoretical exercise."

"But the Führer determined for the cautious approach?" Heinrich asked.

"Didn't so much determine as absolutely ordered it. He was first briefed on this after the big Toronto accident, just before we all relocated here. He'd read the reports of the various seminars and said that the future of the Reich would be placed in jeopardy if so much as one of these eminent scientists was even slightly off in their theories. He said his grandfather had instigated the Nuclear Weapons Project and explained how the scientists involved with that had wondered if, by setting off the first bomb, they would rip the world apart. I remember him being really passionate when he said that the nuclear program was a necessary gamble. I'd never realised that the Reich felt they needed to have the nukes to force the rapid capitulation of the unoccupied territories. But he said now was different. Hence the direct order that Project Thule was only to be used for intelligence and investigative purposes. He even reiterated that when he signed us into provisional-live use last month."

"What do you think?" asked Heinrich.

Leigh gave a rather whimsical look. "I think the tsunami approach. If, for example, we go back and make my mum and dad never meet, then everything they ever did, including me ceases to be. Even though I was here to make the discovery which allowed me to go back, as soon as I do it I would be removed from the timeline. I can't just be if they never met, but I was. Imagine it like a snake eating itself from the tail up. The head exists right up to the point when the mouth catches up with it. Oh, and if you think about it for long enough, your head starts to hurt and you take up smoking." She got up.

"Speaking of which."

21

Leigh had said that she always went outside for a smoke around midday and it was close enough. Heinrich followed her to the smoking-area on the south side of the Todt administration building and sat in one of the half dozen uncomfortable, formed-concrete chairs next to a few metal ashtrays fixed to plinths. Shaking his head at the unsightly bus-shelter-like frame that someone had thought would provide a modicum of protection in the normal event of rain in London, he looked to Leigh. She was standing profile on to him, looking out to the surrounding fields that separated the labs from the old dockyards.

He realised that he had changed his mind from the previous evening. Her prettiness hadn't matured into beauty, it was more than that. She was truly, stunningly beautiful.

He looked at her porcelain pale skin with the high cheek bones, the straight nose, proportioned mouth and full lips. He watched as she took a draw of the smoke. He saw the slight tensing of her neck muscles and watched as her hand moved away from her mouth. He slowly let his gaze traverse her body. Her breasts were full and her slim waist accentuated the curves. She wore a simple white blouse and a black knee-length skirt with flat, yet not drab, black shoes. He found himself wondering if her legs were covered in tights or stockings. He had noticed her legs the night before and now, as she stood in front of him, he found them to be even more attractive than he had remembered. He realised he was staring and looked down at the ground.

"Are you finished?"

Heinrich's head snapped back up.

"Um, p... pardon?" he managed to stumble out.

"Asking questions? Have you finished or do you still want to know more about the project?" She was still looking out at the fields.

"Right," he recovered and continued, "the bits you gave me to read. I have questions about them."

Leigh looked around and said, "Well, we're on our own so fire away." She took a long draw on the cigarette.

"You said you all relocated here after some big accident in the Toronto lab. Was that the last of the experiments you were running?"

"Oh no. We finished the experiments when we had flattened enough trees. The big accident, as we all call it, wasn't really an accident," Leigh looked wistfully at him, "more a complete aberration by one of the junior researchers." She looked back out to the fields and shook her head a little.

"Can I ask what happened?"

"This young researcher had a theory that light is matter and it was causing the Window to open because of its effect on gravity. We were all intrigued with her theory and thought it certainly had merit. But she was young and impatient and had decided that if light and sound waves could pass through the Window, then other matter could pass through and arrive at the time scene currently in focus."

"Okay, I think you lost me there, but you're saying time travel. Sending something back into time?"

"Basically, yes."

"So what did she try and put into the Window, another sandwich?" Heinrich smiled at her.

"Not quite." Leigh turned to look at him. "She lay under the formation of the Time Window and then stood up inside the circle."

"Oh!" Heinrich said it as flat as he felt for having tried to be funny. "I'm sorry Leigh, I didn't mean to... I... Was she crazy?"

"It's okay Heinrich, and no, not crazy, just a bit misguided in her thinking and too young to discuss it properly. So she decided to experiment. Her name was Kristen Zielang, she was twenty-two and we didn't find enough of her to bury."

"The report in the file you gave me said there were deaths. How many?"

"Six. Kristen, a couple of young soldiers on the security detachment and three cleaners working the night shift."

"Seriously? I never even heard about it before today."

"No, not many did. It was well and truly hushed up. The investigation was done by the Central Intelligence Office in Berlin. They sent a team over to Toronto. But because someone leaked some stuff to the local press things got quite rough. The Propaganda Ministry handled it and it was eventually spun as a fire in the institute. However, it wasn't just the deaths. The whole lab was wrecked and half the administration wing with it. It was a big explosion. So we were packed up and shipped out here. Underground, secure and given a budget to get it up and running again."

"Why London? Why not Berlin?"

"They wanted us out of the limelight and literally buried underground. Todt was already here and any similar sites in Berlin couldn't fit us in. They did seriously consider building a new underground lab complex east of Berlin but it would have taken too long and, regardless of PR, people tend to notice a six or seven storey hole being dug in their backyard."

"I assume moving and getting it all setup again wasn't that easy?" Heinrich asked.

"We were back up and authorised as an official project by the October of 2016 but it was nearly two years before we saw any progress. The first task was to rebuild all the equipment and reconstitute the labs. That alone took months. But having done all that we couldn't get it to work. So we spent a long time checking we had built everything properly and were doing everything properly, and it still didn't work."

She finished her cigarette and put it in the ashtray. She looked at him as she fished another out of the pack. "I don't chain smoke, just before you get on that moral horse again. I fit two in at lunch time and that's it for the working day." She poked her tongue out like a child.

Heinrich merely held his hands up in mock surrender. She smiled at him and lit the cigarette before continuing.

"In the April of 2018 Franci flew home to see her family in Quebec. It was a family get-together-weekend and one of her cousin's little boys was having his tenth birthday. On the afternoon of his party she rang us to say she knew what the problem was." Leigh paused.

Heinrich felt like he had got to the last scene in a 'whodunit' film. "Well?"

"Aw, come on Heinrich, you're a tip-top investigator, you tell me?" Leigh teased him.

"Stop it Leigh, I can barely follow your explanation of how a laser works. Put me out of my misery. "Heinrich smiled at her and they held each other's gaze for a fraction longer than they should have. Leigh looked down and spoke again.

"The kid had been given one of those little horseshoe magnets as a birthday gift. Franci realised what our problem was as she watched him play with it. The location of Toronto in relation to the Magnetic North Pole when compared to the location of London. So we ran a few small scale experiments and it bore up. It eventually took us until the September to properly engineer a false magnetic environment that would replicate the field strengths and displacements, but we did it." Leigh said it proudly because she really was. She counted the reconstitution of the working portal as one of the defining moments in her career.

Heinrich looked at her and saw the immense satisfaction that her work gave her. He also saw something else; a resilience and a determination that would never give up. He thought that this woman probably didn't see setbacks and tragedy as anything but challenges. And in that moment, as the scent of freshly mown lawns competed with the smoke from her cigarette and the spring sunshine gently warmed him, he finally understood why the Wilson family had truly believed they could bring the regime down from the inside.

She finished her smoke and they began to walk back to the main doors of the complex. Quietly Heinrich asked, "I assume you included the Standard Operating paragraph so I could see why it isn't that simple just to run the equipment?"

She nodded, "There's no chance of running an unscheduled event without all manner of alarms going off. To start an observation the system needs override keys to deactivate the security protocols and has a series of monitoring logs that must be initiated. That's how serious Berlin were about not having a repeat of the Kristen Zielang event."

"Who holds the keys?"

"I have one, and Konrad has one. Either of those can be used separately to arm the system and carry out routine tests and maintenance but, as you saw, they both have to operate in tandem to initiate a TOW."

"So to run the demo for me you had to get all that in place?"

"Yeah. Konrad was a bit naughty in that he lent me his key but I still had to notify Berlin. When we started up that was who I rang. They gave me the numeric code I entered."

"Berlin?"

"They initiate the system logs. Before the TOW is released they need to know who is running the activation, for what purpose and what time coordinates are being visited. The expected duration of the TOW and the actual time expired are also noted, as is the financial authorisation and the investigation case number. They then monitor the time and location coordinates on their repeating display panels and will shut the TOW if the logged details do not correspond to what they are seeing on their screens. They don't actually see the feed from the Window because it was figured that they wouldn't have the necessary security clearances and the investigation materials will be need-to-know. But they see all the control mechanisms."

"Who are *they*?" Heinrich asked.

"The Office of the Reichsführer's J2 staff. They hold the Master key. Without their numeric code sequence we can't use the system. The Duty Watch Officer has to have their shift up and running and monitoring the TOW. Like I said, they can't see the output of the Projection but an alarm sounds if the time and coordinates don't match with what was registered."

Heinrich shook his head. None of this had been in his handover briefing by Berlin and he was meant to be head of security. He paused and considered his next question.

"So you won't be going back to see your parents?"

"No I won't. I decided last night, well, the early hours of this morning actually, that I'll trust you. My promise to my father was there for my protection. I think you trusted my parents and they you. Going back, even if I could, will not help me."

He reached for her hand and squeezed it gently. Her heart leapt in her breast. She caught the scent of him and she turned to look into his eyes.

"Would you like to go to dinner tonight?" he asked.

Leigh was about to answer when she was interrupted by Heinrich's ForeFone buzzing. Hers also began to ring.

They accepted their incoming calls and turned away from each other.

"Leigh Wilson." She listened to the caller and her face lost the radiance that had been on it moments before.

Her only response was, "Okay, I'll be there," before ending the call and turning back to face Heinrich. He looked like she felt.

"Heinrich?"

"That was my office. I have to call Gestapo Central Office in Whitehall on a secure line. You?"

"That was Wolfgang. He was just asked by Whitehall to authorise an immediate activation of Thule. He's called Konrad and he needs to speak to you. He said Department A4 in Berlin had initiated the request. Who are they?"

Heinrich sighed, "My dinner invitation might have to wait. A4 deal with assassinations. If they want to use Thule, then I think we just lost a high ranking member of the Party."

Part Two

A Time to Seek

and

A Time to Love

22

Konrad, Leigh and Wolfgang stood in the briefing room at the far end of the lab corridor. Heinrich was on one of the secure phones saying little but doing a lot of nodding with the occasional "Ja" or "Nein." When he hung up he ran both of his hands through his hair and blew out audibly. Leigh wondered what he was about to tell them.

"Please," he motioned for them to sit. "Professor Faber, Gestapo Central Office in Whitehall has an authenticated message from 8-Prinz-Albrecht-Straße." Heinrich didn't need to tell them any more than the street address in Berlin for them to know that this set of orders came from Reichsführer-SS Friedrichand himself.

"We have a direct authority to use Thule to investigate the murder of Reichsminister Uwe Joyce, who was killed last night in the Savoy Hotel." He didn't pause but did note the shocked look on the three scientist's faces. "Formally, as it is the first time the equipment is to be used on a live operation, I need to get you to sign off the authorisation and transfer control to the Project Director and Deputy Director."

Wolfgang nodded. Heinrich continued, "I'll then need Professor Lippisch and Doctor Wilson to accept the delegated power of day-to-day operations for the project. Berlin want us to get all this sorted as quickly as possible. They'll take the paperwork straight to the Führer for his final authorisation. You need to be in a position to start as soon as we have it. Any questions?"

There were none. Heinrich lifted the phone again and punched an internal extension number. He spoke rapidly and issued a set of precise orders before hanging up and turning to them again. "My lads will courier the papers down to you and look after their transmission. Then we just need to await Whitehall's nod of approval. However, I'll need to get briefed by the scene of crime team. I'll get back to you as soon as I know where and when we need to be looking. In the meantime, if there is anything else that you or your team needs to do, then I'd suggest you do it." He didn't say it arrogantly or rudely, but there was no doubt who was now in charge.

Leigh was fascinated by the man at the front of the briefing room. The same sensitive man who she had spoken to at length over the previous evening and much of the morning had been replaced by an authoritative, efficient, confident professional. She had known he had to be all of those things given the rank he held but she also realised how much she had begun to think of him as just Heinrich rather than a SS investigator. This other Heinrich was in some ways even more attractive to her than the kind sensitive Heinrich. She instantly knew why this persona struck such a chord with her; he reminded her of her father. She stood up with Konrad and Wolfgang and the three followed Heinrich out of the room. He went on down the corridor to get transport for the trip into the Strand, where he would meet the Scene of Crime Officer. Leigh shouted after him as he headed off, "Heinrich, make sure you pick up a hand held GeoCord station, we'll need the exact lat and longs and an elevation if it's in a building."

By 15:30 Heinrich was back in the briefing room and the seated audience had swelled. It included Wolfgang and six of the Thule scientific team, Konrad, Leigh, Francine, Jerome, Wilhelm and Claire. They were joined by Major Dietmar Heysburgh, the Project Thule Mission Liaison Officer from the British Governor-General's Office, Kriminalrat Pascal Debouchy, assigned from Gestapo Central Office Whitehall, SS-Second Lieutenant Peter Vogel, head of the Prisoner Holding and Interrogation Facility and, seated at a small table off to the side of the front row of seats, a female stenographer. While everyone had their allotted tasks to perform she was likely to be the busiest yet the least visible due to her junior rank.

Heinrich started by addressing her directly. "Hannah, I'd like you to stand up."

Nervously, the young soldier did as she was asked.

"Everyone, this is SS-Lance-Corporal Hannah Tensfeld. You won't have seen her around the labs before but she is someone who you will see a lot more of. Hannah is the official Gestapo stenographer for this use of Thule. Long after we are all gone to our new jobs and even longer after that, it is Hannah's words and recordings that will stand testimony to what went on here today. Thank you Hannah."

The young lady, who had now flushed red, retook her seat.

Heinrich continued, "Her access is unlimited, her clearances as high as anyone in here. She is to receive the full cooperation of all members of this team. If she's in a place that is awkward or inconvenient I would request that you politely point her to a more suitable location. But please be under no doubt, she is to be afforded every safe opportunity to be as close to you as possible. She will be using digital video, audio and standard stenography recording equipment and again I need you to allow her to do her job. I would also ask that you look out for her safety in what is an unusual environment for her. I have often seen before in situations like this where a junior soldier gets overlooked due to the rank they wear. I just want to make sure you all realise that Hannah's authority in this matter outweighs her rank by a vast margin."

Leigh looked at the young soldier. She was dressed smartly in her Gestapo uniform, as Leigh would have expected of a member of Heinrich's team. A pleasant faced, young girl with her dark hair caught up in a bun. But Leigh was watching her expression. Hannah Tensfeld had a half-smile on her face and her eyes were wide. Leigh had seen the look on children watching cartoons, or puppets or magicians or anything that enthralled them. Leigh realised Hannah had no warning that Heinrich was going to say what he just had. She also realised that, because he had started with her, he had made Hannah feel important as opposed to being the most junior in the room. Finally, Leigh realised that she was watching a member of Heinrich's team become totally loyal to him and his leadership style. Hannah Tensfeld would never forget this boss who had empowered her in front of this team of senior scientists and military Officers. Leigh looked back at Heinrich and understood why he had risen in the ranks so quickly. This man knew how to lead people, and the personnel who formed his teams wanted to be led by him.

Heinrich cleared his throat before starting his briefing. "At some time before 03:30 this morning a fire started in a hotel room in the Savoy Hotel on the Strand in central London. The occupant of the room was listed as Reichsminister Uwe Joyce, who is the Justice Minister with Portfolio for all Custody Centres in Great Britain. This includes all rehabilitation facilities and Konzentration-slager."

Leigh noticed that Heinrich used the official German name for the concentration camps.

"Initial response was handled by the London Fire Brigade and the intensity of the fire within a modern hotel room was an immediate cause for suspicion. No alarm had activated until the adjoining rooms had become smoke-filled and the in-room sprinkler system had failed to douse the fire effectively. Once the blaze had been controlled and extinguished by the responding fire tenders it was quickly discovered that the smoke alarm in the Minister's room had been disabled, the in-room sprinkler system had been partially but effectively disrupted and a towel had been wedged into the door gap to prevent smoke exiting into the corridor."

Heinrich paused and looked over at Hannah, who had stopped typing almost as he had stopped speaking. Happy that the young soldier was keeping up with him, he continued, "A suspicious death investigation was initiated and the local Kriminalpolizei Office in Bow Street was assigned responsibility. Given the intensity of the fire and the fact it had burnt unnoticed for some time, it is unlikely that any useful DNA traces will be recovered. However, even though the Minister's body was extremely degraded due to the fire, it didn't take a lot of examining to assess the likely cause of death. The attending coroner indicated that, although he will have to wait for the autopsy, it is probable that the Minister died due to a gunshot to the head. A thorough search of the remains of the room revealed no items indicative of a weapon and at that point the investigation was reclassified as a Murder Inquiry." He paused and looked around the room. Everyone was intently focussed on him.

"Given the likelihood that the body was that of a Reichsminister, all processing of ID was fast-tracked. A confirmed match of lower jaw teeth records resulted in a positive identification being established at 10:30 this morning. Gestapo Department A4 was informed as soon as the ID was confirmed and the Inquiry was reclassified as an Assassination of Reich Government Personnel. Initial investigations revealed no one had been seen in the company of the Minister since he left an official reception in Vauxhall Bridge yesterday at 16:30. He has stayed in the Savoy many times while in London on business and is reportedly a quiet, unassuming guest who stays, has breakfast in the mornings, meets his staff and is never demanding or high profile. However, checks of the Hotel's security logs show an exit from the rear of the building by an authorised, but unassigned, key-card at 02:20 this morning. The same card was used to gain access to the Savoy last night at 22:35. The key-card is a master key-card for the hotel and has been used on four previous occasions in the last two months. Each use of it coincides with the Minister's visits to London. Unfortunately the Hotel's security logs do not go back further than eight weeks." Heinrich paused again and let what he had said sink in.

"The preliminary assumption is, therefore, that the Minister was meeting a person or persons unknown on each visit to London and that on this occasion the meeting resulted in the Minister's death. These findings were presented to the Führer at approximately 11:30 and he, in consultation with Reichsführer-SS Friedrichand, authorised an immediate activation of Project Thule." Heinrich drew attention to a single sheet of paper on the lectern.

"I can now confirm proper authorisation of Project Thule in line with Reich High Command General Order 191/1.3/4 was received by me at 15:15." He scanned the room, "If there are no questions for me, I'll hand over to Professor Lippisch."

Konrad rose from his chair and took up a position to the side of the room's display screen, while Wilhelm moved behind the lectern to control the imagery.

"A handheld geo-coordinate reading for the location of the incident was recorded as 51, 30, 36.54 north, 000, 07, 12.68 west with an elevation of 15.6 metres."

The image on the screen switched to an overhead satellite view of the Savoy Hotel in the Strand. As Konrad continued, Wilhelm highlighted the various locations on the screen.

"Based on the timing of the key-card entries we'll begin by looking between 02:20 local on May 18 back to 22:35 on May 17, centred in the Minister's room. If we don't get an identification from that Projection, given that the card was used on previous occasions, we can go back to attempt identification on the previous dates. This will be made easier as the Minister always used the same room when he stayed at the hotel. That will alleviate any GeoCord tracking issues. However, Dimitri is already deployed into London so that should we require to track across other locations, he can upload the coordinates. This," he pointed to the screen behind him displaying a series of personal ID photos, "is Minister Uwe Joyce and the rest of his family and personal staff. We have these available for recognition if or when they appear in the Projection. The first thing we need to establish is that we are actually looking at the Minister. A printout of them has been prepared for you and is in the lab. Finally, we need to remember that the twelve hour lag will prevent any tracking of a suspect after," Konrad checked his watch, "04:00 this morning. Are there any questions?" The room remained quiet. Leigh did wonder how far a killer could have got in the intervening twelve hours, but held her peace.

"Okay. Leigh, Jerome and Wilhelm, please start the Projection and get Dimitri on a line from the Savoy. Francine and Claire, please escort Major Heysburgh, Kriminalrat Debouchy, Second Lieutenant Vogel and Lance-Corporal Tensfeld into the lab and ensure they are given a safety briefing. Ladies and Gentlemen, we have worked on this for some years now. The Reich has invested a lot of money into our efforts. It's time, if you will pardon the pun, to prove our worth."

23

J erome entered the geo-coordinates that had been supplied by Heinrich's trip into the Strand as the Time Observation Window reached stabilisation. When the image focussed, the scene revealed the Minister's hotel room. Wilhelm controlled the elevation and angular properties of the Projection and manipulated the image so that they looked from a vantage point of the entrance door. The room was simply furnished with a double bed, two bedside tables and a dressing table with cupboards underneath that probably housed the in-room bar. There was a door, shown in the top left of the image, that presumably led into the en-suite bathroom. On the bed was a slumped figure covered with various bed linen. The linen was on fire but the flames had not fully caught yet. The time stamp on the Projection showed 02:20:18May2020BST. Wilhelm tilted the view to look at the in-room sprinkler. It was wrapped in a towel and the in-room smoke detector hung broken on its hinge from the ceiling mount. The fire began to flare as the camera panned through the room and more of the linen caught alight.

In the rear of the control room, but with a clear view of the projected image, Heinrich stood next to Hannah narrating what he was seeing while she entered it into the official record. Leigh looked to him and he nodded. She told Jerome to go back by half an hour, then turned to the non-scientific personnel, "The Window is not a smooth scroll facility. We need to jump to a time point and observe forward from there, so we'll be going back in half hour jumps until we get something of note."

01:50:18May2020BST. As the image refocussed the room was lit by a single bedside lamp. Uwe Joyce was lying on his back while a tall blonde woman sat astride him. It became obvious as Wilhelm adjusted the incoming audio signal that the woman was in the final throws of bringing the Minister to an orgasm. Leigh felt her face blushing and she noticed that the men around her also looked uncomfortable at this unexpected voyeurism. She could hear Heinrich talking in low tones at the back of the room, describing the scene in precise and clinical terms. When the on-screen couple came to the end of their act, the woman rolled off Joyce and lay beside him. Her naked body was exposed and even Leigh could see that she was stunning. The Minister was slightly overweight but she knew he was fifty-two, so for his age he was still in reasonable physical shape. Despite her best effort she glanced to his groin and could tell, even as he was going limp, he had been averagely endowed. She guessed it was the power he was endowed with as a Reichsminister that was his most desirable feature. Leigh realised that she was going to have to look past the imagery on screen.

"Freeze it there Jerome, please. Heinrich?" Leigh turned to him. Heinrich looked to the other military Officers who were part of the investigation.

"Gentlemen, I need you to verbally concur that we are looking at Reichsminister Uwe Joyce and that the other person in that image is not a member of the Minster's family or personal staff as compared to the ID photos you have available."

Dietmar Heysburgh, Pascal Debouchy and Peter Vogel all agreed that the man on screen was the Reichsminister and that the woman was unidentified. Heinrich nodded to Leigh, who turned to her fellow scientists.

"Wilhelm?" She didn't have to tell the scientist what was required. A small arrow shaped pointer appeared overlaid on the screen and Wilhelm moved it until it was positioned on the top of the blonde woman's head. He clicked it and a black dot marked the position. Moving the marker to her feet, he clicked again and a small box appeared on the side of the image indicating a measurement of one hundred and seventy-nine and half centimetres.

"Please note that the measurement will not be exactly right. We would advise that you allow a 5 per cent probability of error on that. So we're looking at a height of," Wilhelm looked to Jerome.

"One hundred and seventy-five through to one hundred and eighty-four centimetres, but more likely on the upper end given the relative height of the Minister. We know he was one hundred and seventy-eight centimetres tall. You can see he's definitely shorter than the woman."

Leigh saw from the frozen image that the woman's figure was hourglass. Her legs were long and shapely, she was toned and her breasts were firm. Her pubic hair was trimmed neatly into a light coloured triangle, making it likely that she was a natural blonde. While sweeping the image with her gaze she could hear Heinrich continuing his commentary to Hannah Tensfeld. She looked around to see how the young soldier was coping with the potential embarrassment and saw that the Gestapo stenographer was completely focussed on her task and looked composed and calm.

Wilhelm manipulated the image to zoom in on the woman's face. Another few clicks and he had cropped a copy of her face into a search protocol, which began to run through the eBü. Leigh stared at the main screen again. The blonde hair cascaded onto the pillow and framed features that were both beautiful and, even allowing for her just having had sex, sultry and... Leigh searched for the right word and was slightly embarrassed as she realised the woman looked available, desirable, dirty.

Francine, who was sitting at her control console, phrased it better when she said, "My goodness me, she's sex on legs. Poor Minister, didn't stand a chance did he?"

Leigh looked at her and 'shooshed' her silently. Francine smiled back in her mischievous way. The men in the room smiled too. Leigh looked around and could see even Heinrich smiling. She knew Francine had that knack of saying things that never caused offence but went to the core of the issue. Leigh also knew she was right. This blonde could have seduced any man with a sideways look. Jerome shook his head very subtly at Leigh as they all continued to wait for the search algorithm.

Leigh concurred with the simplest flick of her eyes and turned to the rest of the room, "Based on the light conditions and the resolution we can get on the imagery, while we might be able to recognise the Minister, it's going to be unlikely that the face-match systems will be able to identify this woman. I just want to warn you so you don't get too disappointed."

A small information box popped a red 'x' onto the screen as she finished.

"No match Leigh," said Wilhelm.

The image unfroze and the scene played on. Joyce pulled a sheet up over himself, for which Leigh silently thought, 'Thank you.' The woman walked out of frame into the bathroom. When she returned, Joyce followed the same route. When he returned and made to lie beside her, the blonde got up and began to get dressed. The audio was faint but clear.

"Mary, you could stay, no one's going to be disturbing me until about seven."

"No Uwe, I need to get home,"

"Are you okay, you seem sort of distant?"

"Distant? I just fucked you, how is that distant?"

24

The military members of the investigation team were back in the secure briefing room. Heinrich had arranged for tea and coffee to be brought in and told them to take a few minutes while he went to check on the scientists. He went back into Oscar and found Konrad, Leigh and the others sitting around a bench. Leigh was still feeling physically shaken from the violence she had seen on the screen. She had always known that on occasion the Time Observation Window would present them with challenges they may not have expected. Francine was sitting next to Jerome, talking very quietly. Claire and Wilhelm sat at the end of the bench, also subdued. Professor Faber came into the lab and joined them. Heinrich looked to Konrad.

"It's okay Heinrich, honestly, we'll just sit here and talk things through. We need to come to terms with the things we're going to be doing from now on, so if and when you need us again, just let us know. We'll be ready."

Heinrich nodded and left the lab. Dietmar Heysburgh stood up as he re-entered the briefing room. The man was tall and broad shouldered, in his mid-thirties with dark brown hair, blue eyes and a strong jaw line. It was easy to see why he had been assigned as a Military Attaché to the British Governor-General's Office. He would have carried a presence for the military in the Political surroundings of the office and probably looked good in his mess-dress uniform when attending social functions. When the need came up for someone to be assigned as a liaison for Project Thule, the Governor, despite not knowing what Thule was, had not hesitated in picking Dietmar.

"Kamerad Colonel, I'm sorry to be asking this, but why can we not continue the track?"

They had followed the unidentified 'Mary' as she left the hotel. With the help of Dimitri at the Savoy passing latitude and longitude information they had tracked her to a taxi parked in Burleigh Street but were unable to track any further as the car had begun to navigate the narrow streets.

"I've checked with Professor Lippisch," Heinrich explained, "The observation Window isn't that dynamic. It takes time for it to track through time and space. All they can do is focus on a set of coordinates, then they can view about a ten-metre diameter range. It can be kept on a target that is walking and manually made to follow but you saw how it was limited in the speed of its movement. The only reason we didn't lose her earlier was because we were able to use the hand-held coordinates being transferred from the Savoy. Even then, as soon as she got in the cab and it began to drive, we have no way of knowing what the next coordinates would be. So we're back to standard investigation techniques. Does that explain?"

"Yes, thank you, it's just," he paused.

"I know Dietmar. It's a lot less capable than you were told in the initial briefing by Berlin?" Heinrich asked.

"Well, yes," Heysburgh said. His shoulders slumped.

"I felt the same way at first, but if we just reflect on what we've seen, it truly is remarkable, yes?"

They all nodded. Heinrich grabbed a cup of coffee and stood at the front of the room.

"Okay, Pascal, what do we know?"

"The uniform was Great Britain's Rehabilitation Service. She said she had handled the processing of Turner prisoners last night. Given the distances and that she was in his hotel in London it could only be the Harrow Holding Centre. I can't imagine there are many Marys and even less that look like her at Harrow. As soon as we know how Berlin want to handle it then I can begin running the information down. I can't see any problems finding out who she is. The problem will be if she's running." Pascal Debouchy had the full power of the Central Office behind him so gaining an identification would not be a problem. He was a career detective with nearly thirty years working various crime offices throughout the Reich and had spent time in London as a young man. When the opportunity came to return to Whitehall for his last tour of duty he had jumped at it. In his mid-fifties, a widower, he was beginning to put on a little weight around his mid-riff but still carried himself with the confidence of experience. Dressed in a well-worn brown suit, his face was creased with lines and his eyes, shielded behind his brown-rimmed square glasses, held a seriousness that came from years of investigating things the Reich would rather pretend did not happen. His slightly thinning blond hair made him look older than he was but Heinrich knew him by reputation as a thorough and professional investigator. His influence within the Criminal Police system was going to be vital for Project Thule.

"Peter?" Heinrich looked at the Junior Officer.

"The interrogation centre is completely ready Colonel." Peter Vogel had personally overseen the establishment of the new single-storey Prisoner Holding and Interrogation Facility that had been built to the eastern side of the Todt compound. Any prisoner processing was going to be done out of the mainstream holding centres as Thule was a compartmented security classification. Vogel was not out of the usual mould for a Waffen-SS officer. He was short and squat, with a shock of red hair, pale complexion and freckles. Most people meeting him were surprised to learn he was a native of Dresden. Despite his physical appearance he had graduated top of his class at Bad-Tölz and had been posted directly from there into Todt. Initially the young man had been frustrated, thinking he had been passed over for more high-profile postings, until he had been briefed on what Thule was. Now he understood he had been given a prime assignment.

"Okay," said Heinrich, "a quick revisit of the ground rules. We cannot allow that we have her identification or anything else for that matter from Thule but that isn't going to be an issue. I have spoken to Prinz-Albrecht-Straße and they want to know if this was a lover's tiff or if what she said about the Turners was alluding to a wider conspiracy. If it's the former then it'll be handled quickly in-house. However, if it *is* the latter the Reichsführer wants a public trial."

The men in the room began to murmur and Heinrich raised his hands to halt them. "It's okay, save your breath gentlemen. I've voiced concerns but he wants to make a public example of her if it's a conspiracy. You'll remember the man who attempted the assassination of the last Führer? Because he claimed God had made him do it, there was no outcome that was acceptable other than a trial." Heinrich did not say show trial although he knew it had been and he knew this one would be no different. "If it comes to that we'll need to make sure we gather enough evidence or a simple confession so that we can mask any involvement of this project. Understood?"

They all nodded.

"Make your calls Pascal." Heinrich indicated the secure phones in the corner of the room.

Pascal Debouchy called into the Central Office in Whitehall. Fifteen minutes later he had a list of all female staff called Mary working at Harrow.

"Colonel, as I thought, it's a short list. Chief Senior Overseer Mary Reid. According to Whitehall she's well known in the Rehabilitation Service. A high-flyer and apparently destined for great things. Mind you, if she was screwing the Minister for a while, then it would explain her career. She has a reputation as one tough bitch. Her father was lifted on paedophilia charges five years ago. According to the report he was transported to Harrow and tried to attack his daughter when he saw her at the facility."

"And?" Heinrich prompted.

"She emptied a Glock-17 into him."

"Nice girl! Is she at Harrow now?"

"Yes. One of my guys phoned in a routine call just to check. She's currently in her office and is due to finish her shift at 18:45. There are no prisoner transports expected so she'll probably knock off on time, if not earlier."

Heinrich checked his watch, it was 17:35. "Well, she would appear to be quite a cool bitch too. Do we assume that she still thinks she's clear of any involvement in this?"

The assembled men nodded. Pascal added, "She must think that she scrubbed the room for trace elements and believes no one saw her arriving or leaving. If we assume from the use of the key-card that she's been having an affair with Joyce for at least a few months, if not longer, and no one knew about it, then she's used to being discreet. I reckon she thinks she's clear for at least a while."

"Okay, Dietmar," Heinrich turned to the Liaison Officer, "We can't risk using the local Kripo for this. We saw what she did in the hotel and she's more than likely to start shooting. They'll be more than likely to kill her. The Reichsführer wants her alive and talking. So, get Northwood on the phone. I want their best snatch squad readied. Tell them we're on our way and we'll brief them when we get there."

Dietmar had also looked at the time. "We'll be pushing it to get her at work. Where does she live?"

Pascal referred to his notes, "Brightwell Lane, Watford. She rents a small townhouse."

Heinrich thought for a moment, "Okay, get a target pack for the home address prepped in Whitehall and have it couriered to Northwood. We'll meet up with it there. We'll need historic satellite imagery and up-to-date obliques. Get a Special-Reconnaissance unit out to the address now and have them do an initial assault pack, then get them to meet us at Northwood. Also, get one of your surveillance teams to Harrow. Tell them to track her from work. We need to keep eyes on her."

Pascal and Dietmar got up to make their calls.

"She comes back here, so Peter, I want a security cordon set up around the interrogation centre and be prepped for her arrival. Get up top please and get a car out front. Also, can you get my sidearm out of the armoury locker?" Peter Vogel nodded and left the room.

As soon as Pascal and Dietmar had finished their calls, Heinrich rechecked the time. It was 17:46.

"Let's go."

25

I'm really sorry, I can't."

Carl Schern was kicking himself and as pissed off with his choice of career as he had been in some considerable time. Since waking that morning he'd managed to occupy himself for a few hours before finally making the call. He had tried not to appear too keen but in the end thought 'Ah, fuck it!' When she answered he had tried to sound as casual as he could. He attempted a little bit of small talk before she had laughed in a really sexy way and asked him if he was just going to talk about the weather or actually ask her out. They made plans to meet at a small restaurant he knew in Rickmansworth. She told him not to worry about picking her up, she would meet him there at 20:30. He had laughed and said that it was always good to make a date with someone who knew her twenty-four hour clock. Now here he was having to call her up again and tell her he couldn't make it. "I'm really sorry, but we've just been given a tasking to pick a target up."

"Sounds all very exciting. So you're standing me up to go get yourself a man?" she laughed.

"Aww, come on, I'm not standing you up. Look the job's in Watford and I'll probably be done by nine, ten at the latest. Seriously, I just need a delay. I could meet you for a late meal. What do you say?"

"Watford? They have fugitives from justice in Watford?" She kept her voice light.

"I don't know; we were just put on standby. Some murder thing, but we haven't even had the briefing yet. Anyway, what do you think?"

"I think it must be some murderer for the crème de la crème of the SS to be sent in to get them."

"Nah, just some high-level crap from Berlin. Probably some Party member that knocked off his wife and they don't want the Kripo to go in all ham-fisted. So, later?"

"I tell you what Carl, let's take a rain check on tonight. I'd prefer to have an earlier meal so we could have more time to," she paused for effect, "umm, get to know one another. How does tomorrow sound?" she asked in as seductive a voice as she could manage. She knew it was very effective.

"Seriously?" Carl asked, almost unbelieving that this woman would want him as forwardly as she had just said.

"Seriously Carl. I tell you what, why don't you think about what I'm going to do with you after our meal. And now you get a whole day to think on it. So, tomorrow?"

"Okay, tomorrow, 20:30, same place, see you then." Carl Schern hung up with a smile on his face.

Mary Reid hung up and checked around her office. She had sat at her desk the whole day trying to come to terms with the emotions and turmoil borne from the previous evening. Not Joyce's murder, that was perfectly acceptable to her and had already been compartmented into its own little box in her mind. No, her emotions had been savaged in trying to come to terms with Thomas Dunhill and the numerous other prisoners she had been responsible for. Now, with Schern's call, her conscience was being neatly tucked away again into its deep dungeon and her mind was reacting to the threat of arrest. She checked her watch.

It was 18:00 and she knew instinctively that Carl Schern and his team were coming for her later that night. The likelihood of another high-profile murder suspect living in Watford was much too remote for her to be comfortable. She imagined that he would get the full details of his tasking at any time and then it was a fifty-fifty chance as to whether he would admit to tipping the target off. If he did, it just meant they would come sooner rather than later. How had they tracked her so quickly?

She had never been seen by anyone in Joyce's company since they had first met in Harrow. She was unobserved last night and had taken a cab to a random drop-off before recovering her own car. How the fuck had they found her? She felt her heart racing and told herself that it didn't matter a damn how they had found her. It was irrelevant. The only thing that mattered now was what she could do. She forced herself to think of the likely courses of action that her adversaries would take. The Special Forces had been put on standby. That meant they didn't know what they were being asked to do. That meant someone had to tell them. No doubt a briefing team were en route to Northwood.

She sketched out the probable sequence of events. They were likely coming up from Whitehall, given it was a Reichsminister's death. They would have put Northwood on standby and then left. She knew Carl wanted to fuck her, so he had probably rung her as soon as he could. She would allow him a fifteen minute window. So, how long did that leave for the briefing team to turn up? She decided she probably had half an hour at best. If they were any closer they would have gone for picking her up at work. What else? If they were going to take her at home they would put a Special-Reconnaissance screen in to her house. If they had left at the same time then they would be in place in twenty to thirty minutes. What else? She drummed her fingers on her desk lightly. What else? Fucking think Mary. What else? Eyes on the target as soon as possible. A surveillance team en route to her location. About twenty minutes until they would be in position, if she was lucky. There was only one gate in and out of the Harrow Holding Centre. Mary looked around at her two administration officers.

"Harold, would you go and get a car and bring it around the front? I'd like to go down to the holding cells and check on the repairs. I'll meet you outside."

Harold Spencer rose to his feet with no hesitation or questions. He had worked for this woman for long enough to realise that when she spoke you just did as you were bidden. "Yes Ma'am."

Mary got up from her desk and went through to the inner corridor of the administration centre as Harold left the office. She stopped at the secure locker that held the small arms for the building. After dialling in the combination she opened the locker and reached under the second shelf. The wooden box she withdrew held a foam insert, set into which was a metal cylinder that was actually longer than the Glock-46 service pistol it was designed to attach to. She slipped the suppressor into her pocket, replaced the box and secured the locker. Then she returned to her office and walked across to what was officially the Harrow document repository, but was just known as 'The Vault'.

It was, in effect, a secure vault much like a bank's with its single door set into the wall of Mary's office. But instead of gold or silver this strongroom held the files of ghosts. Long before the days of the smart tablet computers being used by her administrators, the Reich had kept file records. Even now they still liked to make a hard copy print of each prisoner and 'Process Event'. Each year the vault would be archived into long-term storage and each year it would fill again.

She swung open the heavy door and stepped inside. To her front was a small desk that sat in the middle aisle of seven rows of file storage racks, each having a clear walkway between them. She quickly attached the suppressor onto her service pistol and called out to her other administrator, "Fredrick, could you come in here?"

Fredrick Henly responded much as his colleague Harold had done, for he too had worked for Reid for long enough. She came around behind him as he walked into the main walkway of the vault and blocked his path back to the door. He turned to face her and froze in position as he stared directly at the muzzle of her suppressed pistol.

"Slowly Fredrick, empty your pockets onto the desk. You know me too well to think that I wouldn't pull the trigger and walk away, so do as I ask."

He did exactly as she asked.

"Now, take off your ForeFone and earpiece and leave it on the desk as well."

Fredrick's hands were trembling and he had a frightened, pained expression on his face. He reached up and removed his wireless earpiece but he couldn't manage to undo the clasp to the Fone's wristband.

She waited a moment before saying, "You need to calm down and concentrate. Believe me Fredrick, your future is going to be very short if you do not remove that Fone."

He finally managed to release the clasp and the Fone fell onto the floor. He bent to retrieve it.

"Leave it there. It's fine." She waited for him to straighten up before continuing, "Now, I want you to walk to the rear wall of the vault and kneel down facing away from me."

Fredrick managed to turn around but his gait was unsteady and she could see his hands were shaking. He walked the ten steps until he was at the rear wall and then knelt down. She could hear soft sobs coming from him as she raised the pistol and aimed it at the back of his slightly bowed head. As her finger began to apply pressure to the trigger, she heard, as clear as if it had been spoken to her, 'I love you for who you are.' She paused and considered what she was about to do.

A long moment later, she relaxed her arm.

Taking his Fone with her she left the Vault. She called out to him as she was closing the door that she would tell Harold where he was. The look of relief on his face as he spun round and realised he was still alive made her feel a strange mix of happiness and relief.

After securing the door she slipped the pistol into her blouse and willed herself to walk normally through the building. When she got to the front doors she could see Harold waiting in a pool car. Although it was going to be traceable it was the best she could manage. A black Mercedes saloon with no obvious markings other than the Government plates. She got into the rear of the car and leant forward between the front seats. Harold looked down at his right side when he felt the metal pressing against his ribs.

"Harold, there's been a little change of plans. You're going to drive us out of the gates. If you falter for one moment I'm going to kill you. If you do as I ask, once we're clear of here we shall pull over and I'll let you out. Okay?"

Harold gave a small, scared nod of the head.

She knew he would do what she said without hesitation. He wasn't armed and even if he had been he wasn't the sort of man who was going to fight her. He was weak. The realisation made her feel a wave of regret at having to use him like this. She packaged the regret up and compartmentalised it. She needed to stay focussed. "Take off your Fone and throw it on the passenger seat."

He did as asked with a little less fumbling than Fredrick.

"Good, now drive straight to the main gates then head north. I want you to drive through Wealdstone and up to Harrow Weald. Know how to get there?"

Harold didn't speak.

"Harold!" she shouted at him and he flinched, "Do you know how to get there?"

"Yes Ma'am."

"Right then, let's be on our way and Harold, drive like you have eggs in the back, smooth and safe."

The car slowed to go over the speed bumps at the main gate and as it exited the facility Mary lay down on the back seat but with the pistol never leaving Harold's side. They were headed north on Sheepcote Road and approaching Station Road before she sat back up. "Keep going Harold, you're doing fine."

"Ma'am, what's this about?"

"You don't need to know Harold. It's best that way. Then I can just let you go and you know nothing. Okay?"

"Yes Ma'am, thank you."

They drove north through Harrow Weald before she instructed him to take a left and head for Hatch End. Leaving the narrow streets, with buildings on each side of the road, they entered into more affluent surroundings. "Now Harold, go up through Oxhey Lane, you know the way?"

"Yes Ma'am."

Soon there were no buildings at all on the right side of the car. Mary looked out over fields and golf courses. "When we go up over the hill we're going to be on a section of road that passes a small wood that's off to the left hand side. You know where I mean?"

"Yes Ma'am."

"Good, when we get there pull over, leave the car running and step out. Okay?"

Harold nodded and Mary watched a single tear run down his cheek. She considered what she was going to do with him when she got to the wooded stretch of road. Initially her thought had been to kill both Fredrick and him as no witnesses and no trace of them would confuse whoever was coming for her. But the memory of Thomas Dunhill and what he had said to her had stopped her pulling the trigger in the Vault. She sat back and allowed her mind to consider what would be the better thing to do.

It took them another five minutes to reach the wooded stretch of the road. Harold pulled onto the right hand side verge and stopped the car.

"Okay Harold, handbrake on and leave the keys in it. When you get out, close the door and step around the front of the car to the side of the road. Be very calm. Do you understand me?"

He gave no response.

"Harold!" she shouted and he flinched again, "Do you understand me?"

"Yes Ma'am."

"Good, carry on then."

Harold fumbled with his seat belt before finally managing to release it. He stumbled out of the car, shut the door and walked a few steps off to the side of the road. Mary opened the rear door and stepped out. She used her left hand to flick the car door shut and held the Glock down by her right side. Motioning with her head for Harold to walk a few more steps away, she took the time to have a look around.

The evening was calm with a light breeze rustling the leaves of the oak, ash and poplar trees. There were a few clouds in the sky but otherwise it was a beautiful spring evening. She could smell the woody tones of the bark and the heavier notes of the copse's undergrowth. The road was deserted and the trees of the small wood crowded down towards her like interested spectators.

"Harold, I need you to step inside the tree line and keep walking. That way you won't see me drive off, you won't know if I turn the car round, you won't see anything and that will be for the best. Okay?"

Harold mumbled a soft, "Yes," then crossed the road and stepped into the wood.

Mary followed him and as he glanced round she motioned with the pistol for him to continue. "Harold, if I see or hear of you coming out of these woods until this night is pitch black then I will come and find you and hurt you. Do you understand?"

"Yes Ma'am."

"Excellent Harold. Well done." She watched him walk a few steps further into the darkness, stumbling over the roots and uneven ground before she called out, "Oh Harold."

He turned, tears visible in his eyes. She knew that he believed he was going to be shot. Again she had a physical, painful reaction to the regret she felt at having to bully and scare him.

"When you do get out, Fredrick is locked in the Vault. Make sure someone rescues him before he starves."

Harold stared hard at her, sniffed and nodded.

"Well, on you go. Enjoy the walk," she said and turned away.

26

The Northwood briefing room had a lectern at the front right which Heinrich stood behind. The white screen suspended from the ceiling displayed the imagery Whitehall had provided via Pascal Debouchy and the Reich Security Network. In the audience were SS-Major Johan Lowther, his team leader SS-Sergeant-Major Carl Schern and the other three members of the SS-Kommando squad that were tasked as the point unit for the operation. In the second and third rows were the backup, outer cordon units that would provide the wide security for the house assault. Behind them was Dietmar Heysburgh and next to him Heinrich's driver, Lance-Corporal Wiehaden. Heinrich looked over the room and noted the clock on the wall showed 18:25.

"Gentlemen, I'm Colonel Steinmann. My thanks for your patience while we were en route to you. What I'm about to brief you on is not complete, in fact, the whole thing has been put together rapidly and we're still awaiting the assault photography for the target house. However, I'll give you what we have and the rest we'll fill in as it arrives. The mission is an arrest operation. I need to stress that. It's an arrest operation. If we end up killing this target there are some gentlemen in Berlin who will not be happy. So, if you have to engage the target, I strongly suggest you make your aim very good. Before we bring up the subject's details I also have to advise you that your first impressions will not be correct. The target is a cold-blooded killer, is expected to resist and will use lethal force." Heinrich nodded at Pascal who pulled up Mary Reid's ID photograph onto the screen. Even though it was as anaemic a photograph as could be imagined, the woman was still exquisite looking. Heinrich thought he could guess the reactions that he would get from an audience of Special Forces soldiers.

"Fucking shit!"

"Yes, I know, calm down." Heinrich was surprised at the intensity of the comment from the Kommando in the front row.

"No sir," Carl Schern stood up, "I need you to stop this briefing now. Your plan's compromised."

"What?"

Carl remained on his feet and looked around at his colleagues. He had seen her image on the screen and processed his options immediately; stay quiet and risk his mates when they went in to an aware target or admit his phone call. It was likely to be career ending but he had no choice. He looked back at the briefing officer and knew he was going to be in deep shit with the SS-Colonel but he took a breath and told him and the rest of the room about meeting her last night, arranging a date and then how he had rung her about twenty-five minutes ago. Johan Lowther got to his feet and began to remonstrate with his team leader.

Heinrich brought them to order, "Enough! Sergeant-Major stay on your feet. Major, sit!"

Lowther sat.

"Sergeant Major, what's your name?"

"Schern, Colonel"

"Is this your team?" Heinrich swept his hand over the other three soldiers sitting in Schern's row.

"Yes sir."

Heinrich looked at the three men. It was a standard SS-Kommando team. The three men wore the rank of SS-Sergeants but their rank meant little. Between them and Schern there would be a weapons specialist, an explosives specialist, a communications expert and a team medic trained to paramedic standards. However, all of them, including Schern, could ably fill in for the others if the need arose. He had their names printed on a sheet in front of him. Honecker, Schmitt and Calise. They didn't look like most people expected Special Forces soldiers to look. They were not tall and blond and built like tanks. In fact, Heinrich remembered he had been a little disappointed the first time he had met any of their ilk.

He had been a very young, very junior soldier in the 12th SS Panzer Division Hitlerjugend and had gone on exercise to southern Italy. They had been told the SS-Kommando would be playing roles in the upcoming exercise and he had expected to walk into the company of giants. Instead he found himself surrounded by wiry little men. His Panzer Division friends were a majority of tall, blond Aryan blueprints and so there was a bit of sneering at these 'Special Forces'. The talking behind the backs of the Kommando was that the Panzer Division could whip them and that SS-Kommandos were not really elite but more e-little. He remembered the talk was always 'behind their backs' and never directly to them. There was a wariness. A 'just in case' mentality.

Then had come the fight in the bar in Taranto. Some Italian soldiers had decided to share their wit and wisdom, both of which had been lacking. The Kommando's fuse had been a long, slow burn. They hadn't responded to the baiting they got. Heinrich recalled that it was one of the Panzer Division that had swung the first punch at the Italians and gone down in a flurry of fists and boots. At that point the Kommando decided enough was enough.

Heinrich had been twenty years old and had been in uniform of one sort or another since joining the Junior Hitler Youth at age ten. He thought he had been made shockproof against the effects of violence and hard men. After seeing the pure aggressive savagery of the Kommando that night he had learnt there were violent men that he never wanted to come up against. He had reassessed his thinking about those wiry little men and had never forgotten that four of them had weighed into more than a dozen Italians just to rescue one Panzer Division soldier who had spent the previous week taking the piss out of them.

His focus returned to the briefing room, "You three, do you trust this man?" All three soldiers responded by snapping up to a sitting attention position, "Yes Colonel."

"Well that's good, because so do I. Schern you total fuck-wit. You know you shouldn't have gone into details with an outsider. But I'm guessing you were going to get your leg over and your dick was driving your mouth. You're not the first. Thing is, you could have kept your mouth shut just now and we'd all have walked into a prewarned target. So I'm guessing you just gave up your career for your men here. Is that correct?"

"Yes Sir." Schern answered Heinrich while looking directly at him, then dropped his gaze and looked down at the ground.

Heinrich thought back to Taranto. He thought of the Italian Mountain Division soldier. A big burly son-of-a-bitch who had been about to ram a smashed glass into Heinrich's head. He remembered the oldest of the Kommando team step in front of him and go with the thrust of the glass before grabbing the Italian's wrist and twisting in a circle. The Italian had flipped over his own elbow and the sound of breaking bones and tearing tendons had been gratefully received by Heinrich.

The Kommando casually took the glass from the now limp Italian and drove it into his chest before kicking him in the head with enough force to leave permanent damage. Heinrich had watched awestruck. When the Kommando had turned round to look at him, Heinrich had said the only thing he could think to say, "Thank you."

"No need to thank me son. You'd do the same for me. We're German Soldiers."

Heinrich decided it was time to settle a long held debt. "Right, well, I'll figure out something fun for you later Schern, but I will not be taking your rank, nor will I be ending your career. As far as I'm concerned and as far as everyone else is concerned," Heinrich looked around the room making eye contact with all the personnel, "this little balls-up stays inside this room. Am I clear?"

There were a few nods.

"Not good enough gentlemen. Am I clear?"

"Yes Colonel," the whole group responded.

"Right. Now that's settled, Schern sit down. I need all you SF types to get your shit together and figure out how we fix this. She has half an hour on us now. I want thoughts on what she's going to do. Pascal, when did your guys get out front of Harrow?"

"Ten minutes ago. No sign of her at present."

"Get them in there now and find out if her car's still there. If it isn't then we know something, if it is we'll still not know a damned thing."

Mary turned into her road, aware she would have the advantage of surprise if there was a recce team already there. They didn't know she had left work yet, would be on the lookout for her car and not the black Mercedes and would probably, hopefully, be focussed on their task. What she hadn't expected was to find two of them standing in front of her house taking photographs. She drove down the street and noticed their official vehicle parked near the end of the road. It was empty. Either there was another pair out the back of her house or possibly they had been in such a rush that they had only sent the two. She drove around the block, parked in the road parallel to hers, then cut through the side garden of the house that ran back to back with her small townhouse. She was relieved to see that they had obviously only sent a single Special-Reconnaissance team and they were still out front.

Pascal closed his mobile phone, "Her car's still there but they've run a check on all the pool cars on the site. Three of them are missing and one of them was signed out at 18:05 by a civilian administrator from her office."

Heinrich's options were closing in, "Sod it, we can't dick around anymore. Get your guys into her office now Pascal, tell them to try to get her alive."

The rear gardens of both properties were about ten metres in length so she had twenty metres of fairly open ground to cross to get to her back door. The only possible cover once she made her own garden was a small shed on the left hand side perimeter that had originally been a coal store when the house had been built. It now held Mary's underused lawnmower and even less used gardening tools. Just as she was about to negotiate the low hedge and flimsy wooden fence that separated the gardens, she saw both members of the recce team coming down the side path of her house. She crouched behind the hedge and was thankful for her black uniform.

Pascal's phone rang again. He stood quietly, listening to his men at the Harrow Holding Centre for a moment before looking up at Heinrich again, "She wasn't there. Both of her admin staff are missing. She's running."

Heinrich looked at the map that had been pinned up by the Special Forces. He looked at the distance lines and time lines. "Fuck it! This is unravelling. Get on to your SpecRecce team Pascal and tell them that if she's on her way to the house then she's going to be on top of them very soon. The rest of you, I want routes and options for where she could be now, assuming she isn't heading back to her house."

Mary watched the two surveillance men. They were both dressed in dark suits and both were average height and average build. The quick glimpse she caught of their faces as they had come into the garden told her they were both average looking. Overall they were ideal candidates for close observation reconnaissance duties.

She figured the one on her right was the more experienced of the two only in that he had greyer hair than his colleague on the left. He also had a pencil and was making notes in an old fashioned flip notebook, the pages of which would be ripped out and handed to the assault team. Sometimes computers weren't better and faster.

They stood with their backs to her about six metres distant. The one on the left began to take photographs which would, no doubt, include each window and door and would be used to brief the Kommandos. It would have been a lot easier for the assault team to be here waiting for her return so she knew that their time must have been limited. They had to have been planning that she would beat them home. Well, they were correct about that.

She carefully climbed over the small fence while they remained with their backs turned, staying as centrally behind them as she could. She crouched and then sprinted forward. She was less than two metres away when they began to turn round.

Greyhair dropped his notebook and pencil and went to reach inside his jacket with his right hand while the photographer threw his camera at her and started reaching for his left hip.

Mary half turned to her left and let the camera sail past before bringing her pistol up and pointing it directly at the now camera-less photographer.

"Keep reaching for your weapons and the only question is 'how many rounds will I put into you?' It's your choice."

They both held their positions and Mary kept her aim on the younger of the two. The moment seemed to stretch into a minute. She was about to instruct them on what she needed them to do when Greyhair's Fone buzzed on his arm.

The noise seemed to break the spell and they all moved at once. Greyhair instinctively reached up to his right ear to connect the call. Mary brought her pistol around and at almost point blank range fired through the Fone attached to his left wrist. The younger officer reached for the pistol on his hip and had almost got his weapon clear of the leather holster when Mary turned to him and yelled for him to stop. Whether it was adrenaline or inexperience or both, the younger officer continued to draw his weapon. The muzzle was almost level and bearing in on Mary.

Her bullet went through his right cheek, just below the eye and exited, along with most of the back of his skull, onto the faded green grass. His corpse crumpled into a heap as Mary refocussed on Greyhair who was sunk to his knees and grasping his left wrist. He made no sound save for the noise of laboured breathing.

"Who has the car keys?" she asked.

He merely nodded in the direction of his dead partner. She slowly walked a full three hundred and sixty-degrees around him to check each of the surrounding houses that had oversight of the garden. The suppressed pistol had made very little noise, so no one had come to look out. There were no staring faces at any window and no curtains were twitching. She disarmed Greyhair and advised him to use his own jacket as a binding for his wound. Then she opened the small combination padlock on her garden shed and ushered him inside. Taking the car keys and Fone from the photographer's body, she rolled it over to the shed door and had Greyhair pull it in beside him. Resecuring the padlock, she went inside her house to grab an already prepared backpack. It was 18:45.

Heinrich was still standing at the lectern. Johan Lowther stood next to him and Pascal was on his mobile at the back of the room, pacing and looking concerned. He closed the phone and looked at

Heinrich.

"Nothing."

"Right gents, at worst we can assume she's taken down our recce and she's been at the house for at least fifteen minutes. At best she just got there a few minutes ago. Either way, she's not going to be hanging around. I need options."

"Local Kripo?" asked Honecker.

One of the backup squad answered, "If she's just taken down a SpecRecce team, then what do we think she's going to do with the K-heads? No offence Sir." He spoke towards Kriminalrat Debouchy who had rejoined the others at the lectern.

"None taken Sergeant, in fact I'd agree with you. But we might use them to screen the roads. Force her the way we want her to go."

"Great, but where's she going to run to?" asked Dietmar Heysburgh.

"Ireland." The voice came from the back of the room. Carl Schern was logged onto the Security Directorate Network and had Mary Reid's personnel record on screen.

"Schern?" Heinrich prompted.

"Colonel, her parents are dead and her two living sisters are off the radar. She goes on holiday alone and has, for the last three leave periods, headed to the north Antrim coast. If she gets there and goes to ground we could spend a year trying to find her. Think of how long it took to negate the Ulster Resistance Force in the Fifties and Sixties up and down that coast. The good news is that she's going to have to get there and that means boat or plane. Commercial travel's obviously not an option now so she'll probably go for a boat."

Heinrich looked around the room. No one voiced any disagreement with the theory. "Okay. It's the best option we have, so where's her jump off point?" A general hubbub of conversation and ideas sprang up from around the room as Heinrich asked the question. He let it run for a minute or two before nodding at Lowther.

"Okay!" Lowther raised his voice and the noise stopped. "Possible courses of action?"

"North Wales."

"Southern Scotland."

"Cornwall."

Heinrich looked at the map and back at the room. He hated inaction and indecision. It was now almost 19:00 hours and for the previous hour and a half every plan that he had come up with to apprehend this woman had turned sour almost as soon as he had put it in place. He was playing catch-up and he detested it. He took a breath and thought through his options.

The room waited.

He had combat experience, investigation experience and he wore the rank of a SS-Colonel. All he needed to do was figure out what to do and he knew all the men in the room needed him to do something. He took another breath and began to issue his orders in a calm and authoritative manner.

"Johan, wake the rest of your squads up. I want three helicopters, eight-man teams for each and ready to lift at fifteen minutes readiness. Get the pilots briefed, one each to cover those likely destinations and the routes to them. If we get a trail on her car then I want an immediate interdiction. Get on to your Army Aviation buddies and pull them out of whatever hotel they happen to be pissing it up in." Heinrich nodded for him to start now and Lowther left the room.

"Pascal, put Kripo Vehicle Check Points into all autobahn routes and as many trunk roads as you can in or near Watford. Dietmar, I need military backup at those checkpoints but they are not to engage her. They are not to return fire, understand? If she runs the checkpoint they let her go and we let the air assault take her. Also Dietmar, you're going to be running this end of things while I'm away." Again Heinrich motioned with his head and the two officers started making their calls.

"Schern, get your team and the backups booted, spurred and out front in five minutes. I want an immediate assault on her house. If we catch her there then life is going to get a lot simpler. If she's gone then we find her. Let's go gents."

27

Two Geländewagens pulled into the eastern end of Brightwell Road in Watford. A third entered from the western end and immediately slewed across the street to form a blocking force. The eastern most vehicle did the same and the troops debussed. Heinrich stepped out and began to watch the rest of the operation. He was hooked into the main communications channel and could hear the running commentary.

"Charlie secure."

"Bravo secure."

"Alpha squad, check," it was Schern's voice followed by a series of radio clicks. Heinrich knew that Schern would be sitting in the front passenger seat of the Geländewagen that was pulled in to the side of the road just in front of him. All the man's focus would be on the target address and he only needed to hear the radio clicks of the three other members of his assault team to know they were ready.

"Go."

The vehicle was accelerated hard down the little terrace street until the brakes were hammered on and it stopped just in front of Mary Reid's townhouse. Schern was out and took a kneeling position in the front garden. Honecker went to the front door as Schmitt and Calise headed down the side alley to the back garden. Honecker nodded at Schern and stood to the side of the door frame.

"Alpha callsigns, engage."

The charge Honecker had placed on the front door blew the locking mechanism off the frame at the same time as Schern fired two stun grenades through the lower room window. Calise was a fraction behind putting his grenades through the kitchen window and Schmitt was the last to detonate his charge and blow the back door but it was only a second from first to last.

"Alpha Two, hall clear"

"Alpha Three, rear approaches secure"

"Alpha Four, back clear"

Heinrich listened as the four men moved quickly through the rest of the small house. It was less than thirty seconds worth of repeated 'clears' before he heard Schern.

"All callsigns, this is Alpha One. Status Black. Bravo and Charlie lift the block and relocate here, I want a full sweep."

Heinrich knew it had been a long shot. He checked his watch. Mary Reid had been phoned by Schern less than one and three quarter hours before. She had acted quickly and with no hesitation. He had tried to take a cautious approach and keep her arrest as controlled as possible. So far she was beating him hands down. He waved for the wagon to go on down to the house, he needed the short walk to refocus. He continued to listen in to the comms chatter.

"Warrior Control, this is Alpha One. Request immediate CasE-vac. We have Sierra Romeo One, Cat-six, secured to rear of target. Over."

"Alpha One, this is Warrior, Medivac en route your locale. How so Sierra Romeo Two. Over"

"Negative Warrior, Sierra Romeo Two, Cat-one. Over."

"Roger Alpha One, Backup team moving now. They'll take control of Sierra Romeo Two. Out."

Heinrich understood that Schern's men had found the two surveillance team members, one wounded and one dead. Dietmar, who was operating callsign Warrior back at Northwood, would get Pascal to sort out the clean-up and conduct interviews with the surviving member to find out if he could tell them anything useful.

When Heinrich entered the house Carl Schern was going through the small bureau cabinet in the downstairs lounge room.

"Anything?"

"No. Well, nothing to help us. Some bills and receipts but nothing of use."

Heinrich nodded. It was what he had expected. "Carl, get the backup units to go round the neighbourhood. I need to know what she's driving. If it was me I'd have ditched the Merc. See if we can find it. Also have a look for the surveillance team's car. This bitch is clever and I wouldn't put it past her to have swapped. If she has, get the details to Northwood."

"Sir." Schern nodded, stood up and was about to leave the room but delayed at the door.

"Colonel?"

"Yes?"

"Earlier; I just wanted to say thank you."

"Don't thank me yet, you don't know what I'm going to come up with as a punishment." Heinrich looked at the soldier and saw his eyes look down again. "It's okay Carl, I'm only joking. Let's just say you owe me a favour."

"Anything. You name it and if I can do it, it's yours. But I still want to say thank you."

"You're welcome. Now go do what you do."

***

It was 21:15 and Heinrich, Dietmar and Pascal sat in the briefing room in Northwood. They had put vehicle checks in place on most of the major roads out of Watford and further afield but to no avail. They knew she had swapped over to the surveillance team's Volkswagen but hadn't had one reported sighting of her. Assuming she was driving within the limits so as not to attract attention, then her circle of opportunity was approaching almost two hundred and fifty-kilometres in radius. That put her within reach of a lot of coastline. Pascal sat looking over the various reports that were coming in from his checkpoints, all amounting to nothing. Dietmar was sitting with his eyes closed and Heinrich had sent Lance-Corporal Wiehaden to get him a coffee. When the young man came back in he apologised for the delay.

"Sorry Sir, but had I known the machines here needed change I would have brought some with me. I had to go borrow some from the duty watch."

"No prob..." Heinrich stopped. Wiehaden looked slightly puzzled by the frown on his commander's face.

"Fuck it! We're thick!"

The young Lance-Corporal stepped backwards. "Sorry Sir?"

"No, sorry, not you Wiehaden. Dietmar, Pascal!" Heinrich was on his feet and his two colleagues looked up at him.

"What is it?" asked Dietmar who had obviously just been about to nod off.

"Forethought, planning. We didn't even bring change for the coffee machine so she definitely didn't put all of this together on a whim. She must have known that she might be tumbled eventually. She had to have planned an escape route and last night's killing was not premeditated from what we..," he stopped abruptly realising that Wiehaden was still in the room and was not cleared for Thule.

"Lance-Corporal Wiehaden, can you go and retrieve my car please? I'll be along momentarily. And thank you for the coffee."

Wiehaden handed the cup over and saluted before hurrying out the door. Heinrich continued as soon as the soldier had left, "From what we saw earlier today, last night's killing was on the spur of the moment. She had to have sat and planned her eventual escape and she would only have done that last night when she got home. If we're lucky, and I know we haven't had one piece of luck so far, but if we're lucky she might have done something to help us figure out her route. We can go back and see what she came up with. I've still got a GeoCord unit in my car. Dietmar get on the phone to Professor Lippisch and tell him to get his team back in. Pascal, ring Vogel and get him and Tensfeld in as well. We'll go via Reid's house and get the lat and longs and meet them back in Todt."

28

At 23:05 Heinrich watched the Time Observation Window reach stabilisation. The image focussed on the lounge room that Heinrich had stood in less than an hour before but the time stamp on the display showed 04:30 that morning. Mary Reid was sitting at her bureau with a number of pieces of paper on the pull-down leaf and what looked like a fairly generous shot of whiskey in a tumbler. She reached into the lower drawer and pulled a map out. After a few moments of folding and refolding she sat and studied it with the wrong end of a pencil tapping out an unsteady rhythm on the bureau.

They orientated the image so they had as clear a view of the map as possible. The small desktop lamp that provided Mary with light also allowed an excellent resolution on the Projection. Mary began to run through various possible routes and unconsciously ran the pencil over the roads. Her hand moved out and back along the lines radiating from Watford. Each time she returned to her point of origin and went through another option, checking all four points of the compass. Eventually she stopped and put the map into the front pocket of a small backpack.

"Go back please, two minutes." Heinrich stepped forward to the screen. When the image reset he watched Mary Reid use her pencil to point out the last route she had evaluated on the map.

"Freeze it there." The group of scientists and military personnel looked at the image on screen. Mary Reid's pencil had stopped on a small harbour in the west of Scotland.

"Where's that?" asked Pascal.

"Portpatrick." It was Jerome Mills who answered. They turned to look at him. "We used to go there on holiday, I had an Aunt who lived there," said the scientist.

"Would there be boats capable of crossing over to north Antrim?" asked Pascal.

"Well, it's small but on any given day there are going to be twenty plus boats alongside in its harbour. All of them would be capable of making that trip. It's a great choice if you don't know she's going there." Jerome paused.

"How do you mean?" It was Heinrich asking this time.

"She had to figure we wouldn't know because the downside for her is there's only one main road into the town. Once she got through the checkpoints in the south she must have reckoned for a straight run. If she's heading to Portpatrick she's driving down a one-way street into a cul-de-sac."

"How long does it take to drive there?" asked Dietmar.

"Well, when I go home I go via Cairnryan, which is close enough distance-wise for estimating, it takes me about seven hours to get from here using the autobahns. It's the last bit that takes the time, it's not exactly the straightest of roads." Jerome didn't need to add that Mary Reid was unlikely to have used the autobahns so that gave them even more time before she got there.

Heinrich looked round to Dietmar and Pascal, "Tell Northwood to get two of the choppers in the air, full assault teams, but tell Lowther I want them in civilian clothes, overalls, jeans, jumpers, anything that will fit in with a harbour. We'll go in covertly and take her down nice and quietly when she gets there. Also tell him I want Schern and his team to ride along but they're out of a covert approach as they all met her last night. Get the aircrew to route one of the birds here to pick us up and also tell them to get a route sorted out that gets us into Portpatrick from the sea. I don't want a formation of Special Forces helicopters over-flying a land route that she might be travelling. She's already proved she's not stupid. Pascal, we can't let her just disappear, so get the local Kripo down to the harbour."

"There's not going to be Kripo up there. The best we'll be able to do is the Schutzpolizei der Gemeinden."

Heinrich grimaced at the thought of having to use the poorly trained and under resourced uniformed Police force but knew his options were limited by time and distance. "Okay, but brief them on who we're looking for and make sure they fully understand they are not to engage her. Observation only, just so we know she doesn't fade into the mist. I want them to list every boat in that harbour so if she does take one we'll know what we're looking for. Also, see if they can ID us a potential Command Post. Lance-Corporal Tensfeld."

Hannah sat to attention at her desk.

"Can you please make sure all your transcripts and visuals are finalised for my review as soon as possible?"

"Of course Colonel."

Finally Heinrich turned to the scientists, "Professor Lippisch, thank you again." He caught Leigh looking at him as he made to leave. The flurry of activity that was beginning around them, with the scientists shutting down the Projection and Dietmar and Pascal handling the operational tasking, seemed to fade away as he held her gaze. He motioned for her to come into the main lab space with him.

"What is it Leigh?"

"You're going with them?"

"Yes."

"Heinrich she's already killed two people that we know about and it's doubtful we're going to find her other administrators alive. I just want you to be careful."

"It's okay Leigh, there's going to be four squads of Special Forces picking her up. I'm only going along to observe. I'm not going to be wandering up to her on my own." He tried a smile to reassure her but could see real worry in her eyes.

"I know, but," she hesitated.

"Go on Leigh, what is it?"

"It's silly Heinrich. I've known you for just over twenty-four hours, but," Leigh looked up at him. She couldn't phrase what she wanted to say, so instead she leant up and kissed him lightly on the cheek. He put his hands on her waist and reciprocated the kiss. When she stepped back he still held her waist and looked into her eyes once more.

"I promise I'll be back before you know it. Go home and try to sleep. I'll see you tomorrow."

29

The twin NH92 helicopters kept their rotors turning while refuelling was completed. Straight line flying from London to Portpatrick was well within their range but they were routed over South Wales before hanging a dogleg out over the Irish Sea, passing west of the Isle of Man before a low level approach into Portpatrick harbour. Heinrich was looking at the Air Loadmaster on the chopper who checked his watch and signalled with four fingers raised. The minutes seemed to drag by.

Heinrich re-ran the plan in his head. The helicopters would only momentarily touch down to drop off the troops before transiting to the Luftwaffe base at Aldergrove, in the north of Ireland. They would wait there, far out of sight and sound, for the pick up call or a redirect to track a boat if Mary Reid had beaten them to the punch again. The total flying was right on the limit of the aircraft's range so they had arranged to refuel at the Luftwaffe base, which was attached to Swansea Civilian Airport prior to the 'feet-wet' transit.

Dietmar leant across and raised his voice so he could be heard, "It's okay, we'll beat her there. We've got spare time."

Heinrich nodded, but he also knew it would be tight. The chopper had lifted off from Todt at 23:40 and had flown at its top speed of one hundred and sixty knots to Swansea. They had scheduled a fifteen minute refuel and were now overrunning that by four minutes. He reviewed the maths. Mary Reid could possibly be in Portpatrick by 02:00 but it was much more likely to be 03:00. It was now 01:00 and the transit to the small harbour was going to take Heinrich and his group eighty minutes. That put them on the ground at 02:20. It was going to be tight. He stopped his mental calculations when the aircraft finally began to taxi forward. The Loadmaster signalled him with an OK and then circled his index finger in an upward spiral. Heinrich nodded back.

One hour later he was able to look out of the starboard window and see the Isle of Man passing by. A quarter of an hour more and the Loadmaster waddled across the helicopter floor and handed Heinrich a headset that was already plugged into the aircraft communication system via a trailing long lead. He leaned down and yelled over the noise, "You're callsign Golf -Two."

Heinrich put the set on and listened in to the conversation between the aircraft pilot and the lead Schutzpolizei Officer in the harbour.

"Jackal Control this is Golf-One, please confirm status, over."

"Golf-One this is Jackal Control, Tango Zero, I repeat, Tango Zero, over."

"Jackal Control, I confirm Tango Zero, our ETA your location, minutes five. Golf-One Out."

"Golf -Two, this is Golf-One, did you copy, over."

"Golf -One, Roger."

Heinrich took the headset off and handed it back to the Loadmaster. He turned to look at Dietmar, Schern and the assault team leaders and made a thumbs-up signal. Mary Reid hadn't beaten them to the town. The eight men who would form one half of the arrest team checked their weapons. Carl Schern and his team did the same although they knew they would not be part of the arrest. Heinrich and Dietmar looked again at the imagery of Portpatrick harbour that Whitehall had provided to them before they left. The Loadmaster slid open the side door as the aircraft began to bank for its final run in, and what had been a cool and relatively noisy environment became a freezing cold cauldron of buffeting winds and intense noise. Heinrich could smell the sea and even in the pitch black he could make out the occasional white topped wave breaking in what was a sizeable swell. He had travelled in too many army transports to be even slightly queasy with the violent buffeting and sharp manoeuvres. He also never thought about the likelihood of dying in one of the flying taxis, figuring he was much more likely to be shot and killed by whomsoever he was flying towards.

The helicopters flew in just to the north of the two inner harbours that housed the small fishing boat fleet and the occasional leisure craft that were moored there. The planned Landing Zone was next to two municipal tennis courts and was normally the local lawn bowling green. The pilots had assured Heinrich they wouldn't leave so much as an indent as they hovered just off the surface. Heinrich watched the barely visible horizon pitch to a very peculiar angle as the NH92 flared out and performed a classic assault approach. The Special Forces troops deplaned and deployed out into a fan formation, weapons drawn and moving towards the car parks that catered for the boat crews. The aircraft ascended again as Dietmar's foot left the helicopter and cleared the Landing Zone in time for the second helicopter to perform the same manoeuvre. Both aircraft had dropped off their cargo in less than sixty seconds. Even the noise of their rotors disappeared into the winds of the Irish Sea within no more than two minutes.

Heinrich's ears adjusted to the quiet that surrounded the small harbour. The street lights that illuminated the car park and the quaysides weren't very bright but provided enough light for him to survey the Landing Zone and he saw the pilots had been true to their word. There was not so much as one wheel indent in the flat surface of the bowling green. Carl Schern, carrying a briefcase that held a command network radio system, led his three colleagues over at a trot and joined Heinrich, Dietmar and the local Schutzpolizei unit at the north-eastern end of the car park, which abutted the bowling green.

"Hauptwachtmeister Soria, I'm Colonel Steinmann. Thank you for your time in doing this for us. I took it from your transmission to the aircraft that you have seen nothing of our target?"

"No Colonel, nothing and we've been here since midnight. She's not shown up. Also, I've talked to Kriminalrat Debouchy and we've arranged for you to use a room in a hotel as your command point. It's the three storey building just along the road and the owner is retired Kriegsmarine, a Commander Muller." The Police officer indicated the hotel about four hundred-metres away.

"Excellent, thank you again. Go home and have a good sleep."

The police officer saluted Heinrich and then signalled for his two colleagues to meet him at their patrol car. Heinrich looked around the harbour as they drove off and watched Johan Lowther and his Special Forces troops set about their preparations. Their first task was placing a four-man detachment onto the road leading down to the harbour while the rest of the men deployed to their various observation points that they had picked off the Whitehall imagery. Heinrich was satisfied that if Mary Reid turned up, the four-man team on the access road would spot her and the other twelve soldiers deployed around the harbour would be well placed to arrest her. He led Dietmar and Schern's team to the small hotel on the waterfront. Heinrich rapped on the front door and it was opened almost as soon as he had knocked.

"Commander Muller?"

"Yes, but it's been a while since anyone called me that. Please call me Tobias. You must be Colonel Steinmann?"

Heinrich nodded.

Tobias turned and began to walk along the hallway. Heinrich and the others followed the elderly hotel owner who still bore himself in a manner that marked him as a career military officer.

"I have the front room on the first floor ready for you. The bed has been taken out and I've moved a few chairs and a table in there for you."

"Thank you for the trouble you've taken," said Heinrich but Tobias just waved his hand over his shoulder dismissively.

"No trouble, rather exciting really."

They climbed the stairs and Heinrich could see that the older man had been to quite a lot of trouble when Tobias showed them into the room. Not only were there table and chairs, but a platter of sandwiches was set on a small sideboard along with two full coffee pots and various cups, milk, sugar and even a plate of biscuits. Before any of them got a chance to say anything, Tobias merely smiled at them and said, "I'll be downstairs in the kitchen. Don't scrimp on eating or drinking as I'll bring you fresh rations every so often if that's okay?" His new guests nodded their agreement with the plan.

"Happy hunting gentlemen." Tobias rendered a semi-formal naval salute and exited from the room.

Heinrich pulled an encrypted mobile phone from his pocket and punched a speed dial, "How are we doing Johan?"

"All in position Sir. Two of the Observation Posts had no direct line of sight so we've relocated them. Other than that we're good. We'll make sure the most likely vessels are controlled by us."

"Okay, I'll have Schern set up the command net here and I'll monitor the traffic, but as of now you have operational control. Any questions?"

"No Sir."

"Good luck." Heinrich rang off and when he turned back to check how Schern and his team were progressing with rigging up the command radio he was pleasantly surprised to see it was already complete. A small desk speaker and microphone sat centrally on the table.

Dietmar switched the lights off in the room before parting the curtains and looking at the whole of the small harbour laid out in front of the hotel. He checked his watch and saw it was 02:30, he looked at Heinrich and nodded, "Well, we made it."

"Yeah we did, now all we have to hope is that she's actually on her way here."

"Been a fun night, even if she doesn't turn up." Dietmar laughed and, using the light coming through the window from the street lamps, he began to help himself to some of the biscuits.

30

Carl Schern poured himself another coffee while Heinrich, Dietmar, Honecker, and Schmitt sat on the chairs placed around the room. Marcus Calise was positioned obliquely to the window and was monitoring the harbour. The pitch black they had arrived in was now lightening to a soft grey as sunrise began to encroach on the night. Mary Reid had obviously not used the autobahns but there was also the worry growing in Heinrich's mind that she might not be on her way here at all.

"How long are we going to give her?" asked Schern.

"Until she turns up," Heinrich answered with an accompanying shrug of the shoulders.

"We've still got the blocks in around Watford and patrols along the Anglesey and Cornish coasts, so we'll find her," Dietmar added in his normal up-beat, optimistic manner.

By 06:00 the small harbour was quiet again after what had been a short flurry of activity. Five of the commercial fishing boats had departed for their day of hard work and a few of the leisure craft owners had turned up to prepare their vessels for a day of relaxation. Two of the latter arrivals were directly approached by the Special Forces and removed to the hotel. They readily agreed to assist in the way men do when faced with overwhelming firepower and were now downstairs in the kitchen enjoying Herr Muller's hospitality, breakfast and Scotch. They were delighted to be helping the Reich. The only thing that had changed in the front bedroom was the various positions of the watching men. Calise was pouring coffee and Schmitt sat at the window.

"Leopard Alpha this is Leopard Five, Tango One sighted en route your location, confirm vehicle is Charlie-Two." The command net radio spat out the report they had waited patiently for. It had the effect of an adrenaline shot into all the men in the room. Heinrich picked up the binoculars and scanned the quiet harbour from deep in the hotel room.

"Leopard One and Two, this is Leopard Alpha. Move to Victors Three, Four and Seven."

Most of the soldiers could not be seen but as Lowther began to issue his orders, four men moved to positions on the decks of three of the boats. They were dressed in a mix of clothes that even Heinrich thought made them look like passable fishermen, deckhands or amateur sailors.

"Leopard Alpha, Leopard Five, Tango straight on Main Street."

Heinrich angled his view to look out to his left and observed the junction of Main Street and the Crescent that circumnavigated the waterfront.

"Leopard Alpha, Leopard Five Tango turning right onto Crescent, over"

"Leopard Five Leopard Alpha, Seen."

Heinrich listened to Johan Lowther take responsibility for the target from his screening team on the approach road. At the same time he saw the silver Volkswagen turn right into the North Crescent. He focussed the binoculars on her. Mary Reid looked tired but not scared or distressed. He was reminded again that this woman was very controlled.

"All callsigns, let her run, wait, wait." Lowther's voice was also controlled.

Heinrich and the other men in the hotel room watched as Reid's car passed by and headed towards the car park where they had earlier met the local Police. She slowed and pulled nose first into a parking space. The brake lights illuminated for one last time before she turned the engine off. Other than her arrival there was little other visible activity in the harbour. There were two men working on the deck of the nearest small fishing boat to where she had parked. An older man was on the bow of a motor cruiser moored halfway down the west wall and a fourth was working on a bigger boat in the lower harbour alongside a couple of commercial fishing boat crews preparing to depart.

Mary could see all of this in her rear-view mirror and she scanned each as carefully as she could. The nearest three were easy, she could see them clearly but the furthest boats were more of a challenge. After a good five minutes she had decided everything looked right. The men she could see wore appropriate clothing but much more importantly were carrying out the correct type of duties. She had been a hobby sailor for long enough to spot the right type of preparations. None of them appeared to be watching out for anyone. She relaxed just a little and got out of the car.

Heinrich watched her as she stood up out of the vehicle. She wore low heeled black boots, blue jeans and a black jumper with a loose fitting quilted jacket. She was dressed for warmth and ease of travel. Heinrich watched her stretch and yawn and twist to work the kinks out of her back and to subtly allow her a complete circle of observation. As she moved he saw the shoulder holster under her jacket. From his vantage point in one of the small boat houses to the western side of the harbour wall, Johan Lowther had seen it too.

"Leopard callsigns, Tango is wearing a shoulder holster to her left side."

Mary stretched and turned again. She felt her back relax from the hours of driving and she turned slowly once more to look out over the whole of the harbour. She had spent a lot of time here in the past and she knew what it was meant to look like. The boats that had been out overnight would be returning shortly and the early fishing boats would have left. She had planned her arrival for now. Quiet, not a lot of people about, extremely hard to conceal an arrest team or any other form of surveillance. She also knew that there were always a few early mariners up and about preparing their pride and joy for a day out on the waves. She had been relying on it. She checked round one last time and on this sweep looked more closely at the leisure craft where the older man was working. Tucked into the north-west corner of the nearest inner harbour was a ten-metre, Flybridge motor cruiser. She knew the model and had even looked at buying one for herself, or rather, getting Uwe Joyce to buy her one. She smiled as she thought that, in an ironic way, he was going to provide her one after all. It was ideal for her needs. Fitted with a two hundred and twenty hp diesel engine it was stable, quick and could get her across to the Antrim coast unobtrusively. It even had a decent stereo system if her memory served her right. She smiled at the name written on the stern of the vessel, 'Mers Libres'.

She watched the man, dressed in a pair of dirty grey-blue overalls, move in and out of the cabin and traverse from bow to stern while she stood next to her car. He was being thorough and obviously preparing to go to sea. She thought about how to approach him. He was in his mid-forties, maybe older she guessed, not all that handsome but she was sure she could get down close to him on the deck. It would be easy after that. She reached into the rear of the car and withdrew her small backpack which held some underwear, some ammunition and all the cash she had ever put aside for an emergency.

"Leopard Callsigns, standby, standby."

Mary sauntered down to the harbour and stood on the quayside just above the 'Free Seas'. The owner came back out of the cabin and she waited for him to look up.

"Good morning Miss, how are you?" Mary noted his accent, southern French possibly Provence, and relaxed even more.

"Bonjour Monsieur, and I am afraid that is the limit of my French," she lied and smiled her best smile at him, "but I was just wondering if you would be so kind to provide me some assistance?"

"Mademoiselle, I am French and you are beautiful, how could I refuse? What can I do for you?"

"Well, it is a little delicate. Would it be possible for you to come up or me to come down, so I do not have to talk too loudly?"

"Mais oui, please come down." The man extended his hand to indicate the small ladder draped over the wall that led down to the well of the boat. Mary turned around and began to descend. She found it amazing how even fairly ugly older men thought that when she flirted with them they might actually get to fuck her. She knew it had been a given that he was going to invite her down rather than come up.

She turned to face him as she stepped off the ladder and he punched her, straight-armed, in the solar plexus. She went down onto her knees, gasping as all breath was knocked out of her. The man moved swiftly behind her and pulled both of her arms around, fastening them securely with a plastic tie to the wrists. He reached around her body, recovering the pistol from her shoulder holster, before pushing her forward onto the deck. He took a small tactical radio from his pocket.

"Leopard Alpha, this is Leopard Two Bravo, Tango secured, over," he said with no trace of a French accent.

"Leopard callsigns, this is Leopard Alpha secure to Victor Four. Leopard-Control this is Leopard Alpha, advise Golf callsigns for recovery."

Heinrich looked around the room, "Bit of an anti-climax really." The rest of the men smiled and shrugged.

"Dietmar, advise Vogel we're on our way back to Todt. Also, get him to get a message to Professor Lippisch, tell him just to say 'thank you, it's done.'"

Heinrich keyed the mic, "Golf One this is Leopard Control. Request immediate extraction."

31

SS-Second Lieutenant Peter Vogel closed the door and pushed it firmly to make sure the electronic lock engaged. The Prisoner Holding and Interrogation Facility still smelt of fresh paint and everything had the stubbornness of the new that made the locks tight and the switches firm. He walked a few steps up the corridor and entered the Command Observation Room.

The observation room sat in the middle junction of the K-shaped facility, and was equipped with banks of CCTVs able to watch each of its six cells and three interview rooms. Heinrich was already there, along with Dietmar and Pascal. The three centrally mounted monitors were all tuned to the room holding Mary Reid.

It looked much like every interview room in every holding facility in the Reich. The walls and floor were painted battleship grey and two chairs sat on opposite sides of a rectangular table. All the furniture was unadorned grey metal, and all of it was bolted to the concrete floor.

Reid sat quietly with her hands, secured with metal cuffs, resting in her lap. She was still wearing the clothes she had been arrested in. Her head was down and her eyes were shut. It was 09:00 and Heinrich reckoned she probably hadn't slept in over thirty-six hours. No one had spoken directly to her since the Special Forces soldier had punched and cuffed her.

Heinrich turned to the others, "I'll take the first shot and, if needed, we'll do it in shifts until she gives us something we can use."

189

He swiped his card against the electronic reader and Mary looked up at the sound, staring directly at him as the door clicked open, He was struck that, even tired and slightly dishevelled, she was still strikingly beautiful.

"Good morning Mary, I'm Heinrich Steinmann." He took the seat opposite her. She looked at him but said nothing. "Mary we need some answers to some formal questions please. Could you state your full..."

"Mary Emma Reid, Chief Senior Overseer, TV9586217, February 17, 1995, O-Positive." She cut him off in mid-sentence with the standard responses required of uniformed members of the Reich if taken prisoner.

"Well, that's an excellent start Mary, thank you. Now what were you doing up in Portpatrick?"

No response.

Heinrich sighed and put his hands flat on the table. "Mary, we have you in a car that belonged to two members of a Special-Reconnaissance team. We have one of their bodies at your house, shot with a nine millimetre pistol that will no doubt match yours. The other is currently in surgery. It's unlikely they can save his left hand. He's already confirmed it was you who did the shooting and when he recovers from the surgery he'll attest to the same on the record. We have two missing administration clerks who may turn up one day and I'll bet they have the same small holes in them. Finally, we have a dead Reichsminister who you've been screwing and, coincidently, he has a similar hole in his head. What bit of this is looking good for you at present?"

No response.

She looked straight at him, not defiantly, just a blank stare from eyes that were void of light. Heinrich sighed.

"Mary, Berlin is not happy. They want me to use all manner of approaches on you." He paused to allow his meaning to sink in.

"As you can imagine we have even more toys here than you have in Harrow. A Reichsminister is a big deal Mary. They want a show trial. They want an example made of you. They want to hold you up as the personification of weak morals and weak honour." He saw her eyes flicker slightly and she looked away from him, back to the table top. It was the first reaction he had seen in the woman since observing her in Portpatrick. He decided to push it a little.

"They just want to know what happened. They want a thorough explanation. They want to know why you did what you did, but if they don't get your complete cooperation they've told me to hand you over. You know how it'll go Mary? Your face plastered on every television screen and newspaper in the Reich. Held up to ridicule and pilloried by the State as a pariah. A cheap whore who sold her body to get promotion. There's even talk that your own father had known and was going to warn the authorities and that's why you killed him." Her head came up and she gritted her teeth. He watched her closely as she tried to control her reaction.

"Apparently he was a good man and you arranged for him to be killed. That's what the story will be." He watched her bite down hard and her neck muscles strained with the force. "Of course, Mary, if you tell me the truth then I can't promise you freedom. That isn't on the table. But you'll get your version of events out and at least you'll know where and how it's going to end." He paused. "There is no happy ending. But I promise you I'll make sure it's discreet, swift. A proper firing squad, a funeral. No public humiliation. A good death. Think about it." He got up from the chair and walked out of the room allowing the door to click shut behind him.

Back in the observation room they waited and watched her. She sat quietly and put her head into her cuffed hands. After almost half an hour she turned to look up at the camera, took a deep breath and nodded.

Heinrich went back in and retook his seat, "Do you want to start with how long you've known the Minister?"

"No. We'll start with the fact that both my staff are alive. Harold is somewhere lost in the woods off Oxhey Lane between Harrow and Watford. He's probably wandering around in circles. As for Fredrick Henly, he's locked in the vault next to my office. So don't sit there and tell me I shot them," she said with an angry edge to her voice.

"Okay, well that's good." Heinrich knew that Dietmar and Pascal would set the wheels in motion to recover both Harold and Fredrick.

"Let's move on to the Special-Reconnaissance team. Why did you shoot them?"

"That was self-defence. They made to draw their weapons. I told them not to, it was them or me. They made a mistake. That's all."

"What was their mistake?"

"They saw the woman and not the uniform. I don't get to wear the Death's Head for fun."

"Fair enough. I'd have probably done the same if they'd drawn down on me too. Now, let's get back to the Minister. How long have you known him?"

"Five years." She spoke clearly and looked directly at him, studying him with an intense stare.

"And you shot him in the early hours of Monday morning?"

"Yes."

"Tell me why Mary. Why did you kill him?"

"How did you find me so quickly?"

"That's not how this works. You answer my questions."

"I just want to know. How did you find me so quickly? We were always discreet. No one ever saw me come or go in the Savoy."

"There are cameras Mary."

"Don't lie to me. Uwe chose the Savoy for our meetings because it doesn't have cameras. It's the one hotel in London that's clean of them because he wasn't the only Minister that needed some privacy. You raid that hotel on any given night and you'd disturb a nest of inappropriate liaisons."

"I'm not lying. There's new technology. It allows us to put a camera almost anywhere. It's that simple, we caught you on camera." He wasn't going to elaborate and he considered that it was almost the truth.

"So, Mary. Why did you kill him?"

She shrugged. "He told me he loved me."

"You shot him because he told you he loved you?" He was disappointed. He thought she was going to tell the truth.

"No, not Uwe. Thomas."

Heinrich processed the name. It meant nothing to him.

"Thomas? Who's Thomas?"

"Thomas Dunhill."

Heinrich racked his memory. The name was familiar but he couldn't place it. He raised his left hand as if to scratch his cheek.

He heard Pascal through his earpiece, "That's one of the Turners brought into Harrow on Sunday." Heinrich nodded almost imperceptibly.

It helped to put the name into context but Heinrich was getting confused. "Start at the beginning Mary, please?" He spoke as if to a child.

She straightened a little in her chair, "Thomas Dunhill came into Harrow on Sunday. He was still alive when I got to him." Mary looked across the table but her focus was far away. Her eyes began to harden as she recalled the moment that had changed her life.

"Go on," he prompted.

"He forgave me."

Heinrich was quite shocked to see tears welling in her eyes.

She continued, "He looked at me and told me he forgave me. He was so calm and I was killing him and he just…" Her voice caught and tears tumbled down her cheeks and fell onto the steel desk.

"He forgave you as you shot him?" Heinrich felt a surge of empathy and deep respect for this man who had been a true Turner right to the last.

Mary was nodding as she continued through small sobs, "He said he loved me and he forgave me and I twisted my boot into him and then I shot him. Like so many others. But not like any other." She stopped. The quiet lasted almost a minute. Heinrich waited for her.

"He said he loved me but with a specific phrase."

"What did he say, exactly?"

"He said he loved me and he said that God loved me. He said he loved me like my sister used to."

"He knew your sister?"

"Yes. No. I'm not sure. He said the same thing she used to say to me. I don't know if he knew her but he might have."

"You still shot him."

"It's my job." She spoke with no cynicism or sarcasm to her voice. She merely stated it like the fact it was.

"So how does this link to Uwe Joyce?"

She ignored his question. "Do you know about God?" she asked him and reached up with her cuffed hands and wiped the tears from her face.

Heinrich stared back at her, slightly wary of where this was going to lead. Before he got a chance to respond she continued.

"I've killed many people Herr Steinmann and no one ever forgave me before. He said he loved me and he meant it. The last person who ever said that to me was my sister." She paused and then repeated, "I think he might have known my sister." Heinrich watched as her eyes lost focus again and she drifted in a world of memories. More silent tears welled up. He waited.

"He said I was an instrument of God. But I don't think he meant his God." She gave a sardonic smile as she said it and looked back at Heinrich.

"How many Gods are there Mary?"

"Just the one. I think there's one, but I think he might be different from how Thomas saw him."

"Do you spend a lot of time thinking about God?"

"No." She laughed the answer. Heinrich was a little surprised at her ability to laugh with tears still running down her cheeks.

"So what is your version of God like then Mary?"

"Older." Her answer was cold, stark and said with a cruel edge. "He's much older and vengeful to a point that makes us look like amateurs."

"How do you know about this God?" he asked.

"You just need to consider the facts. Thomas said his God loved me. But if he loved me and he loved Thomas, why did he let me kill him? I've thought a lot about that since it happened. Thomas and his God. The God that told Thomas to love me. Told him, made him love me as I shot him. I'd not heard anyone mention God for a long time." She stopped and once more became lost in her memories.

Heinrich needed to get her to talk about Uwe Joyce's murder but he was intrigued as to where this questioning was going. He decided to let it flow.

"When did you last hear about God?"

"We had a teacher, back in primary school. She spoke about Jesus. Said he was weak and he had made God weak. She said that before him God had been all-powerful but Jesus was weak. I wondered what the world would be like if the weak were strong. I always wondered that as a little girl. One day I found out the answer." Mary looked down at her lap. She seemed to shrink a little and Heinrich tried to think of what he could say to entice the next piece of the puzzle out of her. She continued just as he pondered his next question

"I was weak once and then I became strong. I became so strong that I killed him." Her voice began to harden and as she looked up from her lap he could see her eyes had narrowed. She looked and sounded fierce. "That bastard of a man. Don't you dare let them say he was a good person. He was a fucking sadist." She had real rage in her voice. "The weak are worth fuck all. When I became strong I killed my father." She stopped abruptly. Heinrich waited until her face had relaxed a little.

"Can you tell me why Mary?" Heinrich knew what her file said about the incident. Her father was accused of paedophilia and the assumption was he had abused her but that had never been proven or pursued. The official line was she shot him as he had tried to attack her. He wondered if he could get her to talk about it. He didn't need to wonder. She started speaking again.

"It's not what you said earlier. He didn't know anything about me. I wasn't even with Uwe when my father came to Harrow. In fact, it was the opposite. It was because of my father I met Uwe. Don't you dare let them say it was for any other reason. I killed my father because he deserved to die. He knew nothing about me and he wouldn't have said anything to anyone in authority. Don't let them make out he was anything but an animal." Her voice was raised again and her wrists were straining against the cuffs.

"Okay Mary, okay. I'll do my best but you'll need to tell me the real reason you killed him and Uwe Joyce." He looked at her once more as she reclaimed her emotions. She looked directly at him and held his gaze.

"My father raped me. He raped my sisters and he raped me. Each one of us in our time. He raped me over and over for a long time when I was a little girl. I was small and I was weak and no one stopped him. When I became strong enough to deal with the realities of my life, I killed him. That's why I think the weak deserve to be strong. It gives you power. It makes you free. Thomas should have been strong. Instead he loved me and I shot him. Over and over." She looked almost wistful as she finished, "I shot him like I shot my father. That can't be right." She shrugged her shoulders and looked back down at her lap.

"Mary. Why did you shoot Uwe Joyce?"

"Because he was being disrespectful to Kasey. She was nice to me and loved me."

"Your sister, Kasey?"

"No, not Kasey. Thomas. He was saying mean things about Thomas. But Thomas knew Kasey, didn't he?" She half tilted her head and was genuinely asking Heinrich as if he knew the answer.

Heinrich was suddenly aware that whatever Thomas Dunhill had said to Mary had pushed her over an edge that she had probably been teetering on for most of her life. On one level she was cold, calculating, ruthless. On another she was rational and reasonable. But now she was mixing up memories of her sister and this Thomas Dunhill. The last two people, possibly the only two people, who had ever said they loved her. He repeated his question, "Mary, why did you shoot Uwe Joyce?"

She sighed. "He deserved it. It was just that simple. He deserved it. He was being a prick and I decided that I had had enough of people saying bad things about others. He was bitching about Thomas and that annoyed me. I had grown quite fond of Thomas by then."

"Fond of him?" Heinrich didn't mean the question to sound so incredulous but he couldn't help it.

"Yes. I know I'd killed him but I'd thought about him during the evening. I felt sorry for him. I was sorry I had shot him and I wanted to make it up to him," she said, like it was the most natural circumstance imaginable. "Anyway, you asked why I shot Uwe. Well, Uwe said that the old God used to strike people down when he was angry. He said it just like my teacher used to say it. Thomas told me that I had God inside me too, but I didn't want his weak pacifist God inside me. I wanted the Old God. I wanted that angry vengeful God to be inside me. I was angry, so I just did it. Uwe said God should get angry again and settle scores with people. So I did."

The room remained quiet as Heinrich processed the information. He knew she was tired and stressed but he also knew it was so much more. Although it would take proper assessment to be sure, he reckoned Mary Reid was suffering from post-traumatic shock built up over decades of abuse from not only her father but from conducting the duties of a camp overseer. She looked back up at him and smiled a most beautiful smile as if acknowledging his thoughts, "Life would be different if you could pick which God to follow. Don't you think?"

Something deep in Heinrich's psyche flagged what she had just said but he had to ignore it for the present. What he needed to do now was wrap this up by asking her the question they needed answering for the official record.

"Mary, are you saying God made you do this?"

"No, of course not. I did it." She answered plainly, "Uwe annoyed me, insulted Thomas and said that the Turner's God should get angry. But we all know he can't. So I did it for him." She looked directly at Heinrich before continuing, "The recce team just got in my way. Harold and Fredrick were lucky. Had it not been for Thomas you'd be counting more corpses." Her voice was rational and completely at ease.

"Mary, is it your statement that you'd been sleeping with Minister Uwe Joyce for five years and then you shot him because he insulted a Turner prisoner whom you had dispatched earlier in the evening?"

"Yes. It's a real shame you caught me too. I had plans to start reaping some real vengeance."

"Like what?"

"There's an official visit to London in a few weeks. We received a formal notice of it. The Führer is coming to see us at Harrow. I did wonder if I could get close enough to look him in the eyes when I shot him."

She said it so matter-of-factly it took him a second to properly register her words. Heinrich couldn't believe he had heard her correctly.

"Pardon Mary?"

When she repeated herself precisely he decided it was time to take a break. "Would you like a tea or coffee Mary?"

"Tea, white, one sugar."

She gave her tea order in the same tone and manner that she had admitted to planning the assassination of the Führer.

"She's nuts." Pascal Debouchy was watching her on the monitors.

"Completely," agreed Dietmar, "This isn't a Turner conspiracy and God didn't make her do it. She's been abused since childhood and just snapped."

Peter Vogel made the arrangements for her to be transferred to a cell until Berlin decided their orders.

32

Heinrich sat in one of the concrete chairs around the side of the administration building and waited. At five minutes after midday Leigh walked around the corner and stopped mid-stride when she saw him. He smiled at her and stood up.

"Hello, told you I'd be back."

She walked directly up and hugged him. Heinrich was surprised and it took him a moment to raise his arms and hug her back. He held her tightly and felt her body against his. She tucked her head into his neck and sighed loudly.

"Leigh, it's okay, I told you I'd be okay. Are you?"

He felt her head nodding against him as she continued to hold him closely. Heinrich was conscious of the feelings she was stirring in him and he bent and kissed her lightly on the head. Eventually she released the pressure of her arms.

"When did you get back?" she asked.

"A while ago but we had to go straight in with her. I couldn't get away any earlier. I take it you got the message that I passed through to Konrad?"

"Yes," she looked up into his eyes and held his gaze, "Thank you, I assume that was your way of letting me know you were safe?"

"Well, I could hardly call you, now could I? People would talk," he said and winked at her. She gave him a mischievous smile that caused his heart to skip.

"So did she come quietly?"

"Sort of. It was all a bit of a non-event really. I think the fatigue made her guard drop. But we wouldn't have been close to her if it hadn't been for the time Projection."

"You must be shattered, when did you last sleep?"

"I caught some on the helicopter on the way back, but I'm okay."

"What's going to happen with her?"

"If I handle it properly with Berlin I think she'll just be quietly dealt with here."

Leigh was quiet for a moment. Finally she said, "You know, all these years and I've never been able to share my thoughts. Every time something dreadful occurs and every time my work, or anything I've been working on, is involved, it rips another part of me into shreds."

"I know. She's done terrible things but we should be reaching out to help her. To turn the other way. Yet we still serve and we still do their bidding and the best we can hope for is a swift death for her. And pray for God to have mercy on her soul."

"And on ours Heinrich. And on ours."

He nodded, "And on ours."

Leigh watched him and saw a real sadness in his eyes. She needed to try to find something positive out of the whole episode. "But at least no show trial and the attending circus?"

"No." Heinrich shook his head, "She's wounded and destroyed from the inside out. She really is a victim in this."

Despite her earlier sentiment Leigh bristled at the use of the word victim. "I agree we should show compassion but how much of a victim is she compared to the bodies she left littered around. She killed that man in cold blood just after she had slept with him. How much of a victim was he?"

"I know," he hesitated and realised that watching the Projection had impacted on Leigh and probably the rest of the science team. It may well have been the first time any of them had been exposed to anything like that level of aggression. Even though the Reich was brutal, it managed to keep its violence hidden away. "There's just," he paused again and wondered how much he should tell her. Leigh put her hand on his arm as if reading his mood, "It's okay, you don't need to tell me or justify your thoughts. If you think she's a victim, I believe you."

"It's not just that. She also said some strange things about God."

Leigh unconsciously took out a cigarette then thought better of it. He spoke as she went to put it back in the packet, "Go ahead, I don't mind."

She hesitated, looked at him and when he nodded she decided to take him at his word. She exhaled the smoke and asked him, "What did she say about God?"

Heinrich told her about the strong God and the love that had finally pushed Mary over the edge and noticed Leigh's brow furrow and her eyes drift.

"Leigh, what is it?"

"I'm not sure, just something. You know when you get an idea but it's not fully formed, like a flash of something? Then nothing. Do you know what I mean?"

"Like an itch at the back of your mind and only thinking can scratch it?" he said.

"Yes, that's exactly what I mean."

"I know, I got the same feeling when she said it to me. I need to go back and talk to her more but I need to get Pascal and Dietmar away from there. I want to talk to her about God without anyone else listening."

"That's easy. They were briefed on the project by Berlin, so it was obvious they had the same expectations you had. Even I could see their disappointment when we ran the real Projections. Send them down to me and I'll give them the full tour. It'll take most of the afternoon if I spin it out." She smiled as she thought of taking a few hours to explain and thoroughly confuse another two non-scientific minds.

"Oh, you're good, aren't you?" Heinrich teased her.

"Yes I am, but it comes at a price."

"Name it."

"Dinner?"

"I'd love to. I'll pick you up at eight tonight?"

"No not tonight Heinrich, you'll be exhausted. Tomorrow? Deal?"

"Deal."

Leigh stubbed her cigarette out and they both walked back to the front of the building. She started to ascend the entrance steps while Heinrich made his way back to the holding facility on the far side of the compound. A few steps away he turned his head and caught her doing the same thing. They looked at each other, then smiled and continued on their ways.

33

"Mary?" Heinrich spoke softly to the woman who was sleeping on the suspended cot bed attached to the wall of the cell. She woke instantly and looked at him but did not move to get up.

"Herr Steinmann, more questions? Or are you here to take a little rest and relaxation?" Mary Reid knew how to use her voice and her body to control most situations. She arched her back on the cot and looked directly at him. She was like a sensual cat playing with its prey. He saw her mouth begin to form a smile. He could see the slightly parted lips yet her eyes remained opaque and void of humour.

"No Mary, just questions," he said as he sat down in the small chair bolted to the floor.

Unfazed, she remained lying on the cot, watching him. "Are you sure? It would seem the light on the CCTV camera up there has stopped blinking. Are you sure you don't want a little privacy with me?"

"I want privacy, but just to talk."

"Oh, now I'm intrigued." She swung her legs over the side of the cot and sat up, stretching and yawning. "Go on then, what do you want to talk about that needs all the in-cell monitoring turned off?"

"I want to talk about God."

"Are you feeling holy?"

"No, I just want to know why you think he wanted you to get angry. I thought God was loving and caring and taught all his believers to turn the other cheek?"

"No Herr Steinmann, he didn't. He used to get angry all the time. People used to kill in his name," she said it as a fact. Heinrich studied her face for any sign of emotion or confusion but she was speaking what she believed to be the truth.

"How do you know this? From your primary school teacher?"

"No, she never said anything about killing. I know it from my job."

"Your job? In the holding centres?"

"We had all sorts of people brought in to us over the years. Some of them would have little mementos, some had money, some had other valuables. A few had copies of the Turner Creed." She paused and tilted her head sideways to look at him. "Have Berlin decided yet?"

"No, not yet. It might be a little while, I'm sorry."

She laughed, "They can take their time Herr Steinmann, I'm in no rush to die."

"You said about the Creed, Mary. The Turner Creed speaks of peace and harmony."

"And how would you know that unless you've read it too? Naughty thing to admit Herr Steinmann."

"I had a job that required me to read it and you can call me Heinrich."

"Heinrich," she sounded it out and made it sound sweet and tender. "That suits you."

"Thank you." He smiled at her as he continued, "What did you read in the Turner Creed?"

"It's not the Creed I'm talking about," she tested out the sound again, "Heinrich." Then she continued, "I read other things as well. One of the prisoners a few years ago had an old book. Very old. The Scribes of the Sons of Jacob. Have you heard of that?"

Heinrich knew the book. It was one of the oldest tomes in the Religious Archives. "Yes, I've heard of it and yes, you're right, it's an old book. But I thought you destroyed all the prisoner's belongings?"

"Of course we do. We burn all their money and their gold watches and their jewellery." She raised her eyebrows. "Don't be naïve Heinrich. We keep anything of worth and I thought that old book was interesting. I took it home and read it. I was fascinated by it. So much history and so much anger. The people in it were really persecuted. A bit like Turners I suppose. We're a lot more efficient than the old days and the olden peoples weren't cowards, which meant there was a lot more fighting." She looked up at the ceiling and stretched out her back muscles.

Heinrich considered what to say but said nothing. He wanted to tell her that the Old Book had been full of savages who understood little of peaceful ways. That their savagery had paled in comparison to that of the Reich. He wanted to tell her that the Turner Religion was so much more powerful but, of course, he couldn't. He wanted to say that Turner's were more courageous than any who wreaked savagery on others. He wanted to reach out to her and tell her that to turn the other cheek in the face of evil was far from cowardly. But even here in a cell where no one was listening he had to continue to deny his beliefs. Eventually he asked, "So you've been reading illicit texts and plotting murder on God's behalf?"

"Oh no. Not that at all. It never really meant anything to me until Uwe started mouthing off at me." She yawned and stretched again. He waited. "How do you know about the Scribes, Heinrich?"

"I used to be in Berlin, in the Archives. I read it for my work."

"Do you remember the names of the various chapters?"

"Most of them, not all."

"Do you remember Deuteronomy, Ezekiel or any of the other ones that speak about a vengeful God?"

"Yes, some of them. But weren't the teachings of the later prophets meant to replace the old teachings?"

"That's the problem."

"I'm sorry, I don't understand."

"When Uwe was being a prick, it was like all the pieces of a puzzle clicked into place. I understood. Just like that. I understood. Simple and straightforward. I saw all of the pieces together and realised what should have happened but can't. I understood why it should start with a single action, but it never will. Why Uwe Joyce should be the first of many, but won't be. I knew what the world should and could have been like. It's not that complicated Heinrich. I just understood."

Heinrich hesitated. He wasn't sure he wanted to ask the question. Deep inside he felt worried and nervous. These were not emotions he was used to when he conducted interviews. He was always sure, calm and confident but for a reason he didn't know, he was none of these at the moment. He took a breath, "What did you understand Mary?"

34

Heinrich quietly left the cell, secured the door and leant back against it. His mouth was dry and he knew his pulse was faster than normal. He felt a strange mixture of light headedness and a dire weight in the pit of his stomach. Going via the control centre to rearm the in-cell monitoring system, he quickly made his way out to the car park. He had to talk to Leigh. He reached to the ForeFone to ring her but it had already started to buzz on his arm. The incoming call was from the Office of the Reichsführer-SS.

"Colonel Steinmann!"

"Ja, bitte!"

"Die Kommandantur Berlin ist am Apparat."

"Danke Wiehadden, stellen Sie bitte durch."

"Colonel Steinmann am Apparat!"

"Ah, Heinrich, hier spricht Reichsführer-SS Friedrichand. Ich habe da eine Frage bezüglich Reid."

***

"Leigh, it's Heinrich."

"Hello. I was just about to ring you. Dietmar and Pascal are on their way back over," Leigh said and flicked the door to her office shut with her foot. She came back around her desk and sat down.

"I just wanted to let you know that I have to go to Berlin," Heinrich said it as flatly as he could. He worried Leigh wouldn't be as controlled in her response but he had forgotten that she had been playing this game a lot longer than him.

"Oh, lucky you. When?" She delivered it like it was something she would have looked forward to herself and managed to hide the debilitating fear rising in her throat.

"Now. I'm off to Northolt. There's an aircraft waiting for me."

"Is everything alright, do you need anything from my team?"

"Yes, everything's fine, just a simple request for a face to face briefing about Reid and the order was to come now. I don't need anything but I just wanted to check that you and your team were all okay with the first live use of the project. I'm sure Berlin will want to know." He said it conscious of recording devices, but he had needed to tell her he was leaving. And something else.

"Actually, Leigh there is one thing. I was wondering, could you ask one of your staff to bring my jacket back to me? The one I left in your lab yesterday?"

Leigh continued to control the rising panic she was feeling and kept her voice neutral, "Of course. I'm on my way up to have a cigarette anyway so shall I meet you at the entrance steps?"

"Yes, excellent. See you shortly." He hung up and knew that Leigh would be as scared as he was. There was no sane reason to be summoned to Berlin. The report on Mary Reid had been prepared, reviewed and sent already. Why was he being called over? He knew he would remain outwardly calm. He always did. But it didn't change how he felt inside.

Leigh stood at the foot of the entrance steps and watched him walk across the compound from the prisoner holding facility. Her mind was a discordant noise of parading thoughts, each one worse than its predecessor. In the minutes since his phone call she had been assaulted with sickening worries. She had wondered if his story about Berlin was all a fake. Had he played the long game? Had she given away so much to him in such a short time? Had she broken her discipline and her shield of a lifetime for a handsome and beguiling interrogator? Was she caught?

Each of these thoughts was battered back by her longing for him to be real and to be everything he said he was. She had spent so long alone and since Sunday night she had prayed for him to be her confidant. She had convinced herself over and over that he was. What if it wasn't true? Then she had a new thought, accompanied by an almost crushing sadness, what if he was true and together they were now caught? How cruel an irony would that be? To have found each other and to have it fall apart so quickly.

When he got closer she led the way around the side of the building to the smoking area. Lighting a cigarette she turned to face him, "If anyone is watching us they'll see I don't have your jacket with me. You didn't have a jacket in my lab."

"I know. But we need to talk and quickly."

"Why are you being called to Berlin?" she asked with real concern in her voice.

"I honestly don't know. They have my report, they have the stenography records, they have the digital video copies of the Observation Window. They have it all. If I'm being positive, then they simply want a firsthand account of the first use of Thule. It was ready to go live but just happened sooner than they thought."

"You're not convinced though are you? What happens if you're not being positive?" she asked.

"We both know what that leads to. We've always known what happens if they find us," he said it softly.

"The wheel turns at its own pace?" She said her mother's words and felt deeply sad.

"Yes... And no."

Leigh looked directly at him. "What?"

"The wheel turns at its own pace but Mary Reid might just have turned it a lot faster than we could have anticipated."

"Heinrich, you're worrying me."

"Well, that's an emotion we can cope with. There's potentially a lot worse coming." He paused and reached up to take her shoulders in his hands. He looked deep into her eyes.

Leigh felt an intense surge of heat in the pit of her stomach. Her breath caught and she allowed herself to hold his gaze.

He spoke quickly, "Mary isn't insane. She's fractured. The years of abuse as a child and horrendous duties within the camps have been building up and up. She just snapped."

Leigh flushed with a sudden surge of anger and frustration. In that second before he spoke, in the look that had passed between them, she had wanted, desired him to lean forward, to kiss her or to tell her… Tell her what exactly? She didn't know. But she knew she hadn't wanted to hear about Mary. She looked down at the ground, took a deep breath and then looked back at him. "I know. You already told me all this."

"But she had a... I don't really know what to call it. An insight? A revelation? I don't know." He was visibly frustrated.

Leigh backed away a step, "When? Today, when you were talking to her?"

"No, earlier. I think between her killing the Turners, God rest them, and killing Minister Joyce. She had an, oh, I don't know what she had."

"An epiphany?"

"Yes! An epiphany." Heinrich looked both animated and concerned.

Leigh waited but he didn't speak. She took a long draw on her cigarette and tried to order her thoughts. She spoke with an edge to her voice and realised that she had become angry at the thought of Mary claiming God told her to kill. "So now you're telling me she did find her belief and that she thinks she did this for our Lord?"

Heinrich glanced over his shoulder at the sound of a staff car pulling out of the parking bays. He turned back to her. "Not our Lord Leigh; hers."

Leigh knew she had frowned in confusion and yet she couldn't help it. Nor could she find the words to articulate her thoughts. She just looked at Heinrich and tilted her head slightly to one side.

"Look Leigh, I have to get changed into dress uniform and make the transport for Berlin. I swear to you on all we hold sacred that I am on your side. I knew your parents and I am a Turner like you. But Mary Reid had an idea that's of insane proportions. I don't know why I've been called to Berlin but we have to hope for the best. It could well be a blessing. If I can manage to stay in Berlin for a day or two I want to do some research to verify things. We'll talk when I get back."

Leigh felt her body relax. She watched as he again glanced backwards to check on the progress of the car driving across the compound.

He motioned for her to walk beside him as he continued. "If you can find time to get to see that woman and talk to her, do it. I've told Vogel that you might be across to interrogate her."

"Interrogate her about what?"

"I told him it was part of the project. You have to interrogate her to see if she noticed anything during the times we were observing her."

"Oh, for goodness sake! That's ridiculous." She stopped walking and flashed angry again at the stupidity of the suggestion. But when she looked at Heinrich the outcome was obvious. "He believed you didn't he?"

"Of course he did. How is that any more absurd than some of the other things we interrogate people for?"

She shrugged.

"Look Leigh, just ask her about the way back. That's what she calls it. The way back. But please, be careful. I had the camera in her cell turned off when I was in there. You won't be able to do that, so be careful. Promise?" He turned and looked directly at her. She held his gaze and this time she spoke quietly, with no anger.

"I promise. But the woman's a cold-blooded murderer. I don't want to go and talk to her."

"You might not want to but you need to."

"And what's going to convince her to talk to me?"

"Promise her that we know a way to get her out."

"Are you mad?" Leigh exclaimed.

"No, but just do it. You'll see what I mean. I'm sorry I can't explain more but I've got to go."

He set off again, and as he quickened his pace to meet the car, Leigh called quietly after him, "Heinrich, how will I know you're safe?"

He turned back and smiled at her. "I'll call you on the pretence of work. It'll be okay."

He walked around the corner of the building and she heard the door closing before the car pulled away. Leigh said quietly to herself, "God, please let him come back safely."

35

Heinrich stepped from the staff car and hurried across the tarmac to the waiting VIP transport jet. He returned the salute of the young airman standing at the foot of the fold- down steps and, as soon as he had entered the aircraft compartment, the steps were raised. Heinrich wasn't even strapped into the executive leather seat before he felt the aircraft taxiing.

"Not hanging around then?" he asked the steward who was already strapped into a less plush seat at the back of the small lounge-type interior.

"No Sir, our orders were quite precise. Get you into Berlin as soon as possible."

"That's why we're using this then? Normally I get to fly on Junkers transports."

"Precisely Sir. Welcome on board the Leichen Four." The aircraft turned at the foot of the runway while the steward continued his introduction. "We normally accommodate up to six passengers and a steward. Our seats are a little more comfortable than a Junkers. Our table is solid mahogany and our bar is fully stocked. But unfortunately it's also fully inventoried and my orders were that you're on duty Sir."

Heinrich laughed, "Yes, very much so. I'm so pleased to see the Luftwaffe still know how to treat their passengers."

The steward smiled politely, "Well of course Sir. But strictly speaking, myself, the flight crew and the jet are assigned to the SS, not the Luftwaffe. However, when we're in the cruise I can offer you a lemonade, tea, coffee, water; still or sparkling, orange, apple or cranberry juice?"

Heinrich was enjoying the light banter but as he went to speak again the aircraft rolled forward. The engines began to bite and Heinrich felt like he was in a racing car. The acceleration was startling. The feeling was exciting and a little off-putting.

The steward said, "You may find it more comfortable if you turn the chair to face forward Sir."

He managed to swivel around just as the throttles were fully opened. Forced back into the leather he did manage to turn his head and grin in a rather inane way at the steward.

"It's okay Sir, all of our first time passengers are a little startled. Anyone who has never flown in a small jet always finds the acceleration a little overwhelming."

Heinrich felt the bumping of the undercarriage give way to the smoothness of the air. He heard the gear collapse up and the outer doors close. He noticed that the angle of ascent was much steeper than anything he had experienced before and he couldn't help but stare out the small windows at the speedily receding ground. Heinrich looked at the wall-mounted LCD screen as the aircraft levelled off, and saw they were cruising at nine hundred kilometres per hour at an altitude of twelve thousand metres.

"It takes a bit of adjustment Sir. We get higher and faster than any normal transport. Not as fast as a fighter, obviously, but fast enough."

"I'd like to request that I get this transport every time please, could you arrange that?"

"Certainly Sir, I'll have it waiting for you."

Heinrich began to relax into the seat and enjoy the trip as the steward made good on his promise of refreshments.

Sipping on an apple juice, Heinrich tried to contemplate what he had learned from Mary Reid. The woman was broken, damaged, but even in her mental state she was sane enough to realise that the wish she had spoken was simply a fantasy. She had no way of knowing that Heinrich possessed the skills and Leigh possessed the means to make Mary's wish come true. All they needed was an opportunity.

In little more than an hour the jet touched down at Tegel Airport. Heinrich hustled out of the aircraft and across the tarmac to a waiting Mercedes saloon, the door of which was being held open for him. Heinrich couldn't help feeling a sense of importance and pride. He had done many a thing in his life to draw a sense of purpose but he began to understand how the senior leaders of the Party became seduced by the power. Jets, no waiting, doors opened, doors closed, cars cleared through roads. It was quite intoxicating. It was incredibly attractive. The car stopped and Heinrich was aware that he hadn't left the aircraft apron let alone the airfield. His door was opened again and he could hear jet engines and the tell-tale whup-whup of a helicopter.

"Colonel Steinmann?"

"Ja." Heinrich continued to sit in the car and stare up at the open door and the blank face of the young SS trooper. It took him a second to realise that the helicopter with the blades rotating was for him.

He clambered into the SS-Panther and was directed to a canvas seat, had straps done up for him by a loadmaster, and was given a mic and headset to put on.

"Colonel Steinmann, welcome on-board. Are you good to go Sir?"

"Yes, thank you, I must admit I thought I was being driven in to Prinz-Albrecht-Straße."

"No Sir, we have orders to get you there as quickly as possible." Heinrich heard the open mic line click off and then immediately heard the change of tone in the engine overhead. The rotors whup-whupped to a high pitched whine and Heinrich tilted rearward as the aircraft rolled forward and lifted off, nose down. It wasn't as quick or ferocious as the small Leichen Four jet but it was obvious the pilot wasn't hanging about. Three minutes later Heinrich felt the helicopter enter the hover and begin to circle down onto the heli-pad set atop 8-Prinz-Albrecht-Straße. The wheels touched and the aircraft bounced gently then settled. The side door was opened and Heinrich stepped out, bent in a crouch and jogged across until he was clear of the rotors.

"Colonel Steinmann, please follow me."

Heinrich turned to look at the young woman who had shouted over the noise of the now departing helicopter. She was already turning away and moving toward the stairwell that led down to the offices of the Reich Security Directorate. He followed, still feeling the intoxicating rush of the VIP travel experience.

36

His coffee was served by a dour SS-Private. Heinrich reached out to take the fine porcelain cup in hands that were slightly sweaty. He pondered that he had no need to be nervous. This was not an arrest. This was nothing to do with being a Turner. Not the way he had been transited here. This was about his report on Reid. Nonetheless, the man he was about to meet was capable of making anyone nervous.

He sat stiffly in on a leather settee centrally placed in the large office. It was faced by two matching chairs that were separated by a small coffee table providing enough gap to give a direct line of sight to the Reichsführer's desk. The solidity of the desk dominated the far side of the room and looking around, Heinrich realised the whole layout had been managed to ensure visitors knew their place.

Again he was struck by how pervasive power was. Reichsführer-SS Friedrichand strode in from the door in the far corner as the Private exited into the outer offices. His medals and awards brilliantly offset against the deep black of his formal uniform jacket. He covered the width of the room in a few long strides. Heinrich immediately stood and gave a drill-book straight arm salute. Friedrichand returned the gesture in a casual manner, waving Heinrich back into his seat while he remained standing. His height meant he physically looked down on everyone he spoke to. His character meant he metaphorically did the same. His heavy lidded eyes tended towards being half-shut and he tilted his head back when he spoke. The overall effect was of a schoolmaster sneering at his students. He had become the stuff of whispered threats to small children throughout the Reich. Friedrichand knew of his reputation and worked hard to cultivate it. His demeanour threatened violence and intimidation.

"So, Heinrich, did you enjoy your trip?" The diction was as precise as the man's uniform but the voice was soft, with mellow tones, gentle inflections. It seemed so much at odds with the speaker and his role.

"Yes Sir. I must admit to being very impressed."

"Indeed." A pause as if he was considering the merit of the thought before he continued. "You will get used to it. As you continue to rise through the ranks Heinrich, it will become the norm. We treat our best in the manner they deserve."

"Thank you Sir. Although I must admit to wondering why you needed me to be here so quickly. I assume there is more to this than just a question about Reid?"

"Very astute Heinrich. But just for now, tell me about this Reid. Why did she do it? Do I have to concern myself that she was a Turner? A weak, insipid, malignant creature inside our own house?" He lowered his tall frame into a chair opposite.

Heinrich recounted his on-the-record interview with Mary.

"Yes Heinrich, that was all in your report. But will it serve the Party to put her on trial? Be frank."

"No Sir, it won't. She's bordering on clinical insanity and doesn't profess to be a Turner. Fundamentally, this comes down to the fact she was abused as a child and this incident just pushed her over the edge. Also, if we put her on trial the," he paused and chose his next word carefully, "indiscretions of a Reichsminister will be on the record."

"So you recommend a quick termination?"

"Yes Sir. However," he paused and waited as Friedrichand poured himself a cup of coffee, added two heaped spoonfuls of sugar and stirred it with a delicacy that mimicked his voice.

"Yes? However what Heinrich?" asked the Reichsführer.

"Well, she mentioned a quote that I know but can't remember precisely where it comes from. I read it somewhere in the Archives when I was working in Department B. As you know, those documents and manuscripts are some of the most sensitive and secure records in the Reich. I'd like to return to Oranienburger Straße and review some texts if I may?"

"For precisely what purpose? What do you think it will tell us?"

"When she first said it I knew I recognised it but I didn't have enough background to push her on it. It also wasn't my main line of questioning, obviously. Later, after the interview, I wondered if she'd read it from a banned text or merely overheard it from a camp internee. Even if the latter was the case, I would like to know from whom she heard it but I'm speculating that Reid kept confiscated books from her time in Harrow. A full search of her house turned nothing up so I was planning to reinterview her. Then the call to Berlin came. I know it may be a long shot Sir, but I thought while I was back here I could perhaps take the time to investigate it."

Friedrichand considered Heinrich from under hooded lids and asked, "Why? What will we gain?"

"If I can discover the text in the Archives and identify the manuscript then I can confidently interview her about it. When I name the source and some of its contents I'll know if she shows signs of recognition. If not, then no loss but if yes, we can perhaps track down a document that would be of academic worth as a comparison text for the Archives. I actually don't think it's a Turner text. I think it's much older and if I find it, we can remove another piece of this filth from general circulation." Heinrich paused a beat. Friedrichand continued to direct his gaze toward him. "I also don't like loose ends Sir."

The Reichsführer smiled, a tight, thin expression and gave a small chuckle. "Ha, how very appropriate."

Heinrich looked at him curiously, "Sir?"

"Never mind. Very well, take the rest of today and tomorrow if you need it to tidy up your loose ends. Yes?"

"Yes Sir, thank you."

"But, no longer than tomorrow. I have a job for you back in London and I would like it done without too much delay. However, we shall come to that momentarily."

Heinrich felt a sharp twinge of anxiety at what this man would ask of him but he masked his emotions and simply nodded.

"Now, I agree a quick disposal of the Reid problem suits better. I do not want Joyce's family to suffer the shame and indignation of a public airing of dirty laundry. We should not forget that he did serve us well in the past. His comeuppance may be just payment for his philandering."

Heinrich noticed the way the Reichsführer sounded out each syllable of the last word with distaste.

Friedrichand continued, "But I see no reason to persecute his memory. If we can stop the rumour mill we might even give him a State Funeral. Our Wilhelm Straße colleagues in the Leopold Palace will be pleased. They do so like a little pageantry."

"I know Whitehall already reminded all those involved in the initial response to the crime scene and in the arrest op that they aren't to speak of the circumstances. I think we should be fairly confident they'll do as asked," Heinrich said.

"Yes, I would imagine we can be confident of that," the Reichsführer-SS gave an insidious smile before continuing, "That is settled then. Whether you have found your ancient books or not I want you to look after the Reid matter quickly. Let me see," he paused, pulled his left sleeve up and flicked to the diary page on his ForeFone. "If you are in Berlin tomorrow," he flipped a page across and then another.

Heinrich thought he looked like he was picking a time and a date to meet friends for dinner. If he had friends, which Heinrich doubted.

"Mmm, yes. I think so," Friedrichand said as he flipped the calendar screen closed. "Despite her crimes she too has worn our uniform, albeit in the Totenkopfverbände, so I think a traditional firing squad is warranted. Sunday at dawn."

Heinrich knew it wasn't a suggestion and again nodded confirmation of his orders.

Friedrichand rose and walked casually around the office, stopping at the bookcase to straighten a number of the spines that were slightly out of alignment. Eventually he sat down at his desk whereupon he adjusted four pencils into a precisely ordered row.

On the few occasions he had met the Reichsführer-SS Heinrich had always been struck by the man's luxurious use of time. He wouldn't be rushed. It was noticeable that he didn't even use contractions in his speech. Everything was deliberate and in his own time. Heinrich wondered if the young Jason Friedrichand had been like this naturally or had these habits come with the accumulation of power. The silence stretched and whilst Heinrich wanted to ask if there was anything else, he knew he wouldn't. He merely watched and waited.

Friedrichand completed his pencil alignment and half smiled, half sneered as he looked back up. His upper lip curled back to reveal extended canine teeth that seemed to portray the true menace of his persona.

"Tell me about Doctor Wilson?"

Heinrich felt physically winded. He struggled to control his expression. "Sir?"

"Doctor Wilson. Have you told her you knew her father?"

"Yes Sir. She was rather surprised, but I rather meant what would you like to know about her?" Heinrich was keenly aware that the man who sat opposite was a skilled reader of people. He knew he had to be very careful. He breathed as deeply and unobtrusively as he could.

"Let us be open Heinrich. We are both grown men. It would seem she is capable, but she is also a very pretty girl and her father was influential in the Party. As you know, he was, amongst other things, a loyal advisor to me. Nevertheless, we both agreed that people must stand on their own merits. There can be no carrying of the weak regardless of who they are or who their families are. I want to know your thoughts about her."

"I honestly doubt that she would have the respect of the academics and scientists she works with if it had all been driven by her father's position. It was her discovery that led to the Time Window."

"Ah, yes, the Window. We will come to that in a moment. You know, Heinrich, I am surprised you never met her before. After what her father did for you."

"It just never happened Sir. I knew her parents well but just never met her. But yes, I have had the chance to speak to her and tell her I knew them. She was a little taken aback as she had never heard of me either."

"Does she strike you as a woman who is capable of running the whole project?"

"Well, I know she's comfortable in her role as Deputy-Director and I believe she's stepped into Professor Lippisch's shoes before. However, I have only seen her work in the last few days so it is a very preliminary and superficial assessment. Saying that, I was most impressed with her and the rest of the team on the Reid Projections. Why do you ask Sir?"

"Because she will be taking over as Acting-Director on a temporarily basis. At least until the Technical Directorate can convene a board to determine if she is ready to take the role permanently."

Heinrich couldn't help but smile.

"This pleases you Heinrich?"

"I was just thinking that Donald would have been pleased Sir." He managed to respond quickly and hoped that it would be believable.

"Indeed. Indeed. Ensure you pass my thanks on to her and her team for me." And the Reichsführer also smiled.

"May I ask where Professor Lippisch is posted to Sir?"

"Nowhere. I want Konrad Lippisch arrested on your return to London. No noise. Just remove him when you get back."

"You want him terminated?" Heinrich asked, perplexed.

"Oh no! Just hold him in isolation. There are a few things that have to be arranged and unfortunately our Luftwaffe colleagues are being their normal efficient selves. I expect you will have to hold him in your cells until the weekend. I have already asked for the paperwork to be forwarded to you via Whitehall." Friedrichand resumed adjusting the items on his desk. He lined pens next to the pencils, straightened a small ruler and placed a stapler square on to the end of it. He looked back up at Heinrich.

"You have a question?"

"May I ask why Sir?"

"He is a homosexual." He pronounced the word with unconcealed disdain. It dripped from his mouth.

Heinrich knew his eyes had widened. "Sir?"

"Marseille Kriminalpolizei arrested a young male whore a few weeks ago. They decided to run him for a while to see who they could catch in the net. The operation was about to shut down last week when a certain male scientist came calling. I was made aware of it last night."

"I'm sorry to press this Sir, but are we sure it was Lippisch?"

"Indeed Heinrich, we are sure. Not only was he recognisable from the tapes so the eBü picked him up but it was cross-checked. He was in Southern France at the time. Normally I would have sent him straight to Sachsenhausen but despite his perversions we cannot merely cast him aside. He is a valuable asset. We shall have to convene a combined Potsdam, Munich, Paderborn and Technical Directorate team to conduct a thorough debrief. It could take months. If I merely throw him to the Konzentrationslager system there is likely to be nothing left to question in a few days. So, you conduct the arrest and hold him until I can have him transported safely to one of our debrief facilities. I would imagine it will be Leipzig or somewhere near to there, so as to be central to the participants. Any other questions?"

"Do you wish me to inform Professor Faber and Doctor Wilson?"

"Yes, that would be convenient. I was considering phoning Wolfgang but if you can do it face-to-face that would be better. He can inform the rest of his team as he sees fit. Now, moving on. Tell me about using the Thule Projection to catch Reid." Heinrich was still processing the order about Lippisch but was immediately without doubt that the man opposite had no discernible conscience. He had just issued an arrest order that would eventually end in the concentration camp death of one of the most brilliant scientists in the Reich. Now he was moving on to the next subject as if he had just waved a fly away from his face.

Heinrich forced himself to focus on being composed and spent the next fifteen minutes going through the Projections and processes employed to catch Mary Reid. He made sure that the screw-ups were his and that the innovations and successes belonged to his team. It was how he had always worked.

"Interesting. So it finally begins to pay back on the investments made. I was always sceptical after the initial demonstrations revealed its weaknesses. Everyone else running away with time travel fantasies and, in actual fact, what we have is a series of stilted snapshots of the past. However, it seems to have worked. Now tell me, how did Reid get tipped-off to run?"

Heinrich had kept Schern's indiscretion out of his reports and had also navigated around it when he had retold the story. He couldn't avoid it anymore.

"It was an unlikely fluke. She had arranged to go on a dinner date with one of the Kommandos. He rung her to say he was called out on a job and would be late. She panicked and ran."

"And this Kommando, we have him in custody?"

Heinrich looked directly at the man behind the desk. "No Sir. He didn't reveal any operational details per se and spoke up as soon as he was aware of the compromise. He's rated as one of our best and so I determined to keep him on the operation." Heinrich paused and waited. Friedrichand lifted a letter opener in the shape of a miniature Ehrendegen Reichsführer-SS, the official SS ceremonial sword. He held it in both hands and allowed it to turn slowly.

Heinrich watched the silver blade revolve. On each turn it reflected the now fading sunlight from the windows back into his face like a narrow beam searchlight. He knew his breathing was accelerating and he could hear the blood pounding in his ears as his heart tried to keep the panicked fight or flight adrenaline surge under control.

"Your decision Heinrich?" Friedrichand spoke casually but the tone of the question was anything but.

"Yes Sir." Heinrich held the gaze of the man and realised that he may have made a monumental mistake. He had no choice but wait and as he waited he realised that he was completely confident that his decision about Schern had been the correct one. He also began to realise that he didn't fear the man opposite as much as he first thought. Something else Mary had said played in his mind. He relaxed.

The Reichsführer stood and placed the letter opener back on the desk. He walked over to Heinrich and looked down on him. "Good Heinrich. Very good indeed. I need strong men around me and I like them to make leadership decisions. I also need them to stand by their decisions. Men like that get to rise to real power

Heinrich. Get to experience the type of privilege you have enjoyed coming here today."

"Thank you Sir."

"Now one last thing before you go on your way. I also need my men to follow orders. Sometimes I value their opinion and on other occasions I expect my orders to be followed without question. Do you understand?"

"Yes Sir."

Friedrichand sat on the arm of the settee, placing himself in position to yet again look down on Heinrich. "You are fully aware of the outstanding list of Gestapo priority cases that are to be observed on Thule."

"Yes Sir. We have the preliminary warning orders in place for the Führer's staff visit in June. That was to be the first official use before the Joyce matter accelerated things."

"Good. So you are fully aware we will use the Time Observation Window to investigate various high profile crimes of the past?"

"Yes Sir."

"And you are aware that the list of the so-called, top thirty, priority cases has been agreed by the Führer?"

Heinrich nodded.

"Did you notice anything missing from the list?"

Heinrich hesitated as he tried to think back through the paperwork he had seen. There were murders, child disappearances, art thefts and an infamous bank heist of more than seven million Reichsmark. In the end he shook his head and said, "I'm sorry Sir, but I can't think what you're alluding to."

"I was thinking of our previous Führer's demise in an aeroplane crash."

Heinrich spoke before really considering his words, "But the original investigation found that it was just an unfortunate accident."

The Reichsführer nodded, "Yes, all true and I know you were assigned to a special investigation squad to assist with the original enquiry, so I expect you to defend that report. Remind me of what it said."

"The formal report found nothing of note and everything pointed to the weather conditions causing a failure of aircraft integrity. There was little physical evidence recovered as it went down over the Indian Ocean."

"Exactly. Nonetheless, Heinrich, indulge me. If your parents had been lost in what was an unexplained crash, would you not have thought to use our new project to go back?"

Heinrich froze. He couldn't believe what the Reichsführer was suggesting. It was almost exactly what he had proposed to Leigh about using it to see her parents.

Friedrichand had continued to talk, "...I was expecting it to be the number one case that the Reich Cabinet wanted to be observed by Thule. I thought it would have greatly pleased our current Führer. A chance for him to investigate the circumstances of his Father and Mother's death. Instead, the Cabinet issued the list they did. No mention of using a Thule Projection to go back to make sure the Führer's parents' accident was simply that."

"But it does make a semblance of sense, Sir. Any Projection will be restricted to the ground environment before take-off. As you said, the apparatus is limited. It can't track a moving car so it isn't going to track an aircraft," Heinrich said.

"I know and so does the Führer and so does the Cabinet. We have all seen the project limitations. But if it were me, I would still have asked to investigate the hanger and maintenance procedures in the hours before take-off. I find it," he paused as if considering the most appropriate word, "intriguing." The Reichsführer once more considered Heinrich from under hooded eyes.

Heinrich knew this wasn't finished and so he waited.

"You do not like loose ends Heinrich. I do not like intrigue. So, I would like us to have a small look at a small intrigue. The previous Führer, whom you saved, is in no small way the reason you are sitting here. He is, in absolute ways, the reason I am here. I think it is beholden on us to at least see if there was something suspicious."

Friedrichand leant his head back slightly and considered Heinrich for a long time before he spoke again. Heinrich tried, but this time failed, to hold his gaze. Instead he reached out and took hold of his coffee cup.

"The removal of Lippisch will work to our advantage. Find an opportunity to work with Doctor Wilson. She obviously has the ability to initiate and run a Projection and I think that with her pedigree as Donald's daughter she will, on your advice, assist us. I want you to examine the pre-flight environment. I know you are not an aircraft engineer but Wilson is a scientist and you are an excellent investigator. Between the two of you, you will be able to intuit if anything is amiss. If it is, then I will get you an appropriate technical source from Warton. In the meantime we need to keep the circle of knowledge small and confined."

Heinrich suddenly realised what had been meant by the last remark. He spoke slowly and deliberately, "You don't want anyone else to be aware of this Projection? Not even the Führer?"

"We should realise that the Führer is like a very good lawyer. He only asks questions if he both knows and wants the answers to them. In this case I do not think he wanted the question asked on his behalf."

It was a simple statement by the Reichsführer-SS, but one with huge consequences. The dipping sun cast an ethereal glow across the office and when the Reichsführer steepled his long fingers Heinrich watched their shadow seep across the settee, edging towards him like a black stain.

Heinrich sat still as he thought of the months that had followed the air crash. On the Twenty-seventh of February 2015, Martin Hitler, the third Führer of the Reich, and his wife Heidrun Goebbels-Hitler were killed in an aircraft crash while returning from an official visit to the Japanese city of Perth. Joseph Hitler, the forty-one year old eldest son, had become Führer designate and immediately consolidated his transition to power. He ordered a widespread purge on his rivals within the Party, a renewed and frenzied wave of terror against Turners and a round-up of anyone else he was wary of. The Armed Forces command structure was badly hit and a lot of good men and women fell to the regime. It was a brutal time, even for the Reich.

After a short pause Heinrich looked up, "You think he carried out a coup and then cleaned up the 'loose ends' during the purges?"

"Well, it was always a possibility Heinrich. Even if we discover what I suspect we will, then we will not be able to use the information publically. But I think it will have a value for us." Friedrichand gently patted the insignia he wore at the bottom of his left sleeve. The wristcuff 'Adolf Hitler' surmounted by the Dietrich. It was worn in perpetuity by any former member of the Leibstandarte SS Adolf Hitler. "Do you not agree?"

Heinrich looked down at the same wristcuff he also wore. He recalled the unit's motto called out at the end of every parade, 'Meine Ehre heißt Treue'. He said clearly, "Without question Sir."

Through a smile the Reichsführer said, "Indeed Heinrich, very good indeed. Obviously we shall not document this. Verbal reports to me only. You will have my jet at your disposal. I expect a brief by the end of next week."

Heinrich nodded, "Sir." And as he said it he realised why he had enjoyed such a rapid journey to Berlin. It wasn't about the speed of the transit, it was about the exclusivity. No one would have even a verbal record of this meeting outside of the Reichsführer's immediate and personal staff. The aircrew, the drivers even the stewards were all SS and all handpicked. There would be no logs, no travel authorisations, no transcripts, no knowledge outside the two of them.

Heinrich took a sip of his coffee and was puzzled. He wondered at how or why this was being shared with him. He assumed it was the post he held but he hadn't asked for the post. It just came up. Would the Reichsführer have trusted anyone in the position?

"You look slightly confused Heinrich. Are my orders not clear?" The Reichsführer stood and looked down at him.

"Not that Sir. I just," he stopped, not sure how to phrase it. He took a breath, "I'm humbled by your trust in me. But why me?"

Friedrichand retook the seat opposite Heinrich and actually laughed. "I once asked the same question."

"Sir?" Heinrich was even more perplexed.

"Oh, some years ago a man that I trusted insisted to me that he had met a young officer whom he thought had a certain something. Now, how did he put it?... Ah yes, he actually quoted Von Braun out of context and said this young fellow had the 'Right

Stuff'. He went on to say that we should keep an eye on him. Observe him. Not give him an easy path but just afford him some opportunities. If he took them, then all well and good. If not, then we would only have expended a little time and effort for no real loss. I remember asking him why. Why him? What had made him think this lad was a prospect? He said simply that he had been impressed with him. He could have left it and done nothing about it but he sensed it would always gnaw away at him. He might always wonder if he had missed grooming a future leader. He said it reminded him of a thread hanging down waiting to be pulled and he did not like loose ends. Do you have any idea who I am speaking of Heinrich?"

"No, not really Sir."

"The advisor was Donald Wilson. The young man he met was you. It would seem you share Donald's aversion to loose ends."

Heinrich knew he looked slightly shocked. He couldn't hide it. "I, um, I didn't know that Sir. I mean, I didn't know that Donald and you had observed me. Was this since my, eh, medical discharge, umm, after the assassination attempt?" Heinrich stumbled over his words.

"No, no, no. Much earlier. You were still a cadet at Bad Tölz."

Heinrich couldn't hide his shocked expression this time.

"I know. It is quite strange how things turned out. Donald and I always had it in mind that you would be a Waffen-SS leader. But after your medical downgrading we could not see you lost to us for good. In some ways Heinrich I am very pleased and reassured that you and I both knew Donald as a friend. So, that is that."

The Reichsführer stood, "Well Heinrich, it has been a pleasure seeing you. Enjoy your time in Berlin, enjoy the dusty Archives and of course, enjoy the trip home." He waved a hand in the direction of the outer offices, "Ask my staff to make the arrangements, accommodation, driver, whatever you need. But Heinrich, no more than tomorrow for your loose ends. I want you heading back to London by tomorrow night. Take care of the Lippisch arrest personally on Thursday. Yes?"

"Yes Sir, thank you." Heinrich stood but hesitated in giving the salute that was required. His heart was thumping in his chest and his mouth felt dry but he knew he had to ask. He also knew the man in front of him was a careful, calculating, political animal and that he must have thought of a way around the problem. He calmed his mind and said a silent prayer to the God that he loved and spoke as casually as he could manage.

"Sir, all Projections have to be officially unlocked with the Berlin counter-authority code. The documentary chain is quite precise and the timelogs are exact. That will complicate the running of a secret observation."

Reichsführer-SS Jason Friedrichand returned to his seat behind his desk. "No complication Heinrich. When I had the security protocols designed I kept a back door open. Just in case. Ask Doctor Wilson to enter 636848 at the appropriate time. It will remotely switch the Berlin link off and no one will be any the wiser. After all, we are the Reich's guardians and on occasion we need to have a little," he paused, seemingly savouring the word, "discretion."

Heinrich straightened to attention. He delivered a perfect salute as befitting a previous bodyguard to the Führer. Friedrichand merely nodded in response.

Heinrich reached the door leading to the outer offices as the Reichsführer spoke again, "What was the quote?"

Heinrich turned, "Sir?"

"The quote by Reid, what was it?"

Heinrich held the man's gaze as he said, "My glittering sword and mine hand take hold on judgment; I will render vengeance to mine enemies, and will reward them that hate me."

The Reichsführer snorted in appreciation, "Sounds like something I would write. Goodnight Heinrich."

***

"Leigh?"

"Heinrich?" Her voice was laced with sleep but she was rapidly coming awake.

"Did I wake you?"

"Yes, but it's okay. What is it?"

"I just wanted to let you know that Reichsführer-SS Friedrichand asked me to pass his regards on to you and your team for a job well done."

"Really?"

"Yes really. I'm sorry for ringing so late but I thought that was news that couldn't wait for my return. It's not often that you get compliments like that. Well done Leigh."

"Thanks Heinrich. I'll let the team know tomorrow morning. Where are you?" she asked as unobtrusively as she could.

"At the old 1st Division's Mess. Just about to get my head down."

"Okay, well you get some sleep, you must be shattered. I'll see you back in London. And Heinrich, thanks for ringing and letting me know. It means a lot." The call disconnected.

***

In two separate SigInt analysis centres, in two separate cities, operators finished logging the call details. Almost simultaneously, but entirely independent of each other, they punched a key marking it as Routine Traffic, 'No Further Analysis Required'. In fourteen days, with no follow up enquiries, the call would be erased off the servers.

***

In London, Leigh rolled over and fell asleep, sure in the knowledge he was safe.

In Berlin, Heinrich lay awake for some time trying to process the possibilities that had opened up and dreading how he was going to tell Leigh about Konrad Lippisch. He also reflected on the news that he had been observed since Bad Tölz. He could see with surprising clarity that he had been part of a very long game played out by Donald Wilson. A game that predated Heinrich's conversion to Turnerism by years and was only a continuance of Donald's father's idea for the long term infiltration of the regime.

He felt strangely satisfied and pleased at the audaciousness of Donald and the success of his plan, yet he knew that he should also be feeling resentment. There was a good possibility that he had been manipulated. What if Donald's friendship had just been a tactic? The thought was so naked and profound that it almost numbed him. He sat up and replayed his memories of the years, made fresh by his recounting of them to Leigh on Sunday night.

Before too long he had confidently dismissed the idea of manipulation and couldn't feel anything but gratitude. Donald Wilson may have started out by trying to target him but in the end Donald and Rosalyn had become his true friends. They had given Heinrich the gift of belief. His life since, and because of, being a Turner was worth anything they may have done initially. Heinrich finally fell asleep, considering with pleasure the irony that the Reichsführer's most trusted advisor and now his handpicked confidant were Turners. 'God sends the people you need at the time you need them,' he thought. Even the Reichsführer of the SS wasn't immune.

37

Heinrich's alarm buzzed and he silenced it before it managed to utter its second note. He lay on his back looking up at the ceiling's moulded plasterwork and contemplated his plan for the day. For ten minutes he walked his mind through the next ten hours. He rehearsed the conversations he would have and the procedures he would navigate. Eventually he rose and, once dressed, made his way to the dining room for breakfast.

His walk along the corridors of the Lichterfelde Barracks was tracked by thousands of faces looking out from hundreds of graduation parades, sports teams and Führer's Selection photographs that hung from every available wall space. The home of the Führer's bodyguard liked to honour their alumni. They also liked to acknowledge the historic leaders of the Reich and at intervals along the corridors and walkways were large, golden-framed portraits in oils of the men who were the founding fathers of the regime. Yet in one place on the main corridor, leading from the western accommodation wing to the main reception rooms and dining facilities, there was a gap in the even, almost rhythmic, parade of paintings.

Heinrich, like all 1st alumni, knew the reason. The portrait of Deputy Führer Rudolf Heß had been removed in August 1949, just a week after his suicide by hanging. It probably wouldn't have happened had the suicide not become public knowledge and

232

therefore a public disgrace to the Reich, but it had and so the spot remained vacant as a warning. The apocryphal story was that a committee had been convened to consider which portrait should be put up in its place but the committee chairman had said no one should be hung there as the last man to occupy the spot had done quite enough hanging. He also decreed that each officer or officer cadet should, on passing, make an appropriate gesture to admonish the memory. It always drew a grin in the telling and, like all good stories, was probably not true. Nevertheless, as Heinrich passed the empty wall he reached up and slipped two fingers inside his collar and eased the material from his neck while nodding in mock salute. Traditions took all forms.

Like the case of the slightly larger than life-sized brass bust of Goring that sat on its plinth to the right of the dining room entrance. Touched on the nose by every passing diner since the mid-1950s, the bust now gleamed from the bridge to the nostrils. Erected in memory of the then Deputy Führer a year after his death, it was felt to be a fitting memorial to a larger than life figure. The officers of the 1st thought patting him on the nose was a more fitting memorial for a man who had died from an accidental overdose of cocaine while in the company of prostitutes. Had it been a full-length statue they would, no doubt, have patted another spot as well.

At least the third holder of the Deputy Führer's office, Martin Bormann, had managed to die a more dignified death of old age, in his own bed. That, and the fact he had succeeded in becoming acting-Führer on the death of Adolf Hitler, meant that his memorials were much more grandiose and much more public. Heinrich assumed no one ever yawned up at the Bormann statue that stood in the Avenue of the Führers. But traditions were habits long in the making and so Heinrich, almost unconsciously, patted Goring's nose and entered the spectacularly decorated dining room.

At the far end of the carefully laid out tables was a three-metre high statue of the Nazi Party Eagle but with the Swastika grasped in its left claw and a skeleton key clasped in its right. He was overcome with an emotion he had grown to expect but had not fully understood since his Turner conversion. It was the strange mix of revulsion at the regime and pleasure at still belonging to the enveloping styles, traditions and surroundings of the Establishment. He knew that he had been quietly grateful and a little proud that the 1st Division Mess always kept a room or two available for any of their own who were last minute visitors to Berlin. He hadn't stayed here for some years but the barracks had lost none of their grandeur and it pleased him.

From the sentinels flanking the main road entrance through to the gold plated taps within the bathrooms Heinrich had always admired its ability to project an air of supremacy. Even the carpets were deep and luxurious in comparison to any other Officers' Mess in the Reich. Visitors to the 1st Division were never left in any doubt that their hosts considered themselves 1st by right as well as name. He ate breakfast in the quiet and refined atmosphere of the Mess dining room while reflecting on the strange sense of satisfaction he had felt when the Reichsführer's staff had been every bit as efficient and professional in meeting his needs the previous evening. He had been chauffeured from Prinz-Albrecht-Straße to the barracks in a little over twenty minutes and was told a car was available at his request. He had been pleasantly surprised to find they had rung ahead and on his arrival his room had been prepared for him, as had an evening meal. He had told the driver that he wouldn't need him for the rest of the evening and that he would like an 07:15 pick-up.

He walked out between the four draped pillars of the main entrance at the designated time and, sure enough, the Horch staff car was waiting, purring a clear white exhaust vapour into the early morning briskness. Heinrich's breath clouded in a similar fashion as he approached the car. He noticed it was a different driver to last night but obviously his itinerary had been passed along because as soon as he closed the door and settled into the rear seat the car pulled away. The driver, a female SS-Sergeant, merely glanced in the rear-view mirror and said, "Good morning Sir. I'll have you at Oranienburger Straße in half an hour."

It was nearly six years to the day since Heinrich had been in Oranienburger Straße. His tour of duty had run from 2011 though to 2014 and he didn't expect any of the uniformed personnel to be the same for this visit. But he had assumed a lot of the civilian archivists would still remain and a few phone calls yesterday evening had confirmed his hopes. He walked toward the front entrance of the domed building, gazing upwards at the grand old facade that had been preserved, despite the building having once been a Turner Church. He was met by Jutta Gesele and his old language instructor Albrecht Dollman.

"Heinrich, my lad. It's so good to see you again. You haven't changed a bit. Has he Jutta?"

"Well, perhaps a little more distinguished in his hair colour?" Jutta teased and looked towards Heinrich's head.

"Well, thanks a lot!" Heinrich feigned an offended look. "I come all the way over from a warm and pleasant London, to a cold, if not freezing, Berlin and all I get is that I have a few more grey hairs? Charming is all I have to say on the matter. Of course it is good to see you at least, Albrecht." He winked at the two of them and held out his arms to Jutta who walked forward and gave him a hug.

"Hi you," he said to the short, dark haired, thoroughly bookish looking young woman. She was dressed as modestly as ever in flat shoes, a long skirt and simple plain blouse. Her hair was in the still preferred, but not often seen, plaits and, apart from being heavier than the perfect Aryan specimen, she worked hard to fit the Party's ideal image of a fräulein. Her only departure from the demure norm was the gothic tattoo on her right wrist; ***Ein Volk, Ein Reich, Ein Führer.***

"Hi you too!" she beamed up at him, slipped her arm in his and turned to follow Albrecht.

Jutta had been working in the Archives in one capacity or another since graduating high school. By the time Heinrich was posted to Oranienburger Straße she was a fresh-faced graduate straight out of the University of Posen. Armed with a newly minted Bachelor's Degree in Ancient History she had been assigned back to the place she adored on the direct recommendation of Albrecht. Throughout the three years Heinrich had worked with her he had been singularly impressed with her ability to understand the subtleties and nuances so often present in the ancient writings. Despite not having gone on to do a Masters or a Doctorate, she was nonetheless acknowledged as an expert in the rise of the eastern religions and their embodiment into the Turner ideology. He also knew two more significant details about Jutta Gesele. She had an unrequited crush on him and she was potentially the most fervent and zealous member of the Nazi Party he had ever met.

"So what's happening with you?" he asked.

"Same old, same old. We still argue almost weekly with those deranged Ahnenerbe idiots who want us to move all of our records over to Dahlem. We keep telling them we don't want anything to do with them. They keep making crazy theories up and we keep doing real work." She effervesced enthusiasm and talked non-stop. "I had quite a coup last year, which was pretty good. I found the key to one of the Buddhist translations. It was brilliant. It showed up one of their old monastery hideaways. We rounded up three hundred and sixteen of the weird orange freaks in one go," she giggled.

Heinrich smiled back at her and said, "Well done Jutta, good work. Did we learn much from them?"

"Oh well, it was up in Malaya so we let the Imperial Army take the lead. You know what our little Japanese friends are like. They had decapitated most of them on site before we could convince them to take some down to Changi for a chat. Even then we got little new information before they checked out. But it was an interesting experience."

"Proud of you," said Heinrich and fought to control his revulsion. She continued to babble away as the three of them proceeded through five separate security checkpoints to the level known as the Inner Library.

Heinrich gazed around the room where he had spent almost three years of his life. It was a large open space lined with floor to ceiling book shelves crammed with thousands of bound books. The floor was dotted with multiple further shelves arranged in chevrons across the space. Between these were a dozen stand-alone reader tables. Each of these had a return desk attached at right angles that was equipped with a PC with twin screens. The room was flooded with natural light coming through the central ceiling dome, beautifully supported by exposed wrought-iron stanchions. In the rear wall was a safe door that led through to the Sensitive Archive Room, casually known as the SAR.

Albrecht ushered them into a small room that was set off to the side of the main floor and poured coffees for all of them. Once settled he asked, "Now Heinrich, what can we do for you?"

"I'm sorry but I can't really tell you what it's all about," Heinrich said truthfully. "It's all rather hush-hush but I just need to get some time with The Scribes of the Sons of Jacob. Can't tell you why, but as you can imagine, it is quite important."

"Is it to do with the Minister's death?" asked Albrecht rather nonchalantly.

Heinrich gaped at him.

"Come, come now Heinrich. Don't look at me with such incredulity. We hold the secrets that cannot be spoken about, and I am the grandson of a former Gestapo diplomat. Is anyone better placed to hear whispers in the corridors of power and better capable of keeping them a secret?" He removed his glasses and huffed on them before intricately cleaning each lens. He placed them back on as he looked at Jutta, then at Heinrich, "What? Did I say something out of turn?"

"Albrecht!" Jutta mockingly scolded him. "You can't put Heinrich into such an awkward position. You know he can neither confirm nor deny such a scurrilous rumour."

Heinrich held his hands up in submission. "Okay you two. I feel like I've been ambushed. What on earth have you heard?"

"Oh, nothing much to be honest," said Albrecht. "You know my eldest nephew is employed at the Reichstag Museum? Well, his new boss is an ex-Captain in the SS-Totenkopfverbände. Turns out he heard from someone else that the Justice Minister for Great Britain had committed suicide in Edinburgh."

Heinrich almost laughed but managed not to. "Even if that were true, and I am not saying it is. How or why would that bring me here?"

This time it was Jutta, "Oh, because he left a note saying that God had made him do it and then included another line written in ancient Greek, or Aramaic, or one of the two."

This time Heinrich did laugh. "You know it never ceases to amaze me how we ever manage to keep anything safe in the Empire. If someone isn't spilling our national secrets then someone else is making up better theories and just putting them out there regardless."

"Well, that's all well and good but are we close?" Albrecht asked with a twinkle of mischief.

Heinrich looked between his two tormentors, sat a little straighter in his chair, placed his coffee mug on the table and said with a fake Berlin bourgeoisie accent, "I cannot possibly comment on the nature of unfounded rumour. However," he drew his silence out to tease them, "if a senior Minister was to have become deceased, and if there was perhaps a religious overtone, then it would be reasonable for a fairly senior member of the investigative services to perhaps require access to some archive material." He coughed with a false formality.

Jutta smiled coyly at him across the table. "Would that senior investigator be a full Reigierungs-und Kriminalrat Direktor?" she asked, using as she always had done, Heinrich's equivalent Gestapo rank.

"Might do."

The three laughed at their own joke and finished their coffees.

It was Albrecht who asked more seriously as they stood up, "So Heinrich, what is it that we *can* do for you?"

"I'm very conscious that with you and Jutta helping me I could probably get what I need in a fraction of the time. But I really can't. This is an Eyes Only matter and I'm here with the authorization of Reichsführer-SS Friedrichand. I just need a few hours in the SAR with some of the old scripts. You both do understand the restrictions?"

They nodded and Jutta held out her hand in a sweeping 'after you' motion for him to take the lead across the Library floor. When they arrived at the door to the SAR she swiped her security card and held her right palm on the bio scan pad. Albrecht then stepped forward, swiped his card and leaned in to allow the retina scanner to scan his left eye. The last stage of their elaborate security dance sequence required both of them to key in a nine-digit personal code. Heinrich waited, then heard the 'Grade-6'

Security door mechanism give a small chirp. He handed over his ForeFone to Jutta. "The exit code hasn't changed Heinrich. It's still five zeroes to get out. Good luck and happy hunting."

The tight rubber seal sucked apart and the heavy solid door, finely counterbalanced, swung with a light push from a single hand. Heinrich stepped into the SAR. It was officially titled the Wiligut Room but regardless of nomenclature, its role was clear. It formed the inner sanctum of the Reich's Religious Archives.

He shut the outer door behind him, waiting for the locking mechanism to engage and for his eyes to adjust to the subdued lighting. Directly in front of him a metal walkway bridged a metre-wide gap in the floor that ran the circumference of a thirty-metre diameter inner island structure. Heinrich walked across the metal bridge, then swivelled it onto the inner island to bar the access point. He went through another airtight door into a twenty-metre square room imaginatively called the Central Depository. Shielded from natural light and electronic signals, this temperature controlled room held the Reich's most sensitive and fragile documents relating to religions, sects and cults.

Locking the door firmly behind him, he flicked on the special wavelength lights designed to be as gentle as possible on the ancient documents. Taking a set of white cotton gloves from the wall-mounted dispenser, he moved around the room's two long tables, inspecting the floor to ceiling shelves and the banks of deep drawers. Unlike the Inner Library these held no bound books, only scrolls and papyrus, delicate wafers of paper and thin slates of stone.

He retrieved the Scribes of the Sons of Jacob and turned to the page that contained Mary's quote. Or at least the quote he had told the Reichsführer about. He reached for a pencil and some plain pieces of paper that were the only recording devices allowed and made some scribbled notes. Scattering a few of these across one of the tables, he retrieved a few more old manuscripts, opened them to random pages and placed them carefully next to his notes. Satisfied that it looked like he was busy, he stopped and began to scan the deep drawers set into one of the walls. It took less than a minute to retrieve the documents he wanted.

He carefully placed the Jesus Gospel down on the other table before laying out various fragile whispers of papyrus. Despite his best efforts he noticed his hands were trembling. He turned his head away from the documents and breathed deeply. And again. And again.

Finally, when he felt relaxed enough to focus, he looked down onto the oldest surviving maps of Capernaum and the Holy City of Jerusalem. Maps that had been drawn by surveyors assigned to the office of the fifth Prefect of the Roman province of Judaea; Pontius Pilatus.

38

Leigh walked across the car park, pulling her cardigan closer to combat the morning chill. Entering the Prisoner Holding and Interrogation Facility, she made her way to Peter Vogel's office. At precisely 07:30 she rapped on the door and got an immediate, "Come in."

"Good morning Doctor Wilson," Peter said, rising from his chair.

She swept into his office and took a seat. "Please, Peter sit. And good morning to you too. Are you well?"

"Yes Ma'am."

Leigh couldn't help but be both pleased and horrified that this young man was calling her Ma'am. In one way it marked that she had progressed to a position of authority and in another reminded her of how old she was getting. Although she still considered herself twenty-one, she knew the officer in front of her would see a woman in her mid-thirties and therefore almost ancient. She could inform him that she held an actual SS rank and he should use it but she couldn't bring herself to even acknowledge it.

She shrugged it off and took a breath. "Thanks for meeting me so early. Now, I need to conduct an interview with the prisoner as part of the Thule protocols. It's imperative we properly assess if she had any idea that she was being observed. I know you're probably up to speed on all of this. I'm sure Colonel Steinmann

241

briefed you in. Yes?" She surprised herself as to how easily she had just lied her way through that rubbish.

"Umm, yes Ma'am. He mentioned something along those lines. Do you need to see her now?"

"No time like the present. You know the Reichsführer-SS is personally interested so I suppose I shouldn't keep him waiting. Come along," Leigh said with a matronly flourish and half rose from the chair.

"Yes Ma'am. Of course. But, um..."

She sat back down, gave him a rather stern look and said, "Yes Peter?"

"Well, it's just, I mean... We need to get her up and move her into an interview room. I can get my staff on to it but..."

"Nonsense!" She cut him off, "There's no need to fuss about moving her. I'll speak to her in her cell. That will be more than sufficient. You can just let me in for now and I shall carry on from there. All good?" She paused momentarily and Peter hesitated, teetering on the brink. She needed to make him react rather than think. "Peter?" she said in as brusque a manner as she could manage and the young Second Lieutenant visibly twitched in his chair. "Are we all good?"

"Yes Ma'am."

Leigh almost laughed. "Right, well, if you can show me her cell I'll proceed with my chat. Lead on Peter." With that she stood and Vogel almost leapt to his feet. She placed both her hands into the pockets of her cardigan, led the way out of his office and then let him lead the way into the central corridor and down to Reid's cell.

"I'll call you when I need you Peter, I already have your duty number in my phone. Thank you."

"Yes Ma'am, certainly."

Leigh eased into the small cell where Mary Reid seemed to be asleep on the cot. The breakfast tray that had been placed in the cell was empty so she had obviously been awake earlier. Leigh pushed the cell door shut behind her and nodded to Peter through the small observation window that all was well and he could leave. He threw the lock and walked away.

"Hello Mary."

Without moving or opening her eyes Mary said simply, "Hello. Who are you then?"

"I'm Leigh."

"Hello Leith."

"No, it's Leigh."

"So you said. But I'll call you Leith. I think it suits you better. Now who are you, what do you do and what do you want?" Mary unwound her long frame from the cot and sat up as she spoke.

Leigh sat down on the plain chair, kept her hands in her pockets and looked down at the ground before she replied. "My name is Leigh Wilson. You don't know me and I won't be telling you what I do. What I want will become clear. You can win small victories by getting my name wrong or you can win bigger victories," Leigh raised her head and looked at Mary, "by not being a cunt."

Mary's face registered a look of surprise at Leigh's expletive. She recovered quickly and said, "Charming! You kiss your mother with that mouth?"

"Not recently. No. She's dead. As is my father. I'm an orphan just like you. The difference, of course, is I didn't kill my father. The other difference is, unlike Uwe Joyce, I do actually have your life in my hands."

Mary frowned in recognition of the phrase. "What did you say?"

"I'll ask the questions Mary. Now, I believe you met Heinrich yesterday?"

"Yes," Mary answered cautiously.

Leigh registered the hesitancy and knew she had put Reid off balance. She also knew she would quickly try to reassert herself.

Sure enough, Mary swallowed and spoke more firmly, "He's cute. Did he send you? You'd make a nice couple. I would if you aren't."

"I'm sure you would," Leigh said with a layer of sarcasm. "From what I hear you'd fuck anything from boys to girls to young men to old whores. Single men, married men and, of course, your favourite... your own dear father." She watched as Mary tensed in front of her. "I heard you welcomed him into your bed because your mother was incapable."

243

Mary sprung forward off the cot with her hands raised ready to grab Leigh round the throat. Leigh in response removed her right hand from her pocket and contacted Mary's shoulder with a handheld 200Kv Taser. Reid collapsed vertically onto the cell floor. Leigh moved to bend over her and whispered urgently, "The next time I come to see you I'm going to ask you questions. You're going to tell me everything you told Heinrich. Mary, this is important. I'm on your side. We can get you out of here." Leigh stood up and kicked Mary Reid's prone body in the stomach before backing off into the corner of the cell. She tapped her ForeFone and called Peter Vogel to come get her.

He had been watching and listening to the whole thing on the internal CCTV so was already halfway to the cell when his Fone buzzed. He answered it, acknowledged Leigh's request breathlessly and kept running.

'Silly boy,' thought Leigh, as she recharged the taser, removed a strip of sticky tape from her other pocket, taped the trigger down and then lobbed the unit up so that it contacted the CCTV camera. There was a loud static discharge followed by a very faint pop and a slight smell of smoke. The red diode on the camera mount faded to black. Leigh caught the taser unit, removed the tape and popped both back into her pockets. Peter Vogel opened the door.

An hour later all was calmer, Reid had recovered and was handcuffed to the cot in her cell, Vogel had been reassured multiple times that Leigh was okay and Leigh was insistent that she would continue the interview.

She walked back into the cell and Peter resecured the door and left. Leigh could sense his frustration. He knew he had screwed up. He'd tried to berate her for having a taser but as she pointed out, he hadn't asked her to surrender any weapons.

She simply pleaded ignorance of the rules, "Damn good job I had it on me as it turns out, wouldn't you say Peter?"

"Yes Ma'am," he responded begrudgingly.

Vogel had discovered the camera in the cell had broken as the cleanup of Reid had progressed. Leigh inferred that it had probably shorted out when she tasered the prisoner and was relieved to see that Peter really didn't know anything about electronics. He just murmured his agreement and suggested she should conduct the interview in a different location.

"Peter, she isn't going to be walking anywhere unaided for a while. Your men have already cleaned her up and disinfected the cell. She's handcuffed to her cot. I don't actually have an awful lot of time so I'll just carry on as we are, thank you. If I turn up anything of interest I shall come back later and we can record it for posterity. She seems to be conscious, alert and more important-ly, back in control of her bowels."

"Hello Mary."

"Hello Leigh. Nice work."

"Thank you."

"So, who are you, what do you do and what do you want?"

"I'm a scientist with the Reich Technical Directorate. I work on a specialist project designed to aid investigations and I want you to tell me what you told Heinrich Steinmann about the way back."

Mary worked the handcuffs around the cot end and managed to sit up, albeit crookedly.

"I will if you will," she said. "What was the earlier visit about? You could have just asked me the first time."

"I want to know answers but there are eyes and ears almost everywhere. I had to take care of the ones in here," she nodded upwards at the defunct camera. "Sorry about the kick but it's all in the misdirection."

"You don't look like a manipulative bitch, do you?"

"No Mary, I guess I don't. But looks can be, and if you work at them often enough, are deceiving."

"You said you could get me out of here?"

"Yes I did. But that all depends on what happens when Heinrich gets back from Berlin. Honestly, if they walk in and haul you out, then that's it. But if things are delayed, then yes, I think we can get you out of here."

"And why would you do that Leigh? What would possess you to help and assist an enemy of the Reich?"

"Are you familiar with the writings of Chanakya?"

"Not unless he writes military handbooks, murder mystery novels or soft erotica?"

Leigh couldn't help but smile quizzically, "No, not quite. He was an Indian author who wrote about statecraft a while ago. He basically said the enemy of my enemy is my friend. But a lot more eloquently."

"Naughty naughty Leigh. I could have you arrested for that."

"Yeah! And who the fuck's going to believe a two-bit whore who previously tried to throttle me and I had to taser? Let's not forget, you also murdered a Reichsminister and that I'm a valued scientist."

"Okay, okay, take it easy. Shit, you've got a temper," Mary leant back away from her as much as the handcuffs would allow.

Leigh spoke in a calm and measured tone, "No, actually, I haven't Mary. But it's important you understand that I really am a manipulative bitch. I'll use any method at my disposal to protect myself. The good news is that if I decide to side with you, then you get all the benefits of my protection. Clear?"

"Clear," Mary shrugged, "you win."

"Good. Now, tell me what you told Heinrich."

"It's not that earth shattering. You'll be pissed."

"I'll judge. Come on."

Mary straightened up as best she could and stared hard at Leigh before she spoke, "I don't want to die. This might not be enough for you to help me."

"True, but if you don't tell me I can guarantee it won't be enough. I'm your last chance Mary."

The two women looked hard at each other across a gap of a metre and a lifetime of difference. Yet Leigh could also recognise a woman who had hidden her past behind a mask. In the end Mary shook her head a little and began.

"We're screwed Leigh. We have no chance of changing the regime. I didn't even know the regime was broken before this week. But there are people out there who do realise that this isn't the way things are meant to be. Problem is they're Turners. Do you know what their central tenet is?"

"Yes, of course. Everyone does."

"Exactly. Everyone does. Turn the other cheek. Be kind and loving. Even if I taser you, get up and thank me and be my forgiving friend. That's the problem. All fine if everybody plays by the same rules. Bit of a shit if Hitler comes along and exterminates millions. So what I said to Heinrich was simple. If this regime continues for another generation or two there'll be no one left but us. We'll eventually eradicate the Spanish, the Italians and the Japanese. We only tolerated them because we didn't have enough citizens of the Reich to occupy everywhere. But when we do, it'll be the Reich's world. Dictatorial, authoritarian, complete, global. If you aren't built like an Aryan then you'll be removed from the gene pool."

"How does this come to a way back?"

"We forget that all of this came about because of one man. One man united all the peoples of the world in harmony."

Leigh almost interrupted to say Jesus was no ordinary man but instead held her tongue and let Mary continue.

"He ripped up the old world order. But that was the problem. Before his time there was discord and inter-tribal and inter-faith violence and struggle. It was brutal but it meant no one took complete control. There was a strength and an edge to the old God that departed when the Turner belief became all powerful. The really old prophecies were fulfilled and they brought peace on earth. They called it Pax in Terra. The whole world pendulum swung to peace and reconciliation. Why should we have been surprised that it eventually swung in the opposite direction?"

Leigh was watching her carefully and could only see a lucid and focussed individual totally in charge of her faculties. How could Heinrich have thought she was crazy? Yet this was the same woman Leigh had watched cold-bloodily lean forward and blow her lover's brains out.

"Remember Leigh, all of that era of history fell apart because of one man as well. War and desperation consuming the whole world. When I spoke to Heinrich I told him I'd prefer we went back to a balance between the two. I'd settle for some peace and some war. No more extremes. I told him I had read some old, ancient books. There was one called Ecclesiastes. It said there should be a time of war. But to do that, we'd need a strong God to believe in. We'd need faiths that have mettle in their doctrine. That'll inspire people to pick up weapons and fight back. I want a vengeful God. That's what I meant by going back to the old ways."

"That's it?' Leigh was deflated.

"I told you. It isn't exactly rocket science."

"Is that all you told Heinrich?"

"Pretty much."

"Look Mary, pretty much won't do. You need to tell me everything you told him."

"That was it. I mean, I said I'd killed Uwe as the first step, you know, to show it was possible to fight back. I had seriously begun to consider being a sort of avenging angel but that plan didn't last long. I still don't get how they caught me so damn quickly, but they did. Anyway, the point is, imagine if the millions of Turners that are still out there fought back. They'd sweep the Reich away."

"But Turners won't fight Mary!" Leigh was exasperated.

"I know Leigh, I know. That's why we need new religions or more religions." Mary's voice had risen.

"And that is frankly bloody ridiculous. We can't just start a new religion and wind the clock back two thousand years." Leigh's voice was also on the rise.

"You don't think I realise that? You don't think I said the same to your fucking boyfriend, Heinrich?" Mary was shouting now.

"He's not my boyfriend and frankly if that's your great plan and that's what got him excited I wonder for his fucking sanity." Leigh almost spat the words.

"Well, maybe he just fancied being in my company. Maybe it was me that got him excited." Mary pouted as she yelled it at Leigh.

"Oh, go fuck yourself!" Leigh stood and watched as Mary brought her legs up in defence. For a moment there was silence. Leigh could feel the redness of her own face and realised that she had her fists clenched.

Mary spoke quietly, "Yeah, right. He's not your boyfriend."

Leigh almost laughed. She relaxed her fists. "I'm sorry. But seriously, forming a new religion? That was your plan?"

"No Leigh," Mary sighed. "I didn't have a plan. And yes you're right; we can't start a new religion. The only people in this whole sorry world that are inclined to be religious already believe in Turner pacifism. Like I said to Heinrich, it'd be a different world if Jesus hadn't killed off faith."

"That makes no sense. Turners have the ultimate faith."

"No they don't. Or rather, yes, they do." Mary paused and Leigh gave her a look of frustrated annoyance.

"Well, go on."

"They have belief. They believe entirely. There's no faith required."

"I don't understand you," Leigh said and sat back down in the metal chair.

"It's not difficult; no need for faith means no room for manoeuvre. That's why the religions united and no one dissented. You don't argue about something that's a belief." Mary raised her shackled hands as high as they would go, "I am handcuffed, yes or no? The answer's yes. I love being handcuffed? Maybe yes, maybe no and we could argue about that. Jesus left no room for manoeuvre. Everyone believed in him because of what he did and what he said. Plain and simple acts of wonder and plain and simple speeches of certainty."

"So what's your answer to all of this?"

"I told you, I don't have one. I just know that it's a shame Jesus was so good at his job."

"Yeah, but what would you expect of a Messiah?" Leigh's voice was flat and she felt entirely deflated.

"Ha, that's funny. That's exactly what Heinrich said." Mary chuckled. "I said that if he'd been a little more messy and a little less Messiah we'd be better off." She laughed again.

"Yeah, and what did Heinrich say to that?" Leigh had heard enough. She stood up and began to turn toward the cell door.

"Not much really. I think he said, 'it's a pity someone couldn't go back and tell him not to be so efficient.'"

Leigh sat back down.

39

Heinrich sanitized the room before leaving it to have lunch with Jutta and Albrecht. Afterwards he went back and worked solidly, eventually emerging from the SAR at 17:40 Berlin time.

Jutta bounced across the main Library floor to him. "Wow, that was a shift and a half. You can still put the hours in can't you? Find what you came for?" she bubbled.

"Yes, yes and believe it or not, yes." He looked down at her and winked.

She blushed and once again slipped her arm into his. "Come have a drink, you must be parched."

Heinrich, Jutta and Albrecht spent another half hour catching up over coffee before he got up to take his leave.

"Can't you stay for another evening Heinrich? We could grab a meal. There are some fantastic restaurants not a stone's throw away."

"Oh Jutta, I really would love to. Seriously, I really would, but I'm under orders of the Reichsführer-SS himself to be back in London as soon as possible." He watched the brightness leave her eyes. "What if I promise that the next time I'm coming to Berlin I ring you and we set up a date?" He saw the sparkle return. She smiled such a wide smile and nodded. He knew what he was doing and he knew it was mean. Despite her zealousness she still had emotions and he knew he was playing with them. They said their goodbyes; he shook Albrecht's hand and kissed Jutta on the cheek. She called him as he turned to leave and he turned back. She was holding a perfect straight-arm salute. Her tattoo clearly visible on her wrist, he couldn't help but read the last two words, One Leader.

"Heil Hitler!" she called.

He returned the salute and made his way out. If his research proved to be correct he would likely never see either of them again.

Heinrich's trip back was just as swift and luxurious as his trip out had been but this time the steward poured him a beer. He managed to drink half of it before his lack of sleep over the previous few days caught up with him.

With the saved hour on the return journey Heinrich was entering his apartment on Gloucester Place by 21:00. He dropped his bag in the bedroom and unbuttoned his dress uniform jacket. He carefully unbuttoned his shirt and slipped out the pages of notes he had compiled in the SAR. Placing them under a pile of clothes in a drawer was not the most secure hiding spot but he doubted he was going to get raided. He made his way back into the kitchen and poured himself a generous shot of bourbon. He rang Leigh as the bite of the alcohol kicked in.

"Hi."

"Hi. Are you back?"

"Yeah. Just got in. Listen, I know I'd offered to maybe have a meal but can we pass until tomorrow?"

"You're knackered aren't you?"

"Ah, I love that you use olde English words and yes, absolutely. Do you mind?"

"No Heinrich, not at all. Did you have a productive trip?"

"Yes, very good. How was your day?"

"Oh, just playing with my little toys as usual. Although some intriguing new possibilities seem to be revealing themselves, they're of no real use. To be honest with you I'm slightly disappointed. The person who suggested them should have known better. Maybe I'll try to explain it to you tomorrow at work?"

"Sounds good. I'll see you in the morning and thanks for allowing me to slide on dinner."

"Bye Heinrich."

***

The only difference with this call was that both ends of it were monitored in the UK SigInt centre, where operators logged the call details in two separate rooms. Almost simultaneously but entirely independent of each other they punched a key marking it as Routine Traffic, 'No Further Analysis Required'.

***

Despite his tiredness Heinrich spent long hours of the night lying awake, thinking of what he would have to do in the morning.

Not too far away, in her own apartment, Leigh also lay awake. Her mind had run all the scenarios that she could come up with. Each terrified and disappointed her in equal measure. It was insane, uncontrollable and completely impossible. There was no proof or rational reason to think it would work and even if it did there was no way to make it happen. Yet as she lay awake into the small hours of the morning the ideas and images of a world without the peaceful union of the Turner Church played through her mind.

She knew the history of the Old Book. The wars and factions, the killing and fighting. Could she really leave the world to that? But what if the Reich could be stopped? What if the ultimate evil befalling humanity could be bought off? At a cost of pain and death but ultimately allowing the good of the human race to win through. She knew her reality. Even if she did what she could and it went wrong, how much worse could it be? What could be achieved and what would it mean even to attempt it? Perhaps this was the time and the place that she had been destined for. She just wasn't sure if she had the courage to try.

40

07:30 Thursday, May 21, 2020 – London

"Professor Lippisch?"

Konrad was locking the door to his car and hadn't noticed two of Heinrich's SS troopers approaching him.

"Yes?"

"I'm sorry Sir, but Colonel Steinmann was wondering if he could have a word?"

"Certainly. Where is he?"

"Over in the detention centre with the Reid prisoner."

Konrad checked his watch display but didn't really look at it. He knew that Heinrich wouldn't be asking if it wasn't important and he also knew he had no choice. He picked up his briefcase and began to walk with the two men. Halfway to the building Konrad began to wonder why there were two escorts. The fear he felt gnawing at the back of his mind was something he had been used to for a long time. His lifestyle meant that he had always been vigilant and a little paranoid. Mostly he controlled the anxiety and continued to present the outward image of a confident and successful scientist. One of the SS men held the door open for him when they reached the detention centre's main entrance. Another soldier was waiting inside and escorted Konrad through the central corridor and then swiped him into the north-eastern cell block.

"Straight ahead. End of the corridor on the right."

He'd never had a need to visit the newly built facility before and so hesitated.

"Professor Lippisch? Just to the right at the end of the corridor," the soldier repeated.

Konrad entered the unfamiliar hallway and noted that the escort didn't follow him inside. He saw Heinrich appear out of a door a little way in front of him as he walked forward.

"Good morning Heinrich, what can I do for..." Konrad's cheery greeting stopped short when he looked at Heinrich's expression. He concentrated on keeping his gait steady and resolved to be as strong as he had always hoped he would be. He had often thought about the possibility of this moment and his greatest fear had been finding that he was a coward. Now, at least, he knew he wasn't. His fear dissolved and was replaced with calmness. He walked up to Heinrich and shook his outstretched hand.

Heinrich nodded his head gently toward the cell. Konrad looked into the small empty room. It wasn't Mary Reid's cell. It was his. He felt a terrible loneliness.

"I'm sorry Konrad."

"Me too Heinrich, me too. May I ask how?"

"Surveillance tapes, Marseille."

"Ah, I see."

"I'll need your swipe card, keys and other belongings."

"Of course." Konrad reached into his pockets and began to drop the trappings of his position into the evidence bag Heinrich held out for him. "I appreciate you doing it this way Heinrich. Thank you."

Konrad had to lower his head to enter the cell and then sat on the small fold-down cot attached to the wall.

"I'll need your laces, belt and tie as well. When I've gone you can change into the overalls there on the bed."

Konrad merely nodded and then thought to ask, "No uniform with a triangle?"

"No."

"Thank you again. Why so kind, Heinrich?"

Heinrich shrugged, "You seem like a good person. I see no reason to humiliate you."

"Be careful who you confide that to Heinrich. You'll be in a cell next to me." He shrugged off his tie and looked up at Heinrich with resigned eyes, "How long have I got?"

"I'm not sure. Berlin will confirm later," Heinrich lied.

"No trial? No appeal?"

"No need."

"Is there anyone up the food chain that I can talk to?"

"I only know one higher than the Reichsführer-SS and I'm not sure he'll take calls."

"I feel special already," Konrad gave a flat chuckle and added, "the Reichsführer himself? At least I know they considered keeping me for a moment or two."

"Is there anything I can get for you, do for you?" asked Heinrich.

"Tell me who knows and what the story will be?"

"No one in your team yet and I'm not quite sure what they'll be told."

Konrad was removing his laces from his shoes as he spoke, "Ah well, you can always borrow from history."

"Professor?"

"Never mind Heinrich. Just the fact that some of our brightest and best scientists and, yes, I can now immodestly include myself, have been whisked away to new posts almost overnight. Or at least that's what we were all told at the time. Of course it turned out that those new posts were ones they were tied to before being shot." He stood and removed his belt, "Here you go."

Heinrich almost said thank you but stopped himself. Instead he took the items and went to leave.

"Heinrich, who will take over from me?"

"Leigh," he said and he watched the refined features of Lippisch relax and smile in genuine warmth.

"Good. Not before time to be honest. She's been my protégé since she was a young under-graduate all those years ago. She'll do a great job," he hesitated and then added poignantly, "I wish I could see her to say goodbye."

Heinrich left the cell, closed the door and locked it. He checked through the observation window and watched solemnly as Konrad Lippisch began to weep.

When Heinrich got back to his office Peter Vogel was hovering outside his door. The Junior Officer stood to attention and saluted. "Colonel, I was wondering if I may have a word?"

"Of course, Peter. In fact, I was just about to call you, so well done on saving me the bother," Heinrich returned the salute and ushered him inside. "What's on your mind?" He put the evidence bag on a shelf, set Lippisch's briefcase to one side, sat behind his desk and expected the young man to sit down in the chair opposite but Vogel remained standing and looked a little embarrassed.

"Come along Peter, what's concerning you?"

"Well, it's Doctor Wilson Sir."

"Yes, what about her?"

"She came in here while you were in Berlin and asked to speak to Reid. She said it was important that she checked on the prisoner's reactions to the Projection. But she said it all had to be done straight away."

Heinrich frowned, "Didn't I tell you she was coming in?"

"Yes Sir, you did."

"So what's the issue?" Heinrich was immediately on guard that Peter may have overheard something that could have compromised Leigh.

"May I speak freely Sir?"

"Of course Peter." Heinrich dreaded what was coming.

"I think you need to speak to Doctor Wilson."

"Why's that?"

"She ignored our regulations and tasered the prisoner."

"Pardon!"

"She tasered the prisoner."

Heinrich was momentarily blindsided. He knew nothing of what Leigh had done and so decided to go on the offensive. "And how, Second Lieutenant, did she get a weapon into one of my cells?"

Vogel looked very uncomfortable. "She didn't declare it to me Sir. She just took it in."

"And what, she just used it on Reid?"

"No, not, um, well, yes."

"Make your mind up, yes or no?"

"Yes, she used it on Reid but in self-defence. The prisoner tried to attack her."

"Okay, let's stop right there Peter! Sit yourself down and tell me what happened."

Peter sat and began, "Well she and Reid were arguing from the moment they began to talk. Doctor Wilson was almost baiting her and eventually Reid tried to attack her. That's when she used the taser. Reid dropped like a stone and Doctor Wilson asked for me to come let her out. We had to clear up the cell and clean up Reid before we handcuffed her to the cot. I confiscated the taser and then Doctor Wilson went back in."

"So, Doctor Wilson took a weapon into a cell and although she shouldn't have it, it appears that it was just as well she did?"

Vogel said nothing and looked down at his feet.

"Well?" Heinrich barked the word.

"Yes Sir." Vogel sat straighter.

"Did you tell her there were no weapons allowed in?"

"No Sir."

"Did she manage to conduct her interview in the end?"

"Yes Sir."

"Well then," he said more relaxed, "no harm, no foul."

"I suppose so Sir."

"I suppose so too. Now, anything else?"

"She broke our camera."

Heinrich fought hard not to laugh at Peter's petulant tone. "Reid did?"

"No, Doctor Wilson did. When she discharged her taser the camera shorted out."

Heinrich took a moment to reflect on what Leigh had been up to. She had worked out a way to disable the camera and put the blame on Peter for not having stopped her in the first place. Genius. "Well, I'm sure the budget can stretch to a new camera. Let's not worry about that. Anything else?"

"No Sir," Peter said in a flat tone and looked decidedly dejected.

"Well, I have two things for you Peter. Firstly, well done on all your actions over the last few days. I've been very impressed. We'll let the incident with Doctor Wilson and her taser slide under the carpet of momentary lapse and say no more about it. I was actually very impressed by how you managed the arrival processing and initial handling of Reid. You and your team did well."

"Thank you Sir." Peter had perked up again.

"The second thing is that our prisoner quota has doubled. Rather like proverbial London buses. We have no one and now we have two at once. But I need you to make sure a few things happen." Heinrich flicked a notepad across to Peter and waited for him to get a pen out of his pocket.

"The prisoner is Professor Lippisch." Heinrich waited for a shocked Peter to ask questions but he didn't. He just looked calmly back at Heinrich waiting for more details.

"I want all of your people briefed that if the identity of our prisoner leaks, I will have the source of the leak taken out and shot. There is a team on the other side of this complex who do not know that their boss has been arrested. I need to figure out how to inform them and do not need the information pre-empted. Clear?"

Heinrich received a nod.

"Ring Pascal Debouchy down at Gestapo Central and ask him to assign a team to Lippisch's home address. He should have the arrest and seizure warrants already sent through from the Reichsführer's office."

"Do I assume Lippisch is not returning home anytime soon?"

"Correct. He'll be picked up for transfer over the weekend, not sure what time but Whitehall will let us know. Reid won't be getting picked up. Berlin's authorised us to handle her here. The execution is by firing squad in the central courtyard at dawn on Sunday. Select your firing party and get them down to the range. Run them through their drills. I don't want any mistakes Peter, nor do I want any treatment that is not beyond reproach for either of our inmates. Both of them have served the Reich with loyalty and devotion. The fact they're now in disgrace is neither here nor there. We owe one a dignified short stay and the other a dignified death. Yes?"

"Yes Sir."

"Lastly, you'll have to get in touch with either Bradford or Aberystwyth to find out if they can send over a disposal crew."

"Not Harrow Sir?"

"She worked there and they would have been her clean-up team. I don't think we should make them do that, do you?"

"No Sir, I suppose not."

"Ideally we'll want the corpse taken away immediately. Any questions?"

"No Colonel," said Peter as he flipped the notepad closed and stood ready to salute and leave.

"You don't want to know what Professor Lippisch is charged with?"

"Will it make a difference to how I treat him or what we do for him?"

"No."

"Then if it's all the same, no Sir, I don't." Peter saluted and Heinrich acknowledged it in the typical SS half-arm, relaxed manner from his seated position.

There was a buzzing and vibration from the evidence bag on the shelf as Peter turned to leave.

"Grab that will you?" asked Heinrich.

Peter reached into the bag, retrieved the ForeFone and handed it over. Heinrich saw it was a call from Professor Faber and realised he was probably calling to see why Lippisch wasn't at work yet. Heinrich nodded for Peter to leave and close the door behind him.

"Professor Faber, hello."

"Konrad?"

"No Professor. It's Heinrich Steinmann. Professor Lippisch will not be in. I'm afraid I have some news that may be difficult for both you and your team."

"Is he okay? Has he been in an accident?"

Heinrich hesitated slightly and that allowed Wolfgang to make the next logical assumption.

"Is he dead?"

'Not yet' thought Heinrich but actually said, "No Professor. No accident and not dead. Reichsführer Friedrichand asked me to speak to you directly rather than him phoning you."

There was a pause.

"Ah. I understand." The older man said, suddenly sounding all of his years.

"May I come over and see you?" asked Heinrich.

"Of course."

The line disconnected.

41

What's he charged with?"

"Crimes against the State," Heinrich said.

Wolfgang Faber actually tutted at him, twice. "My dear Colonel, we need to come up with a better excuse than that."

"That's the official charge Professor." Heinrich made a show of the palms of his hands, as if to say he had no more to offer.

"Yes, well, that's all very good for the Gestapo but what's the real reason?"

Heinrich merely shook his head slowly.

"Pathetic is what it truly is. How many times are we going to take our best and brightest away?"

"Professor, I must caution..."

Faber cut him off, "Do NOT dare to caution me young man. I've been around quite long enough to know when and how I can criticise my Party and my Nation and this is one of those times. It is pathetic!" He slapped his hand down on an overflowing in-tray sending papers cascading onto the floor behind his desk. The professor watched them fall before continuing, "It's not the first time and it won't be the last. Leave aside the fact that one of my good friends and colleagues has been ripped away from me, this will set our work back considerably."

"Please Professor," Heinrich said it in as gentle a way as he could, "please, don't put me into an even more difficult place."

The Head of Laser Research for the Reich Security Directorate's Technical Division visibly sighed and his shoulders slumped. "What age are you?"

"Pardon?"

"Indulge me, what age are you?"

"Thirty-nine."

"Well, when you were being born I was at the Arcand Institute in Canada. I assume you've heard of that?"

Heinrich merely nodded.

"I'd started there in 1978 and eventually, around about the time you were celebrating your first birthday, we matured the technology of weaponised Lasers." The professor tutted again, "I can see from your face, you're wondering why I'm mentioning this."

Heinrich gave a small half-shrug of his shoulders.

"Well, let me enlighten you. Scientists had been trying to turn Lasers into weapons since the start of the Reich with no success. It was the University of Toronto that were finally making progress and that's why the Arcand Institute was founded over there in the fifties. Professor Dr-Ing Becker was the project lead. He was an outstanding scientist, the son of a respected General and he'd led his team for over fifteen years. They were on the brink of a breakthrough in the late sixties when he was removed overnight." The professor snapped his fingers to emphasise his point. "It put the research back ten or fifteen years." He shook his head, "I really thought we'd progressed but here we are nearly sixty years later and doing the same thing."

"What do you expect me to say Professor?"

"Nothing. That's the point. We all say nothing. We might fume and rant in private but we say nothing when it matters. We didn't before and we won't now."

They sat in silence and Heinrich waited while Faber calmed a little. He considered the cluttered desk and wondered how the man coped on a daily basis. There was no free space at all. The desk phone poked out of a stack of report files like an island in a sea of brown cardboard waves. Heinrich surreptitiously looked around the rest of the room, or at least all of it that he could see, without making it obvious. The office could have been quite spacious had it not been for the jumble of papers, books and old briefcases scattered randomly on bookshelves, spare chairs and across the floor. There were at least four pairs of glasses that he could see, the insides of what resembled a pop-up toaster in the corner and what seemed to be at least two removalist boxes with various magazines spilling out of their open tops. The wall behind the professor had a pin board that was a blur of notes and cuttings, the one to Heinrich's left had a blackboard with a swathe of scribbled equations and what appeared to be a shopping list chalked on it. Remarkably the blackboard on the right hand wall was clean and unmarked.

Eventually Faber sighed yet again and said, "I suppose it's only because our beloved security services don't change their ways that we are all so well versed in coping." He aimed another look of disgust at Heinrich, shook his head in disappointment and said, "Well, we shall need to make a start."

"What do you need me to do?"

"Firstly we get Doctor Wilson in here. Your organisation's responsible for this mess so you're going to tell her why she's just been appointed Acting Director. I don't envy you your task. You have no idea how incredibly close Konrad and she are," he hesitated, "were."

"After that?" asked Heinrich.

"Other than telling her that you have her mentor and friend in custody, I need nothing from you Colonel. You and your ilk have done quite enough. My scientists and I shall cope and we shall determine the best way for our team to handle our loss." Glaring once more at Heinrich, Faber reached for the desk phone and called Leigh.

***

Tears streamed down her face and she sobbed with silent gasps. Her body heaved with each new wave of misery. She tried to process what was happening, what it meant, how it would resolve but all she could hear in her head, pounding, over and over, was Heinrich's last sentence, "We have him in custody."

Professor Faber patted her on the shoulder and left the room. Heinrich remained. He walked over to her and said quietly, "Leigh."

***

"Francine?"

"Yes Professor?"

"Can you ask all of your colleagues to be in the briefing room please?"

"Of course Professor, what time for?"

"10:00 please. Although we shan't start without everyone being there."

***

She remained bent forward in the chair, almost hugging her knees.

"Leigh."

"Get away from me Heinrich."

"Leigh, please, come on."

She raised her head and looked almost manic. "Come on! Really!" Her voice was shrill. "Come on! That's what you're going to say to me? Come on! You self-centred prick! How could you do this?" She stood up and faced him almost toe to toe. "How could you do this?" she shouted.

He looked down and said nothing.

"Answer me!" She yelled it.

"I had no choice."

"Yes you did. You could have warned him, you could have warned me. You could have..." She gasped for air again as more tears fell.

"I couldn't Leigh. I really couldn't. You know I couldn't."

"But Heinrich," she gasped a little more shallowly, "he's my friend." She wailed the last word in a heartbroken, choked, child-like way. His heart ached for her loss and all he could do was reach out for her and pull her close. She collapsed into him, buried her head into his shoulder and clung to him tightly whilst she continued to weep for Konrad.

***

She knew he was watching her. He sat just under the bus shelter structure but she stood outside of it, wanting to feel anything to take away the numbness. The smoke felt good as it burnt her throat and the slight drizzle stung her face.

"So what now?" Her voice sounded flat and she knew her eyes were still red.

"You have to go into a briefing with Professor Faber and the rest of the team. I think you're all going to decide how to handle things from here on."

"Yes, I know that Heinrich. I meant about Konrad?"

"Berlin have arranged for transport to pick him up on the weekend. He'll go to a debrief facility."

"And when they've taken all they can out of that sweet, gentle man?"

"He'll go to a camp."

Leigh was rather surprised that he hadn't even attempted to sugar-coat it. "What, no SS lies? Not even a lame attempt to make me feel better?"

"What'd be the point? You didn't ask me because you didn't know the answer."

"I assume he's being held for his homosexuality."

It was Heinrich's turn to be surprised, "How do you know that?"

"I told you, he's my friend Heinrich. For a long time he's been my friend. He told me." She finished her cigarette and looked up at the sky, allowing the drizzle to soak her eyes. It was cold and soothing to her still flushed skin.

"Leigh?" Heinrich said her name with a panic in his voice.

She snapped round to him, "What is it?"

"Does he know you're a Turner?"

"No! No, of course not." She could see real concern in his face. She knew it was for her safety and that touched her. Rather more gently she said, "It's okay. No one knows apart from you and me. I almost told him once but to be honest I thought about what might happen if he was ever arrested. So no, he doesn't know." She watched him relax a little. "Will he go to Sachsenhausen?"

"Sooner or later."

She thought about lighting another cigarette but decided against it. "So what happens now?"

"Well, you have to go and brief your team with Professor Faber" he checked the watch on his ForeFone, "in ten minutes."

"Oh, that's going to be a mess. Especially Franci. She loves Konrad."

"All your team seems close, he must have been a great boss."

"No Heinrich, I mean she loves him. Truly, madly, deeply type of love. You may have noticed, she's not backward in coming forward and at some point, I think it was in Toronto but it might have been even earlier, she propositioned him. He turned her down. Apparently, according to her, he did it in the sweetest and most polite way but it didn't change the fact that she had fallen for him. The amount of nights she and I have downed bottles of red discussing the whole sorry saga."

"Did she know he was..."

"Eine Tunte?" The words were harsh and her tone was hardening again.

"No Leigh, I'd never use a word like that!"

"It's what you were thinking, anyway yes, of course she did. She never said a word to him or anyone else, apart from me, but, yes, of course she knew."

"Anyone else?"

"Why Heinrich, you planning on taking them in for failure to declare?" She said it too quickly and regretted it as soon as it was out.

"No I'm fucking not!" His reply seethed with anger and as he stood she took a step backwards.

"Hein..."

"Enough Leigh! All I've had this morning is people having a fucking go at me. I'm not the bad guy. I actually think the way I handled Konrad's detention was as gentle and respectful as it could be. I don't expect a pat on the back but I certainly don't expect sarcasm and snide remarks from you. We have a chance to do something about this, to negate Konrad's arrest, Mary's execution, all of it and all I get is, am I planning on arresting more people? Well, no, I'm not!" He stopped and there was only the faint sound of the drizzle against the ashtrays and chairs.

Her head was bowed and her shoulders hunched in defence against his words. She looked up at him and said, "I'm sorry."

They stood in silence and she decided to light another smoke. By about halfway through he had calmed and said, "I'm sorry too." She looked at him and smiled contritely.

Exhaling a long stream of smoke into the drizzle she asked quietly, "Mary's being executed?"

"Yes. Dawn, Sunday."

"We need to talk about what she said."

"I want to do more than talk."

She stepped a little closer and looked at him. "But Heinrich, I've told you over and over there is no way to do what you're thinking about. Even if we knew where to go and when, even if we could determine what to say and how to say it and even if it meant that faith became disjointed like Mary wants and the Reich never rose, even if all of that was possible we can't do it. Berlin has the ultimate off switch."

"Not anymore."

"What?"

"There's a way around it."

"How?" She was incredulous.

"Look, we need time to talk about this and time to plan what to do and time to act but, we can't do it here. You're due inside in minutes."

"Right, well, I reckon the rest of today's going to be a mess. Not much work's going to get done but I suspect a lot of energy will be spent talking things through. People are going to need time to come to terms with Konrad's arrest. But I'm going to suggest to Wolfgang that we stand the whole team down for tomorrow. Give them a long weekend to get their heads around what's happened."

"So we can talk tomorrow?"

"Yes we could, but I was thinking about dinner tonight?"

"Okay." He said it hesitantly.

"You don't want to?"

"No. I mean yes, I do. It's just I'd have thought being in my company would have been the last thing you would have wanted."

"Heinrich, I'm mad and angry and upset but not really with you. You're the first person I've been able to talk to properly since my parents passed. I'd like to spend time with you, if it's alright?"

"I'd like to as well. Do you want to go out somewhere?"

"Mmmm, I'm not sure I'd feel right going out but I guess we'll have to. You said it would raise suspicions if you came to mine."

"No it's fine," he said rather too quickly. "I mean, I'll take you out but going to yours is okay. It would have been weird on Sunday if I'd just dropped round but that was because we hadn't even met before. We're colleagues now."

"That's all it's been?"

"Pardon?"

"Sunday night. We met on Sunday. It's not even a week."

"A lot can happen in a week." He said, smiling at her.

She held his gaze. Once more she felt the reactions that she had each and every time she made eye contact with him. Her stomach jumped again and she felt the frisson of a tingle running down her spine. She forced herself to breathe deeply. Her emotions were shredded and it wasn't even ten in the morning. "Yes, I suppose it can." She checked her own ForeFone watch display, "I've got to get back in," she turned and began to walk quickly toward the entrance steps. "I'll see you at 19:30 tonight." she called over her shoulder.

"No Leigh. Hang on."

She stopped and turned back, "What?"

"Bring Francine over to my office when you knock off for the day."

"Why?"

"So I can get both of you into see Konrad."

She bit hard on her lip to stop from crying again, nodded at him and walked away.

42

19:25 Thursday, May 21, 2020 – London

Hi," he said, a little breathless.

"Hi, come in." She stood back and opened the door, "You okay?"

"Yes, I think so. That's quite a staircase." He walked past her down the small hallway to the living room.

"You're meant to be a SS Officer."

"You're meant to have a lift."

"Oh, it's not that bad."

"Didn't notice you coming down to walk me up."

"Now, now! I had to press a button to open the door for you so fair's fair."

"I hope you like this?" He turned and offered her the bottle of wine he had brought. He silently thanked himself that he had gone home, had a shower and put on a decent pair of trousers, an open necked shirt and a casual jacket. At least he looked reasonably attired. Leigh, on the other hand, looked simply stunning to him. She wore a cream coloured knitted tee-shirt over a pair of faded-to white-in-places blue jeans and a pair of low-heeled suede boots. A plain gold necklace with a small golden Celtic knot pendant and matching stud earrings were the only jewellery she wore.

"Oh, Cabernet Mitos, very nice, yes I like it very much, thank you. Please, sit." She gestured towards the sofa, "I'll just open this, back in a sec."

He looked about the tastefully furnished apartment. The room he was in had been split into two by clever placement of furniture and formed a dining area and a living room. There were two small hallways off to either side that he assumed led to bathrooms and bedrooms. Beyond the dining area and where Leigh had disappeared to, was the kitchen. He slipped his jacket off and wandered across to the bookshelf. He saw a lot of academic volumes with titles he struggled to understand, a few biographies, a couple of fiction classics and a half-shelf full of Katrin Lieberman novels. Picking out one of the mathematic textbooks he flicked through it hoping to recognise at least something familiar.

"See anything you'd like to borrow?"

He turned with book in hand and watched as she came back in from the kitchen with two glasses of the Cabernet. "Eh, would it offend you if I passed?"

"What, on the wine?"

"No, on the offer of the book loan." He returned the book to the shelf and took the glass offered.

"You could get into this," she gestured to the academic volumes, "you're not a stupid man."

"Thanks for the compliment but each to their own."

He sat on the sofa and she took the small matching chair that faced it at an offset angle. They both sipped the wine and waited for the other to talk.

"I just..." they both started at the same time. Heinrich held his hand out for her to proceed.

"I just wanted to say thank you," she said softly.

He placed his finger to his lips and then pointed to the ceiling. He retrieved his jacket, reached into the inside pocket and took out a small, thin device and set it on the table. It looked like a mobile phone and he reached down and depressed the centrally mounted button on its facia. After watching the LED display for a few seconds he pressed the button again and put the box back in his pocket.

"We're good. I wouldn't have imagined your apartment was bugged but I thought it would be wise to check. I borrowed that little gadget from work," he said as matter-of-factly as he could but he hoped she would be impressed at his forethought. When he looked up she just looked amused and he felt foolish. "You knew it was bug free didn't you?" he said.

"Mmm," she hummed and nodded to emphasise the point, "I work in one of the most sophisticated scientific labs in the Reich. Right next door to Oscar is the best equipped electronics lab anywhere outside of the Japanese Islands. So yeah, I might have managed to make a simple detector that runs a continuous bug sweep for me." She paused and he looked sheepishly at her.

"Is that how you got your hands on a taser as well?" He frowned in mock anger.

"Yeah. And it worked, didn't it? No cameras, no recordings." She smiled at him before continuing, "But seriously Heinrich, thank you. It's quite sweet that you went to that trouble," she said it with no hint of sarcasm but he looked sceptical. "I mean it, thank you for that and thank you for getting Franci and me into see Konrad. It meant an awful lot to us, and him. It was a kind thing to do."

"You're welcome, as was Franci. I also meant what I said to her. I'll try to get her into see him again on Saturday." He paused. "If we're all still here on Saturday." He leant forward and his face became serious. He was about to launch into a discussion about Mary and all that she had said.

Leigh waved her hand at him, "Not yet Heinrich, let's not talk about that just yet. Let's eat first?"

"Okay, yeah sure, that's good." He relaxed back into the sofa, "What are we having?"

"Well, glad you asked. I looked up roast fillet of new season lamb with fennel and liquorice sauce."

"Wow, that sounds amazing."

"Yes it does!" she nodded emphatically and then shook her head slowly, "Except it turns out it takes quite a lot of time and effort and needs a lot of things I didn't have, like lamb, fennel, liquorice," she paused, "culinary skills."

He laughed out loud. "Okay then, so we're having...?"

"Bratwurst sausage simmered in beer and onions accompanied by oven chips and instant gravy," she said enthusiastically.

"Love it. Sounds even better than that bad idea of lamb and liquorice. Can I help?"

271

"Come talk to me while I cook."

They spoke of normal things and laughed and drank more wine, burnt some of the Bratwurst and laughed again. She wanted to know more about him. He told her that he used to play football and, after a lot of pressing him for details, he begrudgingly admitted that he had been selected for the Waffen-SS national team. Unfortunately his playing days had ended after the stabbing. She told him about her love for dancing and how, while her love for it remained, her dancing days had ended with the damage to her leg. She discovered he was an avid reader and he was surprised to learn that despite her mother's talent and her own ability to sing, she had never played an instrument. They talked and laughed and ate and drank and forgot the day that had been and the day that was coming.

***

She set the two coffees on the small table and sat beside him on the sofa. "Tell me your thoughts Heinrich?"

"About?"

"About Mary Reid."

He reached forward and took a sip of his coffee. "Now?"

"Yes, now."

He thought for a moment, hesitant because of the enormity of the conversation they were about to have.

"I thought she was insane at first. On reflection, and I've done a lot of that in the last few days, I think she was still in shock. I know she was really confused over how we'd identified her so quickly. The incident with the Turner prisoners pushed her over an edge that I think she'd been on for a while. But as for the ideas about the religions, well," he hesitated, "I thought it was brilliant. I mean, I know she was only talking hypothetically and she doesn't know what we have access to but," he stopped.

"Go on, say what you're thinking," she encouraged.

"Your parents taught me that we don't force things."

"I know," she agreed, "they taught you what they taught me; the wheel turns at its own pace. God places you where you need to be and sends the people he needs to send." Leigh repeated the

272

sentence they had first said together on Sunday night in the Todt cafeteria.

"Exactly, so I thought about what Mary did and what happened to her mind and how, in the midst of her confusion, she came up with an idea that on face-value seems insane. But like I said, she doesn't know what we have access to. What if we're in the right place now? What if the wheel has turned to where it's meant to be and Mary is the person that's been sent?"

Leigh shrugged in response.

They sat in silence, drinking their coffees, each contemplating the reality that they now found themselves in. Eventually Leigh put her cup down and leant sideways into him. He moved his arm around her shoulder and she laid her head on his chest. They stayed like that, comfortable, secure and lost in their own thoughts. When finally Heinrich moved to put his cup down she had to prop herself up and then sit upright. She reached out to him and hugged him hard as he went to lay back. She raised her face and met his gaze. She felt again the light, yet intense kick in her stomach and the tingling sensation across her whole body. She looked to his lips and back to his eyes. He bent his head forward. As his lips touched hers she opened her mouth slightly and felt the heat of him. Their tongues touched delicately and lightly and she sucked him into her mouth, gently but insistently. She heard him moan a low, feral sound and felt his arms tighten around her, surrounding her, holding her, protecting her. She felt his mouth, his breath, his chest against her and she twisted so she could lie back on the sofa. She pulled him down and felt his kisses grow more passionate. She responded in kind and was aware of his strength pressing against her, holding her pinned. Somewhere deep in her consciousness she knew that she had never felt like this before. The fairy tales she had read as a little girl spoke of first kisses between soulmates but she had never believed in them. She had never had any faith that there was a 'someone' out there for her. But now she was being convinced. He ended the kiss and pulled away a little.

She leant up, holding his gaze and gently, very tenderly kissed him again. Her mouth parted and this time she let her tongue explore his mouth and he bit gently on her lower lip. She pressed hard into him whilst his tongue circled the tip of hers and then ran across her teeth, exploring the inside of her lips. He drew back and ran his hands through her hair, grazing his fingertips against her scalp. She closed her eyes and rhythmically moved under him, sighing as she did. He moved her hair aside from her neck and placed his mouth next to her ear. She tensed in anticipation that he would kiss her or blow lightly against her skin but instead he gently breathed in. The rush of air was something she hadn't experienced before. It was intense and caused her to respond by straightening her back and allowing a small moan from her lips.

"Let's go to bed," she managed to say.

43

fterwards, they slept contentedly in each other's arms. At some point he woke and she was curled up in front of him. He leant forward and kissed the nape of her neck. She murmured something intelligible. He repeated the kiss and she moved to nestle her back against him. When he kissed her a third time she rolled over and faced him. She looked comfortable and at peace. He bent his head to kiss her again. She smiled and stroked his forehead, "Are you okay?"

"Oh yes, more than okay. You?"

She responded with a soft hum and nuzzled into him. They dozed off again.

It was gone 03:00 when he awoke. He eased himself up out of the bed but as gently as he tried, she woke as well.

"Heinrich, what is it?"

"Nothing. I'm just going to get a drink of water. Would you like one?"

She sat up and yawned and stretched, "No, but a coffee and cigarette seem like a good idea."

He was dressed in her bathrobe and she had on jeans and an old, friendly woolly jumper. She sat at the outdoor setting on her roof garden and smoked while he stood gazing out across the city.

"Heinrich?" She spoke quietly in a mellowed tone that barely carried to him on the other side of the small garden. He looked across to her but said nothing and waited for her to continue.

"I'm scared."

"About us?"

"No. Not that. I'm scared to ask you what you meant when you said that Berlin wouldn't be able to stop a Projection. I need to ask you what you meant, but I'm scared. Terrified, in fact. This whole thing's been a game of what-ifs in my mind since I spoke to Mary because I always had the safety net of Berlin. I knew we couldn't actually do anything. It made it safe. I couldn't see a way round the security protocols and I couldn't see them signing off on a Projection that's designed to wipe them off the face of the planet."

"I know."

"It's the same reason I never asked you about what you did in Berlin when you were there." She finished the smoke, crushed the butt in the ashtray and joined him to look out over the cityscape. She slipped her hand in his, "I suppose I have to ask so, go on then, what did you mean?" She sounded defeated, like she had struggled not to come to this point but that it was inevitable.

He led her back downstairs and took a seat at the small dining table. He was about to start talking when she interrupted.

"Hang on, stop. Are we going to sit up the rest of the night and discuss this?" She had looked at her ForeFone and it was 03:21.

"I suppose so, why?"

"Right! Shower, dressed, pots of coffee. Then at least we can sit and talk for a few hours and feel more focussed."

"You're stalling." He said it plainly and without criticism.

"I know, but pander to me. This may be the last chance you get." She winked and sprung up before adding, "We get to share the shower."

It was almost 04:30 by the time they finished with each other in the shower and got dressed. Leigh made toast as well as coffee and Heinrich rustled up some microwave scrambled eggs. Climbing the spiral staircase they emerged into the silver sphere of the pre-dawn light. They decided not to spoil breakfast with talk about plans for an uncertain future that would alter the past and destroy the present. They simply enjoyed the moment.

After they had eaten they sat still and watched the first yellow rays breach the horizon. Leigh sighed deeply, "Did you ever know where my mother's phrase came from?"

"Which?"

"The years leave a mark."

"Not really. I just thought it was a family saying."

"It's from a Haiku."

"A what?"

"A Haiku. It's a Japanese type of poetry but when it's butchered into English it doesn't work as well. There are lots of rules about subject and seasons and all other stuff but the main thing is that it's made up of three lines and seventeen syllables. It's meant to read, five-seven-five."

"I'm sorry, I've never even heard of them before."

"Didn't you get a literary Masters from Oxford?" she teased.

"Yes, in *English* Lit, there wasn't much Japanese on the curriculum."

"Probably would have been if you'd gone to Cambridge and got a proper degree," she said in a mock sotto-voce.

He laughed and stuck his middle finger up at her. "So what's a hack oou then?" He butchered the pronunciation deliberately.

"A Haiku," she corrected and playfully raised her eyes at him, "they were a pastime of ours, my mum, dad and me. I even had a cat called Haiku."

"Did he only have three legs?"

"Oh ha-ha! No, but he had seven toes on his front paws and five on his hind."

"You're serious? Was it a cat or a genetic experiment?"

"Aw! Don't be mean. He was lovely. We got him from Cornwall. He was a polydactyl cat."

"Wow! Well, I do learn something new every day."

"Yeah, most days I bet," she grinned at him and he feigned hurt. "So you never heard the full version of the poem?"

"No."

She nodded at the climbing sun and said, "The years leave a mark, through the Swastika's winter, till the sun rises."

"Your mum wrote that?"

"Yeah."

They returned downstairs and, sitting together on the sofa, Heinrich told her what had happened in Berlin. He took her through his visit to the Reichsführer, the Archives, what he had looked for and what he had found. Finally, he explained what he wanted to do. She argued and he countered. He argued and she countered but in the end, after more than an hour of to and fro, it came down to a few simple questions.

"If we do this Heinrich and nothing changes, then what's the point?"

"The point is we'll have tried."

"And Konrad goes to his death?"

"Yes. And Mary."

"No harm to her, but I'm more concerned for my friend."

"If we don't try they both go to their death. If we don't try we're stuck in a world with no hope of redemption and future generations are damned before they're born."

"And if we try and succeed?"

"You said yourself Leigh, nobody knows what happens. At best we find ourselves in a world of peace and harmony again."

She nodded her head and took his hand, "And at worst, everything is destroyed. Utterly destroyed. We'd rip the fabric of the planet apart."

"Isn't that what you said the physicists that made the Reich's first nuclear weapon worried about?"

"Yes, but they were wrong."

"What's to say you're not?"

She shrugged, "Maybe that isn't the worst anyway. Maybe the worst is that we really do succeed. Me and you, Leigh and Heinrich, cause two thousand years of warfare and death. How's that feel?"

"Honestly? I can't say how it'd feel because we probably won't know a thing about it. Our lives would be forfeit."

"Forget about us; we might kill hundreds of thousands, millions even."

"And how many have the Reich killed so far? Isn't there a balance sheet in play here?"

"What, you're saying that if we kill less than they have then we're winning?" She was getting tense.

He stopped and said nothing for a long moment. "I don't want to argue Leigh. I want to know that you'll do this with me. I can't do it alone."

"I'm scared."

He reached out to her and she snuggled into his chest again. He spoke quietly, "So am I. But maybe that's why we're here, together. I think it comes down to three questions. Do you think Mary's right about needing less certainty? Do you think that saves us from an all-powerful Reich?"

She bit the inside of her cheek to stop the tears from coming, "Yes, probably," she bit harder, "to both." She maintained control of her voice and her tears. "That's only two. What's the third?"

"If you believe we can do something that just might reset this world and we don't try, then when they take Konrad, will you be able to live with yourself?"

She stood up and removed one of the seat cushions. Reaching down she eased a flap of material away from the side of the upholstery. Easing her hand further down into the guts of the sofa she retrieved a wooden box. He watched intrigued as she opened it and then he sighed as he saw. She lifted her family's Wheel of the Messengers out and offered it to him. He set it down carefully on the table.

"Can we say the Creed together before we go?"

Part Three

A Time for Peace

and

A Time for War

44

He drove them both back to Todt, stopping first at his apartment so he could change into uniform and retrieve some items. It was a busy morning in the city so the trip out to the Isle of Dogs took an age but they passed most of it in silence.

He double flashed his headlights when he turned off Eastferry Road. The guards on the gate had grown familiar to his sleek, black BMW and waved him through without an ID check. They saluted as he passed under the raised gate and he returned a nod in their direction.

"You know you're speeding?" she asked him.

"Marginally."

"And no one is going to stop you and have a word?"

"I'm Colonel Steinmann of the Allgemeine-SS, Special Investigations and Security Directorate. Who in the whole of the Todt Laboratories Complex is going to rebuke me?"

"I suppose I should be glad."

"Why so?" he said as he pulled into the closest reserved spot next to the 'Jewel' steps.

"Because that's the same reason no one's going to ask why you and I are going into Oscar when the rest of the team is stood down for the day."

She looked to see if Corporal Dieter Fischer was on duty as they passed the Wehrmacht security detail prior to reaching the

Tubes, but she could see neither him nor young Private Lukas. She knew that meant that their shift was over and Dieter would probably be at home with his beloved Margarethe. She had a deep and sudden pain in her heart and a solid weight in the pit of her stomach.

Heinrich noticed her frown. "Leigh, are you okay?"

"Yeah, I'm fine. Just… Never mind. I'm fine."

They exited the lifts and padded along the rubber walkway. The inner security door was opened for them before they reached it and the soldier on duty stood and saluted Heinrich. He returned the compliment and said briskly, "Carry on."

Leigh walked a little ahead of him as she headed down towards Oscar. Every other lab she passed was busily getting on with their specific fields of study and experimentation. They would be briefed on Konrad's departure in due course but for now they had no knowledge of what had occurred so she had to smile and say 'Hi' and nod at the few people who passed her in the corridor. She tried desperately not to think of what might happen to each and every one of them if she and Heinrich managed to do what they were here for.

He came up alongside her and pushed open the heavy-duty PVC doors. The motion sensors detected them and turned on the lights as they walked into the main lab. She led them across to the cleanroom, through it and on to the High Powered Laser Lab. Leigh swiped her card and keyed in her security code to the door and waited for Heinrich to do the same. Instead he stayed behind her.

"Heinrich?"

"What?" he asked with a tinge of surprise to his voice.

"You need to swipe your access card and enter your code to get into the HP-Lab."

"But I don't have access down here."

She frowned at him, "You're kidding, right? This is a double entry security door. You watched me and Franci swipe to get you through here on Monday. You watched my whole team double swipe to get us in here for the Reid Projections."

"No I didn't Leigh."

"You did, you must have. You're head of project security, how do you not know this?" Her voice was rising.

"I told you, the Wehrmacht secure the property, I don't have jurisdiction over the real estate."

"You are fucking kidding me!" She said it with force and noticed he looked rather shocked. 'Good,' she thought before she added, "We've spent all of this time worrying about what we're going to do and how it's all going to play out and how we have the means to run a Projection and you didn't even think of how we're going to get into the lab?"

"I honestly didn't see you and Franci swipe in here," He said it calmly.

"How could you not, you were standing right there!"

"I'm sorry Leigh but I didn't and as for the Reid Projections, the door was opened for me, I just walked through."

"Well, that's great. We're stuffed before we start." She looked down and shook her head.

"Hang on, I have Konrad's swipe card as well as his Thule key," he said.

"Great," her voice was heavily sarcastic, "only two things wrong with that; one, you need his security access number..."

"He's across in a cell I control. I can go ask him," he interrupted.

She waited for him to finish, "Yeah you could, except the second flaw is that Wolfgang had a set of procedures to carry out yesterday after Konrad's arrest. One of those is to inform your Wehrmacht buddies upstairs that Konrad's access was to be turned off. With immediate effect."

"But when we talked about all of this earlier this morning you didn't mention that," he said, finally sharing her exasperation with the situation.

"I didn't need to. His Thule activation key that you took off him and kept is a physical device. If you have it you have it. His access card wasn't important. I assumed you had access." She stopped and looked at him. She knew she was red in the face again and she knew it wasn't his fault. But, it wasn't hers either. "Ah, sod it! Let's go get a coffee," she said.

He poured two cups from the percolator that she had prepared and they sat side by side on stools at one of the benches in the main Oscar Lab space.

"I'm sorry Leigh. This is my fault." He held his hand out flat on the benchtop and she laid hers over it.

"Don't worry about it. I should have realised. You did tell me that you didn't have control over the physical security. I should have asked if you had lab access." She took a mouthful of her coffee and winced. "Did you put any sugar in this?"

"No, there wasn't any in the bowl."

"No, sorry, I meant the little saccharin tablets I use? They're in a little dispenser next to the percolator?"

He just shrugged so she got up and wandered over to the little bit of bench that was the lab's coffee making area.

"Bugger it."

"I'll assume that's a 'no' then?"

"Yeah. Back in a minute, I've got some in my office drawer." She walked off to the rear of the lab.

When she came back she grabbed a spoon and sat down beside him.

He looked round and smiled a half-hearted, apologetic smile at her. "All good?"

She waved the little dispenser in her hand and popped one into her coffee. Stirring the liquid slowly she said slightly under her breath, "Yeah, all good." Then she reached into her pocket and produced a plain white plastic card and set it on the bench.

"What's that?"

"That Heinrich, is a gift courtesy of the struggle for women's equality."

"What?" he swivelled to face her.

"My access card didn't work on Monday. So I was given a temporary one and they sent mine back down to me when it was fixed. I should have returned this but Franci scared away the young soldier before I had a chance."

He looked puzzled, "Scared away?"

"Don't ask. But what with the rest of this week being a blur I forgot about it. I just found it in my drawer when I went to get my sweeteners."

"That's nice, but it doesn't help. It's only a temp swipe with your details on it. You can't swipe in twice with the one set of details."

"Mmm, yes I'd agree that would normally be the case. But my friend Dieter gave me this and he didn't want to delay me while he coded a temp one. He also trusts me because we're friends. So he just gave me one of the security detail's cards."

Heinrich had been halfway through taking a drink from his cup. He held the position like he had been frozen. Slowly he put the cup back down and turned to her.

"That's a security detail pass card?"

She just nodded, then held her face towards him and winked. He leant over and kissed her.

They left their drinks and returned to the secure door. Leigh swiped her card and keyed in her numeric code. She handed the security detail's pass card to Heinrich.

"Be my guest," she said.

"Why thank you." When he swiped it, the door registered a second authorised access request and clicked open

She led him through to the far end of the lab and into the small hallway that led to the Thule room. As she put her hand out to open the opaque sliding doors, he put his hand on her shoulder and turned her around, "Are you sure?" he asked.

"No. Not at all, are you?"

"No."

"Well then, that's unanimous." She breathed deeply, reached up and kissed him. They parted again and she said, "Heinrich, I've spent all my life working towards something. I believe you were sent to me to make that something happen. So no, I'm not sure but yes, we're doing this and we're doing it right now."

They used Konrad's Thule key and initiated the Window. When it reached stabilisation and hung motionless, the steady circular ring of purple light edging the flat silver disc, Leigh reached forward and entered the Berlin override code. "Well, I suppose we're about to find out if this actually works."

They both held their breath and the image on the screen blanked out.

"So far so good," she said, "now have you decided which year to go for?"

Heinrich knew the place he needed to go to and the day and the time but none of the Gospels and none of the research conducted by the Archive's staff had ever agreed on what year the incident happened. Most put it between AD 26 and 33. He knew when it was in relation to the heralding of Jesus as the Messiah by the Pharisees, Sadducees and Essenes but that didn't help. No one could agree on what year that had happened in either. It was going to be a case of trial and error.

He pulled the papers out from his uniform jacket and set them on the console. He read from his notes, "The Gospel according to Caiaphas says, 'When dusk reached the shores on the shortest day, He crossed over by boat to His home in Capernaum. One of the synagogue officials named Jairus came up, and on seeing Him, implored Him earnestly, saying, 'My little daughter is at the point of death; please come and lay Your hands on her, so that she will get well and live.' And lo the Master said that he would come.' Let's just start at December 21, AD 26, 14:15 GMT, coordinates are 32 degrees 52 minutes 49.07 seconds north, 35, 34 and 28.6 east."

She turned to a secondary keyboard and punched in the numbers, then adjusted a set of controls and flicked on various other switches. The lights in the room dipped.

"What's going on?" he asked.

"It's a power drain. Other than theoretical testing, we've never tried to go this far back, or even a tenth of this far back. The power requirements are a bit of an unknown."

The lights brightened, flickered, dipped and then brightened once more. They steadied but at a dimmer intensity than usual. The image on the far wall began to show, faded at first but then became stronger. After a few minutes, the image stabilised and the lights in the room brightened a little more. They were looking down, almost vertically, onto a small jetty. Leigh panned around to the left and right, and save for a lone child playing in the dirt of a track, the scene was empty.

"It's not it Leigh."

"How do you know? We only just got here."

"Because some of the other Gospels talk about a press of people waiting for Him on the shore."

"Maybe He's late? It's still quite bright, perhaps the sunset times are a bit off."

"No. Let's go forward."

She shut the Projection down and the lights in the room brightened back up. Heinrich watched as the Window spun down. "Why have you shut it down?" he asked her, concerned that something had gone wrong.

"We need to go forward a year, you said so yourself."

"Can't we just jump to the right time like you did for Reid?"

"It's too big a gap. You can't move an active Window more than twenty-four hours in a single jump. We'd have to wait for me to enter three hundred and sixty-five separate command sequences. It's going to be quicker to do it this way." She started to initiate the Window again and once more the lights in the room reacted but more intensely than the first time. He noticed the worried look on her face but left her to concentrate on entering the data. They went forward to AD 27. This time the scene was overcast, grey and fine sheets of rain poured down. Not even a lone child was visible.

Leigh shut the Window down just as a light bulb at the far end of the room popped and went out. "This isn't great."

"What's the problem?" he asked knowing that he was unlikely to understand it even when she told him.

"To initiate a Projection takes a lot of power. The further back the more power. One of the reasons it worked so well in Toronto was that we had a direct feed from the hydro stations at Niagara. Here, we draw from the substation that was built specifically for us up on the Isle but we've never drawn this type of load before. Everything is working at limit."

"Can we continue?"

"Yes, for now. But I'm concerned that if we push it too much we could really screw things up."

"Is this light dimming and surging going to be noticeable in the rest of the complex?"

"No, well, I don't think so. No it shouldn't be. We've got our own direct feed into the HP-Lab and this room. It's entirely separate from the rest of the complex. It had to be because of the extra load we pull."

"Okay. Then let's try again with AD 28."

The lights steadied at a much dimmer level than normal as the image on the far wall stabilised. Once more they looked down onto a jetty but this time they were looking at a small crowd of people, maybe forty or fifty, waiting next to the shoreline. Leigh joined Heinrich, held his hand and they waited with them.

45

W e should have brought the coffee in with us."

He distractedly nodded his agreement. They had waited and watched the scene on the shoreline for twenty minutes and nothing of interest had occurred. Not that that detracted from what they were looking at or waiting on but they both knew the one thing that was going to be a problem was the failing daylight. There were no streetlights in Capernaum in AD 28 and the sun's rays were fading fast. The astronomical data that Leigh had cross-referenced indicated they were in the full moon's quarter but it would still make it extremely difficult to track people in the open.

Leigh wandered off to the left hand bank of consoles to check on the power levels and when she returned she was looking concerned. "Heinrich?"

"Mmm?" He was transfixed by the imagery on the Projection. He had read about the period, studied the manuscripts and Gospels, researched and contemplated, been converted to the Turner Religion when he read them and now he was looking down on the actual place at the actual time.

"Heinrich!" She nudged him and he turned around and saw the concern etched on her face.

"What is it?"

"The power levels are borderline. I'm not sure how long the load can maintain itself."

"Do you want to shut it down again and rest it?"

"No. You saw how much it draws to start up. It's easier on the system to just let it continue playing forward. Shutting down and reopening could really mess things up. I'm just not sure how long we can keep an active Window open."

He wanted to ease her worry but didn't know what to say. The whole experience was overwhelming. He was about to reach out to hug her when there was a surge of noise from the speakers that connected to the Projection. The crowd had reacted to something outside of the Window's view.

They waited a few more minutes and saw three small fishing boats approach the jetty. A number of people jumped from the boats, secured them, then formed a semicircle that gently eased the waiting crowd back. When all was still a figure, dressed in a simple robe, stepped from the last boat. Leigh grasped Heinrich's hand and they watched as the crowd tried to surge forward. The semicircle held fast and then moved like a protective screen, encouraging the crowd back and allowing him to walk freely. Heinrich and Leigh were transfixed as they watched. She rested her head against his shoulder, "You've found Him Heinrich, you've found Him."

"We found Him," he said, incredulous that it had worked.

"Yes we did," she said and laughed.

"To be honest I really wasn't sure it was possible. In all my studies this was the only time and place that I could track down. Even then we had to guess the year." He was babbling and he knew it but the excitement he was feeling was like a current through him. He laughed with her and gestured up to the screen, "But now look at us!"

"We make a good team," Leigh said and hugged him hard.

The crowd had moved back and divided to either side of the cobbled road. Likewise, the semicircle of protection split into two flanking lines and in the middle he strolled unhindered. Then a figure broke through and prostrated himself on the road. The Prophet helped him back up to his feet and they walked together.

"That's Jairus, come to seek Him out," said Heinrich. Leigh merely nodded. They were so transfixed that the people started moving out of the image. Leigh reacted first and sprinted back to the control for the tracking mechanism.

"Quick Heinrich, what direction are they moving, I need to track the Window."

He assessed the image and estimated, "Track 035 degrees and don't worry, they're not going fast."

Leigh slewed the Window too quickly, which in itself was no small effort given the time lag on its movements, and overshot the entire crowd.

"Ahh, nooo, don't you dare do this to me."

"It's okay Leigh, no rush, they're only ever going to walk for us here. Or at worst trot on a horse."

She calmed her breathing and concentrated on the tracking mechanism. She centred the scene and found the Prophet again. Just as the image was refocussing he stopped and turned quickly and his face was lit by the last rays of the setting sun. She zoomed in to the maximum resolution and reorientated the Window. Both she and Heinrich gazed on the smiling face of a man in his thirties who looked handsome, confident, wise beyond his years and above all, kind. He had olive skin, relatively short dark brown hair, a closely trimmed beard and moustache, high cheekbones, broad nose, high forehead and strong jaw. His eyes were alive and he radiated a warmth of expression that made both Leigh and Heinrich gasp.

They watched as he reached out to a woman in the crowd. Leigh zoomed in further as they began to hear the speech from the scene but she didn't understand any of it.

Heinrich shook his head, "It's too quick for me to keep up."

"But we know what this is, don't we?" She said it smiling through tears that spilled from her eyes.

"Yes, that old lady just reached out and touched the hem of His garment."

"Dear God," said Leigh and touched her forehead, heart and abdomen. Heinrich circled his heart with his right index finger. She wiped her eyes with the back of her sleeve and asked, "Do you think the ones keeping the crowd away are the disciples?"

"I suppose so, but this is early in his ministry. So at most there would be ten or twenty. How many do you count?"

"It's difficult; the light is fading really fast. Hang on," she paused the display and looked closely, "I can see thirteen, you?"

"Yep, same. Let it play forward."

The Prophet laid his hand on the old woman's head and then she was helped away by some of the disciples, back to the main throng. Leigh tracked the procession as a group of men approached the crowd and called out. She tightened the focus as Jairus sank to his knees and wailed in despair. The Prophet waved his hand to indicate he wanted his path cleared and helped Jairus to his feet. They walked together towards a Roman style villa set in a clearing in the midst of a copse of trees to the west of a synagogue. The Prophet turned and stopped the crowd by holding his hand up. The disciples moved forward again and formed what was almost a cordon around the house. Then the Prophet and Jairus went inside.

Leigh worked quickly at the console in front of her and the image spiralled down, went to black and then refocussed inside an empty hallway.

"Leigh?"

"I know, I know." She moved the controls and entered into what appeared to be a sitting room illuminated by oil lamps and candles where women were talking together. Tracking forward and right she came across more women in another room that could have been a kitchen. Moving rapidly she overshot the house completely and ended up outside again.

"Fuck's sake," she swore under her breath but loud enough for Heinrich to hear.

"Not really the best time to be swearing, now is it?" he said in a light tone, trying to put her at ease.

She laughed nervously and twitched the tracking control involuntarily. The room that came into focus was quiet and dark save only for a single oil lamp that cast its flickering shadows over a small bed in the corner. Lying atop the bed was the still and peaceful body of a young girl. Leigh guessed she was about twelve and she wore the pallor of death. In the middle of the room, lit in profile by the lamp, the Holy Prophet and Messiah of the Turner Religion stood before the bed with his hands raised and his head bowed.

Leigh looked at Heinrich and could see the tension in his face and jaw. He was clenching his teeth and looked an equal mix of scared and awed. He breathed deeply a few times and his face transformed. He relaxed and looked serenely calm. He looked at her and said, "The years leave a mark Leigh."

"Till the sun rises, Heinrich," she replied.

Then he nodded and she flipped the microphones in the room to transmit.

46

"Morenu Rabenu, avadeicha anu. Nichlamnu midaber imcha."

Heinrich spoke the greeting, calling on the teacher to hear his humble servants, as clearly and as slowly as his nerves would allow. He had learnt to read and write old Hebrew but speaking it was a whole different discipline. He paused and waited. Leigh was holding her breath looking up at the Projection screen and staring in wonder as the Prophet lowered his arms and looked around him. He turned away from the girl, raised his hands again and spoke.

There was a sudden loud noise like the rushing of wind through the Thule Room. It built rapidly and was so loud that Heinrich and Leigh put their hands up to cover their ears. But there was no wind. Just noise. Then it ceased as rapidly as it had started. Leigh yelled out with a sharp, shocked cry.

"What is it, what's wrong?" Heinrich said as he looked round at her and then he also gasped. She was staring wide-eyed at him but around the top of her head, just above her hair and enveloping her like an aura, were tiny tongues of flame. He saw a flicker of fire out of the corner of his eye and when he looked toward it he saw his own reflection in one of the console monitors. He had the same around him. He darted his eyes from his reflection to Leigh. The flames faded and disappeared as quickly as they had appeared.

He felt tears running down his cheeks but he also felt elated. Leigh looked radiant and yet he saw she was crying too.

"Fear not, for I have awaited you. You are the peacemakers, the children of God. Know ye Isaiah's prophesy? Give ye ear, and hear my voice; hearken, and hear my speech."

Heinrich and Leigh looked up at the Projection's image.

"I can understand you!" exclaimed Leigh.

"Of course. The Lord has given the gift of tongues. It would be difficult to know the nations and the tribes and bring them together if Babel was destined to divide us." He laughed in a light, carefree way that was instantly beguiling.

"I...I..." She looked to Heinrich for help but he was as mute as her.

"Be not afraid to speak for it is I who should quake. You have appeared from nowhere as a voice in my head alone." His voice was melodic and light yet had gravitas and purpose.

"Teacher, does this mean you can understand us in our native tongue?" Heinrich asked, finally recovering enough to speak.

"Of course. The Lord our God wants us to converse. For I have been told to expect your coming. But call me not teacher. Call me Y'shua."

"You were told of our coming?" Leigh said in awe of the situation.

"Yes, as in a dream when I prayed on my own in the wilderness some days ago. The Lord our God said to expect a voice as if from angels in the spring that would speak to me in my winter. That I shall not see but yet I shall hear and they will tell me of despair and violence. A hell on our earth that they are living many lifetimes hence."

"Do you know why we want to tell you of these things?" Heinrich asked.

"No, just that you were sent. Neither do I know your names or your number."

"Sorry, um, I am Heinrich," he said incredulous of what he was doing, yet enthralled.

"I'm Leigh and there are only the two of us."

They saw him turn and take a seat next to the girl's bed, reaching out and taking the girl's lifeless hand in his. "Upon which reason do you come in the Lord's name?"

Leigh wiped more tears from her face and sat down in one of the console station seats. She nodded for Heinrich to keep talking.

"We come to seek your help, teach-" Heinrich hesitated before correcting himself, "Y'shua."

"And so does this young girl before me and I must make this right and restore her to her father. Perhaps that is what I am to do for you? To make it right and restore you? What is it that you ask?"

"We speak from many lifetimes removed from you. We know what comes to be the truth. You are heralded as the way and the light, the true Prophet of the Lord. You are recognised as the Messiah who shall bring forth the world to come."

"You know this?" Y'shua sounded surprised which in turn surprised Leigh and Heinrich. They swapped a look and again Leigh nodded encouragement.

"Yes, but surely you are aware that this would happen?" asked Heinrich.

"Not at all. I am merely starting out on a long journey. There were never guarantees. But now you say I am accepted?"

"Yes."

"And is this not what is wanted?"

"It is," it was Leigh who spoke, "it is what we want with all our hearts but it was a false dawn. The foretold world to come doesn't last. You unite all the peoples of the earth but it goes wrong." Her voice was laden with emotion and she wiped more tears away.

"Leigh, do not despair nor weep. Be brave and tell me why the Lord has sent you to me."

"We think we may know a way to change our world from its current misery but..." her voice was breaking on a sob and she stopped and looked to Heinrich.

He continued for them, "It will come at a terrible cost."

"Be at peace and worry not. Tell me how you have come to this way of thinking."

"A young woman who was mistreated and fell into bad, terrible ways had an epiphany of how we might make our world better," Heinrich said.

"What is her name?"

"Mary."

"And where is this Mary? Is she not here to speak for herself?"

"She's in a prison cell awaiting her execution."

There was silence and they watched as Y'shua put his head into his hands. He sat still for what seemed a long time but eventually he raised his head and spoke, "And what did your Mary say?"

Leigh was aware of a flashing alarm light to her left. She nodded insistently to Heinrich to continue as she got up to investigate.

"Y'shua, she knows you bring peace on earth, Nirvana, for two thousand years. Then one man with evil intent overthrew the nations of the earth and cast us down. He founded a regime that is evil and all-powerful. We cannot defeat it by turning our cheek against the aggressor for the aggressor just continues to kill us in our millions."

"Heinrich, you speak of millions? Are you saying millions have died in despair and terror?"

Heinrich's emotions had caught up with him again and at the sound of his name on the Prophet's lips he had begun to weep silent tears of joy. "Yes," he managed to squeeze the word out.

"And what of Mary?"

Heinrich looked to see if Leigh would speak for him but she was bent over a console at the far end of the room. She seemed to be fully focussed on it, so he took a gulp of air and wiped the tears from his eyes. "She knows that in your time, in the time I can see you in now and before, back in the time of the different tribes with their different faiths, they all fought and warred."

"I am aware of that. That is why I started out on my journey of peace and unity."

"I know but she, Mary, our Mary, thinks that if we had stayed with some division and separate factions then all the nations of the world would have maintained their strength. With war and conflict practised within the world, no one man could have had mastery over all others."

"I would agree with her. But I do not understand how I prevent that from happening. Surely if what you said is true then I am heralded by the peoples of my faith. The divisions in the world will remain. I am not a beacon of light for the whole world?"

"You are Y'shua. You are."

"How can this possibly be?" Y'shua frowned and the flickering light of the oil lamp cast his features in sharp relief.

"Because the Sanhedrin anointed you as Messiah and the Roman garrison of Jerusalem began to be influenced by the society that surrounded them."

"But even if that is so, Judea is not the world."

"No Y'shua but Rome is." Heinrich paused and watched Y'shua close his eyes and nod in realisation. "There were no more rebellions in or near Judea and that attracted the attention of the Emperor. As your word spread so eventually you were heralded by Rome. A couple of decades from now you convert the Emperor Claudius and he ensures all the peoples of the Empire hear your good news. It takes generations but succeeding Roman Emperors change the schooling system. They educate the children in the ways of pacifism and turn them from violence"

"How clever. The children become the makers of the peace," Y'shua said. "Go on Heinrich, what else?"

"The tribes and regions on the Empire's borders turn to peaceful ways and when they are no longer needed, the very legions that once fought and dominated lay down their arms. In time, Rome reaches out to her neighbours both near and far. Eventually all the world unites in the spirit of your divine teachings."

Y'shua clasped his hands together and rested his head on them. "You are telling me, Heinrich, that the old prophecies come true. They shall beat their swords into ploughshares, and their spears into pruning hooks; nation shall not lift up sword against nation?"

"Yes," Heinrich answered.

For a moment Y'shua was still. He finally raised his head, looked at the dead girl next to him and continued, "But how? What convinces the people to believe in me so completely? How do they all come together? Why is there no dissent? For there is plenty now." Y'shua stood and looked away from the girl on the bed to a door in the opposite wall. Heinrich could hear raised voices and shouts coming faintly through the Projection. "Heinrich, do not leave. We need to finish this but the crowd outside are growing restless and I need to get us more time to talk." With that, the Prophet walked out of the room and out of the Projection Window.

Heinrich looked down the length of the room to Leigh, "What's wrong? You look frantic."

"I am. The power supply's tripping out breakers. I'm not sure we're going to be able to keep the Projection running. I'm trying to shunt things away from the main load but I'm not an expert on how the power supplies work." She was flicking more switches as she spoke and he could see a real concern on her face.

"Is there anything I can do to help you?" he asked with genuine intent.

"Yes, talk to Y'shua and be brilliant and use all your knowledge to be the person I know you are and that my father knew you would be." She looked at him and held his gaze.

"Okay. I'll try and you try your best to keep the Window open," he encouraged.

"I will."

A few minutes passed while Heinrich waited for the Prophet to reappear in the dead girl's room. Leigh had worked her way round each console adjusting and monitoring as she went, but it was obvious from the increasingly erratic light levels in the room that she wasn't winning.

"Leigh how bad is it?"

"I honestly don't know. Power supplies really aren't my area. It could hang on for hours or it could fail spectacularly and destroy the whole ring laser assembly in the next second. We need to shut it down."

"We can't until He returns."

"I know."

Another few minutes ticked by on the image display and then he re-entered the room. "Heinrich are you still there?" Y'shua spoke with a gentle yet commanding tone.

"Yes, I'm here but we have a problem. The way that I'm talking to you uses a..." he hesitated and wondered how to explain that a laser ring gyro went weird and caused a Time Observation Window to open up. He decided to skip it, "Well it doesn't matter how I'm talking to you but it might fail."

"Will you be able to repair it?"

"Well I won't but Leigh will." He didn't add 'I hope'.

"Then tell me quickly, what is the reason for my uniting the world?"

"Mary said that everyone believed what you taught. That they believed in you because you..."

Leigh yelled from the far end of the room, "Heinrich! I'm losing this. The power's building in a surge, we're going to lose it all if I don't start shutting it down." Three light bulbs above Heinrich's head suddenly shattered in a spray of sparks and glass, as if to emphasise the point. He crouched and covered his head with his hands.

"Y'shua, we're going to have to leave but to come back again I need to know where and when to find you. This was the only place I knew where to find you at a specific time. How do I find you again?" he asked in a rushed and slightly panicked voice as the lights in the room dimmed, fluttered and then surged to a new level of intensity.

"Come back here Heinrich. Come back to here and now. I will gather my closest advisors and..."

There was a crunching noise that sounded like a car hitting a wall and the room went pitch black.

47

eigh?" he called out in the darkness.

"Heinrich?" she replied hesitantly, yet relieved.

"Yes. Are you okay, are you safe?"

"Yes, I'm safe. Don't move, just wait." She turned slowly in the darkness until she could see the faint green glow of the fluorescent sticker that marked the location of the emergency torch hanging on the wall. "Stay still until I get us some light," she called and moved slowly with her arms held out in front of her and her legs sweeping slowly for open space to walk into. She retrieved the torch after only a couple of small bumps, clicked it on and shone it up into the ceiling so that enough light was scattered to faintly illuminate the room.

"I thought that was it," Heinrich said as he moved slowly toward her.

"What do you mean?"

"I mean I thought that I was dead, that we had changed the world and that it was over for us."

"Me too." She laughed a small, slightly sad laugh.

He moved toward the torchlight and took her in his arms. "I'm glad it wasn't."

"Are you? Isn't that what all this is for?"

"Yes, but when the lights went off I realised that if this was the end, I desperately wanted to be standing next to you, holding hands."

She hugged him hard, reached up and kissed him slowly and gently. "Thank you. That may well be the nicest thing anyone has ever said to me." She kissed him again, drew apart from him and played the torch beam round the lab as she said, "But I think all that happened is the power supply breakers have tripped and the surge protection circuits cut in. You're not dead and we didn't save the world. Well, I don't think so. But, we need to get out of here."

"No, we can't. We need to repair this and go back." He checked his watch and calculated how long the Window had been open for. "We need to go back at the same time the Window crashed shut."

"Yes I know but I have no idea if I can fix it yet and meanwhile we may have a slightly bigger problem."

"Bigger?"

"Well, different." She turned and led him out of the Thule Room. "We need to get the number for the power substation and ring them. That surge and then the complete drop of load will mean they'll have had alarms tripped. They'll be in the process of embarking on the procedures set down for such an occasion. Procedures that will require them to start ringing people to find out what's going on."

"Who are they likely to try?"

"Wolfgang, and if they can't get hold of him they'll ring the Head of Thule Security."

"Me?" he said in surprise.

"Yep, you. So if we head them off then everything will be fine." She swung open the security door and led him through the cleanroom back into Oscar.

"All the lights are on," he sounded quite confused.

"I told you, the HP-Lab and the Thule Room are on a separate circuit. It's an annexe to the main Oscar power supply."

"So no one in the complex knows we tripped off all our power?"

"Nope, they shouldn't. Only the external substation." She had reached a circuit breaker box mounted on the wall and released the catch. Inside the front cover were a list of names, departments and phone numbers. "But you're going to have to ring them. Tell them that you authorised a special maintenance check and that all is well."

"Can't you just talk to them on my behalf? You sound a lot more convincing than me with the technical stuff?"

"Not for this. There are strict controls over the power supplies ever since Toronto. Had they controlled it better we could have prevented the original big accident. So now we control it better. Of course, we're about to prove that any system can have its flaws. But you'll be fine. After all, you are Colonel Steinmann of the Allgemeine-SS, Special Investigations and Security Directorate and as you said earlier, that has its advantages." She read out the number and he punched it into his Fone.

He told his made-up version of events to the duty officer at the Isle of Dogs Power Generation Substation 34A as she made her way back to her office. Logging on to her PC, Leigh called up the official news and information websites and opened each in a separate browser window. Scanning the lead pages of *Völkischer Beobachter, Das Reich* and *Das Schwarze Korps*, she could see no discernible differences to their normal coverage. She opened *Neues Volk* and finally *Signal*; all seemed to confirm what she had surmised. Nothing in their world had changed. It was just as oppressed and devoid of freedom as it had ever been. She joined him back in the lab and found him sitting at the bench where they had had their coffee.

"All done with the substation?"

"Yes, no problem. They wanted, in fact, demanded, to know what was going on. I introduced myself with my full rank and title and said that it was nothing for them to be concerned with. They agreed and thanked me for my trouble. Which is both handy for us and terribly sad for the fact that it shows me nothing has changed."

"I know, I just checked the official news sites. All the same as usual."

"Not so bad though."

"What?" She looked at him like he was crazy.

"Not so bad. It means that we have to go back again. We get to spend more time with Him."

Leigh giggled, then laughed and held out her arms. Heinrich stood, took hold of her and twirled her round and round. They laughed like kids in a playground, overwhelmed at the enormity of what they had done and what they had experienced.

"We talked with Jesus of Nazareth, the Prophet, the Messiah," she said in a tone of wonder.

"I know and He called us by our names and spoke to us and we understood Him. I felt so alive when I heard him speak in German."

"English."

"What?"

"He was speaking in fluent English Heinrich. That's why I was so stunned. You'd said this morning that you were confident you could manage in Hebrew but it'd be slow and deliberate and I knew I wouldn't understand a word and then whoosh, we get granted the power of Tongues. I remember my parents telling me the stories of the Apostles when they went out to preach. How they were granted it and I always thought it would be a great thing to have and now we do. Me and you." She laughed again and again and he twirled her round more and more until they both collapsed back onto the stools at the bench.

When he had caught his breath he said, "I heard Him in German. All my responses to Him were in German."

"Mine were in English and so were His." She thought for a moment. "Say something in German now."

"Bitte entschuldigen Sie mich"

"Oh, that is weird. I heard that in German."

"I'm sure it'll come back when we talk to Him again."

"Me too." They both sat for a long moment, contemplating what they had seen and experienced. The moment was broken by Leigh getting up and retrieving a tissue from a box on one of the cubicle desks. Heinrich saw her dabbing her eyes as she came back to sit down and asked, "What's the matter?"

"Oh, I was just thinking how my mum and dad would have loved this."

"Do you want to see if we can go back and talk to them?"

"No! No I really don't. It would tear my heart from my chest. We just need to get the Window working again. Let's get back in and see if I can fix things."

"What would you like me to do?"

Leigh nodded her head in the direction of the coffee percolator.

48

An hour later she sat at the Oscar Lab bench with wiring diagrams spread out in front of her while Heinrich made yet more fresh coffee. Resetting the breakers and restoring the power had been easy. Yet even though the lights were on and functioning normally and the computer systems had undergone a system restore and were back up and running, there wasn't a peep out of the Window. She couldn't initiate the transmission of the laser beams let alone get it to stabilisation.

The reality of the situation had been manifestly obvious to her for the last twenty minutes but she had gone over and over the diagrams and ran as many remote diagnostics as she could. Despite all her efforts she knew that the answer wasn't going to change. She sunk her head into her hands and said quietly, "I need to get into the Ringroom."

He looked round at her, "Well, whatever the Ringroom is, I'm guessing from looking at you that it isn't good?"

"It's where the ring laser gyro actually is."

"You mean the room on the other side of the glass from the control room?" he asked, not seeing the real problem.

"Yes," she said distractedly.

"So what's so bad about that?"

She raised her head out of her hands and looked directly at him. "You remember I told you about Kristen Zielang?"

He frowned. "I vaguely recognise the name but I can't place it, sorry."

"She was the young lady who stood up into the middle of the Observation Window in Toronto. The one that caused the accident?"

He nodded and waited.

"Before her we had all the normal security clearance protocols. I know you know all about the classified compartments and how clearances and all that works."

He nodded again.

"But most of our physical security was established because of what she did and, as we've seen, that side of things is just not in your purview is it."

This time he shook his head but still said nothing.

"When we moved here it was decided to put in a multilevel approach that increases physical protection the closer you get to the equipment. The last barrier is the door to the actual ring laser."

"And I'm not going to like what you're going to tell me, am I?"

She shook her head slowly. "The door's a Reich Security Grade-6."

He closed his eyes and simply said, "Oh!" After a moment he asked, "Are you sure we need to get in there?"

"Absolutely. I've tried everything else. Something in there is broken and I need to get into it. I need to run real-time diagnostics with power onto the system. That's the reason it's a Grade-6. Theoretically, if you were inclined to, you could do what Kristen did. So they made it a designated no-lone-zone, dual approved entry." She drew a breath and stood up to walk in circles as she thought.

"Well, that's that then." He sat heavily onto a stool at the bench. "Not even a security detail card's going to bypass a Grade-6." He watched Leigh continue pacing in circles. "You're sure it's a true Grade-6?"

She continued to pace but said, "Oh yes. Have you seen one before?"

"Yes, in the Berlin Archives," he said sadly.

"Well, then you know. Two separate swipe cards, two separate biometric scans and two separate coded entry sequences. Miss any one of them and the door isn't opening."

"I suppose, given his future prospects, we could've asked Konrad but he's wiped from the system. We're stuffed."

Leigh stopped pacing and turned to him, "What did you say?"

"That there's no use in thinking about Konrad. He's wiped from the system."

"You're right," she said with a tinge of excitement.

"What? What did I say that's just made you all sparky again?"

"We can't get in and we're stuffed and so is Konrad."

"Yeah," he said it slowly, "and?"

"We need to call Franci and get her in here."

"We can't! She'll hand us over as quick as look at us when we tell her what we're doing."

"No she won't. Oh no she won't!" she said it deliberately. "She won't care what we're doing but she'll care why we're doing it if she thinks it gives Konrad a chance."

"You really think so?"

"I know so, Heinrich. It's a win-win. In fact it's better than that because Franci's a much better physical engineer than I am so we should fix it quicker. She gets to help Konrad and we get to go back and talk to Him again."

"You're sure?"

"Yes!"

Leigh punched the speed dial on her ForeFone. "Franci?"

"Hi Leigh," she sounded dejected.

"What you up to?"

"You don't want to know, it's sad and lonely."

"C'mon Franci, tell me."

"I'm in my pyjamas, on my couch, eating ice cream."

Leigh imagined her in her neat apartment in Bethnal Green and felt such a wave of empathy for her friend. "I need your help."

"Really?" Franci said unenthusiastically.

"Yes really. On something that could help a mutual friend." Leigh could almost sense Francine's physical reaction at the other end of the line. She waited. After a few seconds with no response, Leigh was going to repeat herself when Francine finally spoke.

"Are you at work?" she asked and the full weight of the question wasn't lost on either of them.

Leigh drew a deep breath and said, "Yes."

There was a longer pause.

Leigh knew Francine would be thinking she meant to use the Time Window to warn off Konrad. That was unfortunate but advantageous in the circumstances. If she chose to help then they would have to deal with the truth of the matter face-to-face. For now all Leigh could do was hope that her friend actually loved Konrad as much as she had always said. She waited and wondered if she should try to prompt her but decided to give her time.

After a few more moments, a much more focussed Francine said, "Give me half an hour."

49

There was nothing for them to do but wait. He reached out for her and they sat nestled together on the bench. Her head resting against his chest and his arms wrapped around her.

"I wish we'd had longer together," he said.

"Me too, but I don't think we were meant to."

They stayed like that, breathing in and out in a resonant rhythm with Heinrich planting gentle kisses on her hair.

After a quarter of an hour Leigh swivelled about and kissed him.

"I'm loving this and I don't really want to move, but she's going to be here soon. Who knows what happens after that, so I really need to go and have a smoke. Or two. You coming?" she hopped up and he followed.

Lighting her second cigarette, she exhaled the smoke into the fresh breeze and bright sun of a beautiful May day in London.

"Would you mind if I spoke to her alone, it's just..." She hesitated to say it and he filled in for her.

"That to her I'm still the SS-Colonel who was responsible for Konrad's arrest?"

"Yes."

"No problem. You take her back down and ring me. I'll loiter up top in the cafeteria."

She remembered back to Sunday night when they had sat in the cafeteria, "I'm going to have to tell her I'm a Turner." Heinrich merely nodded. "You know it's typical. Tell no one my whole life then tell you on Sunday and now Franci on Friday."

"Wouldn't be too concerned," he said laconically, "if this doesn't work we'll be outed to the whole world on Saturday." Although they both knew he meant it as a joke the correctness of it hit home. They stood quietly with their own thoughts. Leigh remembered her mother and father at her graduation in Cambridge. Heinrich saw his grandmother and mother, each holding a hand and swinging him as they walked up a hill towards the woods that lay just south of his village.

The sound of a car pulling across the gravel and into the staff car park distracted them. Leigh looked quizzically at the cigarette in her hand. "If we get it all working again this could well be my last cigarette."

He smiled at her. "For a strategy to give up smoking it's a bit extreme."

She took a last draw of the smoke and stubbed it out in the ashtray.

Heinrich was surprised it took so little time. He had loitered outside until Leigh and Francine were safely inside and then wandered up to the cafeteria. The smell of the lunchtime servery reminded him he was hungry so he grabbed a handful of takeaway sandwiches. His Fone buzzed just as he was paying for them and three bottles of water.

"Leigh?"

"Come down."

"It's only been what, fifteen minutes? Is it all okay?"

"It's fine. Come down."

Both women were sitting at the bench next to the array of wiring diagrams when he walked in. Francine jumped up and met him halfway. She flung her arms around him, kissed him on the cheek and said, "Thank you."

Heinrich was almost speechless. "Um, you're welcome. What'd I do?"

"You surprised me Herr Steinmann. That doesn't happen often. And you've given me hope. In the world I live in that doesn't happen much at all."

The three of them sat and shared the food and water.

"So you're okay with everything Franci?" he asked.

"Okay? No. Thrilled, excited and a little stunned? Yes."

Heinrich couldn't help but feel good when he saw the breadth of the smile on her face.

"My best friend is a member of a banned religion, her new fella," she winked at him and he felt his face blush, "is also a member of it and he's in the upper echelons of the SS. We're all going to run a Time Projection back to change the world and save the man whom I have loved for years, yet he can't love me back the way I want and we'll probably wipe ourselves out of existence in the process. Less than an hour ago I was eating ice cream and feeling sorry for myself. So yep, not okay, bit shocked but definitely up for it."

Leigh and Heinrich looked at one another and Leigh could see the confusion on his face.

"Ask her why Heinrich."

"You don't need to ask," Francine said, "I'll ask you something. What do you see when you look at me Heinrich?"

He hesitated in answering, not too sure if he was missing something or if he was meant to respond in a certain way.

"It's okay Heinrich, just tell her the truth," Leigh encouraged him.

"I see Doctor Francine Xu, senior scientist with the Reich's Technical Directorate. I don't know what your specialisation is but you must be good to be on this team."

"Aww, he really is a keeper Leigh," she teased and then turned back. "That's nice but let's get down to brass tacks, what do you see?" she stressed the last word, "And be honest."

"I see a woman of about," now he paused again not having a clue how old she was but he decided to take her at her word and was as honest as he could be, "thirty-eight..."

She interrupted, "Oh, I do like him more and more, go on."

"About one-sixty tall, slim, obviously healthy, fit and," he blushed again and gave Leigh an awkward look. She just nodded her encouragement for him to go on. "And very beautiful."

He looked at the two women sitting opposite. Leigh was smiling broadly at him and Francine was looking contemplative and he could see a sadness in her eyes. Albeit that he had only known her for a short time and all of it at a superficial level within the project, this was the first sign of fragility that he had ever seen in her.

"Did I say something wrong?"

She sniffed and said, "No, not a thing. Leigh said you were a good person and now I'm inclined to believe her."

"Because I said you were beautiful?" he asked, a little perplexed.

"No, because you said nothing about me being a half-caste, yellow chink, slant-eyed, daughter of a whore." Heinrich went to object but she held up a hand and continued, "A product of a mixed-marriage that should never have been allowed. Some reject from the Aryan master race that slipped through the cracks." She sniffed again and wiped her eyes, "You know, I only survived because they needed my parents and then it turned out the Reich needed me too. That's my world Heinrich. Apart from my closest colleagues the world, this world, our world as it is, sees me like that. When I walk down a street I get stared at. When I walk into places I get asked to leave. When I walk into worse places I get asked to stay and perform tricks. I've been verbally abused, spat at and on one notable occasion, punched. The last time someone tried to hurt me I defended myself using stuff my dad taught me and was thrown into a cell for four days. The only reason I got out at all was that Konrad came looking for me. Even then the guy who'd started it got nothing done to him."

"I see," Heinrich said.

Francine reached out for her bottle of water and took a drink. "I can get equally passionate about being a woman in a man's world as well." She gave him a mock toast with the bottle.

"Oh yeah, she really can," Leigh added.

"So that's why I'm up for this and that's why I'm excited. I've had enough of what we have and I'd like something new please."

"We're going a long way back," he said, trying not to ask the obvious.

"I know. I thought at first that Leigh was thinking of going back to warn Konrad directly but that only saves Konrad. It doesn't do much for my situation or the hundreds of thousands like me who haven't even had the chance to live."

"Do you believe it will work?"

"Well, I did wonder how on earth we were going to communicate with anyone from back then but Leigh has tried to convince me that you've apparently been blessed. I'll believe that when I see it," she said with a good trace of cynicism in her voice.

"And what about the actual plan of changing things. Do you think that will work?"

"I don't believe in the Godliness of Jesus but I know my history so yes, why not? My dad had some banned texts from the Far-East. He kept them as a curiosity but I thought they made interesting reading. There was one that was about a guy called Siddhārtha something or other. It was only a scrap really but it said that all things that come to be have an end. I always remembered that. I used to wish that one day people being bastards to me would come to an end. Perhaps today's the day."

"Well, if today's the day, we better make a start," Leigh said and got up.

They took the diagrams with them and headed back into the Thule Room. Leigh and Francine scanned, swiped and punched in the necessary data before pushing the Grade-6 door to the Ring-room open. They could smell a pungent, almost acrid odour as soon as they entered. The two scientists said at the same instant, "The transformer's gone."

"Is it fixable?" Heinrich asked, not having the least clue if a transformer that had obviously burnt out was just bad or catastrophic.

"Yes, probably," said Francine, "we have a couple of spares but it's going to take a good twenty minutes to replace it."

"But we can get it back up and running?"

"There's a very good chance," Leigh said.

"Do you need me to do anything?" he asked as he watched them examine a large, square, black box that had a dozen or more silver coloured metal blades protruding from its sides and rear.

"Nah, we're okay Heinrich," Francine said. "We've got this. It's just a simple case of a one for one swap but we have to disconnect it and wire the new one in."

"I'll leave you to it then. What's the code to get out?"

"Five zeros," Leigh said.

Heinrich laughed softly.

"What's funny?"

"Nothing. Just that I should write a memo to SS HQ and ask them to audit Grade-6 exit codes."

Taking a seat at a console desk, he focussed his thoughts on what he would say when the Window reopened. He referred to the notes he had made in the Archives and tried to find a way to explain, in terms that would be understood by Y'shua, what befell the world when the Reich rose. Leigh and Francine came and went between Oscar and the Ringroom with various tools and bits of equipment. True to their promise, twenty minutes later they were back at the controls and ready to start again.

Once more they used Konrad's key but this time Francine assisted Leigh. When stabilisation occurred, Leigh entered the override code and all of the previous parameters save for the time. "What hours and minutes are we going for Heinrich?"

"After the Window crashed I reckoned we'd been observing about forty-five minutes. That puts it at 17:00 local Capernaum time. So if we aim to go back in to the Projection five minutes later, at 17:05 local, 15:05 GMT?"

"Sounds okay to me." She punched in the data and instigated the Projection. The lights dimmed dramatically then came back to an almost normal level.

"Whoa, that's not good," Francine said as she moved between consoles, but Heinrich wasn't listening. Instead he was looking at the image on the wall.

He turned to look at Leigh, "It's pitch black Leigh."

"The crash wiped the last known coordinates. I had to go back to the jetty again." She said.

"So much for the full moon, I can't see anything."

"Don't fret, you said track 035 degrees last time and we only went about twenty metres. Then we followed them slightly northwest as they walked towards the small clearing. We'll find them." She watched her screens, using the tracking controls to move the numbers on her displays. "We should be about there?" she said and looked up but the image screen was still black. "Oh! That's not exactly what I'd hoped for."

"I don't suppose there's a brightness control?" Heinrich asked.

"Have patience. We'll find it. Franci, knock the lights off in the room please and Heinrich, you watch the image. I'll start spiralling out in concentric circles. Shout out when you see something."

Francine put the room into darkness and Leigh adjusted the tracking controls. She moved in the smallest of increments and concentrated on making each movement smooth. Heinrich watched the image and waited.

After what seemed like an age he saw the smallest flicker of light in the Projection. "There! Stop!"

Leigh froze the controls and looked up. They all stared into the near black. It was Francine who said, just as their eyes adjusted, "That's a lamp in a window." Leigh was about to agree when the moon finally broke through whatever cloud cover had been across it. The small house came into sharp focus and they could see the cordon of disciples still gathered round it. Leigh punched in a lock command to capture the coordinates just in case something went wrong again.

"Can we have the lights on please?" she called and Francine obliged. They struggled to come back on and held only a fraction of their normal output.

"What is going on with this power Leigh?"

"I don't know but I'm glad you're here to help," she said and smiled over at her friend. Then she pushed the image Projection down and into the small structure.

They were back in the room and Heinrich could see that it was slightly better illuminated. The single oil lamp had been supplemented with two more as well as a few candles. In the extra light he could clearly see the young girl lying deathly still on the bed.

Y'shua was standing much where he had been. Heinrich looked back at Leigh and noticed Francine standing transfixed by the image. Leigh nodded at him and flipped the microphones onto transmit.

50

Y'shua?"

"Heinrich, Leigh, you have returned."

"Have we been gone long?" Heinrich needed to ask because he had lost all sense of time when they had been looking for the house.

"Only a few minutes, but long enough for me to talk to my most trusted advisors. I want them to be involved in our discussions but will they be able to hear you?"

"Yes Y'shua. If they are near to you then they will hear us," Leigh said before quickly adding, "but will they be able to understand us?"

"I shall have to hope that the Lord's miracles extend to all who need it. I cannot imagine that he would make you capable of talking to me and not open the ears of those who should hear. I shall go get them." He walked from the room and Heinrich turned around to look back at Leigh.

"We're back!" she said and gave him the biggest grin. They both looked round to Francine and were surprised to see her staring wide-eyed at the image Projection of the room in Capernaum.

"Franci, are you okay?"

"I'm... eh..." She stopped and sat down in the nearest chair.

"Franci?" Leigh repeated.

"I, um, I, uh..."

"Franci, what is it?" asked Heinrich.

"This is him, on the screen, right?" she finally managed to ask.

"Yes." Leigh and Heinrich said almost simultaneously.

"I can understand him."

"Ah ha!" Leigh cried out in triumph, "So now you believe me?"

"Oh yes, I believe you."

"Aww, we should have been watching you. I wonder if you had the same aura?"

Before Francine got the chance to ask what aura Leigh was talking about Heinrich interrupted, "What are you hearing Him in, English?"

"Mmm no, not English. I speak French, English and German. But I used to love speaking Mandarin at home with my father. That's what I'm hearing. Mandarin as clear and precise as if it was my father speaking to me."

"That is as it should be. It is your heavenly Father speaking to you through His gift." Y'shua had made his way back into the room and overheard Francine. "And who has joined us?"

She sat dumbstruck for a moment before Leigh leant over to her and whispered, "Go on, don't be shy. You've never been shy in all the years I've known you."

"I'm Francine."

"And did you come to help Leigh and Heinrich, Francine?"

"Yes, um uh, I'm sorry, what do I call you?"

"Y'shua, just call me Y'shua."

"Then please, call me Franci." She was beginning to recover slightly from the enormity of what she was doing.

"Good, well, we have more introductions." He turned and beckoned. A man and a woman came and stood next to him. Leigh slewed the Window to bring the three into the centre of the screen.

"I trust that as Franci can hear and understand then the gift will be bestowed on all who come." He turned to the woman beside him. She was slightly built, stood as tall as his shoulder, had a light olive complexion, refined cheekbones, a straight, slender nose and heavy-lidded eyes that looked up at Y'shua. Her long black hair was tied up in a braid.

"I am Miriam of Magdala."

There was silence for a few moments. It was finally Leigh that spoke up, "Welcome Miriam, we know you."

The woman nodded to Y'shua, "Yes, I can understand the voice. May I ask, how do you know of me? I am but a follower."

Heinrich answered, "You are known in the Gospels as the first woman to follow the way of Y'shua. It is written that Miriam was fair of face, with a fair voice and a fair heart. You relinquished your wealth and titles to live a simple life in the service of Y'shua and of the poor. You are known to us as the Magdalene."

Her light complexion was shaded by the depth of her blush, easily visible in the candle and lamplight of the room. Y'shua smiled down at her and patted her arm. Then he turned to the man on his right. He stood a fraction taller than Y'shua and had much darker olive skin. His dark hair and beard were short and neatly trimmed and his keen features were framed by a wide forehead and a square jaw. He seemed to exude an air of intelligence and purpose.

"With Miriam, this man is my counsel and my conscience, my strength and my support. He is my friend." Y'shua prompted the man to speak.

"My name is Judas of Kerioth. I too can understand your speech."

This time it was Leigh who spoke in answer, "Judas, you are also well known to us."

"May I ask how?"

"You are one who Y'shua counts on within the Holy City when He is heralded. You are the one He sends to speak to Pilate. The one He calls the Rock of the Church."

"I am pleased to know that my friend and my Master can count on me. But what of you?"

Francine and Leigh looked to Heinrich.

"I'm Heinrich," he hesitated and tried to drag a memory from some of the old Roman maps and documents he had studied, "umm, from Germania Magna." He quickly scribbled on a piece of paper and walked back to Leigh.

"I'm Leigh," she glanced down, "from Britannia."

"And I'm Franci from," she looked at Heinrich and held her hands up in a shrug. Under her breath she said, "Go on then, what's ancient worldy for Canada?"

Heinrich said, "She is Franci whose mother was from Gallia Lugdunensis and whose father was from Sinae."

Y'shua spoke, "So, we gather from distant lands and from a time removed. We have much to discuss. You say that the woman Mary said everyone believes what I teach?"

"Yes," said Heinrich. "Because your teachings and miracles were performed in the open, the crowds believed without question or doubt. You encouraged them to tell what they had seen and to spread the word. By the time you came to enter Jerusalem all Judea was with you. When the Pharisees came to take you in front of the Sanhedrin you answered their questions and demonstrated your gifts when they tested you. They heralded you unanimously. Your ministry continued for nearly forty years and each challenge was met with openness and demonstrations of your calling and place in God's world."

"I cannot see how that is bad. Is this not what we want for the Master?" Judas asked.

"It is Judas, but it doesn't last. Imagine a Judea without the Roman army of occupation."

"I would see that as a great thing. To live peacefully with no oppression."

"I agree, but would you still have the weapons of war?"

"Of course," said Judas, "for there are more threats than the Romans in this world."

"Exactly, but imagine a time when there is peace for generations. Imagine a time when there is no war or conflict. When even the Legions of Rome lay down their weapons. How would the people become?"

"They would grow and thrive and prosper," Miriam interjected.

Leigh responded, "Yes they would and they did. But they also became soft in the ways of war. They grew out of the need for weapons; of how to make them and how to use them. This lasted for generation after generation so, in the end, they knew nothing of how to wage war. They were like children in the crib."

Heinrich had struggled earlier trying to think of a way he could explain the magnitude of the losses. He said, "An evil rose in the midst of these 'children' and rained down death. It swept all before it like the Parthians at Carrhae but a thousandfold worse." He paused and drew a breath, "The destruction was a thousand, thousand times that of Carthage. Millions suffered, were enslaved, died. Are still suffering and dying. Y'shua, we have lost more since the rise of this evil than all the souls on the earth in your time."

There was a silence as they reflected on what had been said. Leigh and Heinrich watched the changing expressions of the three companions in Capernaum as the reality of the future world settled on their shoulders. Y'shua and Judas sat on the floor and Miriam took the seat next to the child's bed. Leigh adjusted the Projection's width to include them all. Francine scooted her chair over next to Leigh's and checked on the adjacent screen. The lights dipped markedly and then returned to a dim glow. There was an audible hum from some of the equipment in the room. Heinrich turned and frowned in their direction and got a shrug in reply.

Judas spoke first, "If this came to pass, how did the evil rise? If the world was at peace how did it make war?"

Heinrich looked to Leigh but she pointed to the screens in front of her and gave him an 'I'm going to have to focus on this' look.

He took a deep breath. "We had almost two millennium of peace. The world still had famine, disease, earthquakes, fires, floods. But for most of this time, like in your time, the news of such things spread slowly. Others may not have heard of them for weeks, months, years. The effects of these disasters were evened out, over time and distance." He studied the faces on the image and could see they were listening intently to him. He checked over his shoulder and saw that Leigh and Francine were huddled together over another control panel. He decided to press on, "But almost exactly nineteen hundred years from when you are now a way was developed to communicate news very rapidly and widely. I know it may be difficult to comprehend but it is like being able to tell Rome and Constantinople and Jerusalem the same message in the same hour." He watched as Miriam and Judas shook their heads slightly as if in disbelief. He couldn't really blame them.

Y'shua spoke, "Heinrich, if you can speak to us as you are doing now, then Rome to Jerusalem seems a simple task. Continue."

"There was a series of bad winters and bad summers and the crops and food supplies faltered. Then came a sequence of volcanic eruptions, earthquakes and," he broke off, wondering how to phrase it properly, "tidal waves that swept the coastlines of many countries. These caused blights and pestilence and the food supplies began to fail. Shortages became noticeable and that led to rationing, and ultimately to famine. Throughout the world people suffered, grew weak and many died. When they were at their lowest a disease began to spread. Like a fever but much more severe. It killed millions more. Finally, with the populations of the world weakened by hunger and disease and not able to work properly, the economies failed. Because of fast communication everyone knew about these misfortunes collectively. They felt the impact of them all, even those far away. The man who rose to power promised to rid the world of its ills."

Y'shua stood again and said, "In this time he rose through the misery of death and despair, famine and disease, flood and quake. Like charging horses he swept humanity before him."

"Yes Y'shua," Leigh said through a voice choked with emotion. She came to stand next to Heinrich again and said, "Everything that went before was slight compared to what came next. We couldn't stop him or his followers. We'd no arms to resist him and no way to protect ourselves that wouldn't have gone against our Creed. To keep our belief was our guiding principle. So he eradicated your believers as they offered him love and kindness."

"You said he and his followers?" asked Miriam.

"Yes."

"How could the whole world have followed this man?"

It was Francine who spoke up as Leigh and Heinrich looked to each other to see who would answer. "They didn't all follow him. The world didn't turn away from good toward evil. It's simply that the ones who would have stood against him and who led by example were killed first. They're still being killed."

"Go on," Miriam encouraged, "we need to know."

"The man who started all this, his followers and his successors, are simply bullies and thugs. They are still bent on eradicating those that don't fit their ideal. They're more concerned with their power, their money and their appearance than the terrible things being done on their orders. But every time someone stood up to them they were cut down. Eventually people learnt not to stand up.

So they came to do nothing against the regime. Just as we still do nothing. Like the majority. We're not evil. We're just not good enough."

"You are today," Y'shua said.

Leigh and Heinrich turned to see Francine smiling the widest smile. "Maybe we are," she said quietly.

Y'shua continued, "So I was too well loved and as no evil can stand against me so no good can stand against him. It is as if we have both removed the free choice of the people. That was never the aim. It is not my place to dictate to the people. They must have free choice. What are we to do?"

"If faith is fragile Master, then alternative opinions will prevail. With those choices comes discord," Judas said the words as he was standing back up again.

Miriam said, "How can mistrust, disbelief, and fear cause the tribes of Israel to prosper."

"It cannot, but not one of those tribes became all-powerful and ruled the whole of them," Judas countered before continuing, "So the question is how do we make your message fragile but strong enough to survive?"

"What did Mary say about this?" Y'shua asked.

"She suggested that you keep your own counsel. Don't reveal your miracles in the broad light of day or in the gaze of the crowds. Have those that know about them say nothing. That way it would require faith to believe that you are who you say.

"She is wise," he paused, "and what of you and Leigh and Franci, what think you?"

"We think as Judas said. If faith is fragile then separate churches will compete," Heinrich offered.

Y'shua turned to Miriam, "Your thoughts?"

"If we do this, it would not mean abandoning all we hold true. Just because the religions of our world would not unite, it doesn't mean they would not be there. Good people would still follow their path of choice. Good people would still be following in God's way."

Y'shua placed his hand on her arm, smiled down at her, then turned to Judas.

"Preaching your message to the crowds in less forthright terms will not dissuade them Master. The influencers in our time are still the same. For you to be heralded needs Annas and Caiaphas. For you to be renounced would need them to be convinced you are not who we know you to be. We may need to start speaking with them in the shadows."

"Ah, my friend, you are my consummate political advisor," Y'shua said before continuing, "Heinrich, why have you come to me. There are prophets before and after me?"

"That is true. But Moses, Noah and Abraham didn't unite the peoples. The prophets who come after you built on your foundations. The last Holy Prophet solidified the great union of the Peoples of the Old Book. He honoured you and strengthened the peace. But you are the beginning."

"And so you come full circle. You have come to me to end it before it begins," Y'shua said it not as a question but as a realisation of the truth.

"Leigh, Heinrich!" it was Francine and she sounded panicked. "The power supply's just spiked off the scale and I can't offload the system. We need to shut this down or risk losing it again." Leigh hurried back to the consoles to help.

"Heinrich," Y'shua called out to him, "we have enough to go forward with. We will seek guidance from our Lord through prayer and meditation. But we will not know if this has worked for some time. If it hasn't we shall need to talk again for I will not leave you to the fates of a devil."

"But I don't know where and when to find you other than here," Heinrich said.

"And I don't know where we will be in the future," Y'shua said.

Heinrich leafed rapidly through his note pages. The lights were dipping and brightening with increasing frequency. Scouring his memory for a time and place that he could be certain of was yielding nothing until he finally realised he didn't need to know the details precisely, because they could tell him.

"Wait, wait! They lead you in triumphant procession into Jerusalem on the Sunday before Passover, not next year but the year after. I just don't know when on the day or where they bring you into the city or where you go to."

"Heinrich we're going to lose this," Leigh called to him but in an unnervingly calm tone.

"I need a time and place, quickly?"

Judas spoke, "On that Sunday, one week before Passover, two years hence. At midday. East of the Temple, in the valley of Josaphat, are vineyards and a garden. It falls to the north-west of the old cemetery on the Mount of Olives. It's a garden of great beauty called Gat Šmānê, do you know it?"

Heinrich thought hard to recognise the name.

"We have seconds now Heinrich!" called Francine.

"No, I've never heard of it before."

"It lays on the Jericho Road. You found here, then find there!" Judas said emphatically.

Heinrich turned to Leigh and Francine and nodded. Francine reached out and hit the emergency shutdown. The Window collapsed and the image Projection went blank.

51

13:30 Friday, May 22, 2020 – London

There was a sudden quiet in the room. The lights were on but the rest of the equipment was dark and noiseless. Leigh and Francine were also silent, moving between the control consoles in a mute dance of inspection. Heinrich stood a little apart from them trying to comprehend the conversation he had just been a part of.

Y'shua had undertaken to completely transform his ministry. In order to save future generations from total subjugation he would change the way his message was heard. He had agreed with no real argument or obstacle. The question was had it made a difference? They were all obviously still alive. No massive tsunami of destruction had befallen them, but did that mean it hadn't worked? Did it mean it had but the theories were wrong? He remembered about the head of the snake being eaten by itself. They needed to know if anything significant had changed and see what the world looked like. If nothing was different, then he needed to know where Gat Šmānê was. He slowly gathered up his notes and the copied extracts from the Archives, looking at them, but not focussing. He was shaken out of his thoughts by Leigh.

"Heinrich, are you okay?"

"Yeah, sure, why?"

"You look like the weight of the world has rested on you?"

'Maybe it has,' he thought, but said, "No, I'm good. How's the equipment?"

Leigh turned to Francine and with a shrug prompted her for her assessment.

"We saved it. A self-instigated emergency shutdown. No blown transformers but one major power surge. It's safe to say if we try to turn it on and go back again then we'll wreck it."

Heinrich's whole body sagged at the news.

"But first things first," she continued, "maybe we don't have to go back. What do you reckon?"

Leigh led them into Oscar and across to her office. Once more she logged into the mainstream, albeit Party controlled, sites. Their logical heads knew that because they were here with no perceivable differences then probably nothing had changed on the outside. But logic didn't salve their disappointment when they saw no discernible difference in the world that they knew so well.

"The answer's yes then. We have to go back," said Heinrich.

"That's still impossible. The system will drop as soon as we try," countered Francine.

"You said you had a couple of spare transformers. If we try with this one and it blows, we still have one left?"

Leigh chipped in, "It doesn't work like that. The amount of surge we're looking at doesn't mean we just blow the transformer. It could mean we shatter the whole system."

They sat quietly for a long moment. Heinrich finally turned to them, "I'm going to go and study my notes and the copies I made of the Archive's maps. I need to at least try to find this garden Judas spoke of. Then I'm going to cross-reference it through the Reich's satellite database that you have access to in the Thule Room. Then I'm going to try and think of what to say when we go back in. All I can do is to be ready when you two come up with a way of figuring this out. I know you will." He began to move out of the office, saying as he went, "Heck, I know one of you would solve this, so two of you together, you'll crack it in no time. A burden shared and all that. Can you let me back into the room?" He was halfway across Oscar before he realised no one was following him. He turned and went back to Leigh's office door, "Seriously, can you let me back in?"

The two scientists were staring at each other with a perplexed look on their faces.

"That could work, couldn't it?" Leigh said.

"Yep, most definitely," replied Francine and reached for a plain sheet of paper. As Heinrich watched they began scribbling with pencils.

"So, can you let me back in?"

Francine looked up at him and said, "Shooosh! Take a seat soldier boy. We're thinking."

He stayed in the doorway and watched while they quickly covered the first sheet of paper and grabbed for a few more. From his upside down view he could see what looked like a couple of boxes drawn with a line between them and what he assumed were mathematical formulas. It could equally have been the shopping list he had seen on Faber's blackboard the day before. He decided to go and sit at a bench and look at his Roman maps.

'Near the cemetery on the Mount of Olives, on the Jericho Road, west of the temple.' He thought as he tracked the maps. The Temple was an easy landmark that the Roman surveyors had accurately marked but he couldn't find anything west of the temple that looked like a garden. After a few minutes he realised he must have heard Judas wrong. Jericho was east of Jerusalem and so was the Mount of Olives. Once he had realised his mistake it didn't take long to find a garden on the map in the right place. It was marked '*Gethsēmanē*' but he figured it was a close approximation. Vineyards were noted with the Roman symbol for wine and a stylised pattern drawn to approximate other vegetation. He needed to log the satellite coordinates but he knew he would have to wait for the two scientists to finish before he could get back into the Thule Room.

He was quite startled when his ForeFone rang. After checking the screen his surprise turned to dread.

"Professor Faber, how are you?"

"Frankly, Colonel Steinmann I am a touch concerned." The older man's voice was brusque and slightly out of breath.

"Oh, that doesn't sound so good," Heinrich shut his eyes and hoped that there could possibly be a completely unconnected reason for the call, "What seems to be the problem?"

"The problem, the problem you say. Well the problem is that I have just been rung up at home by the duty watch officer from the power station that provides electricity to my lab."

Heinrich swore to himself and felt his frustration ratchet up another notch or two. He didn't get a chance to respond before Faber continued, "He informs me that there has been another spike in power use from our lab. Another? I said to him. What do you mean another? Imagine my surprise when he said *you* rang him a little while ago after a power surge. He says that you, you no less, you told him not to be concerned and that you were doing some testing. Have you suddenly developed a PhD in optoelectronics Colonel, have you?"

"No Profe…"

"Oh be quiet young man, I know you haven't. Now, look here, the point is this. I didn't think you were on your own. For a start you couldn't possibly be in there on your own. Simply impossible what with our security. So I rang up the entry control at the Tubes and they told me that Doctors Wilson and Xu are in there too."

"Yes Profe…"

"Hush! Be quiet! I'm trying to save your career, though goodness only knows why I should. I've no idea what my two scientists told you but they obviously convinced you to ring up to assuage the power station watch officer. That is a worry. Do you know why? Well, do you?"

"It's prob…"

"Enough! Of course you don't know why. Well, I shall tell you. We have protocols about excessive power usage. The protocols mean that only you or I could have gotten that watch officer to carry on as normal. Otherwise his instructions are to cut off the power going into the lab completely. Completely off after a power surge. Does that tell you something? Mmm? Only authorised by you or me. Head of Laser Research or Head of SS Security for the project. Two of us. Out of all the people on the project. Does that tell you something, anything, well?"

"I th…"

"Be quiet! You have no idea. Of course it tells you something. It tells you that there is a great risk in abnormal power usage. Our project does certain things that you have seen for yourself but, and

331

it is a substantial 'but,' the project could theoretically be used to do other things. I cannot, nor will not, discuss this on the phone to you but it can do things, mark my words. Things that have been categorically ruled out by our leaders but things nonetheless it could do."

Heinrich heard the professor suck in another rapid lungful of breath.

"Given your intervention into my team yesterday there is a reason we stood them all down. Tempers may be frayed and emotions may be heightened and raw. We need to protect ourselves from anyone deciding to do anything stupid or reckless. Something reckless like trying to assist a former colleague, however well-meaning that intention may be. Do I make myself clear?"

Heinrich waited to see if he was about to get interrupted again.

"Well, do I?"

"Not really Professor." He said, hoping to play for a little time, "How do you mean?" he heard Faber draw another, if slower and deeper, breath.

"Are you in my lab now?"

"Yes."

"Are Leigh and Francine there too?"

"Yes Professor."

"Right! This is an order Colonel Steinmann and please do not forget that I hold a Technical Directorate rank that is quite a number of rungs above you. Get yourself and my two scientists out of that lab. You are to escort them up above ground. Go to the cafeteria, in fact. Go there and keep them there until I arrive. Am I clear?"

Heinrich could sense frustration in the man's voice but also something else. Almost a tinge of disappointment.

"Professor, I will of course do as you ask, but may I ask why?" There was a lengthy pause.

"You are my head of security." The professor's voice had calmed somewhat and his breath was less ragged. "I am instructing you to do this so there is no need to bring in outside agencies. You and I shall discuss this. You and I shall reach a mutual understanding and I will not lose two more of my best for no reason. Is that clear?"

"Yes Professor."

"Good, well, do as I say and take my two out of the lab. Heinrich," the professor's voice had flattened yet carried a sense of dread, "get them out of there for me please. I want them to be safe."

"Yes Professor." The line went dead. Heinrich checked the time, then walked back to the office where the women were still huddled together. They looked up as he got to the doorway.

"We can fix it and make it work," Leigh said excitedly.

Francine added, "And it's thanks to you soldier boy. Your little 'two heads better than one' quip. We can use the spare transformer, wire it in parallel, ease the load on the power input circuits and then," she paused, "you have no idea what I mean do you?"

"Nope, but what I got is that you can make it work again and I'm the genius that thought up how to do it?"

"Yeah, something like that," said Leigh.

The two scientists got up and collected all their papers ready to start work.

"Don't go yet. We need to talk."

52

Heinrich guessed his change of expression conveyed the gravity of the moment as both Leigh and Francine stopped looking pleased with themselves. They sat back down, each distractedly clutching papers and pencils to their chest.

Heinrich propped himself on the corner of the desk and asked, "Where does Professor Faber live?"

"Sevenoaks, why?"

"Hang on," Heinrich punched the location into the map display on his Fone and calculated the fastest travelling time from there to Todt. He then quickly recounted the conversation he had had with Faber.

"He thinks we're trying to go back and influence Konrad not to get caught," Francine said.

"Yes. But he's concerned that you two don't get arrested so he wants to handle things a little less formally. He thinks I'll cooperate or face being thrown out in my first month in the job. He's on his way here."

"Oh!" the women said almost simultaneously. They laid their papers back down on the desk.

"If we go against him then there's no going back. This is it. We do this and even if it doesn't work our path is set," Leigh said.

Heinrich nodded slowly. "That's it exactly. Up to this point we could have, if we'd wanted to, pulled out. Now, if we do this we're committed. If it doesn't work then we'll all be joining Mary Reid standing against posts on Sunday morning. So what do you want to do?"

They were all quiet with their own thoughts for less than a minute. Francine spoke first, "I've waited my whole life to have a go at these pricks. This is my first real, albeit surreal, opportunity. I never, ever expected to get a chance to make a difference. So I say fuck 'em! We do this and at least I go out with a fighting chance." Both women looked at Heinrich.

"I say yes too. I had my eyes opened by Leigh's parents and since then I've waited for the time and the place to help chip away at the Reich. Now I have a chance to chip it all away, so yes." He finished and looked at Leigh. In that instant he realised for no sane or rational reason that he could easily fall in love with her.

She looked straight back at him and said quietly, "I was coached and advised by my family that the belief I have would be repaid by God. He would send the people I needed at the time I needed them. I think that time is now. So yes."

He stood up from the desk, "Okay, so we do this. How long will it take to restore the Time Observation Window?"

"Best guess is three quarters of an hour," Francine said.

Heinrich checked his watch, "Professor Faber is, at fastest, going to get here in forty-eight minutes according to the traffic maps. It's been five since he hung up the phone so he probably gets here just as we power up again. I need to get some things ready to cut us some extra time. Can you prop the door open for me if I need to get back in to the HP-Lab?"

"No, you'll just have to ring us. If we prop it open alarms go off after a couple of minutes. We'd have half the 'Jewel' security team down here long before Wolfgang shows up," Leigh said as she stepped up alongside him and kissed him on the cheek, "We'll get started on the transformers. Good luck."

"Just before you go," he said, "the armaments lab that's down here."

"Arnie, yeah what about it?"

"Do they have live explosives?"

"No, not at all." She looked a little taken aback at the question. "Their work is all theoretical. They might do miniscule chemical reactions and thermal investigations. They model a lot of what they do on computers now. But no, no actual explosives. Imagine the disaster that would be in a shared underground facility." She paused a moment, then added, "Why, what are you thinking?"

"Just considering our options, that's all. I'll talk to you later." He returned a kiss onto her cheek and watched the two scientists go back into the High Powered Laser Lab. Then he sat down at a bench and quietened his thoughts.

As far back as he could remember he had known what he wanted to do. He had pestered his poor mother to allow him to join the junior most branch of the Hitler Youth. Dutifully, she had led him down to enlist on the first day he was officially old enough to join. It was the best tenth birthday present he could have received.

By the time he was fifteen he had been recognised and recommended for special consideration with regard to leadership potential. From that day forward Heinrich had been trained and exercised in planning for contingencies. He had been schooled over and over in looking at the 'what ifs' and switching between the big picture and the finite detail. After the intervening quarter century his mind now automatically sorted, sifted, questioned and reviewed. He went from general to specific and back like a corkscrew spiralling in and out. He always planned like an optimist for the best possible, smoothest and cleanest result. In parallel, he expected that the wheels of the plan would fall off in the first thirty seconds. He was adaptable and, when required, he was clinical. Even now, after years of having been converted to the Turner Creed he found he could operate ruthlessly if he needed to. It tore a little piece of his soul away each and every time he did it but he could still do it. The thought occurred to him that perhaps that is what the faithful would be like if their plan to wipe out the Reich succeeded. In a world that had war and peace, then good men and women would suffer torment for doing ill, for the right reasons.

He left the lab and went above ground. He placed a call on his Fone as he descended the entrance steps towards his car.

"Schern."

"Carl, its Colonel Heinrich Steinmann, how are you?"

"Colonel, I'm well, very well. How are you?"

"Good thank you. Are you on shift?"

"Just doing some drills in and around the barracks, bit of range work, nothing much. What do you need?"

"I know you probably thought I'd call that favour in years from now but I don't like debts hanging over people. So are you and your lads up for a small task?"

"Name it."

***

Heinrich drove his car the half kilometre to the holding facility. He reverse parked into his designated parking spot just to the left of the entrance.

"Hello Mary." He stepped inside the cell and dropped the bag he was carrying onto the floor.

"Well hello Heinrich, I thought you'd forgotten about me," she said as she unfurled the length of her body on the bunk and arched her back as best she could with the cuffs that still restrained her. He thought of a caged panther stretching seductively.

"No one been in to see you?"

"No one likely to now is there? Even if I had people that would care enough, they're unlikely to show up to visit an enemy of the Reich. Anyway, you come to tell me the good news? When do I take the short, one-way walk?"

Heinrich bent and retrieved an extendable baton out of the bag next to his feet. For a fleeting instant he thought he saw Mary instinctively flinch and a real, deep-set fear pass across her eyes, but it was gone before he could be sure it had even been there. He pointed over his shoulder to the camera in the corner. Casually extending the baton, he delivered an easy swipe that shattered the camera's casing and detached the cable from the fitting. There was a small crunch as the whole unit landed on the ground in pieces. By the time he turned back the relaxed and confident Mary was fully present again and if it had been there at all, the momentary show of vulnerability was gone.

"Oh, nice. Are you coming to do something else to me?" she winked at him, "I'd quite like that, although naughty Heinrich, Leigh will be upset."

337

He was a bit taken aback and knew he was reddening under her observation. He managed to say, slightly unconvincingly, "What do you mean Leigh?"

"Oh come on, if you two aren't fucking, you should be. Really, you should see how het up she is for you." She laughed lightly and blew him an over vamped kiss.

He tried to regain a little composure, "Quit it. The camera's out because I have a proposition for you."

"I know; you want to proposition me."

"Mary," he said with an exasperated tone, "shut up and listen. I want you to come with me."

"A caring lover as well, how cute," she interrupted.

"Enough! I'm trying to tell you I'm getting you out of here. Are you interested or shall I just leave?" he said bluntly and watched as her eyes concentrated on him.

"Okay, go on."

"You and I are leaving. We're not going far but I need you to buy us some time. If it all works out you get to walk away. If it goes badly you get to go down fighting. Fighting hard."

"So option A is a life on the run and option B is death in a fire-fight? Your sales patter needs to improve."

"Option A is a different life. A new Mary, not on the run."

"Okay, that's better. Option B still sucks."

"There is Option C."

"Which is?" she asked, looking interested.

"Sunday at dawn, you, a post and a well-drilled, fully formed up, military firing squad of ten rifles pointing at you."

"See, your patter is improving. Let's go."

Heinrich slid the bag over to her. "One last thing," he said.

"Yeah?"

"I'm going to take your cuffs off and then you need to change into the clothes you were wearing when we brought you in. If between now and when we get to where we're going you decide to do something strange and unusual I will drop you as quick as look at you. I know your skills are probably good and you think they're probably better than they are. But trust me Mary. You do not want to try me. Are we clear?" He watched her and for the first time she really looked at him. Not in a superficial way but she appraised him properly. She scanned him from head to toe and back again. Then she settled on his face, then his eyes. He stood calmly waiting for her to finish and stared directly back. They held eye contact but this wasn't the light kick and flutter he got when he looked at Leigh. This was two clinical and, when necessary, ruthless people taking the measure of each other.

"Fair enough," she said and offered her wrists up over the cot end. He stepped forward, unlocked the cuffs and stepped back. She stood, kicked off the thin, flat pump shoes and, without any embarrassment, unzipped the front of the prison issue jumpsuit, letting it fall to the ground. Heinrich didn't flinch but couldn't help look and admire the shape of the woman in front of him. She wore only the plain, white, prison issue underwear and yet looked better than the models on any Berlin or Parisian catwalk.

"Last chance Heinrich, take me now and I'll not say a thing to anyone. Would you like me on my knees or on my back?"

He just shook his head and smiled at her, "Can't say you're not persistent. Get dressed and let's get going."

She gave a dramatic sigh and pointed to herself, "You'll never know now, will ya?" and began to pull on her jeans.

When she had finished dressing he stepped outside of the cell, turned left and came face to face with Peter Vogel.

53

Both men stopped abruptly and Heinrich held his hand out and down to stop Mary from coming out into the corridor.

"Colonel, what's going on?"

"Nothing of concern Peter. New rules from Berlin." He paused, "What brings you down here?"

"I was passing the control centre and noticed the camera in her cell was out again." Heinrich watched Peter lean slightly to look around him. From the look in his eyes it was obvious he had seen Mary dressed in non-prison issue. Heinrich also saw his right hand rise slightly towards the waist holster he wore.

"I'm sorry but you can't move the prisoner Sir. We've received no authority to move her. I haven't seen any RF108," Peter said, referring to the official custody transfer form.

Heinrich was about to make something else up when he sensed Mary move from behind him and come around his right hand side. He watched Peter's eyes follow her movement and could see his hand beginning to reach for his pistol. Heinrich felt a shove on his right shoulder as Mary pushed him to his left. He saw that Peter's eyes again followed the movement and his head half-turned to look at Heinrich's stumble. That small distraction meant he didn't see the vicious, downward scythe of a straight right that Mary delivered directly into his left temple. She had at least a fifteen centimetre height advantage over the young SS officer and that extra potential energy was turned into devastating kinetic force. Peter's head snapped away from the blow and his right temple hit and ricocheted off the corridor wall. He stayed upright for a teasing moment and then collapsed straight down, folding into a flopped heap at Heinrich's feet.

"Talking's way overrated," she said.

"Bloody hell, I was only going to manoeuvre him into the cell."

"Yeah, well, he was getting twitchy. What were you going to do, shove him like kids in a schoolyard? In my experience as soon as you realise that it's going to go physical, then the only thing to do is to land the first one. Do it straight away while the other guy's still thinking about building up his courage."

"You can be a vicious bitch can't you?"

"Ah, stop complaining. Would have been even better if you'd given me a gun. I wouldn't have bruised my knuckles." She winked at him.

They both dragged the unconscious Peter into the cell and used the discarded jumpsuit to fashion a makeshift gag. They put his hands behind his back and secured them with the cuffs that had previously been on Mary. Heinrich stopped as they went to leave and turned back, taking Vogel's Fone and keys.

"Here, you'll need this," he said as he handed her the Fone and then led her to the equipment lockers in the administration spine of the building. He opened the main armoury locker using his own scan card and retrieved a double zipped holdall. She held it open while he put in four Sturmgewehr S-98s, the latest design variant of the Schmeisser Company's assault weapon. Then he grabbed twenty loaded magazines along with a dozen boxes of unopened ammunition. He dumped all of this into the bag before adding his own holster and sidearm to the collection.

Mary said as he went to shut the door "Hey, if we're shopping, stick a couple of the Glock-46s in please."

Heinrich did as she asked and threw in a set of twelve preloaded magazines for the pistols as well. He then used Peter's keys and opened a double locker at the end of the row. It was filled with cold weather jackets, waterproofs and odd remnants of uniform. A couple of field caps, a forage cap, a pair of high leg combat boots, a half dozen belted holsters and a couple of combat smocks and jackets.

"Grab a combat jacket and do your best to look like your wearing uniform," he said to her.

"Where are we off to?"

"Across the car park, to the Todt Labs."

"I need a jacket and four assault rifles to storm a nerdy bunch of geeks?"

"Not quite. We're going to walk past a Wehrmacht security point of access. Then you're going to be my shield so I can finish what I'm doing."

"And what are you doing?"

"We're just talking to some people," he said vaguely.

"Yeah, who's 'we' and who're you talking to?"

"Leigh and I and another scientist called Franci. We're talking to a few people who can alter the course of the Reich. I'd love to brief you but we don't have the time." He zipped up the now heavy holdall, slung it awkwardly over his shoulder and walked up the corridor toward the entrance doors. Mary stood still.

"Nah, don't think so," she called after him.

He turned and stopped a few metres from her. "What are you doing?"

"I'm not going till you tell me what the fuck I'm risking my already dead arse on."

"We haven't got time Mary."

"Yeah, we do, cos no explanation, no me. So you have time. Talk to me."

He drew a breath, "Fine. This is the potted version. You said you wanted a vengeful God. What happens if Jesus wasn't as believed as He'd been? You'd still have the old God of the Old Book. They wouldn't all have joined together. So then there would be Jesus and His followers and maybe the next prophet wouldn't have united with Him because he wouldn't be the only ministry. Then the next and the next and finally the Last Prophet. All of them would have their own followers. There would never be complete harmony. There would be conflict throughout the last two thousand years and a need to continue to have military forces. That would mean that the complete and utter victory of the Reich might not have happened."

"Yeah, all interesting and all the sort of stuff we talked about before. I seem to remember you saying it was a shame we couldn't go back and tell him to be less Jesus-like or something like that."

"Yeah, I did. Well, I knew something you didn't. The geeky nerds came up with a way to look back in time and communicate if needed. We can do what you suggested."

"Ha-ha, very good. Now, tell me the real reason," she said sarcastically.

"That is the reason. Mary, you suggested it and we're able to do it."

"Aw fuck off! Tell me the real reason or I'm going back into my cell."

"You do what you like but give me half an hour. If you still think it's bullshit I'll drive you into London myself and you can run. My word on it."

She looked like she was about to dismiss him and the whole idea when he said, "Mary, you said that you were sorry for shooting Thomas Dunhill. You said you wanted to make it up to him. You told me Thomas said you were God's instrument. Well, guess what, he was right. This is your last chance to be brilliant and to do good."

She dropped her gaze to the floor.

"I know every man that has come into your life has hurt you in one way or another. Most have promised much and delivered little and most have betrayed you and shattered your ability to trust. But please, please, trust one to be different. It was your suggestion that started Leigh and I onto this path. Your suggestion that's put us where we are now, please, come with me."

"Because you're the one I should trust?"

"No! No, not me. Him! Y'shua, Jesus. He's already spoken your name. He knows of you in our conversations. He's the one to trust."

Heinrich didn't know if it was his tone of voice or the look on his face but whatever the reason, Mary said, "You're serious. You've either done this for real or you're so crazy you think you've done it?"

"We've done it. Come see."

"Is this all just a ruse to walk me into a trap, shot whilst escaping?"

"Why would I do that? If I want you shot I can wait till Sunday." He glanced at his watch. It was time to force the issue. "Mary,

I don't have time. I need to protect Leigh and Franci. Come with me or don't but it's decision time." He opened the holdall, fished out a Glock pistol and a magazine and set them on the ground. "Here. You'll need these either way. Good luck." He turned and walked off, wondering if he would hear the click of the magazine being pushed home. He kept walking and said a quick prayer for her not to use the Glock. She still had not moved, nor fired when he reached the door separating the corridor from the entrance foyer.

He opened the door and was about to let it swing shut when she called, "Okay, okay. Wait up." She lifted the pistol and magazine and jogged up to join him.

Heinrich briefed her on the layout of the above ground entrance to the 'Jewel' and told her how the Tubes worked. He gave her the security detail's card that Leigh had given him. They passed through with no hassle from any of the guards. His rank certainly helped and the fact she was dressed in what, at first glance, looked like a Special Forces mix of military and civilian attire meant that no one from the Wehrmacht detail got close to asking them any questions. The inner door from the rubber walkway was likewise opened with no hesitation. The duty guard saluted Heinrich and couldn't help but look at Mary as she walked a few paces behind. She made fleeting eye contact with him but merely stared through him with hard eyes. He blanched under his forage cap and blond hair. By the time they were passing the entrance to the Oscar Lab she knew what was going to be expected of her and had programmed a speed dial for Heinrich into Peter Vogel's Fone.

He walked her into the briefing room at the end of the corridor and sat her in a front seat whilst he accessed a small computer terminal marked with an official 'Geheime Reichssache' tag. He pulled up a file and pressed play. The room's secondary display screen lit up with the official digital record of the Thule team looking at the Projection of Mary Reid killing Uwe Joyce. The official commentary of the material had been added by Lance Corporal Hannah Tensfeld.

Ten minutes later Heinrich left a thoroughly stunned, yet wholly convinced, Mary at the front of the Oscar Lab with the zipper bag and he went back to the High Powered Laser Lab, ringing Leigh on the way.

54

How's it going?"

"Good, we've probably got another five to ten minutes left before we can run it back up. What have you been up to?"

"That's was quick," he said ignoring her question. He followed her through the lab and the automatic doors that led to the small hallway.

"I told you Franci was a good practical engineer." Leigh slid the heavy manual doors open and they re-entered the Thule Room. Francine was standing at the entrance to the Ringroom.

"Hey soldier boy. What've you been up to while we've been redesigning the most complex piece of hardware in the history of the Reich?"

"He won't tell me," Leigh said, showing that she hadn't missed his earlier avoidance.

"Reading comics mainly," he said and shrugged at her, "So Franci, Leigh tells me you're making good progress. Not bad for a Canadian I guess?"

"Yes, I know, fuck you very much." Francine flicked a middle finger at him.

"Love your work," he said and winked at Leigh.

"Okay, a bit of focus? We've got to get back to this. Do you need anything?" Leigh asked him.

"Access to the satellite database," he answered and both of them pointed to a console.

"We already logged you in, it's all yours." And with that they went back to their work.

Heinrich called up the satellite imagery of the area he hoped was correct. He tried to correlate the current day imagery with the Roman surveyor's maps but it wasn't easy. He knew that most old temples and monuments had been eradicated by the Reich's architectural cleansing program. Speer had been tasked by the founding Fuhrer to ensure each capital city had a fitting tribute to the Reich and he had further tasked him with eradicating any churches that could be used as rallying points for dissenters. But towns hadn't changed position, or the roads that led to them. It took him a little time but he found the road to Jericho and on it, at the foot of the Mount of Olives and across a valley from where Jerusalem's temple would have been, was the old outline of a vineyard and what could have been a garden. Comparing the features of the image to the markings on his copied map, he noted down what he hoped would be the correct coordinates. He also double checked the dates and times that he had worked out and then he sat still and waited.

Either he was going to be told that the TOW was ready to work again or he was going to get a call from Professor Wolfgang Faber. As it was, both things happened within seconds of each other.

As soon as he saw Faber's name on the Fone display he terminated the call. He knew it wouldn't buy him very long but the more confusion he could generate the better. Another minute and the Fone rang again.

"Professor?"

"Yes! Where are you and Leigh and Francine?"

"We're not coming Professor. It's for the right reasons." And he terminated the call again. He then rang Peter Vogel's Fone.

"Mary, go do it."

"On it."

The door from the Ringroom opened behind him.

"We're all set Heinrich," Leigh said.

"Good. Before we start I need to let you know what's about to happen." He briefed them quickly but didn't mention Mary's involvement.

"Who's out there helping us?" asked Francine.

"Just a favour I called in." Before they could ask any more he said, "We better get started."

***

Professor Wolfgang Faber had been a fervent Nazi as a young man. Born in Munich, still regarded as the home of the Party, he had excelled in the Hitler Youth. A crack shot and, rather surprisingly when compared to the shape he was now, a good athlete. But it was for his scientific studies that he had been recognised by the Reich. He still remembered with immense pride how, on his fourteenth birthday, he had been awarded the Fatherland's Science Scholarship by the Founding Führer himself.

But his zeal for fascism had faded over the years. He had become disillusioned with the never-ending oppression and control the State wielded as friends and colleagues had fallen foul of the regime. Yet in his deep core, he was still loyal, still a Party member of some standing and still held the significant SS rank of Major General. He had been and continued to be fiercely patriotic and intensely protective of his nation.

Wolfgang also knew that he was disorganised and dishevelled yet only in the things that he never considered important. In the scientific realm or in areas that interested him he had a sharply focussed intellect. He was, in all measurements, a true genius with a speed of thought second to none and matched by a mere few in the history of theoretical science. It was this precise and formidable Wolfgang that considered the potential ramifications of what his scientists were up to in the Oscar Lab. He was now convinced that Leigh and Francine, influenced by their great respect for Konrad Lippisch, had decided to use the Time Observation Window to go back and change events. He had no idea how they had convinced Heinrich but he surmised they had not explained what the consequences might be. It was time to put this to an end, there was no more leeway for informal approaches. He just hoped he would be able to save Leigh and Francine from a firing squad.

348

He rang the J2 Watch Officer in the office of Reichsführer-SS.

"J2 Watch, Major Reddick."

"This is Major General Professor Wolfgang Faber at the Todt Laboratory Complex in London."

"Yes, Major General, how may I help?"

"I'd like you to terminate the current TOW immediately."

"I'm sorry," Reddick hesitated, "um, we don't have one in operation at the current time."

"But you have had earlier today?"

"No Sir. The last activation we show on our logs was," Wolfgang could hear him flicking through pages, "eh, it was 23:05 GMT on Monday the Eighteenth of May."

Wolfgang was shocked but managed to say, "Oh, sorry, it must be my mistake. Thank you."

"Certainly Major General."

He disconnected the call and his concern mounted. He had no idea how they had gotten the Berlin protocols turned off but it still didn't change his view on what they were up to. It did strangely mean that he might yet rescue Leigh and Francine from their fate. If Berlin knew nothing about it then there was still a chance. He walked back down from the cafeteria and through to the security detail guarding the entrance to the Tubes. A young Wehrmacht soldier slid his chair over as he approached the small acoustic opening in the security screen.

"Get me your Commanding Officer, please."

"And why do you need to speak to him Professor?" The young soldier said apathetically.

Wolfgang glared at him, "Because I am a SS-Major General, which is the equivalent to a Wehrmacht Generalleutnant. You either do as I ask right now or I will order your arrest, court martial and execution before the day is out. Do I make myself absolutely clear?" he said it calmly yet with an unmistakable tone of authority and menace. He watched the colour drain out of the boy's face.

***

Mary approached the internal security desk that monitored the rubber walkway and was the only regular entrance into the lab complex. The blond soldier she had stared through on arriving was still on duty and turned in his chair to face the approaching footsteps. He was blushing almost as soon as he saw who was coming up to him. Mary walked with both her hands cupped behind her back, looking relaxed and knowing that her hair, loosed from the band she normally wore, was framing her face in a very attractive way.

"Hi," she said in a friendly, light and carefree tone.

"Hi, umm, Ma'am?" he said as he quickly tried to get to his feet.

"Oh, no need for that. You can just call me," she covered the last metre of distance between them and from behind her back dropped a pistol magazine on to the ground to her left. The soldier immediately looked down to the object like his head was connected to it by string. Mary unloaded a similar punch to the one she had hit Peter Vogel with. This time was no less effective.

She reached over the slumped soldier and flicked the switch marked 'Open." The door clicked and she dragged the unconscious body into the rubber walkway. Taking his sidearm from his holster, she laid him prone across the width of the space then returned inside and shut the door. She walked back to the entrance to Oscar and retrieved the zipped holdall before making her way back to the security desk. Once there, she reached for the small metal hammer that hung to the right of a fire alarm break-glass panel. "Oh, I've always wanted to do this," she said to herself and hit the glass with the hammer. The head of the hammer broke clean off and landed on the ground. The glass remained fully intact.

"Well, that's quite a disappointment." She bent and retrieved one of the S-98 assault rifles, reversed it and smashed the butt into the glass. The alarm panel shattered and the sirens went off above and below ground with a loud and insistent 'whoopa', 'whoopa' and between every fifth blast an electronic voice repeated in a casual and relaxed manner, "Emergency Evacuation. Please evacuate calmly to your designated muster point."

***

When the siren first sounded all three of them jumped slightly.

Leigh and Francine made their way over to the tannoy speakers in the corners of the Thule Room and the High Powered Laser Lab and snipped the wires leading to them. Silence was restored. Through the security door leading back into Oscar they could hear a muted version of the alarm. They shared a final confirmatory look as they reconvened and set to work.

55

Heinrich called out, "April second, AD 30, 10:00 GMT, coordinates are 31 degrees 46 minutes 46.01 seconds north, 35, 14 and 20.89 east." The lights held steady with not so much as a flicker and Francine and Leigh shared a small moment of triumph.

Leigh wound out the elevation to cover as big an area as she could manage as the Window stabilised. The Projection was startling. The weather was glorious with blue skies and what looked like a soft breeze ruffling the branches on the trees. They were looking over a shallow valley running north to south between the Mount of Olives to the east and the Old City to the west. She panned left and right, up and down. A vast number of people were thronged along the sides of all the roads they could see. Just to the Projection's right hand side there was a line of people strung across a road, effectively blocking the entrance to a garden that was dotted with numerous squat trees. The extent of the garden ran east up the foot of the Mount and faced across the valley floor to a hill, atop which was a gate into the city. In the middle of the garden were three figures standing, isolated. Leigh tightened the Window onto the location as fast as it would track.

"Y'shua, we have returned."

"Welcome Heinrich. Are Leigh and Franci there also?"

"Yes," the women called together.

In the Projection Window Leigh could see that Judas was looking agitated, Miriam was looking profoundly sad but Y'shua looked as serene and calm as ever.

"What's wrong?" Leigh asked before Heinrich had a chance to speak again.

"Nothing, nothing really," Y'shua answered.

"Yes there is!" It was Judas and as he spoke his eyes seemed to search for where he should look. Leigh centred the image so that it looked straight at the three in the garden.

"Judas, we are to your front and at head height. Speak to us there. Now what is wrong?" she asked and her voice carried real concern.

"We did as you asked. The Master has spoken in parables, concealed his miracles, counselled his followers to be discreet and wary. Yet the people still follow in the multitudes. Thousands of people attend his sermons and thousands more approach Jerusalem to herald him this week."

"Be calm Judas, my brother," Y'shua soothed. He added, "Leigh, we were lacking the ability to divert our course so we began to talk to Caiaphas and his advisors. Do you know who I speak of?"

Leigh looked to Heinrich to take over.

"Yes, I know of him. He is the chief Pharisee and a writer of one of the Gospels. He was the one who proclaimed you to the Sanhedrin."

"Ha! Heinrich you fool," Judas almost spat the words out. The three in the lab saw the look Y'shua gave him but Judas continued, "he is but a puppet of Annas his father-in-law. Caiaphas is influenced in all he says and does by him. After our conversations with you those years ago in Capernaum, the Master asked me to speak to them in the shadows and away from the people. It is a disaster." Judas bent his head and Y'shua turned to him and took him in his arms. Almost cradling him like a child into his shoulder.

Leigh, Heinrich and Francine shared a look of confusion and concern but said nothing.

"Judas went to speak to them for us," Miriam said. "He spent long nights talking to them over this last year. He has gained the trust of Caiaphas and especially Annas. To convince them to act, Judas told them that Y'shua would lead the people, take the power away from the Pharisees and isolate them. All he wanted was to sow seeds of discomfort. But Annas began to worry. He has led

Caiaphas to a different place. They are scared now that, if all of the people unite, then the Romans will see the movement as a threat and crush it. If that happens, Annas fears he will lose influence within our society."

Leigh interjected, "So he's not really worried about the Romans crushing the people. He's just worried about losing his own power base?"

"Yes Leigh that is indeed what he is scared of. But, instead of simply denouncing Y'shua, Annas has convinced Caiaphas that they must go further."

They watched as Judas straightened up again. His face was flushed and he had tears in his eyes but he spoke strongly. "Ten days ago we knew we would enter the city via the East Gate. We set the date for today, just as you had described we would do back in Capernaum. Caiaphas wanted to ban the parade but the pressure and will of the people does not allow him. He cancelled the official reception but the people have simply reinstated their own. They have strewn the roadways with palms and seek to lift the Master on their shoulders. But Caiaphas called for me a few days ago and confided in me. He will not simply advise the Sanhedrin not to recognise Him as Messiah. He is going to ask them to put Him on trial."

Leigh and Francine gave an audible gasp, whilst Heinrich exclaimed, "For what?"

Y'shua reached out his hands to both of his followers. He looked to his front, standing with his hands on their arms and said, "They wish to charge me with blasphemy."

Heinrich relaxed and said, "Oh, but that's almost perfect. It's exactly the thing that will cause division."

Y'shua closed his eyes and nodded slowly, thoughtfully.

Leigh realized something was missing. "What is really happening? You need to tell us," she pleaded.

"Annas has also convinced Caiaphas that to appease the Romans I must be taken in front of them."

"But that can't happen. The Romans won't care about Jewish religious laws being broken," said Heinrich.

"You are well informed. But this morning, as we approached here from our overnight lodgings in Beth-ania, Caiaphas sent Judas a message. We received it not one half hour ago. He believes Judas will work on his behalf and so told him of his plans. They intend to charge me with sedition."

Heinrich physically stepped back from the Projection and bumped into one of the console stations. When he turned to look at Leigh and Francine he could see their confusion. He knew they hadn't grasped the significance of what Y'shua had just said. He didn't know how he could tell them but he did finally understand why Judas was so angry and upset.

56

Wolfgang had been swept out of the building in the exodus that followed the fire alarm despite him trying to advise the guard commander, Captain Fertig, it was a ruse. He knew as he stood in front of the official muster points for the underground staff members that he had to regain a semblance of control and get back down into the building. Seeing Captain Fertig standing with a group of firefighters and paramedics he also knew it would take some time to sort this mess out. He had to act quicker than that.

He dialled the duty watch officer at the Isle of Dogs Power Generation Substation 34A. Identifying himself and his position he quoted an authorisation code that he had written down on a small credit card sized aide memoire. The duty officer acknowledged him and the code.

"Switch off the feed into the Optical Systems Calibration Laboratory Annex and keep it isolated until further notice. No one is to reactivate it except me. The head of SS Security for the project has had his approvals revoked. Me and me alone. Is that clear?"

"Yes Professor Faber," the duty officer said.

"Good. Can you confirm it's off now?"

"Yes Professor, I've isolated the circuit."

"Thank you." Wolfgang relaxed a little. Now all he had to do was get down there and talk to them. He may yet avert a disaster for Leigh and Francine. Heinrich he couldn't care less about. At least he had the reassurance that with no power nothing cataclysmic could be done to the timeline and events surrounding

Konrad's arrest. If he could keep things relatively quiet he may save his two scientists.

The duty watch officer at the Isle of Dogs Power Generation Substation 34A, was called Gareth Smyth and he was originally from Walthamstow in London. He was a thickset man with a quiff of black hair flopping over his forehead, a bull neck and aggressive tattoos on both his forearms. Yet his shaking hand needed two attempts to replace the phone's receiver in its cradle. Once he had managed it he slowly turned around in his chair and looked at the balaclava-clad man sitting opposite.

"Well done Gareth. Now, like I said, you're going to leave that power circuit on, I'm going to sit here and keep you company and my lads are going to make sure no one comes into your little power station to disturb us. When I get the call for it all to go back to normal then it will. Until that happens, just relax and do what you normally do."

Gareth nodded and glanced down at the muzzle of the HK-MP19 that was pointing directly at his forehead.

Carl Schern kept his aim steady whilst he punched a text message through to Heinrich.

Mary had watched the last of the scientists evacuate and then, with her S-98 assault rifle in the low ready, she carried out a sweep of the labs. When she was satisfied they had all left she closed the two emergency evacuation doors at either end of the long straight corridor. Once secure there was no way of opening them from the outside. The only way into the labs now was through the single point of entry that she controlled. She came back to it, silenced the below ground alarms and checked the CCTV of the walkway. The blond soldier was beginning to regain consciousness although he still looked remarkably shaky. She opened the door and dragged him back inside. Frog-marching his unsteady frame down to the first lab to the right of the T-junction, she locked him, quite unceremoniously, into a large paints, oils and lubricants cupboard that she had discovered in her earlier sweep of the complex. She was satisfied that he would be safely out of her way and probably as high as a kite on fumes when he was finally found.

Returning once more to the inner security desk, she took the holdall and retraced her steps back to Oscar. She laid one S-98 just around the corner of the T-junction and placed three loaded magazines next to it. Then she placed the last two S-98s just inside the heavy PVC doors that marked the entrance to Oscar. She dropped a couple of loaded magazines next to them and put a couple more into her jacket pockets. The remainder, along with the rest of the ammunition and the second Glock, she left in the holdall and placed it in front of the door that Heinrich had said would be her exit point. Then she scanned through the labs once more, collecting items that might be useful, depending on how things turned out.

"What does that mean?" asked Leigh.

"It means we need to stop this now," said Heinrich as he glanced down at the incoming text from Carl Schern.

Judas spoke again, "Exactly. That is what I have been saying since I received the communication from Caiaphas. We need to stop now. It has gone too far. We need clear speech and public displays of miraculous, God-given powers to regain the Pharisees."

"Please, stop talking around me. Speak plainly. What does this mean?" Leigh's voice was tense and stressed.

But it was Francine who spoke, "The Founding Führer based a lot of the structures and symbolism of the Reich on the ancient Roman Empire. Ancient Rome was ruthless and he was attracted to it. Sedition in Rome would be the same as sedition in the Reich. It's a capital offence."

There was quiet and Y'shua simply nodded. The moment stretched between the three in the Thule Room through time and distance to the three in the garden. Finally Y'shua spoke clearly, "Alas, I know that you think we must stop, but I have spent a long time in meditation and prayer since your first visits. We cannot stop. Once you told me of the darkness and despair of a never-ending tyranny on earth, my path was set. We had not planned for such drastic circumstances but if that is what it takes then I must follow it to the end."

"But Master, please consider."

"Hush now Judas. It will not be as bad as you fear. We shall talk to the Pharisees in public over the next few days. They will compromise and, even if it does go to the Prefect's office, Pilate is a fair man. He will not cower to madness. Be at peace Judas."

"Master I..."

"No Judas. Be at peace and listen. Listen carefully now and hear what I think to be true. Heinrich, if we succeed and the future is rewritten I have not asked you yet, what will become of you and Leigh and Franci?"

"We're not really sure. Leigh can better answer that."

"Y'shua, it is likely that we will simply cease to be. We will probably not survive the changes. We're not really sure, but that is our commitment and hope."

"Did you hear Judas? Now if the worst comes to pass and Annas and Caiaphas decide not to compromise, then it is only fitting I must follow the path laid by our Lord the Father. We are not sure of the outcome. We share that burden with our friends in so distant a time. If needs be, then I will sacrifice my life for Leigh and Heinrich, Franci and the countless others in the future. If they are to die then so I must die too and it is a small cost. For there will be worse than our deaths."

"What could be worse than your death Master?" Judas asked.

"Oh Judas and Miriam, Heinrich, Leigh and Franci, hearken to me. If we succeed, there will be wars and nation will rise against nation and kingdom against kingdom. And as for those who do have faith and believe in me they will stand before governors and kings and be beaten and will be put to death."

"Then please, let's stop," pleaded Judas.

"No my dearest friend. I have dwelt long on this during the years since Capernaum. The Lord told me these distant voices were coming to us. This is what must be done. So it will be done. We will enter Jerusalem and I will challenge the elders, the scribes and Pharisees. I will challenge them and they will be forced to denounce me. Once they have done that it is likely no more will be attempted. Now it is decided. Leigh, Heinrich, when did they declare me as Messiah, in your time?"

"It was on the Fast of the Firstborn," Heinrich answered.

"That would be this coming Friday. We should meet before then, if only to talk one last time. Judas, please tell them where they can meet us."

Judas wiped his face with the sleeves of his robe and looked hard at Y'shua. Then he bowed his head and said, "Forgive me Master. I will of course do as you ask." After a brief pause he spoke again, "Heinrich, do you know the village of Beth-ania? It lays fifteen stadia east of the city. Less than an hour's walk along the road to Jericho, on a small rise to the north"

"Wait for a moment," Heinrich said and flicked through a couple of pages of maps. He converted the Roman measurement to its modern equivalent and looked about three kilometres east of the city. "Yes, I can see it."

"Near the eastern end is the last road that turns from the Jericho road into Beth-ania. Take it and go to the ninth house along on the northern side. You pass through an arched gateway. It is the home of a friend; we will be safe in there. Meet us, tomorrow at dusk, in the upper room of the house."

"Thank you Judas," said Y'shua, "Leigh, Franci, Heinrich, we shall meet and talk again."

Heinrich turned to Leigh and she began to close the Projection down. There was silence in the room.

Mary saw the four lift doors open almost simultaneously and a gaggle of firefighters began to stream down the rubber walkway. Mixed in with them were a couple of Wehrmacht soldiers and an older man that she safely assumed was the professor who Heinrich had described to her. At the same time the door that she had control of opened on its own accord. That confirmed one of Heinrich's suppositions, that there would be a master override in the ground floor security post. It made sense; how else would they get back in following an evacuation? It also made no difference to what she was about to do.

She watched them pass by the first camera and as they began to approach the midpoint of the pink-pastel painted corridor she stood to one side of the open door and flicked the S-98's safety catch off. She waited until they were just coming into view round the gently sloping turn and fired a full magazine on automatic, upwards along the length of the ceiling. She still wondered why Heinrich was so concerned about not dropping a few firemen and an academic but he had set the rules. She couldn't avoid the odd injury from a ricochet but she doubted she had even managed that. She flicked the 'Close' switch hoping that the door would close, which it did, and rechecked the CCTV. Sure enough, all of her visitors were scurrying back to the lifts unharmed. Except the old professor.

He remained standing upright in the middle of the corridor. She watched him as he looked up into the camera. Like he was looking directly at her, or whoever he thought was watching. He had such a sad look on his face and shook his head slowly as he turned to walk away. Then he stopped. When he turned back his face showed a resolve and an anger that was beginning somewhere deep inside him. He mouthed very clearly, 'Abschied Verrätern', gave a formal salute to the camera and then slowly walked back to the lifts.

Mary texted Heinrich a SitRep.

57

einrich read Mary's report and knew time was running out. He watched as Francine and Leigh worked quickly to reset the Window's controls but all the while he could see Leigh was wiping away tears.

Through them she asked, "I don't understand. How can they charge Him with any crime, let alone sedition?"

"I'm not sure," he replied, "but I suspect it's because He's been called the Messiah."

She stopped and frowned at him, "You need to explain this to me. Please Heinrich, just tell me."

"We know it as a word to describe Him. But in His time it just meant an anointed one who leads. The Jewish scribes used it when they spoke of Kings. If you want to push Him in front of a Roman trial then just call Him a King. They've dealt with so many rebellions in Judea another King is simply another threat. It's like Franci said, the Reich and Rome share similarities. Imagine a leader in our world being held up as a new Royal King. Berlin would destroy him in a heartbeat."

Leigh wiped away more tears and turned back to the control console. Francine nodded that she was ready and Leigh went to initiate the Projection but stopped.

"Heinrich? What do we do if Caiaphas doesn't back down? What if it isn't a bluff?"

"I don't know Leigh, really I don't."

Leigh sighed a deep sigh and said quietly, "Please God forgive us."

Heinrich came and stood behind her, put his hand on to her shoulder and said "April 3, AD 30, coordinates are 31, 46, 11.66 north, 35, 15 and 50.05 east.

She looked up at him, "What time do we go for?"

He was conscious that he couldn't spend too long finding the place and then idly waiting, yet he needed light to be sure of hitting the mark. He compromised with himself as best he could, "Dusk in April is about 18:00 local, so 16:00 GMT but if we arrive when it's too dark we'll never find the place. Go in at 15:30 GMT."

The image opened above a wide track running horizontally across the landscape. Leigh adjusted the Window and a large village came into focus just metres to the north of the track. It occupied a hilltop and then fell away down the reverse slope as the village continued to the north-east. She moved the Projection until they had gone past the last houses before coming back slowly to the last road that went into the village.

"I assume this dirt lane is the road?"

Heinrich was following the image of the Projection on the copies of the Roman Surveyor's maps. "Yes, definitely. You know, these maps are remarkable. Especially considering the lack of technology they had available to them."

Francine and Leigh raised eyebrows at one another and suppressed a giggle at Heinrich's enthusiasm for Roman mapmakers. Even without the maps she would have easily found the ninth house to the northern side. It sat wide and tall on the reverse slope of the hill and was built from a rich cream coloured limestone that, on the upper floor levels, was quickly turning to a luscious golden caramel in the rays of the setting sun. Leigh reorientated the image and confirmed the arched gateway, through which they could see manicured gardens and a neat path that ran up to a solid looking front door. The door and all the windows seemed to have intricate carvings of geometric patterns framing them. Switching the image to look from ground level, Leigh held it in position to allow Francine to assess the likely elevation of the roof line some three storeys above. Using a rough guestimate, they centred the Projection on what they hoped would be the top floor of the dwelling.

After a small amount of adjusting Leigh settled the image into a long, low ceilinged room that appeared to run the length of the house. It was empty of people but shafts of light from the dying sun came through a large window and picked out a pitcher and some rough-hewn cups sitting here and there on a long table that ran almost a third of the length of the room.

"Shall we assume this is it?" she asked. Francine and Heinrich nodded their agreement.

"And so we wait."

58

Mary was waiting too. She'd been busy since the professor had saluted and departed to the lifts. She had surmised as soon as the door had automatically opened for the firefighting entourage that the security detail upstairs might have automatic control over a few other things. Mary had spent a few minutes putting the items she had scavenged earlier into place and a few more rehearsing her planned movements. Then she spent some time trying to estimate how long it would be before they came back.

She figured on them having missed she was even in the building so they would reckon on two scientists and a SS-Colonel. He alone would be enough for them to take their time, gather their strength. Working through a likely chain of events, she estimated how long it would take the firefighters to get back above ground, tell whoever was commanding the detail what had happened, allow him to regroup his troops and try to put a plan into place. She assumed they would work off an immediate action drill to retake the below-ground level and use as many of the security detail as were on shift. Heinrich had said it was an eight-man shift with a senior NCO and an Officer, so a standard ten-man squad would probably be coming out of the lifts. Having run her scenarios a couple of times, she settled on a delay of eighteen minutes if they were dumb like Heinrich had suggested they would be.

When he'd briefed her earlier, he'd said that if they were smart they'd call in reinforcements from the Wehrmacht barracks in Chelsea immediately. Those troops would come with grenades and rocket launchers. If they were really smart they'd call in SS-Kommando from Northwood, but they wouldn't ever call the SS to take back a Wehrmacht guarded site. So it would be Chelsea Barracks. That would take, at the very least, twenty minutes to get from one side of London to the other. So he'd said if they came earlier than twenty minutes then it would be standard troops with small arms only, and that would be dumb.

"And so we wait," she said to herself.

A little bit of her was quite impressed at the 'can-do' attitude of the commander up there when the door clicked open again after only fourteen minutes. As soon as the door servo had driven it halfway open it ceased and all the CCTV displays that monitored the rubber walkway went blank. Then all the lights went off. Mary put her plan into action.

She leant around the door and fired a full magazine into the space but not up along the ceiling this time. She dropped the empty weapon, switched on two of the torches she had found and threw one of them into the walkway. She left the other where she had taped it to the security desk, pointing at the door. She ran back to the T-junction and switched on two more torches she had taped high up on either side of the opening. She turned on a portable 400-watt halogen workshop spotlight she had found in one of the labs. It was covered with a piece of thick black fabric she had found in another lab and positioned to the right hand corner of the T-junction. She checked that a thick cord she had taped to the fabric was still in place and followed it across to the other side of the T-Junction. She dropped prone, nestled herself into the corner, checked the magazines placed around her and pressed her left shoulder into the stock of the prepositioned S-98. She was naturally right-handed but had thought, 'needs must' as she swapped over and got comfortable. By the time she had regulated her breathing back to a steady rhythm she heard a burst of gunfire. The torch in the walkway was extinguished.

The next shots came from her as she sighted the first man through the doorway in the beam of the torch taped to the desk. She aimed at the night vision goggles he had on his head and double tapped the trigger. He fell backwards out of sight and left only a plume of red mist suspended in the torchlight.

Two muzzles came around the side of the door and Mary managed to roll back behind the wall as they fired indiscriminately into the space between them and her. There was a short pause followed by three more bursts that were obviously aimed at the torches she had taped into position. She didn't have to peek back out to know that all of them had been extinguished. She waited calmly in the pitch black knowing that at least two, maybe four of the detail would have night vision equipment. They would be coming into the corridor and making their way down the walls in tight pairings.

She forced herself to wait another three seconds that felt like three hours, then pulled the cord attached to the fabric. The warmed up halogen pumped out a blinding 32000-lumens of light into the corridor. To a non-night vision wearing soldier it would have been dazzling. To one with goggles it was the equivalent of a whiteout. She rolled back into the opening and saw all of the first four soldiers had goggles on and were therefore effectively blinded. She sighted on the nearest two that were on her side of the corridor and dropped each man with a short, three-round burst. Before they could react to the noise she did the same to the two on her opposite side. The next two pairs of soldiers behind, who she was surprised to see also had night goggles, were using their ears and obviously decided their only hope was to fire everything they had as quickly as they could.

Mary ducked back round the corner as bullets whipped and ricocheted around her. It didn't take many seconds for a number of them to find the halogen and once more there was darkness. She had, at best, a few seconds before the advantage slipped away from her so she turned and ran as fast as she could back to the Oscar Lab. The entrance was seventy metres from the junction and she knew she probably wouldn't make it before they came round the corner. She held the S-98 across her body, pointed it back under her left arm and fired randomly behind her. Even then, just as she reached the door of the lab a 7.92mm Mauser round from a Karabiner went clean through her left calf. It spun her halfway around and threw her sideways through the heavy-duty PVC doors like a ragdoll being tossed by a bored child.

She switched her last two torches on and slid one up against the PVC doors. The heavy-duty plastic might stop the light being shot out so quickly and at least it would give her a little warning that her pursuers were coming. She looked down at her leg and saw the red stain spreading alarmingly quickly. Ripping the torn fragment of trouser into two good lengths of fabric, she tied them in a makeshift tourniquet above the wound before grabbing up the last two loaded S-98s, the rest of the magazines and as much ammunition as she could shove into her jacket pockets. She decided it was time to bug out. Taking the final torch and now limping badly, she headed towards the door Heinrich had shown her. When she got there she doused the light and punched the speed dial.

59

Heinrich answered immediately.

"You need to come get me. I'm at the door."

"On my way."

He got up and ran out of the Thule Room, ignoring Leigh and Francine's startled looks. He bolted through to the High Powered Laser Lab door and opened it. Mary practically fell into his arms with three S-98s and the holdall hung about her. He pulled her back inside, laid her on the ground then took one of the S-98s and shot out the card reader access port on the outside of the door. He looked down at her as he pulled the door closed. "Mary, you're hit."

"No shit! There's me thinking it was only a paper cut. Of course I'm fucking hit. You think I didn't notice?"

"Fair enough. How many and what do they have?"

"Probably five left, small arms only. Like you said, they were dumb. How long do you reckon it'll take them to breach that door?" she said looking over her shoulder.

"Without having explosives of some form or other they don't get through at all. With a few well-placed charges then they'll be through in seconds. That means they'll need to call over to Chelsea, or the Woolwich Arsenals or the artillery companies up in the north of the city. Any of them are going to be at least twenty minutes in getting mobilised and over here."

"Unless they called them twenty minutes ago?"

"If they'd done that they would have waited for them."

"You hope."

"Yeah, I hope. Okay come with me." He helped her up, allow-ing her to use him as a support and guided her through to the Thule Room.

"What the fuck's she doing here?"

"Well hi to you too Leigh. No really, the pleasure's all mine," Mary managed to say through clenched teeth.

Heinrich helped her across to the nearest seat and Mary low-ered herself into it gingerly.

Francine was already moving towards the portable first aid box on the wall, spurred on by the quantity of blood that was flowing from Mary's calf.

Leigh stood motionless in the middle of the room and stared. "Heinrich I asked you a question?"

"We needed someone to help us. Someone close by, able to use a weapon and capable of being trusted. There was no other choice." He elevated Mary's leg as Francine knelt in front of her and ripped open the first aid container.

"What about Konrad? You couldn't have used him?" Leigh was angry and her tone of voice was severe.

"No I couldn't. We wouldn't have been able to get him past the security detail. They all know him and they all know his access has been rescinded. No one up top knows Mary. Also, I doubt Konrad can use an assault rifle."

"So we're using a murderer to help us now?"

"To be perfectly honest Leigh, she was the one that came up with the idea that has us standing here." Heinrich could feel his temper rising.

Mary flinched and reared back in the seat as Francine used al-cohol laden wipes to clean the wound area. "You're lucky, it's gone clean through," Francine said and reached for some thick gauze pads.

"And you didn't think to tell me and Franci that you were going to get her out of her cell?"

"No I didn't. I wanted both of you to concentrate on getting the Projection up and running and I don't see I had any other choice."

"What makes you think, in your right mind, that using her was going to be okay? All you did was put loaded weapons into the hands of a potential psychopath."

"Hey, hey, I'm sitting right fucking here!" Mary shouted. She squirmed a little more as Francine bound her wounded calf tightly but she didn't give either Heinrich or Leigh a chance to interrupt before continuing, "I *can* hear this wonderful domestic you two seem to be having about my presence. I've just been fucking shot trying to buy you time for something I'm still not a 100 per cent up to speed on and all you can do is call me a fucking psycho. Thanks. I really appreciate it. The first time I met you," she looked directly at Leigh, "you fucking electrocuted me. Now all you can do is call me names. What is your fucking problem?"

"You're my problem Mary. You murdered people. One of them right after you slept with him. You're a mad bitch. That's my problem and so is..." Leigh stopped in mid-sentence as she saw a wash of flame envelope Mary and disappear almost as soon as it had been visible.

"Welcome Mary. You will forgive Leigh as she will forgive you. Your deeds and actions will be judged not by your fellow woman or your fellow man but by your Father in heaven and he will look deep into your soul. You may be found wanting but that is not for us to say." Y'shua's words came calm and serene into the room.

Mary's eyes had widened as she looked past Leigh to the Projection on the wall.

"I am told that you had an epiphany of sorts and that you believe I crushed the need for faith? I was also told that you had this revelation after doing many terrible things. Mary, I have rescued many of my disciples from lives of hurt and desolation. You are no different."

Mary still sat wide-eyed and staring at the man in the Projection.

"I have but two questions for you. Will you truly repent of your sins and will you place your faith in the Lord our God to forgive you?"

The room was quiet but after Francine took her hand and said, "Go on," Mary finally managed to speak.

"I don't think even you or God can forgive me for what I have done. I don't think anyone could."

"Mary, I am Y'shua, the anointed leader of a movement that according to Heinrich has reshaped the world. A world that was raised into brightness for two thousand years and then was plunged into dark terror. A darkness that there appears to be no way out of. I will not let that stand. I will rather see the suffering of war shared amongst the generations so that the light of humanity can overcome. For it is better to allow light and dark to be experienced by all than to surrender the whole of humanity to an all-encompassing evil. I will rather see my life extinguished if necessary to make this happen. All of this was brought about by a conjoining of circumstances. I saw in a vision a message that is meant for you. Thomas was a meek and loving man. He shall inherit a new earth because of where you were and what you did. He forgave you even in his final second. And you say that God could not. Oh Mary, you are mistaken."

His words reverberated in Mary's head and she saw the face of Thomas Dunhill looking up at her from the cold and blood-drenched concrete. She heard him say he loved her and she heard the echoes of the shots she had fired. Bowing her head she wept with gentle sobs.

"Leigh, you will forgive your sister for she knew not what she did. You will forgive Heinrich for it was important that he brought Mary here at this time. All four of you pay heed to me."

Leigh and Heinrich turned to look at the Projection and saw that Y'shua was sitting cross-legged against the wall opposite the now dark window. He had brought a couple of candles into the room with him and they gave enough light to see him clearly. He spoke in measured and melodic tones, almost an incantation that they all were drawn to hear.

"Listen to me and reflect. For us to be here, for us to be soon to do the things we do, it needed the world to turn so many times and in so many ways. Each turn took us to a new beginning. Each turn was because there is a set time to all. So Leigh, understand that without you and all you have gone through we would not be here. But equally without Mary and Franci and Heinrich and all they have been through we would not be here at this moment. The world turns and there is a time to every purpose."

Leigh had tears welling in her eyes and said in an emotion-filled voice, "Yes Y'shua," then she turned to Mary, "I'm sorry."

"Now we must speak about our plans," Y'shua said.

"You are alone?" asked Heinrich.

"Yes. I sent Judas to see Caiaphas. He will be back soon. Miriam is with the rest of my closest followers downstairs. There is much confusion in their minds. She will soothe them and be along in a moment."

"Have you told the rest what is happening?"

"No. Only Judas and Miriam know of our purpose. The rest of my people do not know what may be coming but they sense the tension. They are scared and I cannot blame them."

"Y'shua I don't understand why we can still be talking. If you are determined to go ahead with this then all the actions are set. The world as we know it should have seen changes sweep through it. We shouldn't be here to talk with you."

"But it is not set until it is done Heinrich. There is much that could be undone."

"I don't understand."

"It is plain. I may be taken and I may be tried but that is not certain. Even if I am, I could lose my will. I could call on God to intervene and through His intervention, with one brush of my hand, I could cast our accusers aside. I could step away from whatever it is they have planned for me and with one demonstration of His power they would have to believe. There would again be no need for faith. It would be as certain and as plain as the sun and the moon. It is not done yet. Do you understand?"

Heinrich considered what Y'shua had said. He realised that the fear of what was to come or what might come could be overpowering. "Yes, I understand."

He looked around as Leigh came up next to him and slipped her hand in his. They both glanced back and saw Francine had applied a second series of dressings over Mary's wound. It looked like the bleeding was stopping. Mary for her part, sitting as upright as she could, had just about stopped weeping and appeared to be intently following the conversation that was playing out in front of her.

Y'shua said, "Even today in the city it was not simple or straightforward. I tried to provoke a reaction from the elders and the scribes. I challenged how they used the Temple and their presumptuous ways but they would not react." He looked up to his right and the candle flames flickered and swayed as in a breeze. Miriam came and sat beside him.

"Of course they won't react to you when you are surrounded by the people," she said in response to him. "They're scared. They see how the crowd are held enthralled by your words and your teachings. Yet those same words make Annas and his House quake."

"It is true that they do nothing. They are the worst hypocrites, rotted by their power. They care not for the poor and the meek but lord it over them with their gold and robes and coins. Desperate to keep in with the Roman authorities yet too weak to stand against me. I fear we may have to prompt them to act."

Leigh asked, "Is that why you've sent Judas to meet with them again?"

"Yes."

"But why must we force them?"

"We do not force them. We merely let them have the die. It is theirs to cast."

"Y'shua?"

"Yes Leigh, be not hesitant."

"Why would we give them the control? You just said they are hypocrites and rotted men."

"Ah, we think that we are the masters of our own destiny all of the time. That we choose to turn right or left, to do this or that, to go here or go there and it is mostly true. You have the wheel and you steer your own ship through life's seas. But sometimes, on vital occasions, when the seas are at their roughest, your destiny is chosen for you. It is on these occasions you need to let the wheel turn at its own pace and God will place you where you need to be…"

"…and send the people he needs to send." Leigh finished Y'shua's sentence.

Heinrich felt the lump in his own throat and he watched her swallow hard. He could feel her gripping his hand tightly as they both tried to deal with their memories.

"And now you understand," Y'shua said softly.

But Francine didn't understand and she was about to ask a few blunt questions when she saw Judas coming into the frame of the Projection. He looked pale and drawn, tired and stressed. Seeing his demeanour Francine simply asked, "Judas, are you alright?"

He didn't answer her, but spoke directly to Y'shua, "They are determined to take you Master but they are concerned that if they reach for you in the daylight, with the crowds assembled, they will be crushed. And they cannot come and take you in the night for they have no knowledge of our movements. They are undone."

"Yet you, my brother, my most loyal friend, you are a shadow of yourself. Tell me what has been planned?"

"They will not come here to take you in the evening for they fear your disciples. They know that they need to isolate you and they also need to have proof of false witnesses against you. So they plan to question you tomorrow in front of the assembled masses near the Temple grounds. They want to trap you in your answers."

"But Judas, you know I have answers for them. All we have done since Capernaum is answer them in ways that they could not deflect yet railed against. This is not an issue."

"Annas is aware of the likely outcome. He is manipulative but not stupid or unseeing. And so tomorrow night they want me to come to them again and plan with them a place to take you to trial."

"Then so be it."

"Master, please, I beg of you, don't make me do this. The people will believe that I have betrayed you."

"Yet I will know you have not. Caiaphas and Annas have come to believe that you are capable of this and they know that you still hold the place as my closest advisor. There is no one else that could convince them. There is no one else who could deliver me. You must do this for me."

Judas looked so profoundly sad but he simply nodded his head.

"Do they wish to take me tomorrow?"

"No, they wish to take you early on the morning following the first day of unleavened bread. They think it will be safer as the crowds will have dispersed in the evening for their meal and will not rise until daybreak. By the time they realise you are gone they will be too late. They want me to guide you to an isolated spot for prayer and meditation."

"Then we shall try to encourage them to act tomorrow when they question me and if that fails we shall give them their dark of night arrest. In the middle day we shall spend time with our followers and our families and we shall be together for what may be the last time. Now both of you go to our disciples and tell them not of the purpose but of the plans."

The candles swayed again in the breeze as out of the Projection image the door to the upper room was opened and closed as Judas and Miriam departed. Y'shua was left alone.

"Leigh, you can find the Garden of Gat Šmānê again?"

"Yes."

"Then we shall meet where we met before, three nights hence, come at the second hour of the new day. I shall light the spot with a trinity of lamps. Heinrich, it is the day you told me that they heralded me in the Sanhedrin. How things have come full circle."

"Yes it seems that they have."

"Perhaps it will not be needed. Perhaps I shall make them speak the words tomorrow but we shall be safe to make these plans. All I ask is that you come to me in the garden. For if it is to be my arrest and if they charge me with sedition then we know that it will lead to my death," he said the words calmly and without emotion.

Leigh turned to Heinrich and leant into him.

From the rear of the room Mary spoke, "You are willing to do this for us? You don't even know us. You don't even know if this will work. You're going on blind faith."

"Yes Mary and isn't that what we desire? That faith can be its own force? And say not that I know you not. We are united in our struggles and therefore we are friends."

"But you could die," she said.

"Yes Mary, I could. But greater love hath no one than to lay down their life for their friends. You are my friends and do not think that you have chosen me to do this for you. He has chosen you and you will all sacrifice yourselves if this comes to pass. You may each have to lay down your lives. We do this for the Father and in my name, He may grant us our needs."

"What can we do to help?" asked Heinrich.

"I do not wish to be alone. Only Judas and Miriam will know of the true purpose. If this comes to pass then Judas will have to lead them to me and fulfil the role he will detest. Miriam cannot come with me to Gat Šmānê after dark for it is forbidden. I know some of my disciples will insist on coming with me but they will not understand what is going to happen."

"We will be there Y'shua," Heinrich said.

"All of you be confident that what we may have to do will be worthy sacrifice. Mary, your sins will be forgiven for the services you render to me. Franci, your persecution will be lifted. Heinrich and Leigh, your belief will be repaid a thousandfold and I will restore hope and light to the world. Now go and return when I need you by my side." He stood and walked from the image Window. Francine reached forward and shut down the Projection.

Just as the translucent disc collapsed and the Ring Laser powered down all of their ForeFones rang at once, including Peter Vogel's that Mary wore. She bit her lower lip and wiped the tears from her face.

"They obviously know that I'm out then," Mary said with a false smile and punched the speaker option on the Fone.

"This is Captain Fertig. Who am I speaking to?"

"Identify your post soldier!" Mary snapped at him.

"I'm the security detail guard commander, who am I speaking to?"

"Chief Senior Overseer Mary Emma Reid. That's Reid with an E and an I. Do make sure you spell it correctly."

"Who else is in there with you?" Fertig asked, a little taken aback.

"Oh just a few good folk that I'm holding hostage against their will. Now go away or I shall start killing them on the hour every hour. I want a car, a suitcase full of Reichmarks and a plane, fully fuelled and waiting at the nearest airport. Ring me back when you have all of that organised." She hung up the call and looked at Heinrich, "How long?"

"Fifteen minutes, twenty tops."

Francine and Leigh were looking puzzled. Leigh was the first to phrase their confusion, "What are you two talking about?"

Heinrich answered, "The reinforcements are close by or have just turned up. Not sure who but definitely somebody. The first thing they'll want to know is if we're all still functioning. They do that by trying to establish communication. They know we aren't hostages. If they tried Peter's Fone then they've found him and he'll have told them that I helped Mary. Wolfgang will already have told them that we three were working together. So now they know we're a foursome and that we're all in cahoots. Negotiation isn't an option. We don't have hostages and they just want this sorted. So, it'll take them a few minutes to figure out how they're going to do this, a few more to get orientated and a few more to run through it a few times. Give or take, fifteen minutes, twenty tops."

"Why haven't they just turned off all our power? Surely Wolfgang or someone up there has thought of that by now?" Francine asked.

"That's true!" said Leigh, "That should have been the first thing they did."

"That's a good point, they killed all the rest of the power ages ago, why do we still have lights?" asked Mary.

"Because they think they already have. It's just I had some friends go and babysit the circuit breakers."

"Are you serious?" Leigh was looking at him like he had grown a second head.

"Yes, seriously. Some people owed me a favour. I called it in."

"That's a seriously big favour. Must have been some debt they owed you," Mary said.

"Mary, you of all people wouldn't believe me if I told you. Alas, I don't have time. We need to get ready."

378

60

Heinrich was in the High Powered Laser Lab laying the heavy work benches over on their sides and forming makeshift firing points with them. He had positioned four of them at staggered intervals near the rear of the room in the hope they would be far enough away from the door to avoid being caught in whatever blast was used to gain entry. He also positioned a fifth to provide cover to withdraw back into the small hallway that led into the Thule Room. He doubted it would get used even as he laid it in place. He looked around. With the tables in position, he had cleared a reasonable expanse of killing ground between them and the door. The smaller workstations and shelving units were still dotted about the lab but it was the best he could manage.

When all was ready he joined the others back in the Thule Room and they sat together in a circle with joined hands. They said neither Creed nor prayer. They merely took a brief moment to be together.

Before they broke the circle Mary said, "I'm truly sorry for what I did and I wish I could have found my sisters. But I'm glad I knew them at all." She looked to Francine.

"I wish Konrad could have loved me but I'm so pleased that I loved him."

Leigh squeezed her friend's hand tightly, "I wish my parents could have spoken to Him with me but I'm so grateful for the life they gave me and the mark the years left."

Heinrich looked at her and said, "I wish I had met you sooner so we could have had longer together but I'm blessed to be with you now. As the sun rises."

The four stood and hugged. Then Mary limped through to the Lab, leaning on Francine for assistance. She got herself into a good firing position and placed the Glock pistol next to her along with a stack of magazines for both it and the S-98.

Francine walked back to the Thule Room and picked up one of the spare assault rifles. She slung it over her shoulder and stuck another few magazines into her pockets. Then she stepped back into the Lab. From the doorway she called to Leigh and Heinrich who were at the console station at the front of the room. "Hey, you two. Do us proud. When I shut this, lock it from your side."

"No Franci, I need you in here," Leigh called.

"No Leigh you don't. You can operate the Projection and Heinrich is the one with the history lessons. We can't leave Mary out here on her own and I used to be handy with one of these," she held up the S-98, "but lock the door, we won't need to come back in."

Leigh made to run the length of the room but stopped short when her friend simply waved a goodbye and slid the heavy opaque door shut. She still hadn't moved when a half minute later a text message popped up on her Fone.

"What's it say?" asked Heinrich.

"Lock the door silly or they'll walk right in. Love you."

Heinrich walked down to the door and eased the manual lock into place. Leigh sent a final text to her friend and turned back to the console station. She reset the Window and reconstituted the Projection for 02:00 local Jerusalem time on April 7, AD 30. When it opened up on the coordinates they had previously used for Gat Šmānê an almost complete blackness filled the screen, save for the very centre of the image, where three lamps shone like beacons.

Just before she started to adjust the display to spiral down she turned to Heinrich, "I wish we could have had longer together as well. I think I would have been very happy."

"And I think I would have been very much in love."

They shared a gentle kiss and then she centred the image on the light.

He knelt alone in prayer on what looked like a large flat rock protruding from the earth.

Leigh fought to control her voice, "We are come to be by your side."

"And I am pleased. For I have prayed this night to be divested of this cup of sorrows but only if it is the will of my Father. If He wills that I should bear this burden then that is what I shall do, but I fear the burden will be a heavy one. Your voices bring me resolve to hold fast to the course that may be set for me."

"They did not act against you at the Temple?" Heinrich asked.

"No, they cowered from us. They asked their questions and they tried to entrap me but again they failed and again they would not denounce me in front of the many. I fear we have been too successful. We have buoyed our many followers and we have scared our few enemies into drastic action."

"But you said that the Roman Prefect wouldn't allow a trial to go ahead," Leigh said.

"I did, but he will have no choice. Our adversaries are imaginative and resourceful. They have lined up their witnesses and aim to take me to Herod first. He will refer me to Roman authority. Pilate will have no choice but to hear me."

"But..."

"Hush now Leigh, for it is not the way of our choosing but the path we are given and how we deal with it that mark us. I came into this world to rid the evils from mankind and I must believe that my sacrifice will achieve that. Be not sad for me but rejoice."

"What can we say or do for you?"

"Just watch with me for they draw close now and when it is done do not follow me but instead comfort my brother. Comfort Judas. Will you do as I ask?"

"Of course Y'shua, but how will your followers know if you are taken? How can we get word to Miriam?"

"Ah, worry not. There are three here with me this night. They are weary and they know not what they watch for and so they sleep a little way off. But if it is to be my fate then they will come to my side. All I ask is that you keep vigil with me as I pray for courage."

They waited with him; alert and silent.

Mary had chosen the upturned bench on the far side of the lab and Francine the one on the near side. They had looked at the fifth bench, designed to give them cover back to the Thule Room and both had shaken their heads.

"Franci, do you want to go there?" Mary had asked her.

"No, thanks all the same. I think both of us know that this is as far back as we get to go."

Mary had smiled and nodded. They had checked their weapons in silence and settled down to wait.

"Mary, I watched you kill Uwe Joyce."

"I know, Heinrich showed me the footage."

"Why did you?"

"I'd had enough of him, them, all of it," she responded then added, "Why are you here?"

"Similar to be honest. I've had enough. Today is my last day living in a world that hates me for my skin and my eyes and my looks and my gender. If this works it will mean equality, true equality."

"Will it?"

"I have to hope, yes."

They fell back into silence and each reflected on how they had ended up in this place, at this time.

Mary also considered what was potentially about to happen. She figured that when the explosions did come, they would neatly pop the main door off its hinges and disintegrate the heavy blackout curtains. But given that it opened outwards, the attacking force would probably still have to pull the door back into the small cleanroom that was between the High Powered Laser Lab and the main Oscar Lab. She knew that would delay their progress. She also thought they would be surprised to see the lights still on. They were out everywhere else in the labs so they would assume the same was true in here. The attacking troops would have donned night vision equipment but with the lights on they would have to remove it in order to function. That would serve to delay them a little more.

"Franci, when they come they'll blow the entry but they'll delay before they come through."

"Okay, what do you need me to do?"

"Just get into position and then drop anything and everything that tries to get through the doorway. It isn't subtle or clever but it's what we've got."

"Well, I've never been that subtle either," said Francine.

"Me neither," said Mary.

"I'm glad I met you Mary Reid, with an E and an I."

Leigh wasn't sure how much time had passed when she noticed a flare of light drawing into the Window. Y'shua did not move but said, "I must drink of this cup and His will must be done."

Leigh repositioned the Projection a little further out. Panning it upward she could see a large group of men approaching the inner garden, their procession lit by numerous torches. The flames reflected in a macabre fashion off many unsheathed swords and illuminated the long sticks and clubs being carried by others. She reached down and flicked off the microphone input. "Heinrich, they look like the torchbearers from the Nazi rallies."

He just nodded and watched the scene unfold. She tightened the Window again and saw Judas walking forward. They could see the tears streaming down his face as he entered the triangle of lamps but those behind him would see nothing other than his actions. Y'shua stood and turned to face him.

"Oh Master, my Master," Judas said with a heartbreaking sadness, leant forward and kissed him on the cheek.

A number of the men in the procession pushed forward and immediately restrained Y'shua, fixing his hands behind his back. Leigh gasped as three men appeared out of the darkness with swords drawn. One of them swung at the men holding Y'shua. There was a faint spray of blood and a scuffle broke out.

"Peter, put up your sword and sheath it! Hear me all of you!" and Y'shua's voice was raised in command, "If it is that conflict and war hold fast in this world it will not be done in my name. It must not be done in my name."

The scuffle ended as soon as it had begun. He turned to the rest of the men who surrounded him, "So you have finally found your courage to come for me in the dark. You are like thieves armed with sword and stave. Could you not come for me in the Temple in the daylight when I was surrounded by my followers?" He tilted his head back and said, "My followers who watch from afar know that God, the source of shalom, will soon crush the adversary under your feet."

He was led away and Leigh and Heinrich did as they had promised. They waited until the garden was emptied, all save for Judas. Leigh flicked the microphones back on. "Judas, we're here."

"Oh Leigh, it is as I had to do but I will be shamed for this."

"You won't be. He knows you did it for Him, that's what's important. You acted out of love and tenderness for future generations. Even if He stands in front of Pilate, He will be released and you will unite with Him again. Everyone will know the truth."

"But no one will know!" he wailed with a pained, distraught cry. "No one will care. My friends and my family will think I have betrayed my Master. They will castigate me and hold me to account for what is planned. We have gone too far and there is no way back."

"What do you mean? What is planned?" asked Leigh.

"They mean to take Him to Golgotha." Judas was crying openly now and spoke between large sobs. "They aim to move Him as soon as the hour allows. They will move Him to Pilate as the sun rises. But the disciples will not know, they will not go with Him. He will be left on His own. They will forsake Him." Judas collapsed down onto his knees, "I cannot go to His side for I will be an outcast." Raising his head, he pleaded, "Leigh, You must go to Him. You must. You must go to Golgotha."

Leigh looked to Heinrich and saw that his skin had faded to a sickly white. "Heinrich, what is it? What's Golgotha?"

He turned to her and held her hand, "It's the ancient site of execution just outside Jerusalem. It's the place the Romans use for crucifixions."

She stared back at him blankly, "What on earth's a crucifixion?"

When he didn't answer she turned back to the Projection but Judas was nowhere to be seen. She scanned out but in the pitch blackness of the valley she knew she was never going to find him.

"Oh Judas, please come back," she said forlornly. "Please come back and be with us this night and into the morning sun." Her pleas were returned with silence. She finally turned back to Heinrich, "What's crucifixion?"

He was about to answer when a series of explosive charges detonated in the High Powered Laser Lab. A small, hesitant pause was ended with a volley of automatic rifle fire that quickly escalated.

"Heinrich, what do we do now?" She looked up at him and he could see no fear, only a determination in her eyes.

He racked his memory for accounts of crucifixions that he had read in the Archives. He tried to remember the hours that the Romans used and when that would correlate to. In the end he made a best guess. "Push the Window forward by twelve hours. I'll get you a location."

She began to set in the time coordinates and he scanned through his maps for what he knew would be the last time, one way or the other. The rifle fire had intensified more and even the triple glazed glass couldn't diminish the sounds of a ferocious firefight. There was an occasional crump of a grenade but given the proximity of the blasts he was guessing that whoever had thrown them in to the lab was getting them thrown back before they were detonating. He knew that wouldn't last.

Francine saw the first potato masher grenade come arcing into the lab and land just between her and Mary. She scrambled forward, grabbed it and hurled it like a discus back to where it had come from. The next two were dealt with in the same manner. Mary continued to fire suppression bursts at the door then Francine switched to doing that while Mary sighted on individual troops hesitating in the doorway and trying to muster their courage to storm in.

"I'm ready," Leigh called and as they looked up they saw the beautiful Garden of Gat Šmānê bathed in the afternoon light.

"How long will it take to track due west for one kilometre?" he asked looking back down at the satellite database.

"About twelve minutes, maybe ten."

"That's too slow. Jump directly to 31, 46, 42.16 north and 35, 13, 46.59 east. He registered the increasing tempo of the firefight raging metres away from him. While Leigh manipulated the controls he put on his sidearm and slung the last of the S-98s across his back. The Projection image blanked, relit and then came slowly into focus. They were looking vertically down on a small rise. Leigh was trying to identify what she was looking at. Heinrich had read about them and knew at once.

Leigh said in a distracted way, "What's that on the hill?" She continued to manipulate the image and zoomed into what looked like three wooden structures. When she finally realised what she was looking at she gave a cry that sounded like her mind and soul were being ripped apart.

Heinrich came to her and put his arm around her. The noise of the fighting so near to them seemed to rescind momentarily.

"My God Heinrich! My God! How could they do that to Him? How could they do that to anyone?" She turned and buried her face into his shoulder.

"I'm so sorry Leigh. I remember reading about what crucifixion was in the Archives. It's barbaric."

The gunfire from the next room intensified yet again. Leigh seemed to suddenly free herself from the shock of the sight in the Projection. She straightened back up and stepped away from Heinrich. "Mary and Franci are in there doing that for us, the least I can do is be as brave as them." She forced herself to look back and orientated the image to look on the face of Y'shua. "Oh Messiah, what have they done to you?" She watched as his eyes flickered open and he cast his gaze around as much as his tattered body would let him.

"My God, why did you forsake me!" he cried in anguish.

"No, Messiah, no! We didn't, we wouldn't! We would never do that. We are come to be your strength and your comfort. Oh please know we are here with you, for you," Leigh cried the words as she looked at him, so pale and drawn. Blood dripped from his hands, his feet, his head and his side. She scanned out a little and she could see women gathered around the foot of the cross including the Magdalene, her face a mask of sorrow. There was a lull in the firefight next door.

Francine and Mary looked over at one another and shrugged shoulders. "Could be they've given up?' asked Francine in a hopeful and sarcastic way.

"Yeah, perhaps," Mary winked at her, "but more likely they've gone off to re-fuse their grenades."

"Ah! Well that's a bit of a downer."

"How're you doing for ammunition?"

"I'm getting through it. You?"

"Yeah, probably fine for all we're gonna need. By the way, Franci."

"What?"

"I'm glad I met you too."

Leigh and Heinrich heard his voice so faintly gasped from parched lips.

"My friends. Stay with me... I need you... To be my witness... I need you to hold faith... As Mary spoke of it... Or I may fail in my courage... To see this passion through... Please stay with me... To the end... So... I may deliver all of us." His head slumped forward and blood oozed from cuts left by thorns that had been pushed into it.

"Of course we will stay with you," they answered.

The troops poured forward through the entrance and raced for the cover of the smaller workstations and shelving units. Mary and Francine dropped most of the new arrivals in the midst of Heinrich's prepared killing zone. But some managed to gain a foothold in the lab.

"Where're the grenades?" Francine shouted as she knelt up and fired another burst into the doorway, knocking a silhouetted figure over.

"Fuck knows. Maybe they just fancy a fair fight?" Mary responded and let loose a carefully aimed three-round burst into the furthest forward workstation. The spray of red told her she had found the slim target of the exposed forehead she had aimed for.

"Yeah right. Cos that's what the fascist bastards have always gone for?" Francine tried to pop her head up to get an aim point but the fire coming their way was intensifying.

"Hey, watch your lip. I'm one of those fascist bastards you know." Mary propped herself up on an elbow and swapped out another magazine.

"Not any more. You're one of the good guys now," Francine yelled and both of them knelt up again and fired into the occupied workstations at the front of the lab. More troopers fell and then the incoming fire stopped.

Mary saw the three grenades sail into the air. They curved up in a perfect arc, tumbling end on end like a juggling act performed by an invisible conjuror. She knew the fuses would be set differently to the ones Francine had managed to throw back. On reflection she decided it was probably just as well. She was down to her last half magazine for the S-98 and had her Glock resting next to her. Running out of ammunition and being taken back to a cell wasn't high on her to-do list. She gazed across at Francine who was on her knees still firing short bursts at the invisible attackers on the other side of the dark gap leading into the cleanroom and further into the Oscar Lab. Francine crouched down to change magazines and looked back at Mary. Their eyes locked as the first grenade fell short on the other side of the tables and exploded on impact. They smiled, nodded and as the final two grenades sailed over their heads and fell just behind them, they both knelt up and emptied their remaining fire into the doorway.

Heinrich was mesmerized by the image of the Projection and yet couldn't fail to feel the heavy crump of the close detonation of three grenades in quick succession. The noise of the firefight ceased. He pulled the S-98 round, checked the magazine was seated, cocked the weapon and flicked the safety catch off. He loosened the catch of his holster so that his Glock was easily drawn. These actions were automatic as he watched Leigh scan in as tight as she could to the cross. They both stepped up to the image to be near him. From the room next door came two short bursts of automatic fire.

"Oh Y'shua, they have taken Mary and Franci to be with you this day. They will take us soon. I am so sorry for what we have done. We have come too late to be with you in your suffering. Oh Messiah you must have thought we had all forsaken and abandoned you. And now we have no time to be with you."

As they watched his shallow breaths there was a volley of shots that shattered the opaque glass doors behind them.

They stood transfixed. Y'shua raised his head and opened his eyes. In their peripheral senses they could hear the manual lock being disengaged and voices ordering them to turn around. In the midst of the noise and violence the clearest and most distinct sound was Y'shua's voice, ringing out to them from across the centuries, "It is finished."

Leigh and Heinrich watched his head bow forward and the rise and fall of his chest slow and then stop.

They turned slowly to see two soldiers standing just inside the shattered doors. Both had rifles up in the aim but both were not sighting along their barrels. Instead they were staring up at the image on the Projection behind Leigh and Heinrich.

Heinrich considered trying to reach for his own weapons but knew it was unlikely that he could bring them to bear before the soldiers reacted. Instead he slipped his left hand into Leigh's right. He looked down at her and she looked up at him but then she looked past him and smiled. He turned and followed her gaze.

In the middle of the Ringroom a silver translucent effect was shimmering around the Time Observation Window. They watched as it collapsed into a magnificent, radiant point of light. A heartbeat later it expanded to fill their world with hope.

Epilogue

Tuesday, July 20, 1995 – Foz do Arelho, Portugal

eriously, we really should think about why we come here."

"Because we like it."

"Don't be daft. You don't like it. You're going to go pink, then red, then back to white with the added bonus of most of the former red peeling off in great chunks of skin dandruff."

"Why thank you. You paint such an attractive picture. Anyway, I'm not the one that goes insane trying to get miniscule bits of sand out from between my toes, belly button, ears and other orifices. That last time you had sand in your bikini top you nearly caused that old fella in the hotel to have a coronary."

"Aye, but what a way for him to go," she turned and winked, "and anyway, at least I look good after a day down here. You, on the other hand, Scottish boy, take a week on this beach just to go from blue to white."

"Yeah, well, I still can't understand how you don't do the same. Why is it that you go all swarthy and beautifully tanned?"

"Don't you know anything? I'm a direct descendant of a swarthy and beautifully tanned Spanish aristocratic sailor."

"Aye, right. Your Ma's idea of an exotic holiday was getting out of Belfast for a run down the shore in your Da's wee car. She never set foot on a plane, so how'd she manage to meet the Prince of Benidorm?"

"Tsk Tsk, you Philistine. Do you know nothing of the history of the Spanish Armada?" She feigned the voice of a movie trailer announcer and said, "When the wild, wicked wind blew them all away and they shipwrecked on the west of Ireland." She dropped back to her normal accent, "Then they couldn't get their travel insurance to pay out as it was considered an 'Act of God' and wasn't covered. So they all had to stay and make merry with the local wenches."

"War's hell, obviously. Although, if they looked anything like you, well, who could blame them." He rolled over on the double lounger and kissed her.

When they broke apart they stayed facing one another and listening to the rhythmic lapping of the waves.

"Um, I am sorry to disturb you." They both looked up into the sun to see a woman, not much older than themselves, standing almost at the foot of their lounger. She had on a light summer dress in a simple, yet attractive, floral pattern. Her hair was long and blonde and she had a round and cheerful looking face.

"It's okay, you're not disturbing us. What can we do for you?"

"You are English, yes?"

"Ha! Well he's Scottish and I'm Northern Irish but we'll forgive you. We do speak English, yes."

"Oh I am so sorry. I mean not to offend you."

"No, no, don't be silly, I'm only joking. Where are you from?"

"Germany."

"Oh I do love Germany. Whereabouts?"

"The Harz mountains. Do you know them?"

"No, I don't think so. Where are they near?"

"Well, a little south-west of Berlin."

"How beautiful. Oh lucky you."

"Thank you. You have been to Germany?"

"Yes, many times. I go there for work. So does this one," she pointed her thumb at her husband and smiled up at the woman. "But your English is much better than our German. Wie geht es Ihnen?"

"Es geht mir gut, und Ihnen?"

"Mmm yeah, that's about the limit." She smiled broadly and said, "So what can we help you with?"

"Ah yes. I am so sorry to impose but I noticed that you have some cream, eh, for the sun?"

"Sun lotion? To protect from burning?"

"Ja, I mean yes, that is what I meant."

"No, we don't," she said and the German woman looked perplexed as she could see it sitting next to the lounger. "We don't have *some* lotion, we have a *bucket* of lotion. Protection factor fifty. Honestly, you'd get more of a tan wearing a wet suit and a motorcycle helmet." She laughed a clear and carefree laugh that caused both her husband and the visitor to laugh with her.

"We need this much as my darling husband will boil and frizzle like an egg on a griddle if we don't. So please, if you would like to borrow some, feel free."

"Oh no, it is not for me. It is for my boy," she turned and pointed to a tall, athletic looking boy of about fifteen who was standing holding a windsurfing board.

"He so loves the water but he goes to burn so easily. I have forgotten and send my husband back to the room to get it but you know how the children are like. They will not wait."

"Yes, of course. Please borrow away. In fact it's about time we got our wee one back for another coating. She's got her father's skin type so we have to cover her in the stuff."

"Oh, and where is your daughter?"

"She's just over there." She indicated a young girl of about ten who was swinging upside down from a set of climbing ropes strung across the frames of a children's play area set a little way up on the beach. Both women called to their children to come back to them.

"Heinrich."

"Leigh."

Glossary

Organisations

Greater Germanic Reich (GGR): The official state name of the political entity that Nazi Germany established.

Schutzstaffel (SS): Protection Squadron. The preeminent paramilitary organisation of the Nazi state.

Waffen-SS: The armed wing of the SS.

Allgemeine-SS: The non-combat branch of the SS incorporating the Gestapo and the Kriminalpolizei.

SS-Totenkopfverbände (SS-TV): Death's-Head Units. The SS organization responsible for administering the concentration camps within the GGR.

Reichssicherheitshauptamt (RHSA): Reich Main Security Office, an organization subordinate to the Chef der Deutscher Polizei (Chief of German Police) and Reichsführer-SS.

Gestapo: Abbreviation of Geheime Staatspolizei, Secret State Police. The official secret police of the GGR.

Kriminalpolizei (Kripo): Criminal Police. The Kripo became the Criminal Police Department for the entire GGR.

Schutzpolizei der Gemeinden: Municipal protection police. Municipal uniformed police in smaller towns.

Ahnenerbe: Inheritance of the Forefathers. The scientific institute established to research the archaeological and cultural history of the Aryan race.

Kriegsmarine: The GGR's naval forces.

Luftwaffe: The GGR's air forces.

Wehrmacht: The Army of the GGR.

1st SS-Panzer Division Leibstandarte SS Adolf Hitler (1st SS-Pz.Div. LSSAH): Adolf Hitler's personal bodyguard. Initially the size of a regiment, the LSSAH eventually grew into an elite division-sized unit. Their motto Meine Ehre heißt Treue translated as My Honour is Loyalty. Their symbol was a skeleton key, in honour of its first commander, Josef "Sepp" Dietrich. Dietrich is German for skeleton key.

Bund Deutscher Mädel: The League of German Girls was the girls' wing of the Hitler Youth movement.

Places
Bad Tölz: A town in Bavaria, Germany and the home of the Officers' Training School for the Waffen-SS.

Dahlem: A borough of south-western Berlin, home to the headquarters of the Ahnenerbe.

Leopold Palace: Situated on Wilhelm Straße and housing the headquarters of the Reich Ministry for Public Enlightenment and Propaganda.

Oranienburger Straße: Location of the GGR Archives.

Prinz-Albrecht-Straße: Location of the headquarters of the Reich Main Security Office, Gestapo and the SS.

Tegel Airport: Berlin's main airport.

Wedel Straße: Street address of the Signal Magazine Publishing House. Named after the original promoter of the magazine, Chief of Wehrmacht Propaganda, Colonel Hasso von Wedel.

Wilhelm Straße: A general term referring to the GGR's overall government administration, housing in particular the Reich Chancellery and the Foreign Office.

Military Hardware
* Denotes fictional device based on modern or historic equivalents.

Glock-17: 9mm pistol with a seventeen-round magazine.

Glock-46: * New generation sub-compact 9mm pistol with a seventeen-round magazine. Replaced the Glock-26 in 2015.

HK-MP5: 9mm submachine gun with thirty-round magazine.

HK-MP19: * 9mm, new generation submachine gun and personal protection weapon with thirty-round magazine. Combines the MP5 and HK UMP capabilities and strengths. Laser sighted.

HK-P8: 9mm side arm pistol with fifteen-round magazine.

Karibiner: * Semi-automatic with a twelve-round magazine. 2015 variant of the original K98 bolt action rifle.

MG-42 Mk6: * Latest variant, designed in 2005, of the MG-42. A 7.92 Mauser general purpose machine gun. Enhanced with laser sighting and an established 1500-rounds per minute rate of fire.

S-98: * Development of the MP-40/41 developed by the Schmeisser factory in 1998. 9mm with a thirty-two-round magazine.

Leichen-IV: * A multirole VIP transport, jet aircraft with a maximum capacity of ten passengers although normally rolled for six plus a steward/crew member. Used exclusively by Reichministry personnel and senior SS officers within the GGR.

NH92: * Latest variant, medium sized, twin-engine, multirole military helicopter used for transport / utility operations.

SS-Panther: SS utility transport helicopter.

Geländewagen: A four-wheel drive SUV.

Horch: * SS staff car.

Miscellaneous
Casualty Categories: Cat 1-deceased, Cat 6-incapacitating illness or injury (part of a 7 category system).

CCTV: Closed Circuit Television.

CP: Command Post.

Det Cord: Detonation cord. A high-speed fuse which explodes, rather than burns, and is suitable for detonating high explosives.

Dr-Ing: Doktor der Ingenieurwissenschaften, denotes holder of a German Engineering Doctorate Degree.

elektronische Bürgerdatei (eBü): * National identity database within the GGR.
ForeFone: * Mobile, smart phone with curved glass display panel, worn on the forearm and connected to a wireless earpiece and in-built mic.

J2: Intelligence Staff Function.

Konzentrationslager (KZ): Concentration Camp.

LZ: Landing Zone.

NCO: Non-Commissioned Officer.

OPs: Observation Posts.

Parteiadler: The emblem of the Nazi Party. The spread-winged eagle atop a laurel-wreath-enclosed Swastika.

Siegrune: The 'double lightning strike' runic insignia of the Schutzstaffel (SS).

SigInt: Signals Intelligence.

SitRep: A situation report. An update of current status.

Subdued-pattern: Low contrast rank insignia used on combat patterned uniforms.

Tango: Designated as a target of interest.

Tempest Cage: A metal enclosure of conducting material formed into a mesh, within which electromagnetic radiation is heavily attenuated or blocked in total.

Acknowledgements

This is the bit most people don't read but I think it's important that I say thank you to those who provided their time to assist me.

To the modest expert on lasers who answered my emails and reminded me that Science Fiction is indeed fiction and not to get too worked up about the science. I trust my readers will follow their advice.

Rachel, for surviving your car crash and telling me what it's like to recover from a serious head injury.

Bernd, Uzy and Norm for your patience in translating my strange requests into your native tongues. All mistakes are mine.

Aliya, for casting your eyes over the earliest version of the early chapters and Anne for taking the time to read and encourage as I progressed slowly.

Phil, your attention to detail during your thorough and multi-lingual proofreading of the manuscript was much appreciated and Kristy, thanks for introducing me to Haiku.

Finally, to Jacki. Thank you for... Well, everything really. You gave me the time to write and you give me the purpose in my life. Thanks honey.

Also by Ian Andrew
Face Value
Flight Path
Fall Guys
The Little Book of Silly Rhymes & Odd Verses
Self-Publishing for Independent Authors

About the Author

Ian Andrew's first crime novel, *Face Value*, won the 2017 Publishers Weekly BookLife Prize for Fiction. Since then he has continued to add to that series, is also a successful ghost writer and has founded the Book Reality Experience, a publishing assistance service that helps writers become independent authors.He is currently working on the next in the Wright & Tran Series of detective novels.

Find extra information at:
www.ianandrewauthor.com

Face Value
The First Wright & Tran Novel

Kara Wright and Tien Tran, former members of an elite intelligence gathering team active in Afghanistan, Iraq, and places still classified, now make their living through Wright & Tran, a PI service that tracks errant spouses, identifies dishonest employees and, just occasionally, takes on more significant cases that allow them to use all their skills.

When siblings Zoe and Michael Sterling insist that their middle-aged parents have gone missing, Kara and Tien are at first sceptical and then quickly intrigued; the father, ex-intelligence analyst Chris Sterling, appears to be involved with an enigmatic Russian thug.

Using less than orthodox methods and the services of ex-colleagues with highly specialised talents, Wright & Tran take on the case. But the truth they uncover is far from simple and will shake Zoe and Michael as much as it will challenge Tien and anger Kara. Anger she can ill afford for she is being hunted by others for the killing of a street predator who chose the wrong prey.

The only constant in this darkening world is that nothing and no one can be taken at face value.

"Ian Andrew is an author who can be relied upon to deliver a good — no, much more than that — a great read. Face Value, once again proves him to be a versatile and gifted writer who delivers books that hold readers from beginning to end."
(Elaine Fry, The West Australian)

Flight Path
The Second Wright & Tran Novel

Wright & Tran are back!

Kara Wright and Tien Tran, combat veterans of an elite intelligence unit, now make their living as Private Investigators. Often working the mundane, just occasionally they get to use all their former training.

"I'd like you to make sure
the dead are really dead."

So it is that the enigmatic Franklyn tasks Kara and Tien to investigate the apparent suicide of a local celebrity. Within days the women are embarked on a pursuit that leads halfway around the globe and into the darkest recesses of the human condition. Kara, Tien and their team will endure mental stress worse than anything they experienced from combat and, like combat, not everyone makes it home.

…Wright and Tran are the best in the business. Andrew's own experience working with Military Intelligence provides his work with authenticity and heart… He is an author who can be relied upon to deliver a good – no, much more than that – a great read.
The West Australian

Fall Guys
The Third Wright & Tran Novel

Kara Wright and Tien Tran, combat veterans of an elite intelligence unit, now make their living as Private Investigators. Often working the mundane, just occasionally they get to use all their former training.

"We want to know why the Brits
are selling weapons to ISIS"

When a break-in threatens Britain's National Security, Franklyn calls on Wright & Tran but Kara will have to take this case on her own. Tien wants nothing to do with the world of Private Investigations and less to do with the world of Franklyn. Kara goes solo, but finding who is responsible for the break-in is the easy part. Finding who the real criminals are is much, much harder.

Isolated in a world of half-truths and lies, international arms deals and power politics, she is quick to discover that she's been working for the wrong side. What she didn't figure on was that making amends will place her, and those she loves, in the sights of those who have everything to lose.

The Little Book
of
Silly Rhymes
&
Odd Verses

An illustrated collection of humorous, daft, sometimes sad and occasionally thought provoking verses from the pen of Ian Andrew. Illustrations by Alison Mutton.

Printed in Great Britain
by Amazon

81897040R00236